The Forbidden Tarot:

The Dark Horse

Patricia Simpson

tor romance

A TOM DOHERTY ASSOCIATES BOOK
NEW YORK

This is a work of fiction. All the characters and events portrayed in this book are either products of the author's imagination or are used fictitiously.

THE DARK HORSE

Copyright © 2005 by Patricia Simpson

Edited by Anna Genoese

A Tor Book
Published by Tom Doherty Associates, LLC
175 Fifth Avenue
New York, NY 10010

www.tor.com

Tor® is a registered trademark of Tom Doherty Associates, LLC.

ISBN 0-765-35324-5
EAN 978-0-765-35324-5

First edition: November 2005

Printed in the United States of America

0 9 8 7 6 5 4 3 2 1

This book is gratefully dedicated to:
My fellow writers—Beth, Dona, and Tonda.
My friends at Wind River—both human and four-footed.
And lastly, my mother June—for always taking the time.

Two urns by Jove's high throne have ever stood,—
The source of evil one, and one of good.

—*Alexander Pope (1688–1744)*

Set O

It may be true that we were taught to never take lives, but after living with these savages for so many years, I believe I have shown remarkable restraint. And on the whole—I must admit—it has been uncommonly easy to set one human being against another and thereby achieve my objectives.

Set, Egyptian God

Prologue

Medicine Valley, California

Jack Hughes dismounted near the cave, his knees shaking and his ears ringing. He hadn't eaten for three days, and a wave of lightheadedness swept over him as his boots hit the ground. He blinked away the dizzying blackness inside his head and urged his strawberry roan forward, seeking shelter from the storm that whipped over the hills in a roiling frenzy.

Jack wondered if the Washoe Indian legend was true after all. Was this place cursed? One moment the sky had been blue, and the next it had turned purple with rage, growing darker and more virulent with every step he had taken in the remote valley.

Wind and hail had forced him toward the yawning mouth of the cave to the east, and now huge drops of rain splattered his back. But even at the young age of thirteen, he wasn't the kind of kid who was easily scared or easily deterred from his path. He would ride out this storm and complete his vision quest, accursed valley or not.

He'd gone three days without food, and had spent every evening of the long ride meditating on his life, determined to find a way to live differently than his folks did, especially his father. He wanted none of his father's greed and anger, and none of his mother's cowardice and complacency.

He'd heard stories about the Native Americans who had once freely roamed the Sierra Nevada and the Great Basin—how boys his age had fasted and prayed, and then sometimes set out into the wilderness in search of a spirit guide. Although no Native American blood ran in Jack's veins, he had come to this desolate valley with that same goal in mind: to find his spirit guide; to find his path in life.

Jack didn't know what rituals the Native Americans performed during their quests. But his lack of knowledge didn't deter him. He knew his heart was in the right place, and he was open to all possibilities. If a spirit guide was to come to him, he was certain it would appear here, in this special place unfrequented by hikers and hunters.

He'd been warned to stay away from Medicine Valley, and told by his grandmother that only powerful shamans dared to venture into the shadowy canyon. But he had come here nevertheless, half of him running from his father, and the other half drawn by the magical stories he'd heard about this valley. He knew in his heart that here was "the place."

Lightning flashed overhead and a roll of thunder crashed soon after as the storm plowed on directly overhead. The echoing boom shook the earth and the surrounding trees, rattling Jack's eardrums.

Terrified, his horse yanked up his head and gave a shrill whinny, dancing backwards.

"Easy, Biscuit," Jack crooned, gently urging him back down. "Steady now, boy."

He stroked the side of the horse's neck and looked over his shoulder into the blackness of the cave. He couldn't see anything, as his eyes had not yet adjusted to the dark. Rain pelted the dry dirt where he stood in the opening, struggling to calm the horse. The sharp scent of ozone hung in the air, and the hair on his forearms raised, charged with static electricity.

Before either boy or horse came fully to their senses, another flash of lightning rent the sky. Jack looked up just as a blinding light streaked toward the metal rings of Biscuit's bridle, hit the horse, and in a monstrous glow of blue, traveled down Jack's arm.

Biscuit reared up, stunned by the bolt of electricity. Jack watched him paw the air as time stood still. Every cell in his body ignited as the glow passed through him. His lightheadedness merged with the searing energy of the lightning, and he felt his body lose all sense of gravity, all sense of form.

He couldn't move. All he could see now was the floor of Medicine Valley, but only in his mind's eye. Through the chaparral pounded a herd of wild horses, their manes flying, their tails like flags. Jack had seen this wary herd before, but only from a distance. This time, they thundered toward him. Or was he only imagining things? Was the noise he heard coming from the horses or was it just the rolling thunder of the storm? Was he dreaming? Had he died from the lightning strike? Where was Biscuit?

Still the horses came, led by a massive black stallion. Jack could see the look in the animal's eyes, wild with fear and fury at seeing a man-child invading his territory. He could see the bulging muscles bunching at the stallion's chest as the horse raised his forelegs, one after the other in a pounding frenzy, almost to the cave now.

Jack knew he had to get away. The stallion could kill him. One blow from the horse's huge hooves could knock him unconscious, leaving him to be trampled to death. He tried to move, but his body would not obey him. The awesome beauty of the stallion held him in thrall. He could feel sweat trickling down his back, even though he was aware that his world stood suspended and he shouldn't have had time to work up a sweat.

And then, in another flash of lightning, the stallion reared up, inches from Jack now, shrieking and screaming, tossing his head, his massive form backlit by the storm.

At that moment, Jack would have prayed to a God, had he believed in one. Instead he just stood there, mute, staring up at the horse, certain it would be the last vision of his lifetime. He had trespassed into sacred territory. He would forfeit his life for the transgression. Jack knew—as surely as if his sentence had been carved in stone—that the old spirits of this place had sent this horse as a messenger of death, to pound the life out of him.

He could not break away, could not pull his stare from the blazing eyes of the stallion. He could feel the horse sucking his courage from him, sucking his will, sucking his life away.

The lightning burst again, shimmering over the stallion and streaking through Jack, burning away every human thought, every vision.

His mind went blank, his eyesight went dark, and he felt himself falling slowly backward—falling into buzzing, prickling nothingness.

THE NEXT DAY, Jack's grandmother found him lying in the meadow behind the barn, his hair singed, his fingernails black, and his clothing missing. Neither of them could explain how Jack had returned to the ranch without his horse in such a short amount of time. All Jack could remember was a vivid dream of running with the wild herd, clambering up the rocky trails and galloping across the high meadows, more powerful and fleet than he had ever been in his life.

As his grandmother helped him into the barn, he said nothing of his wondrous dream, and his grandmother said nothing of his strange nakedness. Odd things could happen to a person when they were struck by lightning, making them forget, making them see things they never saw before. Neither Jack nor his grandmother needed more explanation than that.

But once in the barn, as his grandmother fetched him a horse blanket from the tack room, Jack looked down the aisle between the stalls to the patch of blue beyond the barn and thought back to the stallion of Medicine Valley.

Had he met his spirit guide after all? Or had the wild beast's nature somehow merged with his own during the electrical storm? Was it all just a dream? A vision?

Hungry and spent, Jack sank onto a bale of straw and leaned against the wide planks of the stall behind him. He had been transformed forever by Medicine Valley. He knew it. But he wasn't sure in what way.

TWO DAYS LATER, Biscuit limped back to the ranch, dragging his tattered reins. His red-brown coat had turned completely white.

Set 1

Modern day humans speak of body and soul. Maybe even spirit, if we stretch things a bit. But that's it. I have to smile at such simplicity. We taught the Egyptians much more varied and subtle distinctions of form: the *khat, ka, ba, khaibit, akhu, sahu, sekhem, ab,* and *ren.* From the physical body to the secret name withheld from all the earthly world, the true and full "being" is far more complicated than twenty-first century minds can fathom. Subtlety is lost on these people. Who could fault me for wishing to sleep through the last few millennia?

Set, the Enlightened

Chapter 1

Silicon Valley, California, Seventeen Years Later

I'm here to see Mr. Benton," Claire Coulter announced, raising her chin.

The stylishly-emaciated, thin-lipped receptionist gave Claire a cool once-over, her tiny German-engineered glasses perched at the end of her nose. Claire refused to allow her gaze to waver and betray her nervousness. She had coifed her long ebony hair into a perfect French braid, selected a blue cotton sweater and navy slacks to fit in seamlessly with her coworkers—an outfit that was not too casual but not overly dressy either—and had complemented her clothes with jewelry both conservative and genuine: tiny sapphire earings, set in sterling silver. What fault could anyone find with her appearance? Claire raised her chin a notch higher.

The receptionist took her time consulting an appointment book spread out upon her immaculate desk, a vast, empty expanse marred only by a white and lavender orchid in full bloom and a framed photograph of a smiling man standing in front of the Eiffel Tower. Claire had never seen a desk so neat and wondered if the woman's only task was scheduling Tobias Benton's appointments. It could happen. Everyone at CommOptima was specialized, including herself.

Claire waited, accustomed to enduring that extra excruciating moment she and her brother had always suffered at the hands of teachers, public officials, and even bank tellers. Each time she waited, she worried that the moment had finally arrived, when her true identity would be discovered—

that this time there would be a tiny damning notation next to her name. Though she had no reason to fear such a moment now, she had waited for it to occur for so many years that the expectation was stamped on her psyche like a permanent tattoo.

Today's particular scrutiny was made all the more excruciating because she had no idea why she had been summoned to the office of her boss, Tobias Benton, head of CommOptima and a man she had never met face-to-face.

The receptionist gave Claire a second scathing glance and then reached for her phone, as if it were against her better judgment to allow anyone to pass through to the boss.

"Miss Coulter is here," the receptionist breathed into the phone. She paused for a moment, her eyes rolling toward the two-story ceiling as she listened to the reply. Then she replaced the receiver and glanced at Claire once more.

"He'll see you now."

"Thank you," Claire replied, balancing her voice safely between good manners and chilly impatience at being treated as second-rate.

The receptionist motioned toward the tall double doors behind her, and Claire took the gesture as permission to proceed. She wondered, if she had been anyone else, whether the receptionist would have stood up, showed her to the door, and opened it for her, instead of remaining seated behind her austere desk.

Claire stepped toward the forbidding closed doors, accustomed to doing things for herself, facing great odds, and forging ahead. She was no coward. Still, the ominous summons to appear before Tobias Benton had her worried. What had she done? Was she going to be fired? She could think of no reason to be let go, other than a downturn in the economic forecast. But if she were going to be fired, why hadn't her supervisor done the deed instead of handing her off to the CEO?

Claire wrapped her fingers around the door handle, took a deep breath to steady her nerves, closed her eyes for a moment to ground herself, and then opened the door.

* * *

TOBIAS BENTON BARELY noticed her entrance.

She expected to see him glaring at her from behind a massive desk, her exit papers in hand. Instead, he stood with his back to her, staring out a large window overlooking the huge CommOptima campus, his hands braced on his hips, heatedly discussing something through a wireless headset curled around his right ear. His generously applied cologne hung in the air, musky and oppressive.

As Tobias Benton paced the floor in front of the window, Claire took the opportunity to survey the powerful billionaire, and was surprised at what she saw.

Not that she judged people only on appearance; she'd simply expected more from a man whose disposable income could have easily supported a few small countries. Such a man could have afforded a decent wardrobe or a stylist, or at least a stint in a tanning booth. But apparently Tobias Benton cared little about his outward appearance. His lank, dirty-blond hair was cut in an unflattering, boxy style with bangs, which he pushed to the side as if in afterthought. His skin was sallow, his eyes a dull blue. He wore a pair of wrinkled jeans that hung on his hips and poked out at the knees, no doubt from countless hours spent at a computer or behind a desk. A black polo shirt, stuffed into the top of his jeans, did little to disguise the lack of tone in his shallow chest and abdomen. And apparently he had dressed for the meeting by throwing on a jacket—from what looked like a decent suit—but the charcoal and tan pinstripes clashed with his jeans and shirt. Either he was color blind or just hopelessly unstylish.

Claire stared at him as he droned on, wondering if Benton thought to display his importance by showing her how busy he was, or if he simply didn't have time to spare for her. She heard words like *stocks, leverage buyout,* and *profit margins*. She waited, standing in front of his desk, certain that her job at CommOptima was at an end, and wondering how she would cope with no paycheck and a mountain of medical bills to pay.

* * *

AFTER TEN MINUTES, Benton said his goodbyes and turned around, tugging the wire coil from his ear.

"Tobias Benton," he said in a monotone voice that matched the flat look in his eyes. He raised his hand toward her as his gaze slowly slipped down her figure, lingering on her breasts and hips. She saw a small smile of appreciation blossom on his lips.

"Claire Coulter." Fighting back a wave of anger at being ogled by her boss, she raised her hand to his. She would have thought that Tobias Benton, a well-respected computer genius and savvy businessman, would have been more enlightened than the average guy and might have treated her in a non-sexual manner. But he had just given her the same old perusal she'd received from men since she'd reached puberty.

His handshake was more than what she had expected, though: cool and lackluster.

"I don't believe we've ever met, Miss Coulter," he said.

"We haven't." She remained standing before his desk, hoping he would get her dismissal over with quickly. She wasn't a person who believed in dragging things out.

"Pity." He smiled and placed the headset on his desk. "I had no idea such a beautiful woman worked for me."

"I keep a low profile."

"An even greater pity." He glanced at her sweater again. "Please," he said, waving in the air with a slender hand. "Have a seat."

"Thank you." As Claire lowered herself into the leather chair that faced Benton's desk, he sank into his own chair. Its high back gave her boss the appearance of a king sitting upon a throne—probably the very impression he intended to convey to millions and competitors alike.

He opened a manila folder, glanced down at its contents, and then leveled his bland gaze upon her. "It says here you are a translation technician. That you work for our DigiArch division."

Claire nodded, still not sure why she had been summoned. Was he going to fire her or ask her out on a date? She didn't know which would be worse.

"And that CommOptima has started the paper work to get a green card for you."

"Yes." Claire fought down a flush of fear and alarm. This conversation might get a lot worse than she thought. She was relatively safe from jail time and deportation, but there was always her brother.

"Someone must think very highly of your skills." He glanced at her again.

"My education is very specialized," she replied, hoping her cool voice concealed all traces of her inner turmoil.

Benton nodded in approval. Then he slowly flipped through the papers of her file. Claire could hear the clock ticking on the wall, and she used the sound to steady her pulse. She watched her boss closely, wondering if he was reading the documents in the file or using the heavy silence to make her squirm. He looked like the type to get gratification out of intimidating others.

"You are pursuing a PhD?" he asked, looking across the desk at her. His gaze slipped into her hair and his eyes glazed over, as if he wasn't really interested in her response.

"Yes. In anthropology."

"What area?"

"Linguistics."

Benton nodded and pursed his thin red lips. He surveyed a paper in his hands. "Do you like working for DigiArch, Miss Coulter?"

"Yes, I do." She really did. She loved her work, especially the last year when she'd become a translation tech. Her job had morphed from routine interpretation to fascinating cryptography, as she worked on a team assigned to decipher one of archeology's oldest mysteries, the Nimian Stone, a tablet inscribed with a chronicle of ancient history, much like the Rosetta stone. A year ago, the missing corner of the stone had been discovered in a recently excavated temple in Egypt. Benton had used his considerable wealth and influence to buy the piece on the black market before the discovery had even been announced.

He'd brought the shard to DigiArch, the division of his conglomerate whose sole focus was to digitize artifacts and make them universally available to scientists and scholars. But the discovery of the missing shard of the Nimian stone had not been made public. Claire's team worked in absolute secrecy as they struggled to decipher the strange code chiseled into the basalt. All employees working on the project had signed privacy statements and would face immediate dismissal and ruinous lawsuits if they leaked any information about the stone to the public.

"It says here you've worked for me for two years."

"That's correct."

"Doing what?"

"At first I worked on the Geological Data Bank, in the western division of the North American sector, section nine specifically."

"And now you are—" He consulted her papers again. "Assistant Director of the Nimian Project." His eyebrows rose. "That's heady stuff for a twenty-eight-year-old woman."

"I work hard," she replied, shifting uncomfortably in her chair, still not able to guess where this interview was headed. "And I pay attention."

"Apparently you do." Tobias sat back in his chair. "And would you consider yourself ambitious?"

Claire studied his flat blue eyes, fairly certain now that she wasn't going to be fired. But what was Benton up to? Was he going to offer her a new job? Pick her brain about a coworker? What?

She folded her hands in her lap, pressing them together to keep them from trembling. "Yes, I would say I'm ambitious. But—" She broke off, not wanting to limit her chances, but not wanting to give up her present position either.

"But what, Miss Coulter?"

"I'm also deeply committed to the Nimian Project, sir. The Nimian Stone is the focus of my dissertation."

"Which is why I have asked to see you."

So that was what this was all about. Benton thought she was violating the privacy statement by something she'd written in her dissertation. But she hadn't revealed anything whatsoever about the newly-found shard. Her work focused entirely on the Nimian Stone itself, which was safely ensconced in an Italian museum.

But someone at CommOptima must have believed she'd overstepped her bounds. Claire clenched her teeth and chided herself for discussing her theories with her coworkers. She should have concentrated on her job and never said a word to anyone—as she had been raised to do. Her mother had always told her that the more information a person divulged to another, the harder it was to remain anonymous. And until Claire and her brother were legal, she wished to remain *completely* anonymous.

"My dissertation has nothing to do with the shard," she ventured. "If that is what this is all about."

"It does in a way, Miss Coulter." Tobias Benton leaned back and made a steeple of his fingers in front of his chest. "And as to that, I have a proposition to make to you."

"What kind of proposition?" Claire asked, suddenly on the defensive again. She didn't appreciate the way Benton's flat eyes feasted on her, and she didn't trust the smug look on his face.

"I have a—" Benton paused for a moment as if searching for precise terminology. "A business partner, shall we say, who needs your services."

Claire wondered just what he meant by the word services. Ordinarily, she would assume he referred to her talents in a work capacity, but she was picking up a strange vibe from Benton, and she wasn't sure of him or his motives. He set her senses on edge. "And what services would those be?"

"Translating some code."

"Why me?" she asked. "Why not Randy Rivard?" Randy was the director of the Nimian Project. "He's got more experience."

"And calls himself 'The Code Meister.' I know." Benton waved away her suggestion with a dismissive flick of his hand and an equally dismissive smile. "But the Code Meister doesn't have your skill of synthesis."

"What do you mean?"

"He didn't take disparate facts, such as geological survey

data and a certain archeological find, and come up with a theory that the Nimian Stone may be connected to the Sierra Nevada. Now that's what I call synthesis."

Shocked, Claire jumped to her feet. "You've read my dissertation!" she blurted.

Benton shrugged, immune to her outburst. "Some of your logic is crude and there are plenty of places that could use supporting annotation, but the overall concept is quite astonishing."

Claire gaped at him, indignant to the point of speechlessness. "You read my work!" she sputtered. "Without my permission!"

"Hey." Benton rolled his eyes as he held up a white hand in protest. "You used a company laptop for your school work. Anything on company equipment belongs to me."

"I can't believe it!" Claire paced across the floor, her shoes sinking deep into the Persian carpet. "You've been spying on me!"

"Actually it was your friend and co-worker, Martha McConnell. But that's beside the point, Miss Coulter."

Claire turned on him. "So now what? Are you going to claim ownership of my theory?"

"Not at all. Calm down, Miss Coulter." He motioned toward the chair again.

Claire just glared at him. "Are you going to steal my work just like you stole the shard?"

"That's enough!" He smacked the desk with the flat of his hand. Then he paused, marshalling his emotions to a more even position. He cleared his throat and leaned forward. "What we do is not stealing," Benton continued. "It's getting information about an artifact analyzed and recorded for the good of the public before some government locks it away."

"It seems like stealing to me."

"If the Vatican can do it, so can CommOptima." He gazed at her and smiled. "I am serving the public in the end. And so are you."

Claire looked at him. The smug bastard. He knew he was in control, and that she was way out of control. She hated to lose her cool like this. She was so upset, she didn't know what to do, slap the man or run screaming out of his office.

"Now please, Miss Coulter," Benton said, motioning toward the chair where the soft leather still showed the outlines of her slender body. "Do sit down and hear me out."

Still seething, Claire sighed and reluctantly complied with his request.

"You feel violated. I understand that. But it was all done for a good cause. And don't worry. CommOptima is not going to steal your intellectual thunder."

Claire made no reply. She kept her glare fastened to the edge of his massive cherry desk.

"In fact," Benton continued, "I have every intention of rewarding you for a job well done."

Claire shot a distrustful glare at him. "What do you mean—reward?"

"Okay, here's the deal." Benton put both hands flat on the blotter in front of him. "And I don't have to remind you that everything we say in this room is covered by the privacy statement you signed when you joined the special projects team at DigiArch. Do we understand each other?"

Claire nodded grimly.

"Okay. The business partner I mentioned? Well, he's a bit unusual—unconventional, let's say, and he needs to gain access to a certain area in the Sierra Nevada as soon as possible."

"What does that have to do with translating?" Claire asked, confused. "Or me?"

"It involves an archeological site, one that's never been discovered until now. But it's been found by a colleague of my partner. The only thing is, the place is booby-trapped. And my business partner thinks the way in is by deciphering the code on a door that he believes will lead to an ancient fountain. A kind of fountain of youth, if you will."

Claire stared at Tobias Benton as the words he'd just spouted quickly filtered into her mind and then slowly coalesced into meaning. "Wait a minute," she gasped. "Are you saying the code on this door is connected to the Nimian Stone code?"

"That's exactly what I'm saying. Or at least that's what I hope will be true once you see the actual door."

"You mean my theory may be correct—that the basalt of the Nimian Stone matches that of section nine in the Sierra Nevada?" She slowly rose to her feet as a cool wave of excitement passed through her.

"That's the theory."

Claire felt a shiver run down her back. "And that there existed a people who were in contact with the ancient Egyptians?"

"That's exactly what I'm saying, Miss Coulter."

"My God!" Claire clamped a hand over her mouth, shocked by the information she'd just been given, and soaring with excitement that her theories might prove to be true.

Benton stood up, his smug expression stretching into a smile. "Think of it. You could prove your dissertation thesis, Miss Coulter. You could blow the lid off the world of archeology as we know it."

"Oh, my God!"

"That is, of course, as soon as we 'suddenly rediscover' the missing shard in that Egyptian temple, so we can allow everything to finally be made public—which might take some time, unfortunately."

"I can't believe it!" Claire whirled around to face the wall behind her, and then spun back to gape at her boss. "I truly can't believe it!"

"But that isn't the reward I mentioned earlier." Benton waved her back into her seat. "I will also make this worth your while on a personal level. Something more immediate than announcing the true origin of the Nimian Stone." Benton leaned forward and his expression sobered. "If you get my partner through that door and to the fountain, I will not only procure a green card for your brother, I'll pay for his kidney transplant and all his post-operative care as well."

Claire swallowed, hardly able to grasp what she was hearing. A huge lump formed in her throat as she thought of the ramifications of the offer Benton had just made. He would get Emilio a kidney and make him legal? How could she say no to such an offer? Her life would be utterly transformed if

Emilio wasn't sick any more—and if they never again had to face the fear of being deported to Mexico. An enormous weight would be lifted from her shoulders should she see her brother healthy once more, both of them finally able to live whole, unfettered lives.

But not only that, with this discovery, she would make her mark in the anthropology world. The Nimian Stone would make her famous, even immortal. She would be the first member of her family to rise from the peasant class into the heady world of public recognition, and her name would be forever linked to that of the stone. It was more than she had ever dreamed.

"Well?" Benton asked, tilting his head in expectation. "What do you say? Are you up to the challenge?"

Claire raised her gaze to meet his, her eyes burning with determination. "When do we leave?" she replied.

LATER THAT NIGHT, as snatches of her conversation with Benton echoed in her thoughts, Claire recalled the hungry way he'd looked at her and the worrisome feeling she'd had that set her on edge. She was concerned that all was not right. Just as Benton had "stolen" the missing shard of the Nimian Stone, he and his business partner might have an ulterior and not-so-altruistic motive for breaking into an archeological site. Could she trust the man? He'd obviously been spying on her at work and digging into her personal life. Why? And who was his partner?

Still, she was doing the right thing, surely. To get Emilio medical help, she would do just about anything. And the Nimian code was her specialty. She was the only person for the job.

No matter how she tried to justify her part in the operation, however, she had a strange misgiving about the trip. Though Claire was not a religious person, she closed her eyes and spoke out loud to no particular deity—especially not the unresponsive God her mother had prayed to for sixty years.

"If this is the path I should take," Claire whispered into the night air, "please show me a sign."

Chapter 2

Two days later, Claire tucked her travel hair dryer into her suitcase, did a final pass through her mental checklist, was satisfied that she hadn't forgotten anything for her trip, and then pulled down the flap of her suitcase. Just as she reached for the zipper, she heard her doorbell ring.

Claire frowned. It was eight o'clock at night. Who would be at her door at this hour?

Always careful, she quietly padded down the hallway of her apartment to the front door and looked through the peephole. The face of her friend, Maria, stared back up at her, wildly distorted by the fisheye lens. But even beyond that distortion, Maria's face looked contorted. What was wrong? Claire pulled open the door.

"Hey, Maria," she said in greeting, and was surprised when her small, fiery friend swept past her without so much as a hello and stormed into her living room.

"Hello to you, too," Claire remarked, closing the door.

"Claire!" Maria tossed back her mane of long black hair and pivoted as she flung her purse on the couch. "I am so upset! I could just scream!"

"What is it this time?" Claire asked, indicating for her guest to sit down on the couch. Maria glanced at the cotton upholstery but stomped across the floor and back again, her high heels clattering on the wood.

"Ah, no, Maria," Claire chided kindly. "It can't be that Jonathan again."

Maria spouted a string of Spanish words toward the wall,

as if a god lived above Claire's fireplace and Maria was chewing him out for deserting her in her time of need. She crossed her arms over her chest.

Claire signed and sat down on the couch. "Okay. What has he done this time?"

Maria whirled from facing the wall. "Bought *La Puta* this!"

Maria never referred to Jonathan's wife by name. She called her *La Puta*—The Bitch—instead, as if never speaking her name would keep her out of her reality.

Maria flung a metal box onto the coffee table. The container flew across the glass surface and would have fallen to the ground if Claire hadn't reacted quickly enough to catch it. She picked up the box, which was a little smaller than a paperback novel but much heavier.

Claire turned the plain golden box to view it from the bottom and back around to the top again. It looked old, but not valuable enough to whip up such a frenzy of jealousy. Still, Maria would be offended by anything Jonathan bought for his wife. She placed the box safely in the center of the table. "So what is it?" she asked.

"A deck of tarot cards!" Maria spit. "Really old ones. Gold leaf and everything!"

"How do you know?"

"Jonathan told me all about it. He was so excited. 'La Puta loves tarot decks this,' he says, and 'La Puta loves antique tarot decks that!' He spent a fortune on them. Half a million dollars! But that's not what gets to me, Claire." Maria flung both hands in the air. "He expects me to gift-wrap them for her birthday. For her, Claire! He expects me to wrap a present for her!"

Claire didn't say anything. It was obvious Maria wasn't in the mood to listen to words of caution about affairs with married men.

"He should have given me those cards," Maria continued, her color high as she jabbed a finger in the direction of the box on the coffee table. "I know the tarot like nobody else, especially her! I am the tarot expert. Me!" She thumped her chest.

Claire nodded.

"You know what La Puta can do with that tarot deck?"

Claire raised her dark eyebrows.

"She can stick it up her big white *culo,* that's what!" Maria whirled and stomped to the fireplace and then back to the coffee table. "Wrap her birthday present. Wrap her present!" She tossed her hair again, planting a hand on her hip like a toreador. "He promised me he was going to leave her, and now he asks me to wrap a present for her. Me!"

Claire tilted her head. "You *are* their maid, Maria."

Maria stamped her foot and glared at Claire, but she could not find words to refute the truth.

Claire leaned forward. "When he told you he would leave his wife, you didn't believe him, did you?"

Maria's nostrils flared and the whites around her irises showed like those of an enraged bull. She lifted her chin in an effort to fend off the truth behind Claire's question, and stood there, breathing heavily.

"They always say they're going to leave, Maria—that they're so unhappy, so bored. That their life with the wife is so pedestrian. But they never leave their wives. You know that."

"But I am like a flower!" she sputtered. "And she's but a thistle! Wrinkled and prickly!" She crossed her arms again, her eyes blazing. "How could he choose her over me? Impossible!"

"Because, Maria. You are a maid." Claire rose and put her arm around Maria, squeezing her shoulders gently. "Not that being a maid is bad. And you are the best maid in Silicon Valley." Claire felt the flare of Maria's anger subside somewhat.

Maria sniffed. "I care about my work."

"I know you do, Maria. You care about your work more than anyone I know."

"There is a lot of dust in the hills. But not in my house. Never." She sliced the air with the edge of her delicate hand. "Not one speck of dust!"

"But it is not your house, Maria. And it never will be. No matter what that bastard Jonathan promises you."

For a moment Maria was still, as if Claire was finally getting through to her. And in that moment, her fiery outrage broke. Maria sagged against her friend and put her hands to her pretty face as she slowly rotated into Claire's embrace and hung there, sobbing.

"How could he do this to me, Claire, how? How could he break my heart like this?" Her shoulders shook.

"Ah, Maria." Claire hugged her friend and quietly swept her hand across Maria's slender back and over her glossy black hair. No one had comforted her then, not when she had needed it the most. No one had spoken words of support to her when her world had collapsed and spun out of control at the age of twenty. She had been too ashamed to tell anyone of her affair, not even Maria. But the shame of being spurned still burned her like a brand.

When at last Maria's sobs subsided, Claire urged her to sit down on the couch, and then she slipped into the kitchen to get them both a glass of red wine. Though she knew Maria would have preferred a shot of tequila, Claire never kept tequila in the house. In fact, she never kept anything remotely connected to her heritage in the house, as if purging the past from her environment could purge it from her heart. She'd even legally changed her last name to Coulter to distance herself from her roots. She'd never known the name of her father—which her people customarily added as a third name—so she had made one up, something that didn't sound at all Spanish.

Maria took the goblet of wine in both hands. *"Gracias,"* she murmured, her voice thick from crying.

"You're welcome," Claire replied. She sat down beside her friend and reached for the cards in an effort to change the subject and clear the air.

Maria sniffed beside her. "You are a good friend, Clarita Francisco. I don't know what I'd do without you."

"Hush now." Claire patted her arm. "What about giving me a reading before I go off on my big adventure?"

"You want a tarot reading?"

"Yes. Just the short one. You know, where you have me

pick a card and then you tell me the future?" She offered the box to Maria. "I don't think you're in the right mood for an extensive reading, are you?"

Maria shook her head and set down her goblet. Claire watched her, relieved to see the anger and sadness already ebbing from the large, dark eyes of her childhood friend. She knew Maria well, knew how easily she could be distracted, even by the smallest of gestures. It was both her biggest downfall and her most endearing quality.

Taking a deep, purging breath, Maria reached for the golden box and slowly opened it. She set aside the top section, glanced down, and then swore under her breath.

"Oh my God—," she murmured, her voice lowering to an unusually subdued tone. "Look at this writing, Claire."

Claire leaned closer as she took a sip of her wine and looked down at the deck. Strange writing paraded across the yellow parchment that had been wrapped around the cards. She guessed it was some form of Aramaic. Unfortunately she couldn't make out any of the words, as Aramaic had never been her specialty.

"I don't think we should touch these," Claire whispered, wondering even as she whispered why they had both lowered their voices, and why she suddenly wished to hold the cards in her hands, even though she'd been taught by her years at CommOptima never to subject an archeological object to the destructive oils of human flesh.

"Why not?" Maria, shrugged. "La Puta will touch them."

"I think that's real parchment." Claire leaned closer to stare at the writing. "These cards really are old, Maria."

"So why give them to La Puta? She would not appreciate such a thing."

"Probably not." Claire agreed simply to appease her friend, even though she knew differently. La Puta, known to the non-Maria world as Diana Allman, was a huge collector of antiques, but Claire wouldn't press the point and risk having Maria whip herself into a frenzy again. Instead she added, "She probably doesn't even know how to do a reading."

Maria blew air through her teeth in agreement as she carefully opened the parchment to reveal the deck of cards.

"Wow," Claire gasped, as she caught sight of the top card. Though she knew she was only looking at the back of the cards, the design was magnificent enough to take her breath away. And though she'd never studied much Egyptian history, she'd taken enough general knowledge classes in college to recognize the Eye of Horus staring back at her, exquisitely fashioned with gold leaf.

"Man oh man!" Maria exclaimed.

"You shouldn't have taken these, Maria."

"Pah!" Maria waved her off. "What is Jonathan going to do? Accuse me of stealing?"

"Someone might." Claire shook her head. "Those cards look very valuable. I wouldn't be carrying them around!"

"Why?" Maria's lip curled. "No one knows. The Allmans have left for Paris and won't be back for a month." She dropped the deck into her left hand. "Besides, Jonathan could buy a hundred decks like this. Easy."

"Only if another like it existed." Claire took another sip of wine. "And I doubt one does!"

"Hmph!" Maria shrugged a pert shoulder and fanned out the cards, turning toward her friend. "Okay, think about your big adventure and pick a card, Claire."

Closing her eyes, Claire concentrated on the morning to come, when she would be whisked away to Lake Tahoe by her boss, Tobias Benton, and then continue into the wilderness of the Sierra Nevada.

"Okay. I'm ready." Claire reached out, slipped a card from the fanned deck, and carefully placed it upon the table.

Maria squinted at it. "What?" she murmured, staring at the card, perplexed.

"What is it?" Claire wasn't accustomed to Maria pausing at anything put before her. "Is it bad?"

"The Two Urns?" Maria scowled prettily. "I don't know. I've never heard of The Two Urns!"

"You don't recognize the card?"

"This deck must be a lot different than mine. Hold on." Maria set the golden cards on the couch beside her and reached for her purse. She pawed through the contents of her huge bag until she brought out a velvet pouch that

Claire recognized as the container of Maria's usual set of tarot. "What number is on that card?" she asked over her shoulder.

Claire looked at the roman numeral in the lower left corner. "Fourteen." She glanced over the strange card, which showed a man, standing on bare ground, a huge burst of light behind his head, and with wings on his back as well as at his ankles. He was young and dark-haired, with a flame coming out of the top of his head, and naked except for a striped sheath of cloth slung over his left shoulder. In his hands he held two urns, and he was pouring the contents of the upper urn into that of the lower one while he looked intently at something in the distance. In the top right corner was the astrological sign for Scorpio, and in the top left was a symbol comprised of three concentric circles, which she surmised was the glyph for the sun. The card made no sense to Claire whatsoever.

She surrendered the card to Maria, who absently added it to the pile beside her, and then opened the velvet bag.

Maria expertly shuffled through the top section of her cards. "Fourteen," she repeated. "Just what I thought. Temperance."

"Temperance? What does that mean?"

"Opposites attract, Claire." Maria wiggled her eyebrows at her friend, much more cheerful than she had been a few minutes before. "Maybe you and this Tobias Benton guy are going to click?"

Claire took a thoughtful drink of her wine. She was fairly certain she was opposite in every way to Tobias Benton, at least from what she'd seen of her boss. But she was dead certain she would never pursue a romantic relationship with the man, no matter how much money and power he possessed. Not even if she had to leave the Nimian Project.

"The forces of purification and transformation are in the air." Maria added. "A very fruitful union can be the result."

Claire stared at the card thoughtfully. The card with the two urns depicted a positive outcome. Was this tarot card her window to the future? Was this the sign she'd asked for?

Chapter 3

The next day Claire and Tobias sped through the Sierra Nevada in Tobias's Porsche, en route to his legendary fountain of youth. She had been surprised when her boss had shown up in a sports car. She had expected they would be traveling with a larger group from CommOptima as well as Tobias's business partner. But Tobias had informed her that his associate would meet them later, and that no one else from the firm would be accompanying them. Claire had slipped into the leather seat of the Porsche, her sixth sense telling her to be on her guard.

Claire looked out the window of the car at the rock face of the mountain pass they drove through, and couldn't believe how busy her last forty-eight hours had been. One day she had been summoned to Benton's office—and the next day she was making last-minute calls to her coworkers and friends, going in for medical tests to see if she could donate a kidney to her brother, shopping for the camping trip, and packing for the trek into the Lake Tahoe area. Now she and Tobias were headed for the Dark Horse Ranch, whose owner was supposedly a knowledgeable guide who would take them into the mountains.

Tobias took the curves in the road far too quickly for her taste, as if he were showing off for her or trying to frighten her. Claire kept her expression bland and her head turned away from him as the mountain fell away on her side of the car, plunging thousands of feet into a river valley. She wasn't impressed with Tobias's abrupt driving style, but she certainly wasn't going to admit that she was frightened.

"You sure don't say much," Tobias remarked. He turned toward her, but she still didn't look at him.

"I don't have much to say," she replied, straining to keep her voice level.

"You might try lightening up. This could be an interesting trip. Exploring the unknown, if you know what I mean."

To Claire's disgust, she felt Tobias's left hand slide onto her knee. She froze and then glanced at him. He raised his lips over his teeth. She couldn't tell if the expression was a smile or a grimace.

"I beg your pardon," she said coldly and angled her leg out from under his palm. "But that's my leg."

"Ah, c'mon." He snickered to mask the tenseness of the moment. But he retracted his hand and draped his wrist on his own thigh instead. "This could be like a vacation. You. Me. Nature's playground. Why not have some fun while we're up here? Get to know each other?"

"You might be on vacation, Mr. Benton, but I'm not."

"You could be. Let's say everything's off the record the entire time we're up here." He looked over at her. "How would that be?"

"Inappropriate," she replied. "Uncomfortable."

"It doesn't have to be."

"You are my boss, Mr. Benton."

"Tobias. I insist."

"You're my boss," she repeated firmly. "And there's a lot at stake in this for me."

"For me as well, you know." He raised his hand to the wheel. "My business partner isn't what you would call the easygoing type. If things don't go well for him, he won't be too happy."

"So that's why you're handling this yourself?"

"Exactly." His hands tightened around the wheel. "My idea of fun is definitely not camping. But having a beautiful woman along could take the rough corners off a whole lot of things, if you know what I mean."

Claire didn't follow his logic and didn't care to. "Not really, no," she responded.

"What I'm getting at is, we're going to be stuck in the mountains for a good week. So we might as well get to be friends. Maybe even good friends."

"This is a business trip, Tobias. I intend to keep it that way."

"You want me to help your brother, don't you?"

She turned to stare at him, shocked by his implied threat. "Yes," she finally replied, worried that he was about to put a limitation on the promise he'd made. She should have got the agreement in writing.

"Then I would suggest that we get to know each other." He glanced at her and smiled his watery, red-gummed grin at her. "Because I think we'll be great *compadres. Comprendo,* Princess?"

She turned away again, stung by his use of Spanish, as if he meant to remind her of her place in the world and her subservience to him. Bile rose in her throat. She could always sue Tobias for sexual harassment, but then where would that put her brother and her work with the Nimian Project?

Claire closed her eyes as Tobias took a sharp turn off the highway onto a gravel road. The Porsche fishtailed on the loose rock and then roared onward. Claire kept her eyes closed. Not only was she going to have to endure a rigorous horseback ride through mountain wilderness, she was also going to have to fight off the advances of her boss, who was nothing more than a creep with power—the worst kind of creep there was.

What had the tarot card predicted? A fruitful union? Transformation? Purification? Tobias Benton would have to do a complete one-eighty before she'd contemplate even a casual friendship with the man.

As far as she was concerned, this expedition had just taken a sudden turn for the worse.

JUST AFTER THREE o'clock, Claire noticed the scenery changing as the car sped higher and higher into the mountains, following the valley carved through the rocks by the American River. Oak trees and oleander gave way to red fir and pine. Even the light changed to more clear tones of cerulean and celadon high above the treetops. If the air-conditioning hadn't been on in the car, Claire guessed she would have smelled the vanilla scent of warm pine bark on the air.

She was stunned by the beauty of place, having seen the area only through scientific digital images data, which came nowhere near to capturing the splendor of Lake Tahoe. No pixel count could reproduce the silvery quality of its air.

A few minutes later, they rounded a curve in the gravel road and drove over a small wooden bridge that spanned the boulder-strewn river. The lane wound between tall stands of Jeffrey pine, past a marsh full of cattails and coots, and then through a field white with meadow foam in full bloom. Ahead of them, in a pocket in the hills, Claire caught sight of a cluster of outbuildings, a cedar-shake house, and a perimeter of fence—the only sign of civilization they'd seen for miles.

Tobias let up on the gas as they rumbled toward a ram-shackle gate with an arching sign above and a cattle guard below.

"Looks like we're here," Tobias announced.

Claire looked up at the sign spanning the entry gate. Long ago, someone had fashioned a logo of a rearing horse from a sheet of metal. Over the years, the sign had bent so much, it looked as if the horse were going to launch itself toward the moon. The letters *c* and *h* had completely fallen off the sign.

"Dark Horse Ran," Tobias read out loud, and snickered. "Sounds like a weird Japanese movie."

He shifted down to second gear, rolled over the cattle guard, and continued up the drive toward the house. Claire perused the grounds of the ranch, which didn't seem all that prosperous. The outbuildings were gray with age. The fence swayed and dipped, slung together with rusty barbed wire. The meadow seemed to march right up to the house. She couldn't see a patch of lawn or even a vegetable garden be-yond the waves of slender grasses. The only sign of life was a group of well-groomed horses grazing on a gentle slope behind the house, their tails flicking in the bright April sun.

The place wasn't unkempt, but Claire would have bet it hadn't seen a coat of paint in the past twenty years. What kind of rancher lived here? And did she want to entrust her life and her brother's future to the person who owned this rusty old spread?

They turned the final curve and came into full view of the house. A shiny black Hummer was parked outside, dwarfing the pickup beside it.

"Somebody's got some bucks," Tobias commented, setting the parking brake.

"It looks like an armored car." Claire reached for her purse.

"If they came here to pick up money, they're going to be sorely disappointed." Tobias turned off the engine. "The place looks like a dump."

"Maybe it's different on the inside." Claire rose easily from the low-slung seat of the Porsche, glad to get out of the car and away from her companion's over-familiar presence. Behind her, she heard Tobias grunt with the effort of getting to his feet.

She waited for him to catch up, and then walked toward the front of the house, where she spotted a grillwork entry leading to an atrium. The center area boasted a small pool full of water plants, and a riot of geraniums and African daisies—the first sign of human habitation besides the grazing horses.

Claire couldn't see a doorbell buzzer, but she did find a bell with an old rope dangling from it, and boasting a small metal figurine of a horse much like the one on the gate. She pulled it, and the bell tipped and clanged, splitting the quiet heat of the afternoon with a loud dong.

A tall, thin woman in a rose-colored suit answered the bell. With her polished pumps, stylish platinum hair, and the diamonds at her ears and throat, she looked startlingly civilized in such a rustic setting.

"Yes?" she asked, glancing from Claire to Tobias, her green eyes guarded.

"Tobias Benton," Tobias announced. "I'm here to see Jack Hughes."

She stared at him, taking in his rumpled, informal clothes and lank, unstylish hair, and then seemed to snap out of her initial surprise. "Mr. Benton, of course!" She pulled open the iron door, which squealed in protest. "Do come in, do come in!" She swept the air, motioning them into the atrium.

"Thank you," Claire stepped through the gateway.

"And this is Claire Coulter, my fiancée."

Stunned by Tobias's introduction of her, Claire shot him a dark glare, but he just smirked and looked away.

"How do you do?" The older woman shook Claire's hand. "I'm Susan Hughes, Jack's mother."

Claire tried to smile. "Pleased to meet you."

Susan led them into the cool darkness of the house, and for a moment Claire couldn't see much more than basic shapes until her eyes adjusted to the dim light.

"Jack won't be home until supper. May I get you something to drink? You must be parched, driving all that way."

"Have any Coke?" Tobias asked in answer. He drifted into the living room and gawked at the interior. "Man, this place looks like something right out of a cowboy movie."

Claire followed his glance. Like the exterior of the house and outbuildings, the living room appeared as if it hadn't been changed for a couple of decades either. Paneled in pine, it was furnished with heavy Mission-style pieces upholstered in red, orange, and white stripes. The huge fireplace was built of rough-cut stone, and the windows were hung with heavy cotton drapes with pictures of pheasants stamped on an orange background. Stuffed animal heads—deer, mountain lion, and bear—gazed blankly from every wall. Claire had to turn away from their eyes.

"What about you, dear?" she heard the older woman say.

"Water is fine, Mrs. Hughes," she replied, trying hard to mask the despair she felt for the animals whose now gruesome heads decorated the walls. "Thank you."

"I'll be right back." As soon as Susan Hughes disappeared down the hallway and out of earshot, Claire turned to Tobias.

"How dare you!" she cried, her emotions swinging in outrageous spikes.

"How dare I what?" Tobias's mouth hung open.

"Tell her we were engaged."

"I thought it would make it easier for everyone."

"In what way?"

"People out here are old fashioned. They'd go to a lot of trouble if they thought we weren't an item."

"What kind of trouble?"

"Separate bedrooms, that kind of thing. I don't want to put anyone out."

"I can't believe you told her that!" Claire tossed her hair, realizing she was as fired-up as Maria got when talking about Diana Allman.

"What are you so worked up about?" He gave her a scathing glance. "We're both adults. You can handle it."

"Like you would ever marry me." She met his gaze. "Aren't you worried the news might get out?"

He shrugged. "It wouldn't be the end of the world." Tobias's small blue eyes leveled on a place between her breasts and then wandered up to her lips. "Besides, it would make me look very progressive, choosing a woman like you."

"A woman like me? What is that exactly?" She crossed her arms. "You don't even know me."

"Yeah, but what I've seen certainly isn't hard on the eyes. If you know what I mean."

"I would prefer you cut the comments about my appearance." She clenched her teeth. "If you know what I mean."

"Hey!" He held up both hands. "Don't get so huffy! I meant it as a compliment."

She glared at him.

Tobias gave a short laugh. "You're a knockout. You must know it. I'm just giving an honest opinion."

Claire hugged her arms more tightly around her chest and said nothing.

Then she heard him take a deep frustrated breath. "Wait a minute. You think I'm not good enough for you."

"I never said that." She looked over her shoulder at him.

"Yeah, well." He curled his lip. "Just remember. Women

are incredibly stupid when selecting mates. Don't be one of them."

"I don't except to be. And just for the record, Tobias, I haven't selected anyone, either."

"Then you've never fallen for a pretty boy, I take it."

"No." None that she would tell him about, anyway.

"Pretty doesn't last, you know. But money and power does."

"What are you getting at?"

"Simply this, Bright Eyes." He stepped up behind her. "Don't be so quick to dismiss me. You don't know me either. I think we could work very well together. Very well. And don't forget—we made a bargain."

"A bargain that didn't include anything personal."

"Really? I call helping one of your family members pretty darn personal."

"You know what I'm saying, Tobias."

"And I think you know what *I'm* saying." He cupped her shoulders with his thin pale hands. "If you want me to help your brother, you'll keep your trap shut about our true marital status. *Capite?*"

Claire pulled out of his grip and turned to face him.

He was still holding her glare when Susan Hughes bustled back into the living room.

"There we are!" She gave them each their glasses. "Please, sit down if you like. Or feel free to stretch your legs outside."

"Thank you." Claire took a long drink of water, but it did nothing to douse the fire in her gut. What else would Tobias exact from her? And how could she outwit him? She refused to be at his mercy.

DINNERTIME ARRIVED AND the small group gathered in the dining room at seven o'clock after enjoying a cocktail on the back patio. Though the ranch house was rustic, Jack Hughes's parents insisted on their rituals of civility and good grooming, even going so far as to change clothes for dinner. Jack's mother wore a black skirt and sweater, and his father, William Hughes, had donned slacks and a crisp blue silk shirt. During the cocktail hour, Claire had learned they lived in New York State, and that Jack's father had recently taken early retirement to pursue a private business venture.

Jack Hughes still hadn't appeared.

"It's just like Jack to be late," his father grumbled, pulling out a chair for his wife. He nodded at Claire's chair and glared at Tobias, who finally realized he was expected to treat Claire like a lady.

"I can do it," Claire put in before Tobias had made it around the table to assist her.

"Suit yourself," Tobias muttered, retreating to his seat at the right of their host.

Claire surveyed William Hughes. She pegged him at about fifty-five. She could tell his hair had once been strawberry blond, but it had faded to a gray fuzz tinged in brown. His face was a spidery network of broken capillaries stretched across an opaque tan. Claire guessed he had spent many of his years on a boat. His sharp golden brown eyes were pulled into taut slits, as if he were permanently squinting from the glare of sunlight on water.

William turned to his wife. "When did Mother say he'd be back?"

"Dinnertime."

"I'm not going to wait more than five more minutes for that boy."

Boy? Claire glanced at the doorway of the dining room. Their guide was a boy? Or at least a very young man? She had another wave of doubt about the success of this venture. Going into uncharted wilderness was dangerous enough; going in with a careless twenty-something was madness. Still, Tobias's assistant had claimed Jack Hughes was the most knowledgeable guide in the area.

Then from the back of the house came the sound of the screen door slapping closed, the rumble of a deep male voice, and the approaching clump, clump, clump of a man in cowboy boots ambling down the wood floor of the hallway.

Chapter 4

Claire watched as a tall man appeared in the doorway. His wide shoulders and long, long legs filled up the vertical space, and his barely harnessed energy radiated outward, filling up the remaining edges. When he caught sight of the visitors, he ground to a halt in the doorway and stared in surprise at the crowd around the table. Judging from the dark expression on his face, Claire could tell his surprise wasn't of the pleasant variety.

"What the hell?" he exclaimed.

Jack Hughes was no teenager. He was at least thirty years old and every inch a man.

"Jack!" Susan rose, dropping her napkin to her plate. She hung in midair as if stuck between a desire to embrace him and a fear of rejection.

Jack obviously hadn't been told his parents were coming to visit. He stared at his mother. Then he glanced at Tobias and over to Claire. His brown eyes hung on her speculatively for a moment, and she felt herself holding her breath.

She took the moment to peruse the man beneath the tousled, damp, black hair. He wore a red cotton shirt with the sleeves rolled up on his forearms and a pair of well-worn jeans. From the look of those forearms and his neck, Claire could tell that Jack Hughes was all sinew and muscle, from his square jaw to his wide, knobby wrists and his long, lean legs. Not an ounce of fat clung to his powerful frame. He was the type of man who could sling a woman over his shoulder and effortlessly carry her, kicking and screaming, into the hills.

Claire flushed. Where had that thought come from? She blinked, and it seemed to startle Jack into the present. He reached up and drew his fingers and thumb down his shadowed chin, as if trying to decide whether or not to enter the room.

"For God's sake, Jack," his father remarked, "the least you could have done was shave."

"And you could have called." Jack scowled.

Claire wondered if the cowboy would decide to turn on his heel and leave instead of sitting down with his family and her and Tobias.

"Why would we call?" William countered. "Whenever we do, you make yourself scarce."

"I'm a busy man," Jack replied.

Claire could hear the strain in his gravelly voice, as if his throat was taut from suppressing words of a much harsher kind.

"Jack, darling, try to be civil." His mother swept the air behind her. "We have guests."

"I *was* being civil." Jack glanced at Claire again, and then kept a wary eye in her direction as he ambled to the far end of the table. He had a loose way of walking, as if he'd spent far too many hours on horseback and the time in the saddle had unlocked his hip joints. He slid a chair out and stood there, propping both of his long-fingered hands on top of the ladder back.

"Gran!" he called. "You coming?"

"Be right there, Johnny!" a good-natured voice answered from the back of the house.

Jack flashed a dry smile at Claire. "My grandmother calls me Johnny."

"Mine called me Angel."

"Your name is Angela then?"

"No. Claire." She shrugged. "Go figure."

He smiled again. "Grandmothers are funny that way."

Claire gazed up at him. Just like that, with no introduction and no handshake, and with only the flash of his smile and the rumble of his voice, he'd made her feel completely at home, as if only the two of them were in the room together.

Then his grandmother bustled into the dining room carrying a steaming bowl of mashed potatoes. Susan stepped out of the way and hovered silently behind her chair as if unsure how to proceed.

Jack's grandmother was thin and spry, with skinny little legs. She wore a pair of stretch polyester jeans and a plaid shirt under a long, navy blue cardigan. Her hair was snow white, and Claire guessed that she was well into her seventies. Judging by the standoffish behavior of Susan Hughes, she also guessed the old woman was William's mother.

Jack held the chair for the elderly woman while William jumped to his feet.

"Goddammit, Susan," he admonished, "Are you going to sit down or just stand there?"

She flushed at his harsh tone and scrambled to do his bidding. "Sorry, dear," she murmured, fumbling for her napkin.

Claire watched, shocked by the combative dynamics of the Hughes clan. She had been raised in a deathly quiet, single-parent household by a reserved, religious mother who had constantly worried about the health of her only son. Claire had never witnessed a family being this rude to each other. Or this loud.

After Susan had settled in her chair, she reached for her water glass. "William, why don't you introduce the guests."

"Finally, some civilized behavior!" William looked up. "Jack, this is Claire Coulter and her fiancé, Tobias Benton. They've come up from Silicon Valley." He reached for the platter of steaks. "You may have heard of Mr. Benton."

Jack leveled his dark eyes on the billionaire. "You're the guy who's launching his own probe to Mars."

"The very same." Tobias smiled smugly. "And if there's life on Mars, my rover will find it."

"What are you calling the thing?" William paused, taking a moment to remember his facts. "Red Rover?" He smiled and held out the steaks. "Damn, that's good!"

"I try to keep a whimsical outlook, Mr. Hughes." Tobias

lifted a large steak from the offered dish. "All my products have clever names as well as cutting-edge technology."

"I've been following your career for years, young man," William continued as the others concentrated on filling their plates. "You have a real knack for business."

"And good lawyers, which doesn't hurt." Tobias smiled and then turned to Jack. "So what do you do, Jack? Besides the tour guide operation?"

Jack finished chewing his bite of steak, in no particular hurry to answer any questions.

He swallowed. "I raise horses."

"Not that lucrative a business, I take it?"

Jack set down his fork. "Doesn't have to be."

"Doesn't have to be?" William thundered from the other end of the table. "What a load of crap! You're in your prime, Jack. And what are you doing? Making a decent living? Investing in the future? No, you're out in the middle of nowhere playing farmer."

Jack made no answer. He just sat there, stirring his potatoes.

William leaned forward. "No self-respecting man with a head on his shoulders would be spinning his wheels in a place like this. My God, Jack, the place looks like a dump!"

"I beg your pardon!" Jack's grandmother sputtered.

"No offense, Mother." William's voice softened a notch. "I know you've struggled with the place since Dad died. But I expected more from Jack."

"Training is my priority," Jack said at last. "When I have time to paint the barn, it'll get painted."

"Time? You don't have the time?" William inhaled a big spoonful of mashed potatoes. "That's a bunch of crock! You have enough time to go gallivanting around the countryside. That's what I've heard."

"What I do with my time or my life is my business." Jack slathered butter over a homemade roll with hard, agitated strokes.

"After all I've done for you?"

"I never asked for your help."

"Well, don't come crawling to me, mister, when the horse racing flops and the ranch goes tits-up."

"Who said anything about it going tits-up?" Jack glanced at his grandmother and then back to his father.

"I've heard about Mr. B," William continued, pointing a fork at his son.

"He's just having a minor setback."

"You call not winning a race for half the season a minor setback?"

Claire looked at Jack. So he raised and trained racehorses. That was different.

"He'll get back on track."

Tobias sliced through his steak. "Me, I'd never go into racing. Too much of a gamble. Too many variables. I'll always stick to machines and software. Leave out the emotional aspect of a task, and it's just one less thing to worry about."

"A man after my own heart!" William lifted his wine goblet. "To the future!"

Tobias directed his calculating eyes toward Claire. "To the future," he repeated, never dropping his gaze.

Claire lifted her glass but didn't take a sip of wine. The last thing she wished to do was toast to a future that featured her as Mrs. Red Rover.

"So what do you do, dear?" Susan asked, turning toward Claire. Her eyes were blankly sweet, innocent of the hard undercurrents around her. Or perhaps she ignored the family dynamic as a form of self-defense.

"I work for CommOptima, Mr. Benton's company."

"Really?" Susan replied.

"That's convenient," William drawled.

"What do you do there, dear?"

Claire put down her glass. "I'm a translator. Of old documents, mostly."

"And a vegetarian?" Jack pointed at her table setting. "I don't see much protein on your plate."

"Yes. I make it a practice not to eat anything with eyes." She scooped up some mashed potatoes. "Besides spuds, that is."

Tobias and William fell silent for a brief interval, as if they'd never heard anything so outlandish.

"Oh, my God," William drawled at last. "A goddamned hippie!"

Claire raised her chin, refusing to be intimidated by Jack's blustering father, and said nothing.

Jack must have sensed her discomfort. He turned his gaze back to her. "So you're traveling with my folks?"

"No." Claire put down her fork, surprised that Jack didn't know they'd come to take advantage of his services.

"We came to see you." Tobias leaned forward on both elbows. "To guide us into the hills. You father was kind enough to set it all up for us."

"My father?" Jack glared down the length of the table and then turned to the billionaire. "Wait a minute. He set what up?"

"A trip into the hills. To find an ancient fountain. A spring or something."

"What are you talking about?"

"A spring." Tobias glanced at Claire, as if expecting her to chime in and support him. "I have a map to it."

"What kind of a map?"

"An old one actually. It supposedly marks the spot of a fountain-of-youth kind of thing." Tobias leaned forward and slipped something out of the back pocket of his jeans. He held it up. "I've got it right here."

Jack held out his hand, but Tobias shook his head. "I was asked not to show this to just anyone."

"If I don't see the map, how will I know where the fountain is?"

"First you have agree to take us to it."

"You've got to be kidding!" Jack pushed back his chair with a loud screech and jumped to his feet. "There isn't any magic spring out there. There's hardly any water at all!"

"Maybe not." Tobias looked up at him. "But we'd like to find out if the map is genuine or not."

"I can tell you that without looking." Jack placed his fists on his hips. "Where'd you get it, at a carnival? A swap meet?"

"It was given to me by someone I highly respect."

Jack's brown eyes swept over Tobias's face and across his shoulders. "Map or no map," he said, "I can't take you, Benton."

Tobias straightened. "Why not?"

"I'm busy."

"Surely not too busy to pass up an opportunity like this."

"You'd say no to Tobias Benton?" William grabbed the two corners of the table, as if to keep himself from lunging at his son. "Are you crazy as well as lazy?"

"I'm busy, Dad." Jack's words were laced with anger.

"But I've agreed to pay you a thousand dollars a day." Tobias stood up.

"I told you," Jack said, clumping toward the doorway, "I've got things to do."

"But I've got a signed contract. Your father promised you would honor it."

"My father?" Jack turned at the door of the dining room. "My father has no business writing up contracts for anything, especially taking you and Miss City Girl on some jaunt into the hills. Do either of you know what such a trail ride would entail?"

Claire rose to her feet. "I can do it."

Jack turned to her. "Have you ever ridden a horse for a week?"

"I said I can do it."

"What about your Mars Rover man?"

Claire glanced at Tobias. "I can't speak for him."

"If she can do it, I certainly can!" Tobias countered, throwing back his shoulders. "She's just a girl."

"Girl or no girl, I'm not taking either of you. And that's final!" Jack stormed out of the room.

"Jack!" William called after him.

"Jack, darling!" Susan struggled out of her chair to follow her son, but Betty Hughes, Jack's grandmother, stopped her by clutching her forearm.

"Let me speak to the boy," Betty said. "He'll listen to me."

Set 2

I don't believe I have ever been this tired in all my days on Earth. Then again, I have never met humans as adept as Robert and Rae Lambers, who have achieved remarkable insight and powers during their short lives. I am beginning to suspect they possess a form of genetic knowledge, much like collective memory, and that they will continue to be formidable enemies if allowed to live. I have even begun to suspect that they might be descended from a bloodline that stretches far into the Egyptian past—perhaps as far as mine. Could the blood of the Lady Isis run in the veins of Rae Lambers? I should have done away with the woman, I know, but I was too exhausted after recovering the sword. I had expected a certain power transfer from the sword—and it did give me incredible sexual prowess for a few minutes—but maybe even that great weapon has seen better days.

Set, Son of Ptah

Chapter 5

Jack strode down the hall, through the overheated kitchen, and out onto the back patio. He felt overheated himself—claustrophobic, even. One more instant in that dining room with his father, and he would have lost his tenuous hold on his self-control. Even now, he felt his blood heaving in his chest, felt the familiar throbbing in his thighs and calves as his spirit nature threatened to take hold urging him to kick up his heels and run, to leave behind the bondage of the dinner table, to snort his contempt at every contentious word his father had hurled at him.

Breathing heavily, Jack paced the perimeter of the flagstones, trying to shake off the desperate urge to flee. Ever since he'd walked into the house, he'd sensed something on the air, the scent of something he'd never smelled, something that caused the hairs to rise on the backs of his neck and arms. That something had been in the dining room, sitting there as innocent as a lamb, her black hair long and lustrous, her large black eyes intelligent but very cool. Claire Coulter. He had hardly been able to string two thoughts together when she'd been sitting there, so close at hand. Her scent and bearing had disarmed him. There was pride in her and toughness of character, and yet a hidden softness underlaid it all—

"Johnny!"

Jack ground to a halt and frowned at the nearby hills covered in scrub and pine. Even his grandmother, usually so easy to get along with, was not going to leave him alone.

"Johnny!" She came up beside him and touched his back.

"Gran, don't start—"

"Normally I wouldn't give those two the time of day," his grandmother began. "Bill and Susan, I mean."

Jack nodded, still glaring at the hills, while beads of sweat rolled down his back between his shoulder blades.

"And I wouldn't countenance them making arrangements behind your back either."

"But?" Jack put in.

"We need the money, Johnny. And that Tobias Benton character is willing to pay you a thousand dollars a day!"

"Well, then I'd call him an idiot."

"We could do a lot with a few thousand dollars."

"I know, Gran. But what about Mr. B?" Jack turned and looked down at his tiny grandmother. "The Kentucky Derby is just weeks away."

"And what are you going to do this time that's going to make him run?"

"I don't know. But I'm certainly not going to find out if I take those two city slickers into the hills."

Betty pursed her lips. She was once a beauty, but age had shriveled her face into a mass of brown wrinkles and shrunk her body a good six inches. She gazed out at the hills, where the wall of darkness slowly shadowed the horizon. Then she sighed. "The Derby is such a long shot, Johnny. You know that."

"It's the only shot we have."

"But Mr. B just barely qualified." Betty slowly shook her head. "What are his chances? Be realistic, Johnny."

"I still have to try."

"But Benton's money is a sure thing."

"Maybe."

"And then there's Professor Avare."

"Who's that?"

"A gentleman who wants to study snakes. The Northern Pacific rattler."

"At this time of year?"

His grandmother shrugged. "I tried to tell him, but he insisted."

"Did you make the arrangements with him or did Dad?"

"I did." She shrugged again. "I figured I could take him out, easy. There's probably some rattlers around that rock ledge in Graveyard Gulch. That's one or two days, max. An easy couple-of-hundred dollars."

"You were planning on taking him out yourself?"

Betty nodded. "Why not?" She puffed out her chest. "Think I'm too old?"

"No." Jack had to smile. "When's he due?"

"He should be here sometime tonight."

"So we have three city-slickers and a seventy-five-year-old guide." Jack shook his head. "Hmm. What's wrong with this picture?"

"Nothing, boy. I can do it."

"And leave me with the folks?" Jack glanced at the house. "No way!"

"Then you'll take Benton out?"

Jack sighed. His better judgment told him to back off. But the wild voice inside him—the voice that spoke no language but was often stronger and more pure than his human sensibility—told him to follow the female. The female was a prize like no other. He had to find out who she was and what she was about.

"Okay," he finally said. He stomped to the screen door and grabbed his cowboy hat off the rack just inside the house. He plopped the black Stetson on his head. "I'll take a look at Benton's damn map after I feed the horses."

Grandma Betty nodded.

"I'll let you know how much grub we'll need," Jack continued. "And tell them to be ready first thing in the morning. We'll ride at six. That means breakfast at five a.m."

"Okay, Johnny."

"Whoever doesn't show up, doesn't ride."

CLAIRE WALKED INTO the guest bedroom, dragging her small wheeled suitcase, with Tobias not far behind her. He threw his bag on the bed nearest the door and grinned.

"Just like the Fifties!" he commented. "Like Ozzie and Harriet."

Claire glanced at the two twin beds, dressed in green and red plaid coverlets neatly folded down to reveal white sheets and pillowcases. She hadn't seen a twin bed for years, but was relieved she wouldn't be forced to share a larger single bed with her faux fiancé.

"We could push them together," Tobias continued, crossing his arms. "If you're the type that gets scared in the night, that is."

"The only thing that would scare me would be you getting the wrong idea." She met his gaze as she hoisted her suitcase onto a chair.

"And why would I ever do that, Little Miss Agreeable?"

"Because you think you can bully me."

"Can't I?"

"I agreed only to the fiancée line. And that's as far as it's going to go."

"Really? And who's going to stop me?" He cocked his head. His sneer grew wider. "A little carrot-cruncher like you?"

"Don't underestimate me, Tobias."

For a long moment she glared at him, until she saw his snicker start to fade from his pale lips. The thought of him touching her made her shiver with revulsion, and his superior attitude made her burn. Claire grabbed her purse and headed for the door.

Tobias stepped in front of her. "Where are you going?"

"I need to make a phone call."

"Make it here. You won't bother me."

"I prefer my privacy."

"Have something to hide?"

She took a step forward, but he remained standing in front of her, barring her way until she shot him an even darker glare.

"Look," she said through clenched teeth. "You don't own me, Tobias."

"Sure about that?" he retorted.

She made no answer and she refused to drop her glare. Finally, he backed off and allowed her to brush past him. But as she pulled open the door, his voice stopped her.

"Not that your phone is going to work way out here in the toolies."

She glanced at him over her shoulder. "It might."

"This will for sure." He reached into his pocket and slipped out the tiniest cell phone Claire had ever seen. The flat silver rectangle looked more like a cigarette lighter than a phone.

"It's a prototype." He held it out until she took it from him. "With incredible range. It should work anywhere in the world, no matter how remote a location. Plus it will last forever on a single charge. I call it the Lone Ranger."

Claire flipped it open. The phone was lighter than a tube of lipstick.

"Use it." He nodded toward the tiny device. "Up here in the mountains will be a good place to run it through its paces."

"But I don't want to take your phone." She held it back out to him.

"No problem." He waved her off. "I've got one for me, too. In case you ever need me, my number is programmed in there already."

She glanced at him. "I don't expect we'll be that far away from each other."

"Now you're talking, kitten." He winked at her.

She thanked him and left the room before he could say anything more.

CLAIRE FLED DOWN the hallway to the rear of the ranch house, remembering the patio at the back where they'd had cocktails before dinner. She hoped no one was outside, for she was tired of dealing with rude strangers, especially the obnoxious Hughes family. Quietly, Claire shut the screen door behind her and glanced around the shadowy patio where a single lantern glowed on the table. All the chairs were empty. Behind her, she could hear someone in the kitchen putting away dishes and guessed the household help, Bonita, was tidying up the last of the dinner mess.

Taking a deep breath of the sweet evening air, Claire wandered across the flagstones to the back field. Claire opened her phone. Just as Tobias had predicted, she had no service out here in the mountains. With a sigh, she exchanged phones and opened the tiny Lone Ranger device. After figuring out how to turn it on, she dialed and held it up to her ear as she waited for her brother to answer.

"Emilio?" she asked when he picked up.

"Hi, Claire," he replied. The warmth of his smile traveled all the way from Santa Clara where they lived.

Claire cradled her elbow with her fist as she ambled across the tufts of new grass. "How are you feeling?" she asked. "Did the dialysis tech come today?"

"Yeah." She heard the distance in his voice. Her brother tried to ignore his illness, as much as his mother had been obsessed by it. "How's the ranch?"

"It's crazy here. They're at each other's throats all the time!"

"Is that guy taking you into the mountains?"

"We don't know yet."

"Oh, Claire." Emilio paused as if reaching for something. "Someone called today. They said it was urgent. It was about your friend Maria."

"Maria?"

"Yeah. Apparently she didn't show up for work."

"That's odd. That's not like her."

"I know."

"Did the person leave a number?"

"Yeah." Emilio gave her the name and number of another maid who worked in the Allman household. Claire recognized the name: Fabiola Gonzalez, the head housekeeper and Maria's boss. After chatting with her brother as she did every day, Claire hung up and dialed Fabiola's number.

"Hi, this is Claire Coulter. You called me about Maria?"

"Oh, Clarita!" Fabiola Gonzalez's voice swooped up to an excited pitch. "Oh, my God! Have you heard?"

"Heard what?"

"It's been all over the news! Poor Maria!"

"What about her? I've been out of town." Claire stopped in her tracks as her stomach flipped sickeningly. Why would Maria have been on the news? "What's happened? Has she been in an accident?"

"No." Fabiola sniffed loudly. "Oh, my God!"

"What?" Claire screeched into the phone.

"It's so hard to tell you like this, Clarita, over the phone."

"Tell me!"

"She's been murdered!"

Claire fell back. "Murdered? Oh, my God! How? Why?"

"They found her not far from your apartment complex, in a parking lot. She'd been—" Fabiola paused. "No! I can't tell you. It's too horrible!"

"What, Fabiola? Please—"

"Somebody chopped off her head!" Fabiola's voice came through louder over the phone, as if she were clutching the receiver more tightly to her face. "The police say someone chopped off her head with a sword!"

The starry sky swirled around Claire as she struggled to stay on her feet.

"Why, Clarita?" She heard Fabiola wail on the other end of the line. "Why would someone want to hurt poor little Maria?"

Why indeed? What about the valuable tarot card deck Maria had secreted out of the Allman household? Had someone known about it? Had someone followed Maria to the apartment? Claire tried to breathe, but she felt as if she'd been punched in the gut. She staggered backward and collapsed in a patio chair.

"Are you there, Clarita?"

Claire nodded, and then realized Fabiola couldn't see her response. "Yes," she croaked.

"I thought you would want to know."

"Yes, Fabiola. Thanks. I appreciate it."

"I'm sorry you had to be told like this. I know you were Maria's best friend."

Claire nodded again. "Yes." She choked back a huge sob. "And there are no—no suspects?"

"No. Nothing. The police tried dogs and everything." Fabiola blew her nose. "Will you want to collect her things?"

"Yes, but I'm out of town—on business."

"When will you be back?"

"I'm not sure. A week. Two weeks maybe."

"Then you won't be coming to her funeral?"

"I can't." Claire sank her head onto her right hand. How could something like this have happened? And why when she was so far away, when she couldn't drop what she was doing and attend the funeral of her friend?

"Clarita, are you there?"

"Yes." Claire swallowed and pushed her hair out of her face as she straightened her back. "Fabiola, there's something I have to tell you."

"What is it?"

"Maria came to my house the other night with a deck of cards."

"Not those tarot cards!"

"Do you know about them?"

"*Si!*" Fabiola's voice sank to a hush. "Mr. Allman paid a fortune for those cards!"

"Apparently, he asked Maria to wrap them as a gift for Mrs. Allman."

"He did?"

"But she wanted to show them to me first."

"Oh, that girl! Forever getting into trouble!"

"What I wanted to tell you is that Maria accidentally left them at my house. She'd had a little too much wine, and was so upset, she must have forgotten about them. She left them on my couch."

"Where are they now?"

"I have them. I thought they were too valuable to mail, and I didn't have time to give them back to Maria. I had to catch a plane early."

"You have the cards with you?"

"In my purse."

"Clarita—if they are lost or stolen—"

"Don't worry. I'll bring them back as soon as I can."

Claire switched the phone to her other ear. "Aren't the All-mans in Europe anyway?"

"*Si.* They are."

"Then they won't miss them."

Fabiola paused. "You don't suppose someone was after the cards—that they killed Maria to—"

"That's what I am wondering, too."

"There's been a crazy woman calling here about those cards."

"Who?"

"A woman named Rae Lambers."

"What has she been saying?"

"That the cards are cursed. Oh, Clarita—what if they are?"

Claire frowned, recovering enough not to jump to the same hysterical conclusions Fabiola was leaping toward. "No. That would be ridiculous."

"But this Rae Lambers says it happened to her, that she was cursed, and that no one should even look at the cards!"

"Why?" Claire flushed, remembering how she had looked at the deck. She reminded herself to keep her head, that Maria and her buddies were overly superstitious sometimes. "Why shouldn't anyone look?"

"Because of the curse. They could be really dangerous. This Rae woman keeps leaving messages begging someone to call her."

"Maybe I should talk to her." Claire pressed her lips together. "Maybe she would know something about Maria— why someone might want to kill her."

"Maybe."

"Do you have the woman's phone number?"

"*Si.* I will get it."

While Claire waited for the older maid to retrieve the number, she rose to her feet and strode into the kitchen to look for something to write the phone number on. Bonita gave her a notepad and a pen. Claire scribbled the information down and then hung up the phone.

Claire felt the younger woman's eyes on her. "Are you all right, miss?" Bonita asked, holding a towel in one hand, and a big kettle in the other.

Claire nodded as she dialed the number. All she got was an answering machine. She hung up.

"Are you sure, miss? You look really pale."

"I just need some air. Thanks."

Claire slipped out of the house a second time. She had to get away. She had to be alone. Maria was dead! How could that be? Maria hadn't even made it to the bus stop. Tears welled up in Claire's eyes, and she broke into a run. The barn loomed ahead of her. She dashed up the sandy lane toward the open door, seeking the comfort of the horses she knew were inside. She could feel their gentle energy reaching out to her, offering their friendship and love—something none of the humans in this place could give her.

Maria was dead! Her best friend was gone. She would never see her again. Never talk to her! How could it have happened? What had the last minutes of Maria's life been like? Claire couldn't even think about it. She dashed the vision out of her thoughts.

Claire stumbled into the soft lamplight of the barn, her eyes blurry with tears, and fumbled her way to the first stall. Something shared her shock and grief here. She could feel it as surely as if a voice had called to her. With shaking hands, Claire lifted the latch of the stall.

Chapter 6

"H ey there," Claire crooned as she slipped into the stall. A huge horse towered in the shadows, but she was not afraid. She feared no animal, and none had ever hurt her. In the dim light of the barn, she could see a dark brown horse standing along the far wall, his head flung up, one white-rimmed eye warily checking her out, just as Jack Hughes had checked her out at the dinner table.

"Easy, boy." Claire stood just inside the door, not wishing to threaten him.

The horse shook its head.

Slowly, she surveyed him. The stallion was very tall—the tallest horse she'd ever seen—with elegant, powerful lines, sleek with muscle, much like his master. The horse nickered and lowered its proud, emblazoned head, which was slightly dished between the eyes, showing his faint Arabian blood-line. He took a step toward her.

"I've had some bad news," Claire confided. She held out her hand, and the horse bent toward her, his whiskery muzzle feathering across her fingers and over her wrist. "I've had some very bad news today, my friend."

Two more steps, and the horse had ventured all the way across the stall. Claire looked up at him, at his soft brown eyes, and then down his snowy white blaze to his freckled, questing nostrils. She could smell the pungent odor of his flesh, the sharp smell of fresh straw, the musky fragrance of horse dung, and the sweet tang of oiled tack hanging on the wall—a mélange of smells she loved above all others. It reminded her of her grandparent's farm, the only place she had known unconditional love. But that had been long ago and far away in Mexico.

Claire took a deep, shuddering breath and closed her eyes. The horse sniffed the top of her head and her shoulders, and she allowed his whispery investigation as she struggled to find the calm center that had kept her grounded through all her disappointments—the death of her grandparents, the death of her mother, and the endless periods of illness of her brother.

Now she had Maria to put away with the others—pretty, fiery Maria who had lived life head-on, expecting far too much from it and battling her way forward only to fall back most of the time. Reckless, passionate Maria.

She would give Maria this one night of grieving and then move forward, keeping busy, keeping her mind off things, keeping her worry and fear under tight control. She could live no other way.

JACK HAD JUST come out of the tack room when he saw a dark shape slip into Mr. B's stall. No one had any business being in that stall with his horse. Silently, Jack crossed the floor and reached for the latch of the door. But what he saw before him in the silvery moonlight made him stop in his tracks and draw in a breath.

There was the city-slicker woman standing in front of his prized racehorse, with the great beast's head pushed against her shoulder and her slender arms wrapped around the big lug's neck—just standing there with him as if she were giving him comfort, wrapping him in a golden envelope of understanding and compassion.

Jack caught himself holding his breath, imagining those arms wrapped around his neck, pulling him close in a communion so deep no one would feel compelled to move or speak. A part of him lunged forward, longing for such primal understanding from the woman. He'd never known even an instant of such compassion.

Then she turned her head, tipping the right side of her face to the moon, and he could see tears on her cheek, like raindrops on jasper. Why was she crying? How could she be sad or feel sorry for herself? She had nothing to be sad about. She was beautiful and engaged to one of the richest men on Earth. In fact, she had the three things every woman desired: youth, beauty, and money.

Something in his demeanor must have alerted her to his presence, for she opened her large, dark eyes and slowly raised her head, drawing her palm across Mr. B's cheek in a heartfelt caress as she turned toward him. Jack felt his blood rising at the gesture, and he lost the questions he had intended to ask her: what was she doing here and why was she crying? The power of speech fled from him as he felt his changeling self jostling for dominance.

"This horse," Claire murmured, her lips thick with tears. "This Mr. B—" She stroked his cheek again, and the horse dipped to the small of her shoulder. "He is very sad."

"Really?" Jack glanced at Mr. B's face. He couldn't see any sadness there. But he couldn't really concentrate on the animal. He was having too much trouble keeping himself under control, finding his tongue, finding his breath.

"He is grieving, Mr. Hughes."

"Grieving?" Jack couldn't take any more of watching her stroke the horse or the effect it produced in him. He pulled open the door. "Right. Come on out of there, lady."

"Why?"

"He's temperamental."

"He feels abandoned."

"He may bite."

She glanced up at Mr. B to smile at him, and warmth poured from her face, melting the cool moonlight and threatening Jack's self-control again. He could see Mr. B lean into her with careful tenderness, as if he were aware how easily his brute strength might bruise her delicate frame.

"He would never bite me," she said in a whisper.

"How can you be so sure?" Jack's voice cracked.

"No animal has ever harmed me." She stroked Mr. B's neck and then ran her hand over his withers. "And this one is nothing but a big old pussy cat."

"Pussy cat? Lady, this horse is an athlete in his prime. This horse is Terrell Owens of the racetrack!"

"This horse has a broken heart, Mr. Hughes."

"A what?"

"A broken heart."

"How? He's never even had a girlfriend!"

"Not every heart is broken by a lover," Claire replied, taking a step toward him. "Some are broken by love."

"You're saying Mr. B loved some*thing*?"

"Yes."

Jack tipped back his Stetson and gave a small, uncomfortable laugh. "That's pretty far-fetched!"

"He loved something and lost it. Now, he is very lonely."

"And how would you know all this?"

Claire looked back at the horse, and the movement made her long black hair sweep the small of her back. "I know it just by touching him."

Jack snorted and shook his head in disbelief. But in spite of his contempt for her claim, he wanted to touch her, to put his nose in the fragrant curtain of her long, silky hair.

"Animals tell me things," she added.

"So you speak horse, then?" he retorted. "You're fluent in Thoroughbred, are you?"

"I don't hear words. I see visions. Flashes of images. Sensations."

"Critter TV, eh?" He had to smile at his own wit.

"It's not a joking matter, Mr. Hughes. Especially for your horse."

Jack stared at her. She was serious. This gorgeous woman, who could have been anything from a top-grossing movie star to a foreign ambassador, was nothing but a self-proclaimed pet psychic. A nutcase. Still, she was so serious, Jack couldn't help but feel a sudden stab of shame for making fun of her.

"Okay, so supposing you can communicate with animals—and I'm not saying I believe it—what is Mr. B telling you?"

Claire shook her head, refusing to confide in him, and grimly brushed past him. She walked out of the stall.

"What?" he called after her, wondering why she had suddenly clammed up.

"It's hopeless."

"What's hopeless?"

"This conversation. And the fact that such a wonderful creature has to suffer a master like you!"

"What do you mean, suffer?" Jack slammed the stall shut and flipped the latch, while his stare remained glued to the slender woman marching away from him.

"Hey!" he called after her again. "I'm great with horses! Ask anyone!"

She threw up her arms in a gesture of frustration and kept walking.

Jack rolled his eyes. "Okay!" He trotted after her. "Okay then! What did Mr. B tell you? I'm listening."

She whirled to face him, and even in the darkness he could see anger glinting in her eyes.

"I saw a dog. A golden-colored dog with a black muzzle."

Jack flushed, surprised.

"I saw the dog sleeping with Mr. B."

Jack crossed his arms. How could the woman know about poor old Mavis, his shepherd-chow mix?

Claire glanced at the stall and then back at Jack, her eyes scathing. "Mr. B is distraught. He doesn't know where the dog is. He loves the dog."

"He does?" Jack scowled, confused. He didn't know what to think right about now.

"Where is the dog, Mr. Hughes?"

"She was killed. We think a bear got her. I found her in a gully about a mile from home."

"Oh." Claire's voice dropped in sympathy. "When?"

"Last year."

"And Mr. B doesn't know what happened?"

"Of course not." Jack waved the air between them. "He's a horse!"

"Tell him. Take him to her grave," Claire insisted. "Let him know. Or he will never run again. Never really run."

"You're kidding."

"I am not, Mr. Hughes." Claire lapped her cotton sweater closed over her shapely breasts. "I would consider getting him another companion, too. He is terribly lonely."

She gave him another scathing glance as if he couldn't be trusted to carry out such important tasks, and as if she doubted he was capable of understanding even the simplest concept.

"Goodnight, Mr. Hughes."

He watched her walk away.

Mr. B was terribly lonely? She could tell that just by touching the beast? What about him? What would Claire Coulter be able to see in him, if she ever put her hands to his face? What visions would flash before her eyes? Would she be able to see that he was aching with loneliness, too? That he was a freak of nature? And that he was hiding his freakishness from the world?

She had almost reached the house when Jack remembered the map that he needed to get from Benton.

"Miss Coulter!" he called out, breaking into a trot. "Wait!"

Set 3

The world has changed exceedingly since I last "retired from modern life." It's quite remarkable, actually. I wonder what the old ones will think. I hope they'll be shocked. I'd love to see them be just a little surprised. But then again, Those Who have Always Lived have seen nearly everything. The only downside to all the change is that my usual rejuvenation spots have disappeared, forcing me to seek new ways to regenerate my *khat*. I am getting too old for this much-too-ancient game of reinventing my physical self. And this new country—this United States of America—is simply a God-forsaken wilderness. Pardon the pun.

Set, Egyptian God

Chapter 7

At the sound of Jack's voice, Claire paused and turned, her slender body graceful in silhouette. But in the deepening dusk, Jack could plainly see the sour expression on her face. She was still angry at him for not believing in her crazy-ass theories about his horse.

Jack loped up to her, barely winded from the run, and ground to a stop beside her. "I almost forgot. I need to see that map of Benton's before you two turn in."

He held out his hand, but she backed away like a skittish mare, as if she thought he posed a danger to her. Could she sense his freakish nature without even touching him? Jack flushed, feeling suddenly skittish himself. He lowered his arm slightly, unsure how to proceed.

"He won't show it to you." Claire looked up at him and narrowed her eyes. "Not unless you agree to take us into the wilderness."

"I'm going to." He sighed and glanced to the side, already regretting his decision to serve as her trail guide. "My grandmother talked me into it."

"Oh." Her voice dipped in surprise as her dark eyes studied him. She didn't trust him. She didn't even like him. He could tell by the slight curl of her lip and the flat opacity of her eyes. "I thought you were too busy."

"Yes, well," he said, scowling at her, telling himself that her opinion of him didn't mean a thing. He couldn't care less if the woman liked him or not. "It'll be cutting it close—"

"Cutting what close?"

"My time. I have to get Mr. B into shape for the Kentucky Derby."

"When is that?"

"The first week in May."

"How long will it take to get to the fountain?"

Jack pushed back his hat. "Well now, I won't know that, will I, until I see the map."

"Then you promise to guide us?" She tilted her head and stared at him, skewering him with her eyes. He'd never met a woman whose mistrust ran as deep and as strong as hers. Did she distrust everyone, or just him in particular?

"You think I'd break my word?" he asked, put off by her distrust.

"But do you promise?" she repeated, her tone more intense than before.

"Okay." He flung up his hands. "Okay, yeah. I promise."

She stared at him, her serious eyes raking over his. "All right. I'll get the map."

Without another word, she turned and walked the few steps to the patio where the lantern still burned on the table. A few more strides, and she was through the back door. Jack leaned against the stone wall of the patio, waiting for her to return, and feeling that the night had gone strangely quiet after she'd disappeared into the house.

Much to his disappointment, she came back outside with her fiancé in tow.

"So you've decided to take us for a ride after all." Tobias greeted Jack with a glib smile. "Pardon the pun."

"Yeah." Jack didn't return the smile. He peeled himself off the wall.

Tobias reached into his back pocket for the map and carried it to the table. Then he carefully unfolded it—a piece of leather, scraped to a thin, buttery softness. Claire moved closer for a better look, standing to the right of Benton's elbow.

Jack came up behind her, making sure to stand at a safe distance, even though the curve of her back and the delicate frame of her shoulders called to him to step closer, to enclose her slight figure with his much taller, broader body, to warm his male hardness against her feminine curves, to seek the release he had so long denied himself. But though this woman sang a secret song to his wild nature, he couldn't allow himself to get anywhere near her.

Besides, her fiancé was two feet away.

Warily, he watched Claire's body language for a sign that he'd stepped into her sensory zone, just in case she really could pick up signals from animals. Her posture didn't stiffen and she didn't glance over her shoulder at him, so he moved a bit closer to the table, and came to an uncomfortable stance at her right shoulder, ready to step away if she so much as reached out a hand toward him.

Oblivious to his discomfort, Claire busied herself with spreading the map flat on the table and pushing it into the golden circle of light from the lantern. Jack bent down to read the markings, bracing himself on the heel of one hand as she stood beside him, silently surveying the map as well.

He was surprised by the map's appearance. It was older than he would have guessed, and it looked genuinely aged. The landmarks and symbols had been painted on the leather with a purple stain that had faded to brown at the edges. No words were written on the map. Hills and streams were marked by triangles and meandering lines. A single symbol had been drawn in the upper right-hand corner, comprised of a circle with a dot in it beneath a down-turned U.

He studied the layout of the markings. Only a seasoned guide such as himself—a person familiar with the back country and its labyrinth of streams and canyons—would have been able to make sense of the map, as it covered territory off the main trails of the area. It described one of the drier valleys of the region—Medicine Valley—a place he knew only too well as a destination fraught with danger.

"Sure you want to make this trip?" he asked, glancing to the side at the smooth plane of Claire's left cheek and then on to the pale square of Tobias's face.

"Why do you ask?" Tobias countered.

"This valley," said Jack, running a fingertip over the area

at the top of the map, "right here, where your map ends? It might not be the best place to visit."

Claire leaned closer to his hand. "Why is that?"

"It was thought to be full of bad spirits by the Washoe people."

"The Washoe?" Tobias repeated, not understanding.

"The ancient people who called this area their home."

"And you believe old legends?" Tobias snorted. "That's usually just a way of keeping other people out."

"Maybe." Jack nodded. "But there's often a good reason why native tribes avoided certain places."

"Have you ever been there yourself?" Claire asked, her dark eyes widening.

"Once." He swallowed, not about to divulge what had transpired during that fateful trip. He'd never told a soul what had happened to him when he had gone on his vision quest at the age of thirteen. "A long time ago. And I've never been back."

Tobias snapped him out of his thoughts. "Does that mean you won't take us there?"

"No. But I can't guarantee your safety."

"What could happen?" Claire asked, her eyes wide and her pupils dilated in the dark light, which made her eyes seem more luminous than ever. She had beautiful eyes. Kind eyes. Eyes full of care and intelligence.

Jack shrugged, as a lump in his throat temporarily choked him. He swallowed it back. "Lots of things. Falling rocks, sickness, bad water, no water, storms. You name it."

Tobias stood up straight. "Well, we'll just have to take our chances then."

Jack raised to his full height as well and turned toward Benton, wondering why he would drag such a beautiful woman into such dangerous territory. "Why are you so hell-bent on finding this fountain anyway?"

"Supposedly it's a fountain of youth."

"What do you need with that kind of thing?"

"I just want to find it, is all." Tobias reached for the map, and Claire moved out of the way. Jack stepped to the side, avoiding her elbow.

"Your fountain might not even exist," Jack ventured. "That map might be bogus."

"Maybe."

"So you are willing to risk your life and Miss Coulter's for something that might be a hoax? Why?"

"I've got my reasons," Tobias shot back. "And I'm paying you to guide us. Not psychoanalyze me. Do I make myself clear?"

"Plain as day." Jack touched the brim of his hat.

Tobias slipped the map back in his pocket. "See you in the morning." He turned to Claire. "Come on, Princess."

She hung back. "Go on ahead," she said. "I'm going to get some air first."

Benton shot her a dark look, but she seemed to ignore it. "Goodnight," she said.

"Don't be long," Tobias replied. He turned on his heel.

Jack glanced at Claire, wondering if her zeal to find the fountain matched that of her fiancé, but she had already turned around to walk away, almost brushing his arm as she went past him. Jack flattened against the edge of the table and watched her go. The faint fragrance of her powdery perfume lingered on the air, mingling with the salty undertone of her female scent. The smell tugged at him. His skin tingled and tightened. He could feel a rippling sensation just under his hide and an insistent prickle inching down his spine.

For two long years he had managed to force himself to remain in his human skin. It was the longest stretch of denial he'd ever achieved. But one night with this woman bedeviling him, added to the pressure of dealing with his parents, and he could no longer resist the spirit animal rearing inside. He dashed to the barn, anxious to shield himself from the eyes of his family, but especially from the eyes of Claire Coulter.

Striding toward the small office he kept in the barn, Jack unfastened his belt and then reached for the buttons of his shirt, his hands shaking. Transformation was full upon him now. The roar in his ears thundered and flared. He stripped, desperate to rid himself of his clothing.

Tossing his head, he felt the unfurling of his ebony hair,

felt the longer, larger muscles bunching at his shoulders and flanks. Then, with a shrill call that echoed through the quiet aisle of stalls, he lost all consciousness as he surrendered himself to the spirit that lived within him.

CLAIRE WALKED AROUND the outside of the house following a flagstone path, unnerved by Jack's warning regarding the map. Were they heaping potential misfortune on an already-dangerous situation? If she misread the code on the door, or if she didn't recognize the symbols at all, what might happen to them? Would they even make it to the fountain? Still, the tarot card had foretold a good ending.

Then her thoughts turned to Maria. Her friend certainly hadn't come to a good ending. Tears welled up again, and all Claire could do was keep moving forward to try to outrun her grief. She walked down the gravel lane, thinking about her best friend and what might have happened to her, until the sound of a horse whinnying brought her out of her daze. She jerked to attention and glanced around, surprised to find that she had walked a good distance from the house. She could see no sign of civilization, except for the rickety fence on her left. Chiding herself for taking such a careless risk as walking alone and unarmed in the night, she turned around and hurried back toward the ranch house.

Quietly, Claire slipped into the house and padded down the hall to the room she shared with Tobias. She prayed he was already asleep. But when she opened the door, she could hear the repetitive sounds of a computer game in progress. She heard Tobias give a victory cry as she turned to close the door.

"Three million!" He grinned. "My highest score yet!"

"Good for you." Claire crossed the floor, hoping he wouldn't be able to detect she'd been crying.

"You're not impressed." He stood up. He was dressed in an olive green tee shirt and a pair of teal-colored shorts, both of good quality and bearing all the right logos, but clashing in color. Obviously, some assistant had purchased Tobias a respectable wardrobe, but unfortunately that same assistant wasn't there to coordinate it.

"Don't you play games?" he asked, oblivious to her perusal of his clothing.

She glanced at him. "I never got into them."

"That surprises me." He reached for the can of Coke on the maple nightstand. "With your IQ and all."

"Working an eight-hour day, spending a lot of time in hospitals, and going to college doesn't leave much time for fun."

"You didn't get any scholarships for college?"

"A few. But only to schools too far from my mother and brother."

"But that's what college is for!" He took a swig of his soda. "Breaking away from la familia!"

"I didn't wish to."

"So serious!" Tobias tilted his head. "What's to be so serious about all the time?"

"I've got plenty." She set the phone on the nightstand. "Excuse me."

Claire walked into the bathroom and closed the door, and then sucked in her breath, more out of alarm than surprise.

There on the counter was a set of lingerie in garish tones of tangerine and lime green, with ruffles at the hips and lace arching across the cups of the bra. Not only did Claire never wear such racy undergarments, but she knew the color would look terrible against her olive skin, and the style was better suited to a brothel than to a ranch-house bedroom. What did Tobias expect to occur should she prance out of the bathroom wearing such an outfit?

Added to her distaste for Tobias's sense of style was her reluctance to accept any gifts from the man. She wanted his charity and her debt to extend only as far as Emilio. She thought she'd made herself clear earlier in the day.

Ignoring the fluorescent undergarments on the counter, Claire took a quick shower and then dressed in the long, white tee shirt she usually wore to bed. For good measure, she pulled on a pair of her plain white panties. Then she picked up her hairbrush and ambled out to the bedroom.

Tobias came to alert at his stance by the window where he'd been waiting for her, holding two flutes of champagne in his hands, and trying to appear nonchalant. When he caught sight of what she was wearing, however, his eager expression collapsed.

"Didn't you see—," he began, pointing toward the bathroom with one of the slender glasses.

"Thanks for the thought, Tobias, but they were not my size."

"But I know your size. Thirty-six–twenty-four–thirty-six. And that's what I bought!"

Claire refused to look at him. He was whining like a little kid. And besides that, how did he know what her dimensions were? Had he sent someone to rummage through her dresser drawers? "Sizes are sometimes off," she replied, struggling to keep her voice calm. "Especially in lingerie."

"Oh yeah?"

"Women sometimes don't wish to admit to their true measurements, so manufacturers fudge a bit."

"Oh." He stared at her for a moment as she sat on the side of the bed, brushing her hair, relieved that he'd so readily accepted her excuse.

"What about the champagne, though?" He stepped closer. "One size fits all."

"Thanks, but I just brushed my teeth."

"Aw, c'mon!" He held a flute under her nose. "I bought it especially for you. It's vegetarian."

She glanced up and saw the neediness behind his witty repartee. It was obvious that Tobias Benton, technology whiz kid and billionaire, didn't know how to handle himself when it came to women. It was common knowledge that he hadn't dated much and had spent all of his time building the CommOptima conglomerate. Could he possibly be a virgin? She felt a small amount of pity for him. He had made an effort to impress her this time.

"All right," she finally replied. "But just one. We have to get up early."

He sat down across from her and gulped his champagne while throwing nervous glances around the room. He had no idea what to say to her, and she wasn't about to make it easier for him. She'd spent enough hours coming up with conversation starters for men, drawing them out, listening to their stories about their work and their bosses. She was tired of taking the initiative for males, of trying to find common ground, only to discover later they were interested only in her body and never her mind.

As she and Tobias sat on their respective bunks, she closed her eyes and said a silent toast for Maria, and then took a thoughtful drink of champagne. It was sweet and smooth and refreshing. After a moment, she opened her eyes to find Tobias flagrantly feasting on her physical attributes again.

"Don't you have to shower?" she asked, finishing her drink.

"Naw. I don't feel like it."

"I always find a shower or bath refreshing at the end of the day."

"Yeah, well us computer geeks don't work up that much of a sweat."

"Do you really think so?" She raised an eyebrow at him, sure now that she held a certain power over him.

He glanced at the bathroom as if it contained torture devices. Then he looked back at Claire and shrugged.

"There is nothing more provocative to a woman than a man with clean skin," she added.

"You're joking." He gulped his champagne. "I thought diamonds were a girl's best friend."

"Not this girl."

He set down his glass and glared at the bathroom again.

"But it's your life, Tobias." She set her champagne glass at the back of the night table and heard the squeak of the bed springs as Tobias rose to his feet. As she settled into bed, she heard the shower burst on. She closed her eyes and pulled the sheet and blanket over her shoulders. If Tobias Benton thought one shower would change her mind about him, he must not be as intelligent as he thought he was.

When Tobias strolled out of the bathroom with a towel wrapped around his hips, Claire feigned sleep. She could hear his breathing as he stood above her, staring down at her.

For a long, horrible moment, she worried that he might pluck up enough courage to confront her. But after an extended pause, he sighed and moved away.

Claire said a silent prayer of thanks, and then her thoughts drifted to the day to come.

Chapter 8

The next morning, Bonita served a simple breakfast of bacon and eggs. Claire ate two eggs and some toast while she gazed out of the window at the mountains to the north, where the trail would take them.

She lifted a forkful of egg while Tobias ambled into the dining room. He picked up a can of Coke as he surveyed the room. She wondered if the man ever drank anything healthy—water, milk, or juice.

"Good morning, Mr. Benton," Susan said in greeting. She was dressed in crisp, pleated jeans that appeared as if she'd never worn them, and a pair of shiny, high-heeled boots. Jack's father wore khakis and a long-sleeved cotton shirt with a sweater thrown over his shoulders. Susan looked as if she'd been up for a couple of hours and was waiting to go on a Sunday drive.

"Morning." Tobias glanced at the older couple. "You two are up awfully early."

"You're telling me," William growled.

"Jack said five and so here we are!" Susan sat down with a plate that held a scant few ounces of food in lonely little piles.

"Wait a minute." Tobias stood near the chair next to Claire and glared at Jack's folks. "You're not going on the ride."

"Yes we are," William countered.

"I thought I made myself clear last night. The location of the fountain is secret."

William waved him off. "Your secret'll be safe with us. We just want to come along. Haven't seen Jack for ages."

"We used to ride all the time when we were first married!" Susan put in, her smile almost too bright for the breakfast table. "I'm looking forward to seeing the old sights."

"No, I can't allow it." Tobias set his soda can on the table and turned back to William. "My associate will not stand for it."

"We don't have to go the entire way," William shrugged. "If that will make it any better."

"You can't stop a man from riding his own land." Jack put his fork down. "The Hughes property goes almost all the way to Medicine Valley."

"Medicine Valley?" William interjected. "You're taking Benton to Medicine Valley?"

"That's what he wants," Jack replied, leveling his gaze on the billionaire. "Right?"

Tobias glanced from William to Jack and then back to the older man. "Yeah."

William picked up his orange juice. "Well, I don't have any intention of stealing your secret, Mr. Benton." He sipped his drink. "And I'd be more than happy to put it in writing, if that'll make you feel better."

Tobias squinted as he mulled over the other man's words, and then he shook his head. "As long as you understand, Mr. Hughes." He slumped into the chair next to Claire. "When we get to the valley, only two of us are going in."

"Not a problem, young man. Not a problem."

JACK MADE QUICK work of his breakfast without saying another word to anyone. As Claire attended to her breakfast, she heard an odd, low noise in the hall behind her. She froze, intently listening. She'd never heard anything like it. All she could compare the sound to was someone playing a low note on a cello, but playing it deep underground, with the sound echoing back upon itself off ancient, crumbling walls. Whatever it was, the noise made the hair raise on the back of her neck.

"What's that noise?" she commented to Tobias, so only he could hear.

"What noise?"

"That." She stared at the hallway leading to the kitchen. "Don't you hear it?"

"No." He followed her gaze as he put down his Coke can. "What's it sound like?"

"Creepy. A low thrumming."

"Sorry, Princess. I don't hear a thing." Tobias picked up a crisp piece of bacon. "Too much heavy metal through bad earphones as a kid."

Claire barely registered his words as she noticed Jack Hughes look at her, catch her expression, and then glance over his shoulder at the hallway.

At that moment, Jack's grandmother Betty and a slight, brown-haired man walked into the dining room.

"Good morning, everyone," Betty announced. "This is Simeon Avare, who arrived late last night. He's a professor at the University of Washington."

Jack rose to his feet and extended his hand. The guests introduced themselves in turn, but just as Claire held out her hand to shake the professor's, Betty offered him a cup of coffee. He stepped aside to accept it.

"Thank you," he said. His soft voice held the trace of a northern-European accent, and his slender, well-groomed figure spoke of his European background as well. He wore his hair longer than the current American style, and combed it back off his forehead and behind his ears. He had the smooth, assured bearing of a person confident of himself in regard to the rest of the world, the kind of bearing Claire aspired to.

Claire suddenly realized that during the time she had been gawking at the professor, the ominous noise had faded.

"And you are—" He smiled at Claire. He seemed to have a lot of teeth—small and white and straight.

"Claire Coulter." She retracted her hand. "I work with Mr. Benton at CommOptima."

"We're engaged," Tobias interjected.

"How lovely," Simeon murmured, his attention focused on Claire. "I did not expect to have such an attractive traveling companion." He winked at her. "Life is full of marvelous surprises, is it not?"

He smiled again, and his face broke into creases—around his mouth, at his chin, and at the corners of his intelligent gray eyes. Then, as all men did, he ran a slow and appreciative glance down the contours of Claire's figure. But his gaze spoke of fine wine and cigars, of women in evening gowns and elbow-length gloves sipping martinis, of grand pianos and marble floors—the kind of world she had never stepped foot in and a world Maria and her mother had only dusted.

"You flatter me, sir," she answered, looking back down at her plate, unaffected by his charm and his wink, but completely fascinated by his poise and grace. Simeon Avare would make *some* college professor. She had trouble picturing the man standing in front of a class, doing something as banal as delivering a lecture.

Tobias leaned forward, intent upon deflecting Simeon's attention away from his 'fiancée.' "You're the guy that's looking for snakes?"

"A certain genus of snake, yes." Simeon pulled out a chair and sat down as Bonita slid a plate of bacon and eggs in front of him.

"What kind?" Claire asked.

"*Crotalus viridis oreganos*, commonly known as the Northern Pacific rattler."

"A rattlesnake?" Susan Hughes lifted her coffee cup. "Why in the world would you want to study such a horrible thing?"

"I am doing research on the medicinal effects of venom, Mrs. Hughes."

"I've heard of that," Tobias put in. "Some scientists believe venom holds the key to curing neurological disorders."

"Quite right, Mr. Benton." The professor smiled at him. "And halting the aging process as well."

"You're trying to stop aging?" Claire asked. "Is that possible?"

"Why not?" Simeon narrowed his eyes. "Cancer cells

don't age. They are designed not to degrade. Why is that? Is there something special about those cells that we can tap into? And why do some organisms degrade more quickly than others? I hope to find the answers to such questions with my research."

"Well, I'll tell you one thing." William Hughes waved his fork in the professor's direction. "Any rattler that gets close to me isn't going to live more than a few seconds!"

Claire stared at the older man, wondering why some people thought they were entitled to kill any creature that threatened them, even if in mere self-defense. She felt someone's gaze upon her and found Jack Hughes thoughtfully regarding the side of her face. As soon as she glanced his way, he turned back to his breakfast and concentrated on scraping up the last bit of his eggs.

"Then you'll be shooting from here to Sunday," Betty retorted. "There's hundreds of rattlers out there."

"Great." Tobias screwed up his features.

"Not in the Hummer," William proclaimed.

Jack looked up. "You're not taking the Hummer."

"Yes I am." William jerked a thumb over his shoulder. "That vehicle can go anywhere. If it can take on Kuwait and Iraq, it can damn well take on anything."

"Not the trail we're riding."

"I thought you said we're headed toward the Two Sisters."

"We are."

"Then the Hummer will be fine."

"The trail's changed, Dad. Besides, we're going beyond the Two Sisters."

"How far?"

Jack shot a glance at Claire. "It's hard to tell from the map."

"So why can't I have a look at it?" William turned his hard eyes upon Tobias. "What's the big secret anyway?"

Claire rested her wrist on the table and answered for her boss. "It's a sacred place, Mr. Hughes. We would like to keep it that way."

"So only the three of you can look at the map?"

"That's right."

"So I can never see it."

"No."

"You think I can't keep a secret?" He shot a glare around the people at the table, as if daring anyone to voice a doubt about his character.

"I never said that," Claire replied.

"That's what it sounds like to me!"

Claire sighed. "You are entitled to your own opinions, Mr. Hughes. Nevertheless, you are not seeing the map."

"Here, here!" Simeon raised his glass of orange juice in the air. "A woman of beauty and spirit. How enchanting!"

"Enchanting my ass!" William jumped to his feet, rattling the china on the table. "Bull-headed is more like it. What happens if something goes wrong, missy? What if Jack runs into trouble? What if something happens to you or your boyfriend? How will we find this goddamn fountain of youth then?"

Claire pushed back her chair and stood up, refusing to spend another moment at the same table as William Hughes. "If something happens to me or Tobias," she said through clenched teeth, "there will be no reason for you to continue the search." She raised her chin. "And don't call me missy again. My name is Claire."

She swept past Jack, angry with him for allowing his father to berate his guests.

"Claire, wait!" Tobias called after her.

She stormed toward the bedroom to brush her teeth, all the while trying to calm herself down. William Hughes had no reason to swear at her or belittle her. No one did. But then again, she didn't have to let the man get to her as he did. She took a deep breath and concentrated on banishing William from her thoughts. It was all about perception and her place in the world, she knew that. She could alter her perceptions and survive, just as she had always done.

"Claire!" Tobias caught up to her, stepped in front of her, and flung open the door to the bedroom.

She marched through it. "Thanks," she said.

"You sure told him off!" Tobias trailed her toward the bathroom, chuckling. "That was priceless."

"It wasn't meant as entertainment. The man infuriates me."

"He's an old fart. Old school. He's just full of himself."

"Well he doesn't need to take it out on me."

"You've got a point."

"You could have said something. You are my boss."

He stared at her. "What, and spoil the show? Never!" He laughed.

She turned to face him. "Listen, Tobias." She paused for a moment to tamp down her anger. She had no reason to be upset with him, at least not this time. "Don't share anything with William Hughes. I don't trust the man."

"He was just taking precautions."

"He's the type of guy that shouldn't be allowed anywhere near a dig. Do you know what I mean?" She reached for the bathroom door. "Now if you will excuse me?"

"Sure." Tobias put up his hands in a gesture of surrender and backed away.

TOBIAS WATCHED CLAIRE shut the door, telling him in no uncertain terms to stand clear of her. A moment later, Tobias heard the lock click. Didn't the chick trust him? He might not have bought her the right size of underwear, but he had enough sense not to invade a woman's bathroom space.

Tobias paced to the center of the bedroom while he idly scratched the right side of his face, just in front of his ear. Being away from his company and all contact with email made him feel adrift and disconnected, but at the same time he was feeling very much alive. He had to admit that Claire's fiery nature challenged him, gave him that jolt of adrenaline he thrived on, like the old days when he'd scramble to figure out a way to steamroll a rival and then watch CommOptima stock soar when he succeeded. Man, he used to love that feeling. He got the same sensation from games sometimes, but never like this, and the digital rush never lasted that long. With Claire, the challenge would never end—unless she somehow changed her entire personality, and he couldn't see that happening.

Doing the favor for his "partner" had seemed like a real headache at first, right up to the moment he'd met Claire. After that one interview with her, however, he couldn't wait to be alone with her—alone in the high sierras, in a car, any-where. It didn't matter. He just wanted to get his hands on her and possess her.

Tobias felt a surge of arousal just thinking about her. Since that first meeting, he had fantasized about what it would be like to finally get between her legs—and he had every intention of making it that far. He'd never had sexual intercourse with a woman, and he couldn't visualize having sex with Claire without getting a raging hard-on.

He'd always been partial to blondes, but Claire had changed his personal preference. Her dark hair, glowing olive skin, and big, luminous black eyes had created a new standard of beauty for him. And her mouth—ah, he couldn't even look at it for more than a few seconds without losing complete control.

So what if her family background lacked money and bloodline. So what if her mother had been a housekeeper all her life and had never got her green card. Once Claire became Mrs. Tobias Benton, no one would dare make a comment about her poverty-stricken childhood, her absentee father, or her shabby relatives.

Tobias didn't expect Claire to fall in love with him right away. Maybe she never would come to love him. She might not even come to like him. She'd made it painfully clear that she was not interested in a relationship and only wanted to help her brother. But he didn't care. He would change her mind.

For now, just to be seen with her was enough—to have other men gawk in surprise and jealousy that he had scored such a babe was reward in itself. And then to have a couple of kids with IQs off the charts to carry on the Benton name and fame—that's all he wanted. And that's what he'd get if things turned out like he planned.

It was a lot to look forward to.

Besides, going on this quest was like playing a computer game, complete with buried treasure and a beautiful princess to save. It was going to be great. He was good at games. But best of all, he couldn't lose this one.

Chapter 9

Later that morning, as Jack, Claire, Simeon Avare and Grandma Betty plodded north, the other travelers drove the Hummer somewhere in a nearby valley where Jack had said an old logging road cut through the forest. Claire tried to ease the ache in her leg by moving it slightly, but the pain continued to throb in her knee and thigh.

Though her watch read only eleven, it seemed as if they had ridden for days. The early part of the morning had been spent climbing ever-higher into the hills, on a narrow trail through an expanse of lodgepole pine, growing as straight and close together "as the hair on the back of a dog" according to Jack's grandmother, who spouted occasional commentary as they plodded along. No one except Claire seemed to listen to the old woman, but she welcomed the information, having a natural curiosity about her surroundings.

The horses carefully picked their way up the rocky switchbacks, swaying and blowing, until they reached a ridge, where they took a short break. Claire could see the turquoise sparkle of Lake Tahoe miles away to the southwest, and the drier mountains to the north. Up on the ridge, the April sun warmed her head and shoulders, but a stiff wind soon blew away that small comfort.

Jack checked the three extra mounts and the two pack horses, while his grandmother claimed she had to "drain her radiator" and then took off for a pile of boulders. Tobias, Susan, and William were somewhere down below in the comfort of the Hummer.

Dr. Avare sidled his mount up next to hers.

"So your fiancé doesn't ride?" he asked, scanning the stunning view below them.

"I think he's more techie than trail hand," she replied, glancing at the attractive man beside her. Avare rode a horse beautifully, straight and elegant in the saddle, with expensive gloves on his hands that fit him like a second skin. He even wore a cowboy hat, but it was a flat-brimmed, Spanish-looking hat that perfectly complimented his gray jacket, and was tilted rakishly over one eye.

"What man would chose comfort over a beautiful woman?" Simeon tipped his head to shade his eyes from the sun and looked toward the north. "Mr. Benton should use better sense."

Then he turned and gazed at her, his warm expression open and friendly. "Much can happen in the wilderness. Danger. Injury. Even romance. Wouldn't you agree?"

Claire nodded. "It's certainly a change from my quiet little lab."

Avare chuckled. "Had I a betrothed as beautiful as you, I would guard her well. From everything."

Claire saw Jack watching them, and wondered if he could hear snatches of their conversation on the breeze.

"I can take care of myself, Dr. Avare. Don't you worry."

"Simeon. I insist." He gave a small bow.

"Simeon."

She shifted in her saddle, trying to find a more comfortable position, but her bottom ached almost as much as her leg. Then, before she'd found any relief, Grandma Betty reappeared, and Jack made a clucking sound at his horse, Brutus, urging him back to work. The string of riders and pack animals headed down the trail, going north.

They continued to ride down a gradual slope as the forest thinned around them, changing to sparse Jeffrey pine and prickly chaparral. The sound of the horses changed from a muffled clumping to a more hollow clatter as their hooves kicked up lichen and gravel. They spotted fewer ground squirrels as the landscape grew more and more dry. Granite blocks jutted up around them, like fortresses between the scrawny trees. They had entered a completely different world, that of the high eastern Sierra where rain rarely fell.

Claire was glad for her fleece jacket and the ball cap she wore over her braided hair. Though it was April and the sun shone brightly, it was chilly at this high altitude. She wished she had worn gloves like the sturdy leather pair covering Jack's long, capable hands or the fashionable ones Simeon sported. She hadn't thought of gloves.

From under the bill of her cap, she could see dusty blue hills in the distance and sand-colored ridges on either side of her. The wide valley they had ridden into during the last hour was surprisingly full of vegetation—although most of it appeared to be half-dead. Many of the shrubs were tangles of dried, brittle branches and thorns, and another prickly plant with dried seed pods grew all around them—a vicious groundcover.

As they rounded a rock formation, the chilly wind shifted and once again, Claire caught the deep thrumming sound she'd heard earlier that morning. What was it?

She turned in the saddle, the leather creaking at her movement, and expected to see some wild animal standing on the rocky cliff beside her, waiting to pounce—an animal she had never come in contact with and was therefore producing an unfamiliar sensation in her. But she saw nothing except rocks, scrub, her fellow riders, and the string of horses.

They clomped onward, and in another half hour, rode down a steep hill toward the sandy channel of a dry creek bed. The grade was so precipitous, Claire felt as if she were going to plunge headfirst over the neck of her horse, Peanut. She jammed her feet deep into the stirrups and leaned back. Her right leg throbbed in protest and seemed unnaturally bent around the ribcage of her mount. She grimaced, grabbed the pommel of the saddle for dear life, and forced herself to ignore the pounding agony in her leg as the horse trotted down the slope.

Peanut came to a lumbering halt at the bottom of the creek bed, and Claire breathed a sigh of relief that she hadn't toppled to the ground, especially when Jack looked over his shoulder to see how everyone had fared coming down the bank of the ravine.

Claire surveyed the creek bottom. Bits of green and a row of small alders grew on the far side, where the water table must have been close to the surface, or where the last of the river water had remained in a pool until it, too, had dried up.

When she saw Jack get down from his horse, she dismounted as well, and hobbled back a few steps, rubbing her thigh.

"You okay?" Jack asked, leading his mount past her.

"Sure."

He paused and glanced at the leg she'd been rubbing and then looked at the horse behind her.

It was at that moment Claire realized Jack had never given her the smarmy once-over she was accustomed to receiving from men. In fact, Jack seemed unusually disinterested in her, even standoffish. Was he shy around women? She couldn't imagine the six-foot horseman being shy about anything. Maybe he had a satisfying relationship with a woman already, and that's why he stayed clear of her, even in the "just looking" department. But what kind of relationship could a man have with someone when he lived out in the middle of nowhere?

To Claire, Jack's lack of interest was wonderfully freeing. People didn't realize how often her privacy and personal space were trespassed by men who wanted to catch her eye or make a connection. She could be on a bus, at a restaurant, or even standing in a line for the women's restroom, and guys would appear at her elbow in an attempt to make small talk and get her phone number.

As a teenager, she'd been flattered by the attention. But as she had grown older, the onslaught of males had become more annoying than enjoyable, and their come-ons were always far too predictable. Then came her shattering love affair with her wealthy boyfriend, and her heart had hardened against men forever.

"Are you sure you're okay?" Jack repeated.

"Of course." She reached for the reins, hoping he would leave her alone.

"Looks like your right stirrup may be set a little low. That's why your leg is hurting."

"I didn't say my leg was hurting." Claire urged Peanut forward. She wasn't about to reveal the extent of her ignorance when it came to riding, as she'd had enough ridicule from the Hugheses.

"You don't have to. I can tell just by watching you walk." He came up beside her again. "Hold on there."

Peanut betrayed her by obeying his master's command and coming to a halt. Deftly Jack flipped up the saddle flap, gave the narrow belt a lift and a gentle tug, and then settled the stirrup back in place.

"There. That should do it."

"Thanks," Claire said. "But you didn't have to trouble yourself, really."

"You want to be more saddle sore than you have to be?"

"Who said I was going to be sore?"

Jack looked at her and then broke into a grin as his brown eyes sparkled at her. He looked right at her—not at her face, not at her hair, and not at her breasts, but at *her*—easily making a connection without spouting a cutesy phrase or an insincere compliment. Then without saying anything more, he walked away in his loose-hipped amble, leaving her to stare after him.

What was it about Jack Hughes that could draw her in so quickly—with a mere exchange of eye contact? She'd felt the same tug the first time she'd met him at the dinner table. What was it about Jack that made her aware of his gaze on her face and his quiet presence in a room? Judging by the expressions she'd seen cross his face, she knew he picked up on her thoughts as well and paused to consider what she was saying while others just talked. She'd never experienced anything like it with a man, and it surprised her.

Yet he seemed oblivious—or at least impervious—to her outward attributes and to the physical effect he had upon her as well. What kind of man was he? A man of steel?

Claire watched Jack as he set his horse to graze before joining his grandmother near a tiny pool of water in some rocks at the side of the ravine. Claire followed, guiding her horse to the water, and told herself to quit wasting time thinking about Jack Hughes. He was just a guy who was going to lead them into the wilderness and then go back to his regular life, and that's all.

A few minutes later, the Hummer rolled up, its shiny black paint dulled with dust. William, Susan, and Tobias climbed out looking fresh and cool, having spent the past six hours in a comfortable bubble of air-conditioning.

"Hey, Princess." Tobias joined her. "How is it going?"

"Slow and bumpy," Claire admitted. "But I'll live."

"Why don't you just give up this proving-yourself thing and join us in the Hummer?"

"I think it's you three who will be joining us."

"Says who?"

"Jack says we'll be heading into some hills soon, where there aren't any roads."

"The Hummer doesn't need a road."

Claire shrugged as she watched Jack and his grandmother prepare lunch: peanut butter sandwiches, apples, and water from plastic jugs. Neither Jack nor Betty seemed overly stiff after six hours of riding. Then again, they were probably callused in all the right places. But if a seventy-year-old grandmother could make the ride, Claire vowed that she could endure it as well, and without complaining.

"Is this lunch?" William exclaimed as Jack handed him a tin plate containing his food.

Jack glanced at the plate. "You don't have to eat it."

Claire said nothing. She was surprised at how ravenous she had become just riding a horse. Maybe it was the cold spring air that had given her such an appetite. She accepted her plate gratefully and stood near the tiny pool, gulping down her sandwich.

Susan Hughes minced up next to Claire, her heeled boots sinking into the caked sand of the creek bottom.

"You know you're crazy to be riding when you could be with us in the Hummer, dear," she said.

"That's what I've been trying to tell her," Tobias chimed in, rolling his eyes.

"I'm just practicing for when the Hummer won't make it." Claire took a bite of the crisp, juicy apple.

"Don't believe everything Jack tells you," William put in, "like that crap about there not being a road. He likes to think he's a mountain man, and wants us all to follow suit."

"He just likes the old-fashioned ways." Susan shook her head, as if Jack's choice of life was heartbreaking to her.

"Well the guy should come into the twenty-first century, if you ask me." Tobias glared at the apple and put it in the pocket of his coat. "In fact, why couldn't a helicopter get us where we want to go?"

"Because," a dry voice answered behind Claire. She knew without turning around that it was Jack speaking. "The Park Service doesn't allow choppers in that part of the wilderness. Or four-wheel drives or ATVs. Horses are our only choice."

Chapter 10

For the rest of the day, the vehicle and riders followed the dry creek bed, plodding onward until the fading April light would soon force them to stop. Claire wondered how far they'd ridden. It felt as if they'd gone as far as the Canadian border, though in reality they probably hadn't ridden any farther north than Carson City, Nevada.

As they approached a bend in the creek bed, Claire heard an engine revving up and then the echoing whine of spinning tires.

Betty Hughes pulled her mount to a stop and looked over at her grandson.

"Didn't take long," she commented.

"Nope," Jack replied.

"It's a good thing you brought the extra horses along."

Jack nodded, his expression impassive as they continued riding toward the curve in the river.

Claire studied him, amazed at the lack of triumph on his face. The Hummer had obviously got stuck up ahead, just as Jack had predicted. He had been right, his father wrong. Didn't he derive any sense of satisfaction from the sound of the Hummer's wheels spinning? Most men would be gloating by now or at least feeling smug. But Jack showed no emotion whatsoever.

Sure enough, Claire soon spied the Hummer, tilted to the driver's side, its rear wheel sunk deep in a rut of the creek bed. Dirt sprayed out as William Hughes desperately gunned the engine, determined to break free by applying brute force to the problem. Tobias stood at the rear of the vehicle, shouting instructions and advice, but the Hummer merely rolled up the side of the rut, spun some more, and then rolled back down.

Betty nodded at the huge machine. "The patience gene definitely skipped a generation in our family."

"You can say that again." Jack sighed. "There's no way that Hummer's coming out on its own."

"And it'll cost a fortune to tow it out of here," Claire remarked. Jack glanced down at her.

"It's a rental, too," Betty added, shaking her head.

Simeon sidled closer. "How do you say it?" He clucked his tongue as he pushed back his hat. "Tenderfeet." He shook his head in mock disgust.

Jack said nothing. Instead, he urged his horse to a trot and rode up to the Hummer, his tall figure straight and relaxed in the saddle, as if he were physically melded to the horse.

Claire watched him, envious. If she tried to trot like that, the bones in her bottom would break in two. They felt half fractured already. She couldn't wait to climb down to solid ground. The image of a nice warm bath popped into her mind, teasing her with the promise of soothing hot water. She instantly dashed away the thought. There would be no baths for her tonight and for many nights to come.

"YOU'RE GOING TO have to leave it," Jack was saying as the rest of the riders came abreast of the Hummer.

Jack's father and mother stood outside the vehicle. William glowered at the Hummer, fists on his hips, his face flushed a deep scarlet.

"Four-wheel drive, my ass!" he exclaimed, giving the front tire a swift kick.

"The trail's only going to get worse."

Tobias stuffed his thin white hands in the pockets of his jacket. "So what do we do, just leave it here?"

"You're going to have to." Jack scowled.

William glared at the Hummer and then turned his hot eyes on his son. "Out in the middle of nowhere?"

"It'll be okay," Jack said, untying the last three horses in the string.

"Yeah." Tobias swept the air beside him. "Who would come all the way out here to vandalize a truck? They'd have to be crazy!"

Jack led a horse up to his mother and offered her the reins. "Need help mounting up?" he asked.

She nodded and hesitantly put a hand on Jack's shoulder.

Claire watched Jack display considerable patience and gentleness as he guided Susan's boot into the stirrup and then boosted her up to the saddle.

"Goddamned horses," William grumbled, heaving himself onto a large bay.

"They'll get us where we're going, Billy," Betty chided him.

"Tobias?" Jack held out the reins of the palomino to Tobias.

The billionaire eyed the reins and then glanced at the horse, as wary of the animal as he had been of the shower at the ranch house.

"Ever ride?" Jack inquired.

"Not really." Tobias took the reins and headed toward the right side of the horse.

"You mount on the left," Jack instructed, without a trace of ridicule in his voice. As Tobias strode to the correct side of his horse, Jack continued the short equestrian lesson. "Bud's gentle. He'll do what you say. So use a light hand. Just pull back to stop. Pull to the side to turn."

Tobias nodded and adjusted his position in the saddle as he held the reins high in the air, his elbows poking outward like chicken wings. Claire noticed Betty sputter and grin, but the old woman nudged her horse to a gallop to hide her laughter from the younger man.

Claire had to agree that Tobias cut a comedic figure on horseback, dressed as he was in his black leather jacket and turtleneck—all stiff and straight, with his feet jutting wide on each side of his mount.

Then Bud moved, startling his rider, and Tobias panicked. Instead of using his legs to steady his position in the saddle, he swayed backward, jerking the reins to keep from falling.

The bit tore into Bud's mouth, and he yanked back his head, anxious to rid himself of a human who didn't know what he was doing. Claire watched in horror as the horse danced sideways, frightened of Tobias's harsh treatment. Tobias cried out, still yanking frantically at the reins while Bud dipped backward on his haunches, bunching his flanks to rear up.

"Whoa!" Jack shouted. He reached for the bridle, leaping up to grab it as the horse reared into the air. Tobias clutched the pommel of the saddle, almost sliding off the horse, while Jack pulled Bud's head downward. "Whoa, Bud!" he commanded. "Steady, boy!"

The blond horse pranced and blew, his eyes white-rimmed, his nostrils flaring, but Jack quickly got him under control.

He turned to look up at Tobias. "I said a light hand, Benton. Light!"

"Hey! It just tried to kill me!"

Jack shook his head in disgust and then said something to Bud while he stroked the horse's neck. Bud's ears twitched back and forth as he listened intently to his master. Then, still holding onto the bridle, Jack urged Bud to a walk.

"Come on," he said, waving on the other riders. He guided Bud down the creek bed, his gloved hand next to the palomino's jaw, his own horse obediently trailing beside him, until both horse and human had recovered from the incident.

AN HOUR LATER, Jack held up his hand, motioning the group to stop. The riders came to a creaking, jangling halt. By then, Tobias was riding on his own, but he remained uncharacteristically quiet. Judging by the frown on his face, Claire guessed he didn't enjoy being in the saddle.

Claire glanced around at the shadowed ridges and scrawny trees. Everything was bathed in lilac—even the sky—as a full moon rose above the distant hills. Lavender moonlight caught on the pattern of rocks of the creek bed, which had narrowed considerably, and was now only a few feet across, including the banks on either side. Sand had turned to dirt and boulders as the riders had begun a gradual ascent into the mountains again.

"We'll bed down here," Jack commented, nodding toward a flat area on a slope above the dry creek. He turned his horse to head for the campsite.

"Wouldn't that sandbar be more comfortable?" Tobias challenged, pointing up the creek.

Jack narrowed his eyes as he surveyed the slight rise in the middle of the creek, where a soft, sandy hump lay sparsely covered with dry grass.

"I wouldn't recommend it," he finally replied.

"You'd rather sleep in that gravel pit up there? Not me!"

"Well, then Benton," Jack drawled, crossing his gloved hands over the pommel of his saddle, "you be my guest. Sleep on the sandbar. But one of these days, we're going to have our next spring storm."

"So?" Tobias glanced at the sandbar and back to Jack.

"When that happens, that sandbar will be under four feet of water. Raging water."

Without waiting for Tobias to make another comment, Jack rode up the bank to the flat area he'd selected and then dismounted. A moment later he reached for the cinch of his saddle, seeing to the comfort of his mount before his own.

Claire and Simeon followed his lead, and the others trailed up the bank behind them, with truculent Tobias bringing up the rear.

Tobias slid off his horse and stood to the side as Jack reached down to loosen the cinch of the palomino. Betty walked up to do the same for Claire's horse, Peanut.

"I'll do it," Claire said to the older woman. "If you just show me how."

"You don't have to." Tobias reached for Claire's elbow. "I'm paying them to take care of this kind of stuff."

Claire shrugged out of his grip. "I want to. Peanut's my horse. I want to take care of him. I like doing it."

Again, Claire had the feeling that Jack was listening to every word she said, even though he appeared busily engaged with taking the saddle off Bud and settling it upon the ground nearby.

"Suit yourself," Tobias grumbled and stomped away.

* * *

WHILE TOBIAS, SIMEON, William, and Susan stood to the side chatting, Jack, Claire, and Betty set up camp. Jack unloaded the equipment and sent Claire off to gather wood. Tobias trailed after her.

"Why don't you just relax and let the Hughes clan get the firewood?" he asked. "Is this some genetic hang-up you have, wanting to do all the dirty work?"

She ignored the insult. "I like to keep busy."

"After all that riding?"

"Especially after the riding. It's best to walk off muscle stiffness." She picked up two hefty branches. "Here," she said, holding them in front of the billionaire. "Take these, would you?"

Tobias did her bidding, but eyed the rough gray bark with suspicion. "Are there creepy crawlies on these?"

"No doubt." Claire reached for more fallen branches. "There are probably even ticks up here."

"Ticks?" Tobias held the armful of wood away from his leather jacket. "Like I could get bubonic plague or something?"

"I think Lyme disease would be more likely," she replied, stacking more wood in his arms. "But you're wearing leather. Just brush yourself off when we get back."

"You owe me," he retorted, scowling.

"You want to eat, don't you?" she shot back.

"Yeah, but when I signed on to this gig, it wasn't as a pack mule."

"Well, the way I look at it, Tobias, the sooner we get a fire going, the sooner we get fed. And I don't know about you, but I'm ravenous."

"You can say that again," he murmured, leveling his gaze at her. "For something hot. Something tasty."

Claire turned away, doing her utmost to ignore his sexual innuendo, and busied herself with gathering up the last of the firewood. His hungry expression had sent a shudder down her spine.

"Come on," she said, leading the way back to camp. From

now on, she would have to remember to keep alone-time in the forest with Tobias to a minimum. She hurried back to the safety of the camp, where she knew Jack Hughes would be close at hand.

Set 4

I wish I weren't so alone. I know, I know, I have always considered myself a lone wolf—an individual—and I never did fit in with the Golden Ones, who were as close to soul mates as I will ever get. And yes, I remember how I loathed them. They treated me shabbily even though I was every inch their equal. But I grow weary of this constant waiting, this constant vigilance, this constant battle to retain my physical form. Who would have guessed that something here on Earth held a secret toxin that poisoned all the others? Only I, with my thick hide and solitary ways, was immune to the slow and agonizing decline of my brothers.

Set, Lord of Chaos

Chapter 11

As Claire walked back to camp, the moon sank deeper and deeper into a bank of clouds. Darkness closed in upon the forest like a black fog. By the time Claire got back to camp, she could hardly see any detail in the ground in front of her shoes. And when they sat down around the fire to eat their dinner an hour later, all Claire could see were the fronts of her companions and the barest line of the backs of their hats and jackets. The crackling fire threw shadows at crazy angles, lighting up demon masks on everyone around her, even Grandma Betty.

No one talked much during the evening meal, as most of the travelers weren't on conversational term with each other. Only Betty seemed cheerful as she cut into her pork chop and ate with gusto.

"There's nothing like a meal cooked over a real fire," she commented, grinning.

"The chops are excellent, Mrs. Hughes." Simeon smiled at her.

"But where's the Coke?" Tobias inquired, holding out his tin cup. "I don't do water."

"I'm sorry, young man. We didn't bring Coke along."

"You didn't bring Coke?" Tobias jumped to his feet. "Why not?"

Jack raised his glance to Tobias, his expression impassive. He didn't seem overly concerned, and he certainly didn't seem afraid of the billionaire's wrath.

William put his plate down in the sand. "Jack, why didn't you pack soda for Mr. Benton?"

Jack finished chewing his bite of meat. "I don't do specialty foods."

"Specialty foods!" Tobias plopped back down. "You call Coke a specialty food?"

Jack put down his fork. "Soda is heavy, Benton. And the cans cause a lot of trash. So we don't bring it on trail rides. You're going to have to suffer and drink water."

"Suffer?" Tobias seethed. "I'm paying you a thousand dollars a day, and you expect me to suffer?"

"I'll be happy to turn back any time." Jack stood up and placed his plate on a nearby rock. "You just tell me when."

For a long moment, Tobias glowered at Jack, unaware of how ludicrous he seemed raising a fuss over a soft drink. Jack stared back, unruffled and unconcerned.

Claire touched Tobias's arm. "There's caffeine in coffee, Tobias," she put in, trying to diffuse the situation. "If that's what you need."

"I hate coffee!" Tobias spat as he plopped back down on the rock he'd been using as a chair. "I can't believe there's no Coke!"

"I can't believe there's no gin and tonics," William growled, staring down at his cup of water. "What kind of outfit is this?" He glanced at his son.

"As I said, we can turn back any time." Jack turned on his heel and walked away, and within seconds was swallowed up by the gloom.

"What's eating him?" Tobias asked, returning to his dinner of chops, beans and fried potatoes.

"Poor Jack has never been right since the accident," Susan put in.

Claire's interest piqued. "What accident?"

"Oh, it was about a year ago."

"Two years," William corrected. "As of March thirteenth. Jesus, Susan, how could you forget?"

"Oh, yes. It was March. My, how time flies!" Susan reached down beside her foot and pulled a wallet out of the purse she'd brought with her. "March the thirteenth. A Friday." She slid a photograph out of its clear sleeve and sat gazing at the little rectangle. "Why would Jack have picked Friday the thirteenth as his wedding day?"

"Because he's ornery," William said, stabbing a big piece of pork. "That's why!"

"So there was an accident on Jack's wedding day?" Claire chewed the last of her grilled cheese sandwich, hoping one of Jack's parents would continue the story.

Susan nodded. "He wrecked his car on the way to the church. The medics found him in a field nearby. Both of his legs were broken. And one arm."

"Tell them the other part." William goaded her with his elbow.

She brushed him off. "No, I couldn't!"

William looked across the fire at Claire. "He was naked. Not a stitch of clothing on him."

"Kinky," Tobias murmured, half smiling.

"His tux, his underwear—everything—tossed on the ground."

Susan leaned closer to Claire, and held out the photograph. "This was his fiancée, Linda Edmonds. Isn't she a doll?"

Claire studied the face that looked back at her. Jack's ex-fiancée was beautiful, with a flawless smile, big blue eyes, and gorgeous, shoulder-length blond hair. The only thing missing in the picture to round out the vision of the perfect beauty queen was a tiara.

"She's lovely," Claire murmured, knowing how often such a woman was tapped for marriage by powerful men, men who passed over women such as Maria and herself with astounding predictability.

"She's the daughter of our best friends." Susan slipped the photo back into the picture section of her wallet. "It was the perfect match. It really was."

"But they never got married?" Simeon asked. He held his plate in one slender hand. He hadn't eaten his beans or his potatoes.

"No." William grimaced. "It was an outrage. A slap in the face. Marge and Daniel barely spoke to us for months afterward."

"Why?" Claire asked.

"They claimed Jack wanted out. That he used the accident as an excuse to back out."

"That seems harsh," Tobias commented.

Betty rose. "Jack must have had his reasons," she stated. "He's not the kind of fella to leave a woman in the lurch."

"Then why did he run?" William countered. "Why did he throw everything away and come out here—to the middle of nowhere?"

"And the poor girl!" Susan added. "Linda was absolutely devastated. Can you imagine being left at the altar?"

Claire shook her head at Susan's question. Inwardly, however, she knew there were much worse things than being jilted at the altar. At least Linda had been chosen for marriage, not lied to, used, and then laughed at.

"Excuse me." She jumped to her feet, her voice quavering. "I didn't realize how late it was! I have to call my brother. Excuse me!"

Before anyone could make a comment, she rushed from the ring of light, hoping no one had seen the color draining from her face. She'd thought that after all these years, she would over the incident. But she'd never really dealt with it or talked about it. She'd simply stuffed it away, out of sight, just like everything else.

CLAIRE DIDN'T RUN far. It was too dark to go anywhere. She'd never been outdoors where there were no streetlights or house lights to dispel the gloom of evening. Out here in the mountains, she couldn't see anything but cold pinpoints of stars in the cloudy sky, which did nothing to help her find a path.

She stumbled past a boulder, tripped on a rotting fallen log, and swore under her breath, hardly recognizing the frustrated stream of Spanish expletives that burst from her mouth.

"Too dark for you?" a dry voice asked, disembodied in the blackness.

Startled, Claire ground to a halt, searching for the man she knew was somewhere on her left. Slowly, the tall, lanky form of Jack Hughes materialized before her straining eyes. He was standing on top of a boulder the size of a small sedan.

"Sorry," he continued. "Did I scare you?"

She nodded and then realized he probably couldn't see her all that well.

"I didn't see you there," she answered. "I've never been in such darkness. It's so opaque!"

"Once your eyes adjust, you can see a little. Not a lot, though, when the moon's not out. There's so many clouds tonight."

Claire fumbled for the phone in her pocket. She wasn't in the mood to make small talk.

"You, um, need some privacy?" Jack asked.

He must have thought she'd come out here to relieve herself.

"No. I was just going to call my brother."

"Your voice sounds funny," Jack commented. "Are you all right?"

"Sure."

"So my folks haven't got to you yet?"

"They're okay," she lied. She held the phone in her hand, keeping it closed so the device's wan green light would not illuminate her face and reveal the fact that she had just lied to him. His folks had got to her. Big time. But it wasn't their fault.

Out here in the wilderness, detached from everything she knew, separated from her routines and the people she loved, she had begun to feel adrift. The world was shifting beneath her feet like her own personal earthquake, rattling her. Thoughts of Maria encroached from all sides, a churning indigo cloud, bringing with it the thoughts she usually held at bay by keeping every moment occupied. But in this vast darkness, where nothing visible could distract her, she found herself facing the painful wall she usually could pretty much ignore.

She felt Jack's gaze on her and prayed his human vision was too weak to detect her very human wounds. And though he stared at her, she could not move out of his sight and

could not think of a single remark to deflect his curious regard. The sudden onslaught of her personal troubles had
robbed her of the ability to speak or move.

She heard a scraping sound at her left, like boots on
granite.

"Come on up here," Jack said. "You should see this."

"What?" she managed to croak.

"Just come up."

Claire looked his way and could see the silhouette of the
cowboy on the boulder. But she couldn't see how she would
be able to scale the rock in the dark.

"Use your sense of touch," Jack added, as if he could
read her mind. "It's an amazing faculty we humans rarely
employ."

"I don't know." Claire studied the rock, trying to make out
a ledge on which to step. Falteringly, she shuffled forward as
she slipped the phone back into a pocket in her fleece jacket.

"Can't you just give me a hand?" she asked as the toe of
one walking boot stubbed against the base of the rock.

There was a pause above, as if Jack were trying to come
up with an answer to her question. Why was it so difficult to
say yes, to reach out and grab her hand?

"Just feel the rock. There to your right."

Sighing, Claire reached out and dragged her fingertips
along the weather-beaten surface. Sure enough, she found a
ledge large enough to climb upon. She stepped up.

"Now feel to the left," Jack instructed above her head.
"There's a small cleft. Just walk up the slope and you're
there."

Claire found the cleft and scrambled upward, using her
hands to support her as she crawled to the top of the rock.
She looked up, assuming Jack would offer a hand to help her
climb the last few inches, but he stood back, nearly to the far
edge of the boulder, clearly out of reach.

Claire struggled to her feet and brushed her hands on her
jeans.

"Okay," she puffed. "Now what?"

"Look over there," Jack said, stepping up behind her. "At
eleven o'clock."

Claire turned slightly in the direction he'd indicated. And at that moment, the full moon sailed out of the clouds, illuminating the nightscape like a cold spotlight. Claire sucked in a horrified breath.

"Oh, my God!" she cried, reaching frantically for the man behind her but clutching empty air. "We're on a cliff!"

Chapter 12

We're on a cliff!" Claire repeated hysterically, "I could have fallen!"

"You could have."

"And you let me climb up here, half-blind?" She turned to face him, afraid to make a sudden move and lose her footing. Her legs ached at the thought of tumbling over the precipice behind her.

"You did fine."

"Fine?! I did fine?" She would have slapped his face had he been standing closer to her.

"I wouldn't have let you fall," Jack admonished in a warm tone. "Now turn back around and take a look."

Fuming and frightened of the great height on which she stood, Claire slowly rotated, her boots crunching upon the granite. She steeled herself for her second look at the chasm and tried not to sway back in horror.

"Eleven o'clock," he reminded her.

Claire swallowed her terror and glanced in the eleven o'-clock position and then adjusted her gaze to a more downward angle. There on the valley floor, thousands of feet down, were two silver lakes, gleaming in the pearly light thrown down by the moon. The landscape far below her feet looked utterly desolate, utterly alien, and the lakes looked like twin silver eyes staring back up at her, daring her to make a wrong move.

She stepped back a pace. Jack didn't move or speak. They

stood there together, with the night breeze rustling their clothing, rushing past their faces, lifting tendrils of their hair.

Then Jack's voice came soft and low beside her. "My soul, living," he said beside her, "is like a courser of the night; the swifter its flight, the nearer the dawn."

Claire let his words drift away on the wind. She let them echo in her thoughts, finding that they comforted her in a strangely dark way. Then she glanced over at Jack's sharp profile. "I didn't know you were a poet," she said, just above a whisper.

"I'm not. Those words were written by a favorite philosopher of mine. Kahlil Gibran."

"I've heard of him," Claire said, brave enough now to really gaze at the midnight valley. "'A loaf of bread and thou . . .'"

"That's Omar Khayam."

"Oh." She was surprised he knew any poetry at all. "So how does a cowboy like you know Middle-Eastern poets by heart?"

"I wasn't always a cowboy."

"What were you then?"

"Various things. Nothing exceptional."

"Did you live back east most of your life?"

"Yes. New York."

"Your mother showed me a picture of your former fiancée. She was very pretty."

"Yes, well, pretty isn't everything." Jack eased back down to a sitting position. "And I don't care to talk about her. So just skip it, okay?"

"Your mother also said you were in a bad accident?" Claire lowered herself to the rock as well, and felt much safer.

"Yeah." He sighed. "It forced me to look at my life. Establish priorities."

"That's why you got into racing?"

She saw the outline of his cowboy hat tilt as he nodded.

"I was always interested in horses. I spent every summer out here with Gran, riding the hills. But I didn't buy Mr. B until I got out of the hospital. I spent everything I had on that horse."

"I'm sorry he's been a disappointment."

"That's what I can't figure out. He just stopped winning." Jack sighed again. "He came in dead last in the Hill Rise Stakes at Santa Anita this winter when he was the favorite to win. He won't even challenge the nags around Tahoe. He's made the Dark Horse Ranch a laughingstock. Me included."

"What about getting a different horse?"

"With what?" Jack laughed bitterly. "My credit card? It's maxed out. Like my dad said, the ranch is hanging on by a thread."

"Then your only choice is to get that dog for him."

"Right. A dog will change the future of the Dark Horse." He looked down at her. "Not to throw you into a snit, Miss Coulter, but your theory sounds like a bunch of shit."

"Maybe. But look at it this way, Mr. Hughes—what could it hurt to get a dog?"

"Jack." He shifted his position and drew up a knee to his chest. "Mr. Hughes is my father. Call me Jack."

"Jack then."

As if saying his name had pushed them into a far-too-uncomfortable intimacy, they both fell silent and stared down at the two lakes on the valley floor. Finally, Claire turned to her quiet companion.

"So are those lakes the Two Sisters your father talked about?"

"Yep."

"And beyond that is the valley the Native Americans avoided?"

"Yep."

"Which one?" She pointed at the valley floor. "The one on the right?"

He nodded. "The narrow one on the right is Medicine Valley. The one on the left is Dead Man's Gulch."

"Dead Man's? Why is it named that?"

"Snakes. Floods. Indian ambushes. You name it. Over the years the whole area got a bad reputation. Nowadays people just avoid going there."

Claire studied the narrow canyons that bordered a low ridge and opened onto a wider plain to the north. It didn't look all that formidable from her viewpoint high above. But Jack knew this land, and she assumed he knew its history as well.

She hugged her knees. "How long do you think it will take to get to the fountain?"

"Two days. Maybe three." He tipped back his hat. "Horses only do about twenty miles a day. Less in steep terrain. It'll be slow going."

"But you were right about the Hummer."

"For whatever that's worth." His voice fell flat. "I don't get all wrapped up in my father's decisions. I learned long ago that we're as different as the sun and moon."

"He certainly is a character."

"Character?" He shook his head, still staring at the lakes. "You're far too kind, Claire."

"No, I'm not."

"Why do you say that?"

"I'm just not all that kind. Hardly anyone is who they claim to be. Or appear to be."

Jack's head whipped around, and he stared at her.

"We're all pretty much faking it," Claire added, wondering why he was staring at her. "Wouldn't you agree?"

"Yeah," he said at last. Then he got to his feet in a quick, fluid motion that seemed impossibly agile for someone so tall. "Well, I'd better let you make that phone call."

"Gosh, I'd almost forgotten about it!" She reached for the second time. "Emilio would think I was dead if I didn't call."

"You call him often?"

"Every night." She opened the phone. "We're all we have in the world, my brother and I."

"So he lives with you?"

"He has to. He's pretty sick."

"What's wrong with him—if you don't mind me asking?"

"His kidney is failing."

"Is that such a problem? We all have two kidneys."

"Not Emilio. He was born with a congenital defect. He has one overly large kidney that is seriously deteriorating. He needs a transplant. Really soon."

"Jesus."

"If he dies, I'll be alone in the world. I don't know if I could handle that." She swallowed. "So you see? I'm not kind. Deep down, I'm just plain selfish, worried about me."

"We all are. It's human nature. Don't beat yourself up about it."

He scaled down the face of the rock and turned to look up at her. "Can you find your way back okay?"

She nodded. "As long as the moon is out." She looked down at him, surprised to find him smiling with a relaxed expression on his usually hard countenance.

"Well, don't stay out here too long. There might be bears looking for leftover pork chops."

"Great." She stood up and glanced around, her nerves on edge again. "Thanks for telling me."

He chuckled. "Just make a lot of noise on the way back. Sing some Led Zeppelin or something." He waved. "They'll steer clear."

Claire watched him walk away and quickly pass through the curtain of darkness in the trees. She could hear his boots crunching on the trail long after she'd lost visual contact with him.

She listened to his fading footsteps and suddenly realized that his company and conversation had banished her bad memories. She felt much more grounded, more like her usual self, and marveled that a dispassionate cowboy could have such a calming effect upon her. It had been a long time since she'd had such a connection with anyone, especially a man.

Taking a deep, relieved breath, Claire looked down at her cell phone. Just as Tobias had predicted, the monitor showed no service available. She exchanged her phone for the tiny unit in her other pocket. The Lone Ranger connected immediately. Shaking her head at her boss' ever reaching genius, she punched in her brother's phone number and held the small receiver to her ear.

*   *   *

"HI EMILIO," CLAIRE said when her brother picked up the phone. Her voice sounded overly loud in the wilderness, but the signal came in clear and steady.

"Hey, Claire," his voice rasped.

"Are you okay?" Her brows pinched together in a worried scowl. "You sound tired."

"I didn't feel so great today."

"Did you go to class?" she asked anxiously.

"I tried to, but—"

His words trailed off. Claire's frown deepened. When Emilio skipped his college classes, it was a telltale sign that his health had declined once again. Emilio hated to miss class. He was driven to finish college early and with honors, as if he knew death snapped at his heels, threatening to cut his time short.

"You have dialysis tomorrow?"

"Yeah. I changed the appointment to first thing in the morning."

"That should help. But don't you be afraid to go to emergency."

"And slap you with another huge bill? No way."

"Don't you ever worry about that." Claire squeezed her eyes shut, blocking off the tears of frustration that welled up behind her eyelids. She was so far away from her brother right now, there was nothing she could do to help him. She steeled herself, forcing her voice to remain at its normal pitch, so she could continue the conversation without letting him know how worried she was.

"Look, Emilio, don't worry. Tobias Benton's people are setting up your operation. As soon as I get back, you'll have the transplant. You'll get all the best doctors, all the best care. You'll be better than ever soon. Just hold on."

"I will," he promised, but his voice was laced with more weariness than she'd ever heard in him.

"In a couple of weeks, you'll be dancing the merengue."

He chuckled hollowly. "I wouldn't go that far."

"And when you're well enough, you can get a job—maybe even at CommOptima, make some money for yourself. Go on a date or two for once."

"That would be something."

She could hear the sad smile returning to his voice. She smiled herself, but her cheeks ran with tears she could no longer hold back. She pressed her lips together.

"Are you crying, Claire?" he asked.

"No." She dashed away the teardrops with the fingers of her free hand. "I'm just allergic to something out here. I think it's the pine needles."

He paused. Then he finally spoke. "Hey, sis, I'm going to be fine. I always bounce back. Don't worry about me."

"Just concentrate on a positive outlook, Em, like you always do."

"I will. And you find that magic fountain and get your fanny back to civilization."

"I will. As quickly as I can." Claire squeezed the phone, wishing she could give her small, slight younger brother a big hug.

"Love you," he said.

"I love you, too," Claire replied. "Bye."

She clicked off the phone, worried even more by her brother's last statement. Emilio rarely ever expressed deep sentiment. Was he dangerously ill this time and sensing his own death? Was he not telling her the full story about the state of his health?

Claire's stomach turned as panic swept through her. She would have to find that fountain as soon as possible—no breaks, no dallying, and no extended, easier trails. She would ask Jack what was the swiftest route and convince Tobias to take it—no matter what.

Chapter 13

When Claire got back to camp, she was surprised to see four small brown tents in a ring around the campfire. Flames still flickered merrily at the fire and three of her companions lingered around its orange glow. The horses were strung on a line tied between two Jeffrey pines, and Jack strolled among them, making sure every animal was set and secure for the night. Claire felt comforted by the quiet scene and Jack's steady presence. She made sure her cheeks were dry, and then stepped forward into the clearing.

"There you are." Betty greeted her with a smile. "Thought you might have been eaten by a mountain lion."

Claire paled. "Are there mountain lions up here, too?"

Betty nodded. "A few. But they mostly stick to the back country."

"Aren't we *in* the back country?" Susan inquired, her face lit up by a flare of flames. The fire popped and crackled, sending a red shower skyward.

"I guess we are, Suzy Q."

Claire glanced around the fire. Both Simeon and Tobias were absent—probably relieving themselves in the woods.

"Well, I think I'll turn in." Claire glanced at the tents. "Is one of those tents mine, Betty?"

"Yours and Tobias's," Betty answered.

Claire did a quick assessment of people, affiliations, and the number of tents, and came up short. Surely Jack wouldn't bunk with Simeon or his grandmother. "Why are there only four tents?" she asked.

"Oh, Johnny hates them. Says they spook him."

"Spook him?"

"You city folk probably call it claustrophobia."

"Oh."

"He's not one for confined places. Or crowds."

"I see."

"But we put your things in the far tent, the one on the left. In case you and your sweetheart want some privacy." She nudged Claire's elbow and wiggled her white eyebrows, giving her a mischievous grin at the same time.

"Thanks," Claire mumbled, embarrassed by the old woman's antics and her assumption that she and Tobias would be making mad, passionate love in their sleeping bags. She glanced at Jack's parents and then at the man himself on the other side of the clearing, wishing she might have the chance to thank him for their chat in the dark. But Jack was busy, and she didn't want to draw attention to herself by walking across the clearing just to say goodnight to him. People might get the wrong impression. She dragged her regard off the tall man and back to his family.

"Well, goodnight everyone."

They echoed her goodnight as Claire turned toward her tent. It was set off a good distance from the others and glowed from within like a boxy beacon. As she stepped closer, she could see a figure moving inside, backlit by the light of a lantern. Her flagging spirits sank even lower.

Tobias, with his sarcastic remarks and persistent attention, was the last person she wished to talk to. What was he doing in the tent, moving around like that—zipping together the sleeping bags so he could reach out in the night and touch her? Her skin crawled at the thought.

As she padded closer to the tent, she heard the ominous thrumming sound again, not quite a hum and not quite a growl. The hair on her forearms rose in alarm. She glanced around, but could see nothing in the surrounding brush. Behind her she heard Susan laugh and then a horse nicker—the normal sounds of a night at a campsite. No one seemed bothered by the strange noise. Obviously she was the only one who could hear it.

Whatever growled nearby, she hoped it would be fearful of the lantern. And it would be better to be inside the tent where she could see, than to stand outside in the dark and make herself an easy target for a creature with superior night vision.

Claire flipped back the tent flap and stepped inside, shocked to find Simeon Avare bent over her purse. For an instant, he just stared at her, frozen in place, and then he slowly straightened, and his expression eased into his customary attractive smile.

"What are you doing?" Claire demanded. A hot flush of outrage flared in her cheeks. She looked at the man's hands and the pockets of his gray slacks but could see no evidence of thievery.

"I am checking for snakes."

"What?"

"Since I'm the expert on vipers, I volunteered to make sure all the tents were free of reptiles before we all retired for the evening."

"You think a snake would crawl into a tent? In April? At night?"

Simeon nodded, nonplussed by her challenging tone. "It was an unseasonably warm winter, Miss Coulter. Many reptiles have come out of hibernation early. And on cool nights such as this one, they are attracted to heat."

"I wouldn't think my purse was all that warm."

He glanced down at her black leather bag. "I was just being cautious. There have been reports of scorpion sightings in this area as well."

"Scorpions?"

"Yes. Scorpions. Their stings can be excruciating, sometimes fatal." He gestured with an open palm at her purse. "Thus the need to check the pockets of your bag."

"I see."

"I am sorry if I startled you. It was not my intention."

She studied him, full of distrust, and realized the ominous noise had faded. Then again, she may have been too upset from discovering Simeon snooping to be aware of the subtle vibrations she received from animals. She had to be open and grounded to receive such sensitive feedback.

"Always shake out your sleeping bag, your shoes. Check under your pillow." He leaned over, picked up one of the small white pillows, shook it, and then checked the sleeping bag below. "Nothing there," he announced. "Thank goodness." He stood up and briskly brushed his hands together.

She still wasn't sure about him or his explanation. "Thanks."

"My pleasure." He bowed slightly and slipped past her to the tent opening. Then he turned and nodded toward her bag.

"Be sure to finish checking your purse. I did not get to the inside sections."

"I will," she promised, intending to make a thorough inspection of her belongings—and not because of snakes and scorpions.

"Sleep well, Miss Coulter."

"I'll try," she replied.

Simeon stooped to let himself out of the tent, leaving a great deal of unease in his wake. His search of her purse reminded Claire of the tarot deck she had hidden away. Then her thoughts jumped to Maria's murder, and Claire's failed attempt to contact the person who might know something about her friend's death.

Claire reached for her purse, checked to make sure the tarot deck was still tucked safely in the zipped inner pocket, and then retrieved the paper that bore the phone number of Rae Lambers. She glanced at her watch. It was nine o'clock—a bit late for phoning a stranger. But she dialed the number anyway, hoping Rae Lambers would pick up and wouldn't be too angry at being disturbed during evening hours.

TOBIAS STOOD IN the clearing a good distance from camp, eyes closed, his body humming with a seductive but familiar vibration as his natural rhythms were amplified by the small electronic device he had placed like a headband on his skull. He and his engineers had dubbed the device the KarmaKazi, as the amplifier could send a meditating person into a deep trance state in a matter of minutes. Tobias, ever searching for new worlds and new ideas to develop, had served as the beta tester for the device, and had used the KarmaKazi for the past five years. It was during one of his theta-wave trances that he had come in contact with his spirit "business associate."

It wasn't long before Tobias felt a change in the air and knew his "associate" had arrived. Still, he kept his eyes closed and his mind as clear as possible. Only through years of meditation and the elimination of all outward distraction had he discovered the world that existed just outside his consciousness and the sentient energy that resided there, ready to guide him. It was hard work to cleanse one's mind of all thought—but his determination and power of concentration had served him well. And in return for his dedication and perseverance, his associate had come to him, counseled him, and helped him become one of the richest men on earth. He'd be a fool not to keep in touch or return a favor—as much as his puny human efforts could manage anyway.

"Lord," Tobias murmured in deference, but with his head held high. His associate was not into humility and servitude, but rather strength of focus and independence of thought—just the kind of higher being Tobias appreciated, as it mirrored his own personality.

"You've done well," his associate said. The statement was conveyed not through words but in a knowing that Tobias could not define. If only he could invent a computer that worked on such a level, he'd be a gazillionaire. But he had to quit thinking such temporal thoughts. It was a sure way to lose the valuable connection. "Things are falling into place, Tobias."

"Good. I owe this to you," Tobias replied. He had to communicate the old fashioned way, by speaking actual words. "I owe you big time."

"One does what one can for those who are deserving."

"Exactly."

"I must impress upon you the importance of expediency."

"I know." Tobias nodded, his eyes still closed. "We'll get there. Don't worry."

"I also must warn you."

"About what?" Tobias felt the air shifting again, felt a swirling coolness around his skull.

"This place you go to. It is powerful. Very powerful. That is why I seek it."

"To rejuvenate yourself. I know."

"Only as a last resort. Otherwise I would avoid it. But there are so few places like it left. And I am—" His advisor broke off with a frustrated sigh. "Desperate."

"Don't worry. Everything will work out. And my tech will get you through that door."

"But it may not be as easy as you think. There are those with us who have been touched by the place. They may be more powerful than you imagine."

"You think I'm worried? With you on my side?"

"I may be unable to help you on a physical level, Tobias. Not until my *khat* is restored. That is why I urge you to be careful."

"So who do I have to watch out for—Grandma Betty?" Tobias smiled to himself.

"It is not a laughing matter, Tobias."

Tobias felt a cold chill pass through him. Perhaps humor wasn't the best approach with his companion. He shrugged. "Sorry."

"It is the man Jack. And your employee Claire."

"Claire's never been to the fountain."

"Don't be so sure. There is something about her. You sense it yourself. You are drawn to her."

"Why wouldn't I be? She's beautiful."

"Forget her outward appearance and remember the plan, Tobias. The woman is expendable. There can be no witnesses."

Tobias shuddered. Surely there had to be a way to keep from killing Claire once she'd deciphered the code. But he would get to that issue when the time came, and figure out a way to convince his associate that Claire could be trusted to keep a secret just as much as he could. Then again, did his associate trust him in that regard? Now there was a chilling thought.

"Tobias? You stray."

"Sorry." Tobias willed away his intrusive thoughts.

"The place called Medicine Valley," his associate continued, "is unlike any place on earth. It has powers even I have not experienced. It may be drawing others like us toward it for its own purposes. Beware."

"I will."

"Good."

Suddenly Tobias felt alone. Just like that, the shifting air had vanished, leaving a strange silent void. He clicked off the KarmaKazi, opened his eyes, and glanced around the dark clearing for a visual trace of his associate. But as always, he saw nothing. He felt stupid for even having looked. What had he expected to see?

Tobias was intelligent enough to know that the being he'd connected with was so evolved, it could exist outside human form. And he himself was so evolved, he was able to communicate with it. That made him pretty special, but then again he'd always known he was a cut above average. Why Claire couldn't see it was a big disappointment to him. He thought she would have been more perceptive.

Tobias took a deep breath and let it out as he slowly pulled the unit off his head. A guy like him didn't need women, didn't need a normal life full of sex and kids and mowing the lawn. Such a life was for lesser beings, for people who couldn't see the big and invisible picture. There was a world out there that most people knew nothing about, a place that had nothing to do with physical bodies and possessions, a place that he knew was far more important than the life he lived on earth. It was a world he intended to master as well as he had mastered this earthly one.

Yet, he wanted Claire Coulter in a very earthly way. He wanted her on the most basic level imaginable, in fact. He wanted to thrust himself into her and explode, just like an animal. The thought of it thrilled him but shamed him at the same time, as he had always considered himself above such gross physical acts. But he had to know what sex was like with her. He just couldn't talk himself out of it this time.

* * *

THE PHONE RANG four times. Then Claire heard the ring break off. Someone had picked up, or she was being transferred to a slow-to-activate voicemail system.

"Hello?"

Claire was relieved to hear a real female voice.

"Ms. Lambers?" Claire looked up at the pitched ceiling of the tent, hoping she had finally connected with Rae.

"Yes?"

"Hi. My name is Claire Coulter. You don't know me—" Claire stepped toward the tent flap and kept an eye on the people at the campfire as she explained her connection to the Forbidden Tarot and Jonathan Allman. Rae Lambers listened without interrupting.

"And I think because of the cards," Claire said in conclusion, "my best friend Maria was murdered."

"It's quite possible," Rae replied.

"That's why I called you. I thought you might know something. Anything."

"I'm sorry no one contacted me sooner," Rae replied. "I've been calling the Allmans for weeks!"

"Mr. Allman is a very busy man. He may have written you off as a prank caller."

"Prank caller?" Rae heaved a quick sigh of exasperation. "Those cards brought a monster into my life, Miss Coulter—one that destroyed a historic house, maimed a friend of mine, and nearly killed my sister and me."

"Was there a sword involved in any way?"

There was a long pause on the line. "What do you know of a sword?"

"Only that Maria was apparently beheaded by such a weapon."

"Oh, my God!" Rae exclaimed. "We saw that on the news!"

"That was Maria. She was Jonathan Allman's maid." Claire sank down upon the end of her sleeping bag, gripping the phone tightly to her head. "I thought you might have some idea who might have killed her."

"Then the monster is still at large," Rae murmured, her voice full of alarm.

"Wait a minute. What is this monster you're talking about?"

"You'll think I'm a nutcase if I tell you."

"Maybe not. Go ahead."

She heard Rae Lambers take a deep, steadying breath.

"My sister and I found the Forbidden Tarot in Egypt, buried in the silt of an ancient, dried-up oasis. And when we looked at one of the cards, we apparently called forth a demon."

"What card did you look at?"

"Typhon. The Devil."

A chill coursed down Claire's spine. She licked her lips, which had suddenly gone dry. "And what makes you think you raised a demon?"

"Lots of things. Almost immediately a man came into our lives. He was charming, and I'm ashamed to admit that for awhile I fell for his bullshit—hook, line, and sinker."

"Don't we all," Claire murmured, rolling her eyes.

"It wasn't until later that I began to see him for what he really was. I mean to really see him, Miss Coulter."

"Call me Claire, please." She shifted the phone to her other ear. "So he was a creep?"

"Oh, he was much more than a creep. We had reason to believe we'd raised an ancient Egyptian god from the dead."

"A god?"

"Set. Do you know who he is?"

Claire thought back on her history lessons. "Don't people call him Satan these days?"

"Yes."

"What made you think the guy was Satan?"

"He had superpowers. He could make you see things, do things that you wouldn't normally do. He almost seduced me, and I'm about as seduceable as a brick."

"What kinds of things did he make you see?"

"Hoards of bats. Lizards. Fire."

"But they weren't real?"

"Only illusion—just as his human form was only an illusion."

"So what was he, if he wasn't human?"

Rae paused again. "He looked just like the image on the tarot card. He was a huge lizard with wings and a snout like a crocodile. He carried a sword and had cloven feet."

"Okay." Claire held up one hand. "Okay, now you *are* sounding like a nutcase, Rae."

"I know. I know it sounds crazy, Claire. But it's true!"

"If he was Satan and had superpowers, why didn't he just kill you?"

"Apparently age had caught up with him. He was old and weak. And desperate to rejuvenate himself."

"A likely story." Claire had half a notion to hang up and forget she'd ever heard the name Rae Lambers.

"Claire, listen." Rae's voice was grave. "I am not crazy. You have to believe me. Everything I have told you is the God's honest truth. And the worst truth is, my sister Angie is pregnant, and I'm ninety-nine percent certain the father of the baby is Set."

Claire's blood chilled as alarm and horror sank even deeper into her bones. She could think of nothing to say.

"You didn't look at any of the cards in the Forbidden Tarot, did you, Claire?"

"I'm afraid I did. Maria and I both did." Claire's mouth went even drier.

"Listen, Claire, I don't know what card you saw first, but everything—and I mean everything—on that card will come into your life."

Claire thought back to the images she'd seen on the tarot card—the sunburst; the dark-haired man with wings on his feet pouring the contents of one metal container into another, naked but for a striped wrap he'd thrown over one shoulder; the strange symbols at the top of the card that matched the one on Tobias's map. Her heart did a crazy flip flop. Was the card already influencing her life?

Rae's voice brought her out of her wandering thoughts. "Where are the cards? Do you have any idea?"

"I have them."

"You have to get rid of them, Claire. ASAP." Rae's voice was sharp with insistence. "You have to throw them into a deep body of water."

"But Jonathan Allman paid half a million dollars for the cards. I can't just throw them away!"

"You must! It's the only way to break their hold on you!"

"But if Jonathan ever finds out, he'll think I stole them. Or at least that Maria stole them, and I was her accomplice. I could go to prison!"

"It won't matter, especially if you're dead!"

"Rae, I've got to think this through." Claire swallowed, barely able to comprehend all that had just been divulged.

"Don't take too long. You are in danger." Rae paused, but only for a moment. "Call me if you need to. Anytime. Night or day."

"Okay."

"Let me know when you get rid of the cards."

"I will."

"I'm not a nutcase, Claire. You'll see."

Set 5

I wait and I prepare. It is ever thus. But sometimes when I look into the heavens and see all the moving bits—the satellites, the jets, and the space offal, I find myself wondering if the others will really, truly return. A lot could have happened since I arrived here with the Golden Ones. Our planet may not even exist anymore. But I must hope that it does, and that it survived the war, as I have survived my stint here on this strange orb. Leaving this place and seeing my home is what keeps me going, it really is. But I look forward almost as much to that delicious moment when Those Who Have Always Lived step onto this land and look around, expecting to see all their little points of light—their precious Golden Ones—and all they will see is me. Me. Set. Talk about a cosmic joke. I love it, actually.

Set, Bringer of Change

Chapter 14

Claire hung up the phone at the same moment Tobias ducked into the tent.

"Remind me never to do this again," he commented.

"Do what?"

"Camp."

She smiled hollowly, still upset by her telephone conversation with Rae Lambers.

"My ass is so sore I can barely walk, and now I have to spend the night on the ground." He kicked the edge of the sleeping bag with his leather boot.

"At least there are pads under our bags."

"Like that will help." He shrugged out of his leather jacket. "And I nearly pissed on my boots out there in the dark."

"It takes some getting used to."

"You got that right." He reached into his saddlebag and pulled out a Game Boy. For a few seconds he punched buttons and then swore under his breath.

"No power." He scowled. "I hate it when my assistants forget to put in fresh batteries. They do it all the time!" He threw the small silver gaming unit on his sleeping bag. "Somebody's going to get fired."

Claire glanced up at him. "Maybe it's a sign that you should try to rest."

"Rest? I never go to sleep without playing! It calms me down." Then he paused and looked down at her, a new light in his eyes. "Unless you have something else in mind to help me sleep."

Claire scrambled to her feet. "Actually, I need to get some air. I'm going to sit by the fire for awhile." She stepped for the tent opening.

"I'll go with you."

She looked back at him, not wanting his company. "You don't have to."

"What am I going to do here? Contemplate my navel?" He grabbed his jacket.

THEY FOUND JACK alone at the fire, hunched over on a rock, his long, capable hands wrapped around a metal coffee cup. He didn't speak as they sank to their respective seats. He only nodded.

For a long moment, Claire took the chance to study him. Under the brim of his hat, his nose plunged strong and sharp from between his expressive black brows. A healthy growth of day-old stubble shadowed his cheeks and chin, accentuating the lines around his mouth, the sharp plane of his jaw, and the small circle of muscle at the right side of his wide mouth. Claire remembered seeing that muscle in action, when it had quirked his lips into a quick, lopsided smile. She could see very little of his dark eyes, only an occasional glint when the fire flared at their feet.

"Jack," she began, and he turned to look at her. "What's the quickest way to the fountain?"

"Depends upon what you mean by quick."

"The least amount of time."

"That would be through Dead Man's Gulch."

"But you won't go that way?"

"Nope."

"Why not?" Tobias challenged.

"Because." Jack's cowboy hat rotated in the billionaire's direction. "I generally avoid places that start with the word 'Dead.' "

"I take it it's a dangerous route?" Tobias continued.

"It can be."

"In what way?"

Jack sighed and placed his cup on a rock. The metallic scrape rang through the clearing. "A person can get caught by surprise in Dead Man's Gulch."

"How?" Tobias pressed for information.

"By a cloudburst. After a few minutes of heavy rain, the gulch can become a raging waterway."

Claire leaned forward, her forearms on her thighs. "But aren't we okay this time of year?"

"Like I told your fiancé a while back," Jack replied, "we're due for rain. Maybe even snow. Any day."

"But until then, we could take the shortcut and save time?"

Jack turned and studied her for a long moment. "Why the rush?"

"My brother's taken a turn for the worse."

He remained silently regarding her.

"And my ass won't take much more of this riding," Tobias put in. "It really won't."

Finally Jack looked away. He rubbed his grizzled chin. "It's too dangerous. We've got too many inexperienced riders."

"I'll chance it," Tobias declared. "If it means cutting this camping gig short."

"No." Jack picked up his coffee cup and rose slowly to his feet. "It's too risky."

"But it might not rain." Claire jumped up. "It's a risk we could take. Please, Jack!"

He glanced at her, his face unreadable in the shadows.

"I don't know how much longer my brother can hold out." Claire went on. "Please."

She reached for his arm, realizing he intended to leave and determined to stop him. But Jack stepped nimbly away from her, avoiding her grasp.

Claire let her hand fall to her side as she stared at the cowboy, frustrated by his flat refusal, offended by the way he shunned her touch, and confused by the wild look in his eyes as he warily regarded her.

"C'mon, Jack," Tobias said, struggling to his feet while he rubbed his backside. "We're talking dying brother here. The lady wants to take the shortcut!"

"Then she'll have to take it herself," Jack retorted. With a sharp motion, he flung his coffee into the sand and stomped away.

Claire ran after him, but this time she did not reach out for his arm.

"Jack, wait!"

He kept walking.

"Do you always walk away from everything?" She flung her harsh words at his broad back. "Don't you have the guts to ever stay and fight?"

Jack stopped. Then he slowly turned around to face her, his boots crunching on the gravel, his expression stormy.

He didn't say a word. He just stood there, staring at her, as if her question didn't merit an answer. Claire felt a hot flush of shame for calling him a coward, but the shame was not strong enough to blot out the frustration and fear for her brother that burned in her stomach.

When he didn't speak, she raised both hands at her sides to waist level, offering herself up for review. "What is it about me that you dislike so much?"

"This isn't about you," he growled.

She could feel his glance raking across her figure.

"Part of it is," she countered, raising her chin. "I can tell."

He took a deep breath and then let it out in a long, exasperated sigh. "It doesn't matter what I think of you. I'm the guide here. I have to consider the safety of the group."

"Even if my brother dies before we get to the fountain?"

Jack nodded, his mouth grim.

"But there are times in life you just have to take a risk!"

"This isn't one of them." He pulled off his hat and ran his fingers through his silky black hair. Then he stood there, tapping his hat upon his thigh.

"Your brother has medical care, right?" he asked.

Claire nodded.

"Well, if anything happens out here, we don't," Jack went on. "So we minimize risk." He tilted his head and looked at her as he bent closer to her, his eyes as stony as his expression. "You got that, Claire?"

His unfriendly tone sent a spike through her, obliterating any warm feelings she might have harbored for the man since their conversation on the boulder. With a few curt words he had thrown up a wall between them. She could feel it as surely as if it were made of concrete.

Claire had never felt so thoroughly rebuffed. Stunned by his coldness, she stood before him at the edge of the clearing, absolutely mute.

Jack plopped his hat back down on his head. "Go to bed," he said, his voice still frosty. "Get some sleep."

Claire didn't move. Her boots seemed frozen to the ground by Jack's icy response to her questions. She watched him disappear into the darkness and chided herself for allowing the man—any man—to get to her. There was no reason for her to seek Jack's approval, but there was certainly no reason for him to treat her like a child.

Tobias ambled up behind her and framed her shoulders in his slender hands. She didn't shrug him off.

"He's certainly no Mr. Wonderful," Tobias commented.

Claire didn't say anything.

"He looks good. Like a cowboy right out of the movies," the billionaire continued. "But the man has issues. You can see that a mile away."

Claire stepped out of Tobias's light grip and turned to face him.

"I'm going through Dead Man's Gulch when we get close to it."

"But Jack said—"

"I don't care what Jack said. I'm going!"

"How will you find it? Is it on the map?"

"No, but I saw where it was this evening. Jack showed me. I could even see where the gulch came out on the other side of the hills."

"You'd go without him?"

"You're damn right." She stormed to the tent and flung open the flap as Tobias hurried after her. She pulled off her fleece jacket, untied her boots, and sat down on her sleeping bag. Tobias stood near the tent opening, staring at her.

"Will you come with me?" she asked.

"Sure. I'm game." Tobias shrugged and stepped forward. "The sooner I get a Coke, the happier I'll be."

"What about your business partner? When's he going to meet up with us?"

"He'll be there. Don't worry."

"But how is he going to get there?"

Tobias shrugged again. "Didn't ask. But trust me, he'll be there."

Claire stared at her boss, puzzled by the unusual resourcefulness of his associate. If she and Tobias couldn't take anything but horses into the wilderness, how was his partner going to get there? But she had enough to worry about. She slipped out of her boots. "We'll ride with Jack and his family one more day. And then we'll take the shortcut."

"But I don't see how that will help us." Tobias pulled off one of his shoes. "We'll just have to wait for Jack to catch up to take us back to the ranch anyway."

"Not necessarily." Claire settled into her sleeping bag. "Once we're there, can't you call someone to send out a helicopter for us?"

Tobias paused, his left boot still in his hand. "Didn't Jack say the Park Service doesn't allow choppers in the area?"

"But what if it's an emergency?" Claire lifted one brow. "Something medical?"

Tobias stared at her and then grinned. "I like the way you think, Miss Coulter." He dropped his boot on the floor of the tent and flipped open the flap of his sleeping bag. Then he turned and smiled at her. "See? We're going to make a good team, you and me."

Tobias turned off the small light.

Claire could tell he was still standing between their sleeping bags, and she wondered why he hadn't sat down. As her eyes adjusted to the dark, she saw him kneeling down beside her.

Every cell in Claire's body jumped into alert mode.

Chapter 15

C laire?" Tobias said in the darkness.

"What?" She rose on one elbow.

"I was serious about getting to know you better."

"You *are* getting to know me."

"That's a joke."

She pulled the sleeping bag up over her breasts.

"If you keep this behavior up, the deal's off. Do you know what I'm saying?"

"What's wrong with my behavior?"

"Plenty. For one thing, you spent more time with that cowboy today than you did with me."

Claire rolled her eyes, amazed that Tobias could be jealous. "That's because you spent most of the day in the Hummer!"

"What about tonight?"

"I took a walk!"

"But you ran into him out there. You said so yourself."

Claire sat all the way up. "If you're saying that I can't carry on a simple conversation with—"

"I'm just saying that I'm your boss." Tobias thumped his chest. "Me. The guy that can help your brother."

"I know that," she retorted in a cool tone. He didn't have to remind her of her impending debt to him.

"So you need to pay just a bit more attention to my needs."

"Your needs?" she repeated, incredulous at his choice of words.

"I'm going to do you a huge favor in the very near future. The least you can do is treat me nicely."

"What do you mean? In what way?" Claire backed toward the wall of the tent behind her, because she had a pretty good idea what he did mean.

"I want you to kiss me."

Claire's blood went cold. She could feel a strange tightening in her chest, as if she could no longer take a deep breath.

"I want to know what it feels like to touch you," he continued. "Naked."

Claire sat all the way up and yanked the sleeping bag securely over her breasts.

"I don't believe in premarital sex," she retorted.

"Right." Tobias snickered. "Then why aren't you a virgin?"

"How do you know I'm not?"

"Your medical records. You were even pregnant once, weren't you?"

Claire stared at him, wondering if knew everything about her, if he had snooped into every aspect of her life. She pressed the coverlet to her breasts, knowing she was trapped, and wondering how far Tobias would take this new tack.

"I tried to break the ice last night with the champagne and stuff. But you wouldn't play along."

"Did you think I would?"

"My assistant said it would do the trick."

"The same assistant you are going to fire?" she asked sharply.

He laughed again, apparently enjoying their verbal sparring. Then he suddenly sobered. "Undo your hair."

"What?"

"You heard me. Undo your hair."

She didn't move. She just raised her chin and stared at him, anger and alarm heating and chilling her at the same time.

"Listen, Princess, I can rescind my offer any time—just like Mr. Cowboy out there." He leaned closer, his breath on her face. "So undo your hair."

Claire pulled her long braid over her left shoulder and slowly unraveled the intertwined tresses while Tobias watched with a smug expression on his face. Then she sat there, rigid with aversion, as Tobias reached out and pulled the glossy, crimped strands through his fingers.

"You have beautiful hair," he murmured. "You shouldn't tie it up like you do."

She didn't answer him. Instead, she centered her powers of concentration on blotting out the sensation of his touch and praying he wouldn't go very far.

Tobias raised a long length of her hair and dragged it over his sallow cheek. Claire fought back a rolling heave of revulsion. He closed his eyes, oblivious to her reaction to him.

"Mmm. Smells good, too," he commented. He didn't seem to care that she had quit making conversation.

Then he took two handfuls of her hair in his fists and drew her toward him. Claire resisted until his tugging burned her scalp too much for her to bear. Slowly he forced her to bend toward him, and then he leaned forward and sank his wet mouth over hers.

His kiss was sloppy and awkward and hard, and Claire immediately struggled to get away. But Tobias grabbed her shoulders, his fingers still tangled painfully in her hair, and forced her to remain where she was. She pushed against his chest and clamped her mouth shut against the onslaught of his tongue, but he slowly forced her down with his weight. She sank back onto the sleeping bag as his torso and hips trapped her against the ground.

"No!" Claire gasped. Tobias's mouth slid over hers as he fumbled with her sweater, all the while writhing against her thigh. He seemed desperate and suddenly out of control as if he hadn't made love to a woman for a while and couldn't contain himself.

"Tobias, no!" Claire cried.

His hands plowed under her sweater and grabbed her breasts, squeezing them roughly. She felt the resulting surge of his erection upon her thigh. Claire kicked, trying to dislodge him from her legs, but his weight pressed down upon her and his male strength overwhelmed her attempt to wriggle free. "Bastard!" she exclaimed, reaching up to scratch his face.

Then a loud snap outside broke off Tobias's sexual assault. "Everything all right in there?" a dry voice asked.

It was Jack. He must have heard her cries. Claire had never been more grateful to hear a man's voice in her entire life.

"Sonofabitch," Tobias mumbled. He raised up, his eyes wild.

Claire took her first real breath and struggled backward, away from him. Tobias rolled off her and got to his knees. "Don't you say anything," he warned in a whisper.

"You all right, Claire?" Jack asked.

She glanced at Tobias, who collapsed onto his sleeping back with a heavy sigh of frustration. He flung his arm over his eyes.

"Yes," she answered, her voice cracking. "I'm fine."

THE NEXT MORNING, after a quick breakfast, the group packed up and rode down the mountain toward the Two Sisters. Still upset by the events of the previous evening, Claire kept her horse at a good distance from both jack and Tobias. At lunchtime she dismounted and walked over to Betty Hughes to lend a hand in meal preparation. She could feel more than one set of eyes on her back as she walked away.

"Anything I can do for you, Grandma Betty?" she asked.

"Sure." Betty pulled out the ingredients for cheese sandwiches. "You're a nice girl. Always helping."

"I like to keep busy."

Betty held out a weather-beaten knife. "Here, dear, why don't you slice the cheese for me?"

Claire undertook the task with the worn, but very sharp knife that looked as if it had been on hundreds of trail rides.

Betty squeezed mayonnaise and mustard on the slices of whole wheat bread. "You're not anything like that good-for-nothing fiancée," Betty muttered.

"You mean Tobias?"

Betty glanced over her shoulder at the billionaire who stood talking to William and Susan. Then she glanced back at Claire, seemingly confused. "No, dear. I was talking about Johnny's former lady friend."

"She went camping with you?" The photo Claire had seen of Jack's fiancée had portrayed a woman highly unlikely to enjoy the great outdoors.

"Her? Good God, no!" Betty waved the plastic mustard bottle in the air. "She wouldn't have been caught dead out here, much less on a horse!"

"Didn't she know how to ride?" Claire asked, curious about the woman Jack had nearly married, but not able to justify why she should be interested.

"She didn't know one end of a horse from the other. She hated 'em, as a matter of fact."

"And yet she was going to marry Jack?"

Betty nodded and clucked her tongue. "I told that boy it would end in tears. They weren't suited for each other. It was plain as day."

"But your daughter-in-law said they were the perfect couple."

"Bah!" Betty brushed off the remark with a wave of her liver-spotted hand. "They don't know Johnny. They never have. And that's a real heartache—when parents don't even know their own son."

Claire frowned as she continued to slice the cheese. No one had known her either. After working a physically demanding job, her mother had spent what little energy remained in her to care for Emilio. Claire had been the invisible child, the helper, the partner, the confidante—never a daughter. But she had understood the reason for her mother's focus on her brother. As for her father, she knew nothing of the man, only that her mother would not speak of him.

Betty clucked her tongue again. "I don't like to talk dirt about people, but I tell you—that girl, that Linda, she was a real bad apple." Betty scowled. "When Johnny was in the hospital, all broken up, she never once visited him."

"She didn't?" Claire glanced down at the old woman.

"No, she didn't. She was too embarrassed because of the media coverage. It was in all the papers about how Johnny was found in the nude. He even lost his job over it."

"But Jack didn't commit a crime in any way, did he?"

"No, but folks are strange sometimes. Everyone just sort of assumed he was a pervert. Even his girl. She didn't want to have anything to do with him after that."

"No wonder Jack doesn't want to talk about her."

"You're darn right." Betty distributed two sandwiches on each of the circular tin pans that served as plates. "She let him lay all alone in the hospital, a place he could barely stand, and never spoke to him again."

Claire didn't say anything as she thought about Jack—who loved open spaces—trapped in a small hospital room, probably in traction, unable to even get out of bed by himself. It must have been hellish for him.

"I heard Linda used the fact that she'd been left at the altar as a reason to break it off," Betty continued, adding apple slices to the tins. "But I think she was just plain ashamed of him. And you know what, Claire?"

"What?"

"I say good riddance. Had he married that shallow little bitch, he would have been miserable."

Claire stared at Betty, amazed at the swear words that had just spewed from the old woman's mouth. Her gentle, pious grandmother in Mexico had never used such language. Neither had her mother.

"Yes, he probably would have been miserable," she murmured.

"Well!" Betty wiped her hands on a towel. "That was short work with you helping. Thanks, dear."

"You're welcome."

Betty lifted two tins and handed them to Claire. "You want to take these over to Bill and Susan?" She winked. "I don't like getting too close to 'em!"

"Sure." Claire smiled, glad she wouldn't have to serve any of the younger men.

AT THE END of the day, they set up camp on the edge of the western lake of the Two Sisters—or the West Sister, as Betty called it. Claire pulled Peanut to a halt and looked across the emerald expanse of the lake. Ordinarily the unusual color and the clarity of the water would have taken her breath away. But all she could think of was the extra hour of sunlight they were wasting by stopping before dusk. They could have plunged onward, past the lake, and gained valuable miles. Instead, Jack had surprised her by holding up his hand, signaling a stop, when they had reached the northern edge of the lake around five o'clock.

Claire urged Peanut ahead. "Why are we stopping?" she asked.

Jack turned and gave her a chilly look. "Because this is a good place to camp."

"But we could go on—"

"The trail up ahead's too tricky in the dark."

"But it's not dark yet!"

"Look. I'm the guide." Jack turned his horse and trotted away, leaving Claire to glare at his back.

William scowled. "What's eating him now?" he asked, glancing at his wife.

Susan shrugged. "Male hormones?"

WILLIAM AND JACK set up tents on the sandy beach, and Claire looked forward to a night spent on a softer surface than the previous evening. Her muscles still ached from her night on the ground. But her bottom and the insides of her legs ached more.

She hobbled out of the clearing to gather firewood, taking small steps so her jeans wouldn't chafe the tender flesh on her inner thighs. Crabby, hungry, and still angry at both Tobias and Jack, she welcomed time alone in the surrounding trees. But she hadn't gone more than a few paces into the woods when she heard a twig crack behind her.

Chapter 16

Startled by the sound, Claire rose up and looked over her shoulder to find Simeon walking toward her.

"Sorry!" he exclaimed, holding up his hands. "Did I frighten you?"

Claire forced down a wave of dismay at the prospect of sharing her foraging task—especially with someone from the male population of their party. "I didn't know you were there."

"I thought I would accompany you this evening, what with all the wild beasts about."

"As to beasts, I haven't seen you catch any of your friends, the *crotalus viridis oreganos*."

Simeon's eyes widened. "You have an excellent memory, Miss Coulter."

"Not really. I recently took some biology courses in college."

"I see." Simeon nodded. "As to the friends you speak of, it may be too cold for the reptiles I seek after all." He stooped for a chunk of a fallen tree.

"And yet they are all around," she commented.

"That is my belief, Miss Coulter."

She *knew* there were snakes all around them. She could sense them—their coldness, and their lack of peace and good humor that most animals emanated. "As a matter of fact, I saw one go under that rock, there." She pointed to a large, flat rock, hoping to make Simeon prove himself. After the incident in her tent, she didn't trust the man, and wondered if he was all that he claimed.

She wanted to see him approach a snake, maybe even catch it. Not many people had the stomach for such danger. If Simeon was a scientist accustomed to handling vipers, he would not show as much fear as would a layman.

Simeon twisted his torso to look up at her and then stood up as he settled the wood in his arms. His gray eyes clouded to a darker color as if he could sense her distrust.

"A rattler, you say?" Simeon placed his armload of firewood upon the ground. He walked toward the rock. "Under this rock?"

"Yes."

"Let us just see about that." Simeon bent to pick up a sturdy limb and jammed one end of the limb under the edge of the rock.

She readied herself for a quick dash away should the viper shoot out in her direction.

"It will be sluggish," Simeon commented, as if reading her mind. "Cold." Then he leaned his weight onto the stick, and with a grunt, toppled the rock onto its side.

Sure enough, a rattler lay coiled on the exposed ground, its triangular head held high, its tail clattering.

"Get back!" Claire shouted.

Simeon made no answer. She wondered if he was frozen in place by fear, forced to suffer the consequences of his bravado.

Claire gaped at him, unsure of what to do as Simeon stood unmoving, staring down at the reptile. Then, much to her amazement, the snake stopped its persistent rattling. After a moment, Simeon slowly reached into the pocket of his slacks for a small container.

Claire took a tentative step forward, not believing her own eyes as Simeon reached down and picked up the snake with his bare hand.

"Oh, my God!" she cried.

The rattlesnake hung limp, as if in a trance, while Simeon deftly milked the venom from its wicked-looking fangs.

When he was satisfied with the amount of venom he'd collected, he dropped the snake to the ground and stepped back as the viper slowly zig-zagged away.

Simeon glanced over his shoulder at her. "Do not try that at home."

"How did you do that?" she gasped.

"Years of practice." He capped the little bottle, slipped it back into his pocket, and smiled at her. "I also have a way with some creatures, especially snakes."

"I've never seen anything like that!" She ran a quick glance over his slender, well-manicured body. "Haven't you ever been bitten?"

"Me?" His smile grew wider as if he were enjoying a private joke. "Of course not."

Claire nodded toward the vial in his pocket. "What will you do with that venom?"

"Perform some tests." He reached for his abandoned firewood. "I have a theory that venom from hibernating vipers, and vipers in the wild especially, has different properties than that taken from snakes raised in the lab. It's like the difference between wild salmon and those that are farmed. There is no comparison in the taste and texture of their flesh."

"So you think the snake's venom will be more virulent?"

"If by that you mean more concentrated and powerful—yes, I do."

"And yet you risked your life back there, just like that!"

"It makes my work more interesting, Miss Coulter."

Claire shook her head in amazement and bent down to continue gathering wood. When she rose up again, she found Simeon staring at her, his gaze hard and probing.

She met his glance and for a moment felt a sudden lapse of time and space, as if she'd lost a handle on who she was and what she was doing. She felt her body and mind being swept away as if by a warm but powerful whirlpool, and she had to use all of her concentration and will to pull herself away from the sucking sensation.

"Yes, well!" Claire exclaimed, flustered, breaking away

from his powerful gaze. "That's enough excitement for me. I'm taking my load back to camp."

Without waiting for his reply, she headed toward the line of tents. Once again Simeon had made her uncomfortable. Her mind felt oddly numb and sluggish as well, which was not like her.

The less time she spent in the company of the professor, the better.

BY THE TIME Claire had gone out for a second load of firewood and stowed her belongings in the pitched tent, she could smell dinner cooking on the fire. A sweet, pungent fragrance drifted on the air. It smelled as if they were having some kind of ham for dinner. Her stomach growled in response, even though she would never eat any of the meat. She hoped Betty was making some substantial side dishes, as she was starving after the long ride. Slipping a packet of dried soup mix from her personal supplies, Claire let herself out of the tent.

She walked to the fire, where William and Susan were drinking coffee, and Tobias had just picked up the gray and white enamel coffee pot, using a towel wrapped around the handle.

"Want some?" he asked, barely looking her in the eye.

"Yes, thanks." She handed him one of the empty tin cups sitting on a board near the fire. Simeon strode into the clearing and stacked his firewood as Claire took possession of her cup. She sucked in a deep, grateful breath of the earthy steam.

"Still tastes like shit," William commented.

"I like it strong like this," Claire replied.

"It's cowboy coffee." William shook his head. "The worst in the world."

"I'll drink to that," Tobias remarked sourly, raising his mug.

Simeon poured himself a cup as Jack strode toward them, pulling off his gloves.

"Betty says dinner will be ready in an hour."

"An hour?" William thundered. "That's a hell of a long time! What's she making—Crepes Suzette?"

As usual, Jack ignored his father's ill-humored remarks. He stuffed his gloves in the back left pocket of his jeans.

"There's a hot spring over there." He nodded to the west. "If any of you want to wash the dust off. We can all take turns."

"I'd love a bath!" Susan exclaimed.

"Some of us can clean up before supper. Some of us afterward."

"Why don't you go on ahead, then, Susan?" William suggested.

Susan beamed and set her cup on the plank. "Nobody has to ask me twice." She stood up. "I'll just get my things."

"I'll show you where it is, Mother, and then you can show Dad while I feed the horses."

WHEN JACK'S GRANDMOTHER called out that supper was ready, Jack ambled across the sandy clearing to the campfire where his family and his clients sat on logs pulled to the fire to serve as seats. His stomach growled, but he watched with aversion as Betty topped the tin plates with Canadian bacon. He could stomach the fried potatoes, pan bread, and peas porridge—but not the meat, now that his other nature had risen so close to his skin, drawn to the surface by Claire's disturbing presence. He would have to dispose of the meat without drawing attention to himself.

His mother, father, and Simeon had all bathed before supper. Claire had relinquished her turn so she could help Betty prepare the meal. That left Tobias, Claire and himself to use the hot spring after dinner. He intended to be the last one in the stream, so he could linger as long as he wished without anyone interrupting his solitude. Last night's encounters had ruined his sleep, making him toss and turn upon the ground, unable to rest. Now all he wanted to do was sink back in the warm water of the hot spring, close his eyes, and banish all thoughts of the strangers from his mind.

His father's curt voice brought him out of his musings.

"I don't see how you can survive on that," William commented, indicating Claire's cup of soup.

Claire gazed down at her meal, happy with the savory side dishes that would please any vegetarian. The repast looked like a feast to her. "There's plenty of complete protein in the peas if combined with this corn chowder." She sipped her soup. "It's all I need."

"I know human beings should quit eating meat," Susan said with a sigh, glancing down at her Canadian bacon. "But I like the taste so much!"

"I didn't mind giving it up," Claire replied. "It wasn't that hard."

"Sounds like a prison sentence, if you ask me!" William glared at Claire. "I can't see why you aren't as thin as a rail."

"Horses don't eat meat, and they're certainly healthy."

"But how long do they live?" William shook a piece of pan bread at her. "Not long, compared to man!"

"I believe that is a function of their natural lifespan, Mr. Hughes, and not their diet."

Jack listened to the conversation, secretly pleased to hear Claire holding her own with his father. She certainly didn't allow him to dominate her.

"Diet does affect the lifespan, young lady," William continued, determined to win the argument. "It's a proven fact!"

"And high cholesterol—due especially to ingesting meat products—clogs arteries and is a leading cause of death!" Claire set her plate on her knees. "Must you insist on having this discussion at every meal? What I eat is my business, Mr. Hughes!"

"Here, here!" Simeon exclaimed. "Freedom of choice. It's the American way, is it not?"

"As is drinking Coke," Tobias grumbled. "But I don't see anyone protecting that right."

"You could have brought your own." Jack reached for a second helping of peas. "Claire brought her own stuff."

"Yeah, well, who would have guessed I'd ever be in a place that didn't have Coke? It's an American staple, for Chrissake."

"You can say that again." William chewed the last bite of his bread. "God, I wish I had invested in that company when I was young. I'd be a billionaire, too. Able to live anywhere I wanted. Do anything I wanted."

The group veered off on a tangent about where they would live if given no limits, and Jack tuned out their chatter. Instead, he watched their faces as they talked: Claire, with her serious but thoughtful countenance; Simeon, who made affable remarks and had impeccable manners, even out in the wilderness; his mother, whose fluttery replies never contradicted anyone—especially not her husband; his father, who thrived on verbal abuse and always made sure his opinion reigned supreme at the end of any discussion; and his grandmother, who was always direct but kind—the way he aspired to be, though he always fell short of the mark. Then, finally, Tobias.

Jack quit chewing as he slowly surveyed the billionaire. Tobias could have been a good-looking guy, but everything about him—his posture, his hair, his skin, even the look in his eyes—showed him to be a man who used only his brain to take the quickest route to his goals, forever eschewing the physical challenge for the mental. Granted, his cerebral route had garnered him a fortune, but it had left him with a body that was slack, lazy, and untried. What did Claire see in him? His money? His mental prowess?

Jack lifted a forkful of fried potatoes to his mouth, puzzled by Tobias and Claire's relationship. Claire didn't seem like the type of woman who would compromise her ideals for money. And she sure as hell didn't seem like a woman who would chose a physically lackluster man like Tobias, not with her commitment to good health. So what was the real attraction to Tobias Benton?

Even more disturbing was what Jack had heard last night, when Claire had cried out in alarm. Jack was certain that she had not solicited Tobias's sexual advances, and that the man had been forcing himself upon her. But weren't they engaged? Didn't they sleep with each other?

Ordinarily, Jack couldn't have cared less about what went

on between two people. It wasn't his business. In return, he didn't want people snooping around his life. But there was something about Claire—her natural beauty; her pride; her obvious intelligence; even the way she spoke in that firm but musical tone, aloof but seductive at the same time—that drew him forward. Each day he found himself inching closer to her, when he knew full well he should run far away.

The previous evening, when she had challenged him and all but accused him of cowardice, he had struck back with cold, harsh answers, hating himself for every word that wounded her but knowing no other way to keep her at a safe distance. He'd been labeled a freak by a woman who had claimed to love him. He didn't need another female to ruin the precarious calm he'd finally achieved here in the mountains.

Still, he should have found a kinder way to keep her at arm's length. His grandmother would have known how to handle the situation. Jack scowled into his coffee mug. The way he'd treated Claire smacked of his father's high-handed tactics. His ears burned with shame at the thought that he might be turning out to be just like his old man.

AFTER DINNER, JACK suggested that Claire use the hot spring while he helped Gran clean up the dishes. Susan volunteered to guide Claire down the trail to the hot spring, and the two women left the campsite, taking a large flashlight with them, even though darkness hadn't completely fallen yet.

Jack washed the tin plates and cups in the lake, enjoying the quiet of the moment. All he could hear was the soft splash of water and the metal clink of the dishes—and not a scrap of chatter from his human companions. But then he heard a faint whinny from the wild herd, far off in the distance and his ears pricked to attention.

Over the years, Jack had learned that such a sound heralded danger—either because of the emergence of the spirit animal living inside him or because of an actual physical threat to his human self.

Without moving a muscle, Jack allowed his awareness to

sharpen and blossom, spreading out to the periphery of his immediate surrounds. It was then, out of the corner of his eye, that he caught a movement behind the tents off to his right.

Set 6

When I see the human father and son doing silent battle over sovereignty, I remember the day Horus handed over the reins of leadership to his youngest human son, Menes. What a day that was. I was sad after a fashion, because after all, Horus and Thoth and the rest of them were my comrades. And they were in terrible shape. It had taken centuries, but they had aged—and not well, mind you. They had taken to wearing masks and costumes so the people couldn't see their lesions and their wasting bodies. Pitiful, really.

Never in my wildest dreams would I have thought I would witness the physical disintegration of the Golden Ones. Weren't they invincible? Weren't they immortal? The best of the best? But mortification quietly seized them neverthless. And on the evening of the final ceremony, after Horus passed on the royal crook and flail of Egypt to his half-breed, the Golden Ones committed themselves to the universe by drinking poison, thinking I would do the same. But I had not spawned a half-breed to take my place. I had not lain—ever—with an Earthling. And to this day, that is why I believe I remained unblemished and long-lived.

Set, Unfairly Referred to as Satan

Chapter 17

Jack moved his head just enough to spot the tail of a black leather coat and a boot heel disappear into a screen of manzanita. Where was Tobias headed?

He stood up, his senses on fire. His animal nature warned him that things were not right, that the alarm he felt was real.

Tobias could have a reasonable explanation for where he was headed. But Jack's sixth sense told him that Tobias was headed for the hot spring where Claire bathed naked and unaware.

Something hard clutched at Jack's guts. During supper, Claire hadn't mentioned anything to Tobias about sharing her bath. And she sure as hell hadn't seemed to welcome his advances the night before. What was the guy planning to do—spy on her? The thought of Tobias ogling Claire when she believed she was alone sent bile burning up Jack's throat.

Surprised at the outrage flaring inside him, Jack gathered the dishes and strode up the gravel beach to his grandmother's makeshift kitchen. Then, without answering Betty's question of "What's wrong, Johnny?", he slipped soundlessly through the bushes after the billionaire. He planned to shadow Tobias until he knew for certain if the man was a welcome visitor or a voyeur.

Tobias had left the underbrush and had made his way back to the trail. Jack soon spotted him moving stealthily along the rocky path, carefully choosing his steps so he wouldn't snap a twig and betray his presence.

A few yards beyond, Jack could see wisps of steam rising

through the trembling leaves of the alders growing alongside the stream bank. He paused and ducked behind a boulder as Tobias moved off the trail, craning his neck to find a good vantage point from which to watch Claire.

The burning grip in Jack's gut clenched tighter. "Bastard," he muttered to himself, as he watched Tobias sneak behind a large incense cedar and peer around the trunk. Jack could sense the other man's arousal, could see the taut lines of his body as he stood on tiptoe, fascinated by the view below.

Jack crept closer, making every step a soundless advance toward the man hiding behind the tree. *Bastard,* he kept thinking. *Creep.*

He'd never been so angry that his vision blurred, but it was blurring now as his own personal cloud of steam roiled inside him. He was so close now, he could hear Benton muttering to himself.

"All the way, baby," Tobias was crooning, his breath taut with excitement. "C'mon now, all the way."

Jack couldn't see Claire from his crouch behind a clump of young alders, but he could plainly see Tobias reaching for the zipper of his pants.

Red-hot rage enveloped Jack. He rose up and plunged through the trees.

"What do you think you're doing?" he shouted.

Tobias whirled around, his jeans unfastened and his face crimson, and gaped at Jack in shock.

"You bastard!" Jack cried.

"Hey!" Tobias held up his thin white hands. Even his palms looked soft and unused. "I was just looking. You can't blame a guy for looking!" He fumbled with his zipper, but Jack didn't give him time to fasten his pants.

Jack lunged for the billionaire, knocked him to the ground, and threw punches into his ribs. Tobias writhed, desperate to get away, but he fought like a wimp, merely holding up his arms to fend off the blows.

"Get up, you!" Jack grabbed the lapels of Tobias's jacket and dragged him to his feet.

Tobias struck out, but Jack dodged the blow, turned

slightly, and delivered a crushing left to the other man's stomach, knocking the wind out of him. With a choked *oof*, the billionaire fell backward, clutching his stomach and rolling in agony on the ground, just as Claire appeared on the trail behind them.

"What's going on?" she exclaimed, glancing at Tobias and then at Jack. Her raven hair was dripping wet, and she wore nothing but her long sweater and boots. She'd obviously jumped out of the water and thrown on the barest amount of clothing. Jack dragged his stare off her long, shapely legs and slender knees.

"Ask your boyfriend what's going on," Jack growled, struggling to catch his breath.

Claire looked at Jack and then at Tobias, who lay on the ground, moaning. Blood trickled from his nose.

To Jack's utter amazement, Claire fell to her knees beside the billionaire.

"Are you all right?" she asked, brushing the bangs off his dusty forehead.

"The guy beat me up!" Tobias moaned again and shut his eyes as he hugged his stomach. He rolled closer to Claire, taking advantage of her solicitousness to put his head on her thigh.

Claire shot a dark glare at Jack.

Stupefied by her reaction, Jack held out a hand. "Wait a minute! He was—"

"I don't care what he was doing," Claire cut in, her voice frosty. "That's no reason to hurt him!"

Jack clamped his mouth together, muffling the sharp response that sprang to his lips. Yes, he'd hurt the bastard. In fact, he could very well have killed Tobias. Rage had consumed him. For a few moments, he hadn't been able to think or even see his opponent—he'd just stood there, pummeling the creep.

"What's wrong with you?" Claire's eyes burned holes through Jack's heart. "That you have to pick on someone smaller and weaker than yourself!"

"But he was—"

"Yeah." Tobias rose to a sitting position, obviously anxious to keep Claire from the truth. "You shouldn't hit anything with eyes. You've got an anger management problem, Cowboy."

"You and your father," Claire put in.

As if Jack needed to be reminded of his father's worst fault.

"You'd better get some help before you kill somebody." Tobias wiped his nose with the back of his hand.

Claire helped him struggle to his feet. He looked down at his pants.

"God," he exclaimed. "You probably ruined my jeans!" He gave the zipper a hard tug and fastened the button.

Jack watched, his lip curling in amazed disgust at how easily Tobias had swung the incident in his favor. He glanced back at the woman to find her staring at him, her eyes hard and cold. Claire didn't want his help, and he was never going to offer it again.

He'd seen enough. He'd had enough. And he wouldn't bother to explain his actions, either. She wouldn't believe him anyway. Without another word, Jack turned and strode back down the trail.

LATER THAT EVENING, Tobias sat on his sleeping bag, alone. Every muscle in his abdomen throbbed. As he sat there suffering from his wounds—without the benefit of a Coke or a single ibuprofen tablet—his mind whirled with thoughts of revenge. Cowboy Jack had no business interfering with his affairs, particularly those that concerned Claire Coulter. If Tobias were playing one of his computer games, he'd get out his biggest weapon, load it with tons of ammo, and blow the know-it-all cowboy out of the water.

On a more realistic plane, he intended to fire the cowboy's ass at the first possible opportunity, but he couldn't do anything until he got Claire to the fountain.

The scene at the hot spring played over and over again in his mind, enraging him and shaming him. He thought about what he should have done and didn't, and after a while the entire incident became Jack's fault in Tobias's mind. He thought about how he could get back at the cowboy if the bastard ever challenged him again, and what clever rejoinder he would say the next time he saw him.

Frowning, Tobias reached into his saddle bag for his Game Boy and switched it on. The screen lit up for an instant and then went black, as the small amount of charge that had built up in the batteries trickled away once more.

"Dammit!" He flung the unit at the side of the tent, just as someone lifted the flap slightly.

"Mr. Benton?"

It was the professor, Dr. Avare.

"Yeah?"

"May I come in for a moment?"

"Why in the hell not." Tobias sighed.

The flap lifted all the way up, and Simeon Avare ducked into the small space.

"May I sit?" he asked, sweeping the air with his hand.

"Why in the hell not." Tobias indicated Claire's sleeping bag.

"I'm sorry to hear of your injuries."

Tobias shrugged in answer as Simeon settled on the end of the bag, looking as clean and crisp as ever. Tobias thought of his own dirty clothes and dusty hair, and his abdomen covered in bruises, and felt sorry for himself.

"To what do I owe the honor?" Tobias asked.

Simeon's gaze traveled swiftly over him and then he looked up. "First off, I would like to say that Mr. Hughes's treatment of you was dreadful. Appalling."

"Thanks." Tobias looked down. Simeon's remark reinforced his belief that he was the victim.

"Would you like a pain reliever?"

Tobias raised his aching head. "Do you have some?"

"Certainly." Simeon reached into his jacket pocket, took out a small white bottle, and shook three red pills into Tobias's hand. "That should help you feel better."

"Thanks, Doc." Tobias popped all three tablets into his mouth and swallowed them, wishing he had some soda to wash them down.

Simeon sat back and smiled. "I don't know about you, Mr.

Benton, but I've found in life that the fewer cooks there are in the kitchen, the sooner one gets to eat."

Tobias glanced at the professor. "What do you mean?"

"Let me put it another way." Simeon crossed his legs. "Your goal is this mysterious fountain, am I not correct?"

"Right."

"What would it take to get to there, at the barest minimum?"

Tobias shrugged, not exactly following Simeon's line of thinking. "Food, water, horses, and the map, I suppose."

"And not the Hughes clan."

Tobias took a deep, disgusted breath. "I suppose I would need Jack."

"Can't you read the map by yourself at this point?" Simeon glanced down at Claire's purse and back at Tobias. "Do you really need a guide now?"

"I don't know." Tobias frowned. "The map is a bunch of symbols and not much else."

"Don't you think you and Miss Coulter could go on alone?"

"Probably." Tobias frowned, remembering how Claire had spurned him the previous night, and his head throbbed as painfully as his gut. "If I can drag her away from Cowboy Jack, that is."

"May I suggest that the woman is clouding your judgment?"

Tobias's head shot up. How did the professor know about his trouble with Claire?

"Listen—" Tobias forced a chuckle. "I only wanted to see her undress. You can't blame a guy."

"I'm not blaming you. I'm simply exceedingly disappointed in you."

Tobias searched the professor's face, struck by the man's choice of words. The delivery and tone seemed all too familiar—frighteningly familiar.

"Wait a second." Tobias swallowed, his stare devouring the well-dressed man sitting across from him. Then he looked down at his KarmaKazi unit to make sure it hadn't been accidentally switched on. It wasn't. A dark thrill shot through Tobias, and he glanced up at the professor as his mouth went dry. "Who are you—I mean, really?"

"I think you know."

Stunned, Tobias scrambled to his feet, all of his body aches and pains forgotten as he edged toward the entrance of the tent. He stared at the man sitting on Claire's sleeping bag, fascinated but afraid at the same time.

"Where do you think you are going?" the professor asked with a quiet smile.

"I—" Tobias broke off, as all power of speech drained away. His associate, the voice in the ether, had been with him all along, in the guise of Simeon Avare. How could he have been so blind? "I'm not sure—"

"You know it is useless to go anywhere. I am everywhere."

Tobias paused, his heart pounding. The appearance of his associate had really taken him by surprise. And he didn't like surprises.

"Do not lose your head, Tobias. I warn you."

"I'm not!"

The professor slowly shook his head in sad disagreement. Tobias crept back toward the center of the tent, anxious to hide his intentions regarding Claire from his associate, but anxious to be in his good graces once again. Avare looked up at him, his eyes hard and all-knowing, as if he could read what was in Tobias's mind and heart.

"You know what's in store for her, Tobias. Why make it hard on yourself? Emotional attachment is a fabrication of the mind that only binds you to the earth."

"And the earth is illusion."

"Exactly." Avare sighed. "I know what you want of her." He shrugged. "And it disappoints me. I had thought you were above all that."

"Hey, I've been strong for thirty years!" Tobias took a deep breath and winced. "Thirty goddamn fucking years!"

"But you're not going to let this one woman negate all that, are you?"

"I don't see it as a negation."

"It will be a huge step backward. You will be seduced into thinking you have feelings for her. It will take everything you have to break away from that falsehood. In fact, you might never break away at all. And such ruin will follow. She will bring you to your knees." Avare clucked his tongue and shook his head again.

"I just want to fuck her," Tobias blurted. "That's all. To know what it's like."

"But don't you see?"

"See what?" Tobias glowered, hating the fact that the entity thought he could rule over his every move.

"You are being used."

"I don't think so."

"Why this particular woman then? Why now?"

"It's just a coincidence."

"I think not." Avare rose. "It's the fountain, Tobias." He waved a finger in front of Tobias's nose. "It's the fountain at work. And it's hopeless for you."

"What do you mean?"

"Do you honestly think Miss Coulter will look at you twice with that Jack Hughes around?"

Tobias flushed at the insult.

"This is his territory," Simeon continued. "How do you Americans say it? His turf. Miss Coulter won't see you for the man you are until you are out from under Jack Hughes's shadow—if ever."

Tobias fell silent. He could feel the professor's intense gaze.

"Use your head. Forget the woman! The only way you are going to have her is by force." Avare ducked past him and turned at the entrance to the tent. "And it will eat you alive not to be able to win her."

"How do you know?"

Avare's lip curled. "I have watched such melodrama for millennia, Tobias. It never changes, this senseless interaction between male and female. And it's so incredibly boring."

"Maybe to you," Tobias flung back. He'd had it with being lectured. He hung his head and heaved a big sigh, dismissing his associate and hoping he'd get the message.

"It pains me to see a good man go bad," Avare remarked after a long pause. "Promise me you will consider my advice."

"Fine." Tobias waved him off without looking at him.

"And when the time comes, we will take the path to Dead Man's Gulch. We will leave the Hughes clan behind."

"Great. Fine. Whatever you say." Tobias shifted again, daring to show his back to his powerful associate.

Set 7

That is to say, in the past, I had not lain with a woman. But as the time draws nigh for Those Who Have Always Lived to return, I was forced to make a snap decision—something I really loathe doing. But I was awakened prematurely by Robert Lambers, and now I truly have become in desperate need of a new body. Only the sheer force of my will sustains my corporal manifestation these days. To acquire a new body, I have been forced to father a son—but not a half-breed as my brothers produced and raised. No, I have fathered a shell, a *khat,* which I intend to inhabit very soon with all the manifestation of my being. I await my son, who will soon inherit the crumbling *khat* of his father during a spiritual transfer, and who will die a weak old man, an old man who has seemingly lost his mind. I have never been forced to replenish myself in this way. But as I said, I am desperate this time. And no human will be the wiser.

Set, Happy Father-to-Be

Chapter 18

After calling Emilio, Claire returned to the fire where Susan Hughes sat sipping a cup of tea. Claire could smell the scent of chamomile wafting on the air.

"Can't sleep?" Claire asked, sinking onto a log near the flames. She poured herself a cup of coffee, even though she knew it might keep her up. She needed something to warm her hands.

"I keep thinking about Jack."

Claire flushed and stared at the fire. She didn't deserve to be blamed for what had happened by the hot spring, but she felt partly responsible for it nonetheless and was bothered by the thought that she hadn't done the right thing by Jack.

"It's just like the old days," Susan continued.

"What do you mean?"

"Losing his temper. Being at odds with everyone." Susan nervously fingered the curves of her cup. "He grew up all sideways with the world."

"He doesn't seem that bad to me."

"Even though he just beat up your fiancé?" Susan stared at her.

Claire looked back at the fire, not sure why she felt the need to defend Jack but wanting to all the same. "Tobias had it coming."

"Still, Jack has always gotten into scrapes of one sort or another." Susan sighed. "Ever since I can remember. Even though his father punished him, he was always getting into trouble. It was hard. On all of us."

"I don't think William understands Jack."

"No one does." Susan sighed again and took a gulp of her tea. "Jack's a hard person to get to know. He always has been. Like there's a barrier between him and the rest of the world." She frowned. "It used to break my heart." She shrugged one shoulder. "But now, I'm used to it. After thirty years, you just get used to things the way they are."

"I don't know," Claire said, propping her elbows on her knees. "I think if my child were at odds with the world, I'd want to know why."

"I used to think the same thing. But he's always just pushed me away. And now, well Jack's not a child any more. And the older he gets, the more closed off he becomes."

Claire glanced at the subject of their conversation as he cared for the horses across the clearing.

"It's the best place for Jack, out here," Susan mused, more contemplative than Claire would have guessed. "Where he can have the freedom he needs. Where he can be away from the rest of the world." She glanced over at Claire. "As long as the world stays away from him."

Claire met Susan's eyes and for a moment felt the sting of her motherly warning.

Susan broke off the stare and rose. "Well that tea did the trick." Deftly, she brushed off the seat of her jeans. "Goodnight, Claire."

"Goodnight."

CLAIRE REMAINED AT the fire, reluctant to make her way to the tent. She was worried that Tobias, having had his pride hurt earlier that evening, might try to re-establish his dominance by repeating his performance of the previous evening. She would rather sit all night on a log by the fire than suffer another one of his wet kisses.

Claire squeezed her mug tightly and gazed down at the fire. Every cell in her body was wide awake, and her mind whirled with visions of Tobias and Jack, tormenting her. Had she any choice in the matter, she would have stood up and walked away from the whole affair. But she needed both men now, and there was no turning back. Another day's ride would take them to the entrance of Dead Man's Gulch. And it was then that she would have to make her choice.

She would have to either go with Tobias through Dead Man's Gulch, leaving herself wide open to his sexual advances or stay with Jack, taking the longer, safer route which might put her brother in danger. Ordinarily she wouldn't be forced to make a choice like this—she'd go by herself. She'd handle the problem without the help of a man, as assistance from males always came with a price. But this time she couldn't go it alone. She was dependent upon Tobias for just about everything important in her life.

The fire popped, and Claire placed two more pieces of wood on the bright orange embers, seeking strength and wisdom in the purity of the intense glow.

Tobias had the means to help her brother and the willingness to go along with her plans. But Claire's gut told her to trust Jack Hughes. He had shown himself to be solid and capable, offering his aid without the usual sexual overtones. However, he had revealed a dark side tonight when he'd lashed out at Tobias, and that kind of unbridled anger alarmed her. She was concerned that Jack might be suppressing dangerously dark facets beneath his deceptively quiet exterior.

Yet Tobias had shown himself as a dangerous man, too. From the moment he'd put his hand on her thigh during the drive to the Dark Horse Ranch, he'd blatantly pursued her, ignoring her objections. Worse, he was getting bolder by the hour. A shiver ran down Claire's spine. She had no doubt that Tobias had followed her through the woods, and she had a pretty good idea what he had been planning to do. She was certain the time would come when he would simply overpower her and ravish her, no matter how much she protested.

Claire glanced over her shoulder at the tent set off from the rest of the travelers, and remembered the way Tobias had forced himself upon her. If it hadn't been for Jack's well-timed interruption, who knows how far Tobias would have gone?

Shuddering again, Claire dragged her gaze across the clearing to where Jack stood in the shadows at the line of horses. She could tell by the movement of his arm and the play of firelight down the side of his body that he was brushing Bud, his head close to that of the palomino. For a few minutes, Claire watched him brush the animal and evaluated his long, gentle strokes. Why had this patient, attentive man lost his temper so thoroughly at the hot spring?

Bud nickered softly and nudged Jack's shoulder in a friendly gesture that shot a hot bolt of shame through Claire. Deep in her heart, she knew she had misjudged Jack. It was obvious that his animals trusted him. A man didn't get that kind of reaction from an animal by being cruel or unpredictable. In fact, the horses seemed to not only respect Jack but to also love him. They listened to his every word and followed him around like puppies. She'd seen them do it.

Claire swallowed and looked down at her hands, her stomach burning. Perhaps she'd been the cruel and unpredictable one. She'd repaid Jack's cautious ways by calling him a coward and rewarded his gallantry by accusing him of violence. What kind of woman did that make her?

She set her coffee cup aside and stood up, knowing she owed the man an apology.

NOISELESSLY, CLAIRE AMBLED across the clearing, not sure what she would say to Jack and half expecting he would take one look at her, scowl, and walk away.

As she came up behind him, he acted as if he didn't hear her and continued to brush the muscled flanks of the palomino.

"Jack?" Claire ventured, struggling to keep both frustration and doubt out of her voice.

He made no reply and kept up the brushing routine. But his strokes became shorter, quicker.

"Jack?" Claire repeated.

He didn't look at her. "Don't you have a fiancé to take care of?" His harsh tone cut through the chilly night air. "Go to bed."

"I can't." She stepped closer to his broad back, wishing he would turn around and look at her instead of ignoring her so thoroughly.

"I won't be able to sleep," she ventured, still unsure how to proceed. "Not without clearing things up with you."

"There's nothing to clear up." He slipped a tool out of his back pocket, lifted Bud's left foreleg, and picked the hoof clean. "You've made your position plain enough."

"It was a knee-jerk reaction." She stepped closer, frustrated by his cold attitude. "At seeing what you did to Tobias."

Jack said nothing. He walked around Bud, and for a moment Claire thought he was going to leave camp again. But he bent over and raised Bud's right foreleg and continued the hoof cleaning.

"There you were," Claire went on, trailing after Jack, intent upon explaining herself, "not a hair out of place. And there was Tobias, bleeding and beaten. What was I to think?"

Jack's cowboy hat tilted backward as he glanced up at her for the first time. "Lady, I don't give a rat's ass what you think."

Claire flushed from the iciness of his stare, and it took all her self-control to remain standing in place before the force of his hard gaze.

Jack rose up and moved to the back of the horse.

"Well, I just wanted to say that I'm sorry," she ventured. She tried to catch a glimpse of his face beneath the shadow of his hat as he bent, supported Bud's back leg on his thigh, and took a look at his hoof. She wondered if her apology had made any difference, or if he was even listening to her. "Violence has that effect on me."

"We're all affected by something." He dropped Bud's hoof and circled the horse, running his hand over the horse's rump as he moved to the other side. "Just leave it alone."

"I can't." She trailed him and watched him lift Bud's other hind leg to clean the hoof. "I'm trying to apologize."

Jack picked something out of Bud's foot and tossed it aside. She glared at him, angered by his ongoing dismissive attitude.

"But you're making it really difficult," she finally said, determined to make him recognize her presence. "When you won't stand up and face me like a man."

Jack lowered Bud's foot and remained bent over, his left

hand braced on his thigh. Claire stared at his back, wondering if her challenge had shut him up for good.

Finally Jack straightened, but slowly, as if arming himself on the way up. He turned to face her, and she could see his dark eyes blazing beneath the brim of his black hat.

"Lady," he said, his voice deadly quiet. "You don't know what a man is."

His statement took her aback. She opened her mouth, but no words came. The air between them congealed, like something she could reach out and touch. For a long, breathless moment, Claire was aware of every line of Jack's body—his sharp nose, the lump of his Adam's apple in his neck, the way his shirt collar opened to reveal the tiny ring of white of his tee shirt, the shirt buttons that marched down his supple abdomen and disappeared into the top of his jeans, the glint of his silver buckle stamped with a bucking bronco, the jeans that weren't too tight—but just tight enough, his long, lean legs, and his big, booted feet set in the dirt in a way that dared any man to mess with him.

"And you never will," he continued. "Until you start acting like a woman."

"What are you talking about?"

"You don't know whether to lead or whether to follow."

"Well I'm certainly not following you right now."

"Then let me put it this way. As far as I see it, you don't know who's boss, and it's getting things all riled up around here."

"Don't know who's boss?" She felt as if he'd slapped her. Angry, she crossed her arms.

"Yeah. You don't know your place."

"What a condescending chauvinist!"

"No, I'm a naturalist. I take my cues from nature."

"You don't say!"

"Have you ever seen a mare leading a wild herd of horses?"

"We're not talking about horses. We're talking about men and women. People!"

"Well, as far as I'm concerned, if people were more like animals, the world would be a whole lot better off."

"You mean stuck in the Stone Age, don't you?"

"So is your modern life all that great?" His lip curled with derision. "I don't think so. I've never even seen you smile."

"Maybe because I don't have much to smile about."

"Maybe because you're trying to do everything and be everything! What in the hell are you trying to prove?"

Claire gaped at him. "Oh, you are something!"

"I'm only telling it like it is." He shifted his weight onto his right leg. "Your pervert of a boss hires me to guide you into the hills, and then you demand to take another route. Against my better judgment."

"For my brother's sake—"

"Yeah. Well, then, don't ask me for advice!"

Claire stared at him.

"And to top it all off, you have the unmitigated gall to call me a coward!"

"Jack, I didn't mean it—"

Jack was on a roll and didn't seem to hear her apology. "You come out here with your fiancé—God knows why—and treat him like a piece of shit."

"I beg your pardon!"

"I haven't seen you say more than two words to Benton. You ever kiss the guy?" Jack's stare burned across her mouth.

"That's none of your business!"

"It is when the guy's balls are so blue, he has to follow you around and beat off in the bushes!"

Claire flushed again. No one had ever talked to her in such naked terms.

"What kind of crazy-ass relationship do you have with Benton, anyway?"

"That's none of your business either!"

"Well, you got me confused, lady." He scowled down at her. "And you sure as hell got Benton confused. So maybe you should try straightening out your business with him before you come bothering me."

"Tobias knows where he stands."

"You're wrong about that."

"What makes you so sure?"

"I'm a man," Jack replied, his voice gravely. "Although you seem to think differently." He nodded toward the far tent. "And I can smell a male in rut a mile away."

"That's cowboy talk for horny?"

He didn't smile at her sarcasm. "If you think you can handle Benton, you're crazy."

"So I need you to defend me? Is that what you're saying?" Claire planted her hands on her hips. "You don't think I'm capable of taking care of myself?"

"I didn't say that," he retorted.

She glared at him. "But you implied it."

"Maybe you don't know how bad a man can want something. Maybe you just don't get it."

He stood there staring down at her, his eyes smoldering, but she couldn't tell if the heat in his expression stemmed from anger or from an unfulfilled hunger of his own.

"Maybe you don't have all the facts," she finally replied.

"Maybe I have enough to make my own decision."

"So are you trying to scare me?" she asked frostily. "Or just make me mad?" She glared up at him.

"I don't know, Claire. You figure it out. Since you're the one with all the answers."

"You bastard!"

He scowled and turned away. She wasn't about to be dismissed by him. She wasn't about to let him walk away from her like this.

"Jack!" she cried. She grabbed his upper arm.

For an instant Jack stood there as if frozen, and Claire froze as well as an incredible image flashed before her eyes. All she could see was a magnificent black horse in a blinding flare of light, rearing up and pawing the air, his eyes burning, his nostrils flaring. As she stood there, the horse trumpeted a shrill cry and looked deep into her eyes. She felt him staring straight into her heart, blazing through to her very core. She stood there, her hand fused to Jack's arm, her soul mesmerized, immolated, every shred of their argument forgotten.

Chapter 19

My God!" Claire gasped, staggering backward. She had never received such an intense reading before, and never one from a human being. Her hand slowly dragged down the sleeve of Jack's coat. As her fingers passed over his, Jack clutched her fingertips and held her fast.

"Claire?" he asked, tilting his head for a better view. "You okay?"

"You—" She broke off, too stunned for words. Her mouth was full of cotton. Her legs were shaking. A chill of fear and awe coursed through her, setting her teeth chattering. Through a haze, she glanced at Jack's face to find him staring at her, his gaze boring into her as if seeking the image she still held in her head. He grabbed both her arms, intent on keeping her on her feet, even though her body hovered precariously out of her control, as limp as a rag doll.

"Claire?" he whispered, his voice cracking.

"I saw a—," she gasped, until an even more incredible image appeared before her: Jack bending down to her. She couldn't believe he was going to kiss her, not after all the angry words they'd flung at each other. And yet, still caught in the spell of the vision, she couldn't pull away, didn't want to pull away. Her senses swam in a roiling mélange of anger, outrage, attraction, and utter confusion, even as an awareness of Jack's undeniable maleness began to unfold around her.

He spoke her name again as he drew her against his tall frame. His warmth enveloped her frozen torso, his big hands steadied her trembling limbs, and then his wide mouth sank upon hers, claiming her, demanding that she come into the searing reality of his embrace.

Again Claire saw the horse, heard each heaving breath as horse and man merged into one—felt the hot gasps and silken hair on her neck, the hard muscles rippling beneath her palms, the heat and power crushing her breasts as she was gathered against what she could only define as a pillar of strength.

The kiss shocked her into the here and now, tearing through her body with the force of a wildfire. Confusion and anger flamed into desire, confounding her even further. How could she react this way to such an frustratingly stubborn man? Her body was betraying her, aching to melt into Jack's embrace, wanting to meet every searching stroke of his hands with her own, wanting to taste his flesh, and breathe in his very essence. She couldn't believe her overwhelming re-action to him, and fought to regain control of her senses.

As Jack slowly rose up from her mouth, Claire pulled back, her hands pushing against his red wool shirt, her lips still bruised and glowing from his kiss. For a strange, extended moment that seemed to stretch into eternity, they stared at one another, both of them astounded at what had just occurred.

Then Claire stepped out of his hands, stumbling back-ward, her gaze still locked with his.

"You all right?" Jack asked, his voice husky.

"I've got to—" She swallowed, her throat dry, as her world spun off center. "I've got to go!"

Then, like a school girl, she turned and dashed away before he could reach out for her, before he once again breached the wall she had so carefully constructed around her heart. He had broken through that wall with a single kiss and had shat-tered her illusion of strength with a simple embrace.

CLAIRE HURRIED TOWARD the tent, only to draw up a few feet from the opening. Regardless of what had just hap-pened with Jack, there still was no way she was going to crawl into the tent and sleep next to Tobias.

And sleep? Who was going to sleep? Every blood cell in

her body still vibrated from the vision she'd experienced during Jack's embrace, and every inch of her skin still tingled where he'd touched her.

Sighing in frustration, Claire threw back her shoulders and glanced around, knowing she had to make a choice from a meager set of options: spend the night in the tent next to Tobias, go back to the fire, or find shelter in the forest.

She turned her gaze toward the lake. Perhaps the shoreline would have a stretch of sand where she could find more comfort and solitude than the gravel surrounding the campfire. She turned around and carefully picked her way across the clearing and down to the beach, conscious of Jack's regard on her back.

Once out of the canopy of pines, Claire found that the moon provided enough light to illuminate her way along the shore. Soon she soon discovered a small inlet where a crescent of sand stretched up to a stand of alders. She padded across the pulverized granite and sat down. Then she looked out across the wide, empty lake and hugged her knees to her chest, feeling very small, very confused, and very much alone.

AFTER CLAIRE RAN off, Jack forced himself to brush every horse on the string, from his own large gelding, Brutus, to the plodding pack horse, Cocoa. All the while, he stroked each horse, he brooded about what had gone on with Claire.

He'd been a damn fool not realizing he had been making her angry enough to grab him. And why had he provoked her? To teach her a lesson? To find out if she was capable of anger? Of passion? To shock her out of her icy aloofness, to make her see that not every thought and action could be controlled by a sheer force of will?

Well, she'd cracked, all right. But then, so had he. And that hadn't been part of his plan.

Jack wiped the side of his face with the upper sleeve of his coat and stood up for a minute to ease the kink in his lower back.

He glanced over his shoulder at the silvery lake where

he'd watched Claire walk along the shore. He should have gone after her and warned her of the danger of bears and big cats that might wander down to the lake for a drink during the night. But he'd come to his senses enough to know it was best to leave Claire Coulter alone. He'd done enough damage for one night.

As he braced his left hand on Cocoa's withers and brushed the mare's neck, Jack remembered how Claire had felt in his arms—how she'd transformed from icy rigidity to melting surrender. He'd nearly lost his grip on his own self-control when he'd felt her breasts crushing into his chest and the slight pressure of her delicate hands pushing against his ribs.

He'd been an absolute fool to kiss her, even though he'd wanted to taste her mouth from the moment he'd seen her in the dining room back at the ranch. But he knew women well enough to realize how important a kiss could be to them. If a man wanted to stay clear of trouble, he could give a woman a quick peck or a friendly smooch, but not a searing, full-on, I-want-everything-with-you kind of kiss—like the one he'd just shared with Claire.

Jack scowled as he picked a tangle out of Cocoa's mane. No wonder Claire had run off. The kiss had shocked him, too. He hadn't been aware that his appetite for Claire was a wolfish, ravenous hunger flaring not only in his loins but also somewhere deep in his gut.

But his romantic broadside had been effective, and had been the reason Jack had grabbed her in the first place. The kiss had squelched any question Claire might have asked, once she'd recovered from whatever she'd felt while touching his arm. It had been obvious she'd witnessed something—all color had drained from her face and her eyes had gone wide with amazement and shock. He'd even been afraid that she was going to faint right there on the spot. Had he not done something drastic, she would have skewered him with questions, none of which he cared to answer.

So he had stooped to the oldest trick in the book: to distract a female, kiss her.

The problem was, the trick had backfired. He might have

shut Claire up for a while, but now a new voice whispered in his head, insisting upon being heard, demanding to be obeyed. He had to quell that voice immediately or go stark raving mad.

Jack was in trouble. He was on fire for Tobias Benton's beautiful fiancée. Even now, he felt his cock tightening, his lips tingling, and his breath going shallow with need. He brushed his face with his sleeve again and realized that though the night was chilly and his coat hung open, he was sweating like a bull in rut.

AFTER BRUSHING THE last horse, Jack picked up a lantern and headed for the hot spring where he intended to sort through and then forget all that had gone on in the last few days. He eased into the water, and the steam rose around him like the cloud of his thoughts. But though the hot water soothed his muscles, it did nothing to ease his troubled mind.

He was still thinking about Tobias and Claire when he rolled out his sleeping bag between the string of horses and the tent where his grandmother lay snoring. After taking off his boots and coat, he pulled the horse blankets over him and lay back, but he was too upset to sleep. Claire had all but called him a coward and had labeled him a bully from a dysfunctional family. Her words still stung.

He'd been called a coward before. In fact, he'd been called worse things. Irresponsible. A bastard. Even a liar. From an outsider's perspective he knew he appeared to be all those things. But that was the way it had to be, and the way it always had been. He had often been punished by his father for lying and had been publicly humiliated many times because of his inability to divulge his reasons for ducking out at the last minute, or not showing up at a prescribed time, or for not being able to explain his sudden absences, his ripped clothing, or his crippling claustrophobia. Had he divulged anything of his other life, he would have been called the worst thing of all: insane.

That's why he lived where he did: out in the middle of nowhere, with no boss to be accountable to, no office to be trapped inside, no cars or planes to limit him, and no one to ask him probing questions about where he'd been. He'd spent enough of his life running from all that, and he'd made a vow to himself to never go back.

But for the first time in his life, Jack ached to explain himself to someone. To Claire, specifically. If she knew the truth, perhaps she would not judge him as harshly as everyone else. Perhaps the gentleness she extended to animals could be extended to him.

But until she knew the truth, she would continue to stare at him with frustration and hurt in her eyes, misjudging his every move. Her accusation had cut him, and the wound had gone deeper than any he had suffered since he was a child.

Jack yanked the horse blanket up around his ears and shut his eyes. If he concentrated, he could banish the vision of Claire's beautiful but confused face from his thoughts. For his own sanity, he had to keep the woman out of his head.

CLAIRE DRAGGED HERSELF back to camp after a cold and fitful night spent curled up on the beach. She had a trail of mosquito bites on her cheek and down the side of her neck, and every joint in her body cried out. Claire stumbled up the gravel beach, her clothes damp with dew and her body frozen to the bone.

Not a sign of life stirred in the four tents in the trees, and Jack slept like a toppled obelisk near the horses, his hat covering his face. Even though she knew he was sleeping, she sensed he was aware of his surroundings, and would awaken at the slightest noise. Quietly, Claire carried firewood to the pit and knelt upon the ground to start the morning fire. What she needed most was warmth, inside and out. Her hands were so cold, she found it nearly impossible to pick a matchstick from the plastic bag she pulled from the pocket of her damp jeans. Shivering, she finally managed to extract a match and set the kindling aflame.

When at last she got a decent blaze going, strong enough to leave alone, she located the coffee pot and coffee in the neatly stacked pile of equipment near Betty's tent.

Claire filled the pot in the nearby stream, carried it back to the fire, and sat down to wait for the water to boil off any impurities. She held her hands above the fire, melting away the ice in her fingertips. The temperature during the night must have fallen well below forty degrees. She'd been lucky she hadn't frozen to death on her little beach.

Just as she spooned the coffee grounds into the pot, Claire noticed Betty walking her way, pushing the stiffness out of her lower back with the heels of both hands.

"You're up awful early," the old woman remarked, arching outward at the waist and grimacing. Her belt bore a an oval buckle made of the most flawless piece of turquoise Claire had ever seen. It looked like the buckle-maker had lassoed a piece of the Tahoe sky inside the band of silver.

"I couldn't sleep."

"You look a sight."

Claire hadn't thought about her appearance. She ran a hand over her hair and found it full of little leaves and bits of twigs. She brushed them out and then dusted off her fleece jacket as best she could.

"You didn't sleep in the tent, did you?" Betty queried, holding out two tin coffee cups.

"No," Claire answered.

Betty glanced at the tent where Tobias slept and then back at Claire. "Because of the ruckus last night?"

Claire nodded, not anxious to discuss the matter.

"Is Johnny getting in the middle of something he shouldn't? Should I have a talk with the boy?"

"He's all right." Claire's cheeks burned with the memory of the previous night. How could Betty refer to Jack as a boy? Claire had never met a man as solid and as undeniably all-grown-up as Jack Hughes.

"Seems to me a nice young woman like yourself shouldn't be sleeping alone in the woods."

Betty lowered her tiny frame to the nearest log and huddled close to the cheerful flames.

"That fiancé of yours seemed to have gotten the worst of the fight," Betty continued, clearly fishing for information. "But it looks to me like we didn't get the whole story. Or maybe even the right story." She ducked her head to get a better view of Claire's face.

Claire remained silent and checked the cowboy coffee she'd made. It looked done. She wrapped the towel around the handle of the steaming pot and poured two cups of coffee. She gave Betty one of them, and kept silent, not ready to divulge her problems to anyone.

"Thanks," the old woman said.

Clare nodded and gingerly sipped her own cup of scalding coffee.

"You know," Betty raised her cup and blew the steam over the rim. "I'm about as old as these hills. And I've seen everything, too. Nothing much would surprise me. Especially about people."

"Thanks, but I'm not ready to talk about it, Betty."

"Fair enough." The old woman pursed her lips and took a tentative sip of the dark brew. For a moment the two women sat looking across the lake, where the pale yellow sky met the lavender hills on the horizon. Far out on the water, a loon laughed in the mist, sending its crazy cackle echoing through the hushed stillness of the dawn.

Finally Betty turned her way. "There's no reason for you to be sleeping out in the open, young lady. It's dangerous. If need be, you just come to my tent next time. No need to explain."

Claire turned to her, warmed by the offer. "That's kind of you. Thanks."

The old woman nodded and took a longer sip of coffee, squinting against the steam. "And if you need me to say a few words to Johnny, you just let me know."

"He was only trying to protect me."

"From your intended?"

Claire nodded. "It's a long story. And like I said, I'd rather not go into it."

"I understand."

"Just don't blame Jack for any of it. He's a good guy."

Betty nodded. "That he is. And it's about time someone realized it."

Claire glanced at Jack's prone figure, where his stocking feet poked out from under two horse blankets. She wondered what the morning would bring, and what the two of them would say to one another, should they ever find themselves alone again. The mere thought of being alone with Jack Hughes set her heart racing.

Chapter 20

Claire kept busy during the breakfast preparations, glad to have something to occupy her hands and mind. When at last she returned to the campfire, she looked down to find Tobias giving her a dark glare. But he didn't say anything, obviously not anxious to make a public display of his strained relationship with her.

Not once did Claire meet Jack's eye, and she guessed he hadn't looked her way the entire morning either. Regardless of his studied avoidance of her, she could feel the air heavy with tension, as if Jack's silence enclosed her in a smothering cloud. Claire was glad when the group packed up and the horses were saddled.

Though it was still early—seven-thirty in the morning—Claire had been up for hours and was anxious to hit the trail. She checked Peanut's girth and swung up in the saddle, feeling worn out and old from the past two evenings of physical and emotional hardship.

All morning Claire and her companions clomped along a narrow trail that bordered the lake, sometimes riding single file along a rocky ridge above the water and sometimes plodding around damp bogs ringed with corn lilies and cattails. A variety of birds lived in the lake area: dark-eyed juncos, tanagers, and yellow-headed blackbirds, as well as stately Canada geese floating on the placid water.

The swaying rhythm of the horse beneath her and the heat streaming down on her head and shoulders lulled Claire into a trance. In her ordered world, where she spent each day on a strict schedule of school, work, and care of her brother, she never had free time like this when thoughts could run wild. Her mind wandered in a jumble of memories and impressions from the last few days. And no matter how hard she tried to concentrate on the high Sierra landscape around her, she found herself drifting back to thoughts of Jack and the startling kiss they had shared.

She couldn't explain why he had pulled her into his arms. He'd always acted as if he disliked her and had made a blatant effort to stay clear of her. As for her—she'd certainly been less than friendly to the man. In fact, the only instance of camaraderie they'd shared was the time on the rock that night, high above the valley.

That brief interlude seemed years ago now.

Claire let her gaze settle on the man at the head of the column of riders and thought of the peculiar bond that seemed to draw them to each other. No matter how unfriendly they'd been to one another, no matter what silence now roared between them, there remained for them an undeniable awareness of one another. From the moment she'd arrived at the ranch, she'd been conscious of Jack watching and listening, just as she'd been aware of his every move and word.

Could it be a form of animal magnetism that Jack possessed—a magnetism that drew females toward him because of his obvious maleness? Was he so close to the earth and nature that he had developed more of an animal spirit than most people? Had that strange nature produced the vision she'd seen when she had touched his arm? Claire frowned at the preposterous notions passing through her mind. When it came to Jack, she ended up with more questions than answers.

Claire studied his wide back and the way the shadow of his cowboy hat played across his shoulders. She wondered, if she were to touch him a second time, if she would see a horse again or some other kind of animal—or nothing at all? Even as she considered the idea, she remembered the wild look in the stallion's eyes and felt the same sharp spike of fear and awe that had turned her limbs to water. Claire clenched her reins tighter and sat up straight in an effort to shrug off the sensation.

She knew better than to go testing such theories about Jack. Touching Jack would only cause trouble. And the last thing she needed was more trouble.

BY MIDDAY, CLAIRE struggled to keep awake by counting the birds she saw and was up to fifty-five when Jack signaled a stop for lunch.

The group watered the horses, quickly ate sandwiches and stretched their legs before setting out on the second half of the day's journey. Late April sun beat down upon them. Claire finally had to take off her fleece jacket and tie it around her waist.

An hour after lunch, Jack led the group away from the lake, following the inlet of the West Sister, a sizable river they would eventually have to cross to get to the final range of hills that barred their path to the fountain. The inlet was similar to the American River, which Claire remembered from the drive up to Tahoe—a coursing flood full of granite boulders, rushing cataracts, and deep green pools.

For hours, it seemed Jack guided them in the wrong direction, going westward along the river directly toward the bright ball of the sun, away from Medicine Valley. But Claire said nothing this time. Jack likely had a good reason for the detour. He was probably hunting for a place to ford the perilous river.

At three in the afternoon, Jack took them down a sandy slope toward the river. It stretched in a wide band before them, at least half a block wide. The riders jingled and creaked to a stop as Jack turned Brutus to face the others and then pushed back his hat.

"We'll cross here," he announced.

"Isn't there a bridge?" Simeon looked down his nose at the torrent of water racing by. "I don't really know how to swim."

"It shouldn't be all that dangerous. Just don't hurry your horse. Let him find his way." Jack glanced over his shoulder at the water and then back again. "It's swift but shallow here."

"Still, I don't like the look of it," Simeon commented.

"It'll be all right." Jack placed his left hand over his right, covering the pommel of his saddle. "If anything happens and you fall in the water, don't panic. Just find your feet. Don't fight the current. Walk with it until you get to the far side."

"I'm with the doc," Tobias remarked, visibly pale around his mouth. "I'd rather wait until we get to a bridge."

"There is no bridge," Betty put in. "We're in unimproved wilderness. No toilets, no trash cans, no bridges."

"That's just ducky." Tobias scowled and shifted uncomfortably in his saddle.

"Let's get this over with," Jack said. "I'll lead. Dad, you and Gran bring up the rear. If there's any trouble, give a whistle."

Without waiting for any more protests, Jack wheeled his mount around and walked down the shore and into the swirling water. Waiting her turn, Claire watched as Brutus picked his way through the shallows and then stepped into deeper water, sinking all the way up to Jack's stirrups.

"This could ruin my boots!" Susan cried.

"I told you not to wear your fancy duds," Gran retorted. "It's not sensible out here."

"They cost a fortune!" William glared at the river. "Doesn't Jack have any idea how civilized people travel?"

"Apparently not," Tobias answered. "Come on, Claire. We're next."

Claire guided Peanut after Bud as Tobias entered the river, holding his elbows out as if ready to flap himself into the air should he run into trouble. Peanut was smaller than Brutus and Bud, and Claire felt cold water creeping through the seams of her boots. She kept one eye on Jack and Tobias and the other on the rippling water at either side, all the while wondering, if she were to fall, if she could swim out of the churning eddies downstream where the river narrowed between two sheer rock walls. Her heart thudded with fear at the thought of being sucked into the mass of whirlpools in the gorge a hundred yards away.

"Come on, Peanut," she urged, more to herself than the horse. "You can do it."

She touched the gelding's neck and picked up a vision from the animal, who wasn't concerned all that much about the current or the depth of the water. What Peanut's thoughts focused upon was the patch of succulent young grass he could see on the far shore.

"That's it," Claire murmured. "You just keep thinking positive." The little horse's attitude cheered her considerably.

Ahead of them, three-quarters of the way across the river, Bud stumbled and Tobias panicked, pulling back on the reins again, disregarding Jack's warning about being rough on his mount. For a terrible split second, Claire watched as Bud bunched his haunches, his tail floating on the current, as he prepared to rise up on his back legs. But then he apparently thought better of rearing upward, and instead plunged forward, almost unseating his rider. Tobias swore and locked his arms and legs around the horse as Bud splashed into the shallows and raced past Brutus. Snorting and shaking his head, Bud galloped up the far bank, his hindquarters straining, as Tobias held on for dear life.

Jack galloped after him and grabbed Bud's bridle as Tobias slid off the horse.

"I'm telling you!" Tobias shouted, his face white. "That horse wants to kill me!"

"For good reason," Jack replied, his sharp words cutting through the air so even Claire could hear them over the roar of the river. "You mistreat him!"

"You bet I do. When an animal tries to kill me, I fight back!"

"He isn't trying to kill you," Jack growled. "He's trying to survive. Now get back on that horse. And lighten up or I'll put you on a lead line!"

Tobias's countenance darkened from white to red during Jack's lecture, but Jack didn't pay any attention to the billionaire's angry expression. Instead, he cantered back down to the water's edge to supervise the rest of the company's arrival. As he passed Claire, he gave her a quick inspection but never met her eyes for more than a second.

Simeon trotted to a halt beside Claire and pulled a handkerchief from an inner pocket of his light jacket. He dabbed his forehead and neck. "I will count myself fortunate not to ever repeat that experience," he remarked.

"You're going to have to," Claire answered. "If you want to return to the ranch."

"There has to be a better way than that." The professor looked over his shoulder at the torrent of white and green.

"Oh, quit complaining!" Betty chided, pulling her mare to a halt. "You survived, didn't you?"

"Marginally." Simeon lifted his left foot. "My shoe is soaked through."

"In this heat, it'll dry." Betty raised the reins in both hands. "And you know what they say—what doesn't kill you makes you stronger." She nudged her horse to a canter, following her grandson as Simeon shot a dark look at her back.

"I shall remember that," Simeon muttered in a voice that matched his dark expression.

Claire glanced at the gentleman beside her, surprised by his menacing tone.

Set 8

I don't know why I keep looking back on my life. Maybe it's just what old men do. And heaven knows I am the oldest living creature on this planet. But there is a lot to look forward to; I've got a lot of living to do, and some planning as well. I must be ready when they come. I must be strong. They will think I am the best of the lot, the only one to have survived. My form must be perfect: a lamb crossed with a lion, oh yes. Then I will at last be given what I truly deserve: a place in the upper echelon where they never thought I belonged.

As for those humans who treated me with such ignorance, with such unbridled fear and repugnance—they shall get what they deserve as well. How do they say it these days? They will all burn in hell? Yes. That's the ticket. They will all burn in hell.

Set, The Merciless

Chapter 21

Thoughts of Jack still churned in Claire's head as the group stopped for the night at the base of the mountain range. To the west lay Dead Man's Gulch, slicing through granite and pine to Medicine Valley beyond. To the east lay a high pass above the valley floor. She knew Jack aimed to ascend to the pass and then ride down the north slope to the forbidden valley.

As they set up camp in the dying light, Claire's thoughts jumped forward to the morning when she would either strike out with Tobias or follow Jack through the longer pass. Jack had warned her that her willingness to take a risk would endanger whoever followed her down the shorter trail. She realized now that she could never take the more dangerous route and ever look Jack in the eye. She imagined that he would be so angry, he would never speak to her and would forever hold her in his memory as a headstrong fool. Such a prospect seemed unbearably bleak.

"So, are you going to ignore me all night, or what?"

At the sound of the nasal tone behind her, Claire frowned, dragged the saddlebags off Peanut, slung them over her shoulder, and turned to face Tobias, the last person she wished to talk to.

"Are you going to stop sexually harassing me?" she countered.

Tobias' eyebrows shot up. "Harassing?"

"You know exactly what I mean." She stepped away from her horse, but Tobias blocked her path.

"Like I told you, Missy, this trip is about getting to know you. And I have to say, this ignoring routine is not giving you many points."

"And how many points do you think *you* have?" She brushed past him, anger hot in her throat.

"Hey," he said, following her, "I'm the one keeping score here." Tobias caught her right elbow. "This is my poker game, Princess, and don't you forget it."

"And you think you hold all the aces."

"Better than that," he replied, smiling. "I've got a royal flush." Though he grinned, his eyes remained hard, and Claire was reminded of Jack's warning that she could not handle Tobias. "So don't go thinking you can call the shots," Tobias continued. "You're nothing. You're a piece of shit from across the border. I can make you or break you, Princess! And don't you forget it!"

"Do you think I ever do?" Stung by his words, she yanked her arm from his grip.

"I'm warning you!" Tobias jabbed the air in front of her nose with his right index finger. "You sleep one more night on your own, and the deal's off."

Claire raised her chin, considering the notion of telling him that he could stuff his deal. As if he read her mind, he wagged his finger in front of her face.

"Remember, you will have nothing if you cross me. And I mean nothing."

"I didn't agree to become your slut."

Tobias laughed. "Is that what you think I want? You are so wrong." He flicked the soft skin under her chin and strode to their tent. Claire stood in the clearing, suddenly aware of the heavy weight of the saddlebags on her shoulder, but she refused to follow him.

Instead of stowing her things in the tent, Claire walked back to Peanut and slung the saddlebags over his back. Then, sighing with frustration, she shoved her left foot into the stirrup and mounted her horse, even though her chafed thighs cried out in protest.

At the movement, Jack looked up from his task of raising his grandmother's tent. Claire glanced at him, knowing her eyes and heart were still stony from her encounter with Tobias. She turned Peanut's head toward the trail beyond the camp.

William stepped into her path. "Where do you think you're going?" he demanded.

"For a ride," Claire answered.

"To forage for dinner?" he chided. "Something without eyes?"

"Oh, leave her alone, Bill," Betty grumbled, clanking her cookware into order. She looked over her shoulder. "Are you all right dear?" she asked.

Claire felt a wave of gratitude for the old woman's unfailing kindness. Her hard expression softened as she looked down at the white-haired woman who held an iron griddle in one hand and the coffee pot in the other. "I just need to be alone for a while," Claire answered. "I won't be long."

"We need firewood, you know," William countered, throwing an unfriendly squint at Claire. "And water."

"Then that's a good job for you and your lovely spouse," Betty retorted. "Claire has helped me fix every meal on this trip. So, if she wants a little break from the routine, she can damn well have it!"

William glared at his mother for using such strong language with him, but she didn't let his stormy expression bother her.

"Don't go far, dear," Betty added, looking up at Claire and smiling. "It'll be dark soon."

"I won't."

Claire urged Peanut to a walk and soon left her contentious companions behind—all except one: Jack. His face and words haunted her every step.

Claire wound her way through the stand of lodgepole pine, the tall, straight trunks echoing onward as far as she could see in the gray light of dusk. She sighed heavily, her stomach still burning from her short conversation with Tobias and her confrontation with William. She could hardly wait for the day when she could put all of this and her fellow riders behind her and return to her old life. What limited life she had, anyway.

Long ago, she had dreamed she would someday be her own person, far away from the responsibility and shadow of her brother's illness, maybe even married with children of her own. But that dream had died long ago, when her mother had passed away and the last shreds of Claire's truncated childhood had vanished forever.

Claire continued to ride slowly down the trail, so deep in thought that she lost all awareness of her surrounds, until the ominous noise she'd heard at the ranch and on the trail suddenly broke into her consciousness.

Startled out of her musings, she jerked to attention, squinting her eyes to see through the trees from where the sound emanated. As hard as she trained her senses upon the sound, however, she could see nothing but trees and underbrush. Not a single movement betrayed the animal that made the sound. A slight rise blocked her view and she wondered if the creature lurked behind the hill. But what kind of animal was it?

She ran a hand along Peanut's warm neck, checking the horse's reaction to the sound, but Peanut's easygoing nature gave her no clue as to how to proceed. The only sign the horse made to tell her he was aware of the strange sound was the way he pitched his ears forward and then flicked them back and forth, as if he were trying to identify the creature as much as Claire. But though she could sense Peanut's curiosity, she could detect no fear, as if he did not recognize the sound as dangerous.

As she hesitated on the path, trying to decide what to do, the sound began to move farther to the left. Claire straightened in the saddle, both hands propped against the smooth leather as she strained to see in the deepening dusk. The ominous growling broke off. She thought she saw movement a hundred feet away, but then again, it was more like a shadow flitting than the darting form of any animal she'd ever seen.

The hair on the back of her neck stood on end.

Peanut shifted beneath her as Claire rotated her torso, straining to pick up any movement in the forest that surrounded her. Then she heard the noise again—this time behind her in the trees. Whatever kind of creature was trailing her, was now positioning itself between her horse and the campsite.

"Great!" Claire muttered, urging Peanut to pivot upon the trail and face the danger head-on. Why had she been so foolish as to ride alone through the dusk in unfamiliar territory? Early evening was the time many wild animals chose to feed, to hunt.

For a moment she tried to calculate how far from the others she'd ridden. She wondered if Jack might be able to hear the noise and come out to investigate. But then with a sinking feeling, she remembered that it was she alone who had been able to hear the noise back at the ranch.

Sensing her disquiet, Peanut took a backward step, his hooves ringing through the eerie gray prison of lodgepole, but Claire pulled him up.

"No, Peanut," she commanded. "We've got to make a run for it."

She had no weapon. She had no idea what kind of animal she faced—whether it was a cat or bear or what. She'd heard tales of manlike creatures that roamed remote mountain ranges like these—the Sasquatch—and wildly wondered if such tales could be true. But she couldn't sit there and run through a list of carnivores while the creature outmaneuvered her. She had to outrun the beast before it cut her completely off from the others.

With a shake of the reins and a quick nudge of her knees, Claire commanded Peanut to a gallop. She saw movement in the trees again, a dark bulky shape that couldn't possibly belong to any of the carnivores indigenous to the Sierra Nevada. Fear spiraled up her throat and shimmered down her torso.

"C'mon, Peanut," she cried, leaning forward. "Run!"

The deep growl rumbled through the trees on her right as they thundered down the trail. Claire stared over her shoulder. Whatever it was, it was keeping up with her, crashing through the underbrush with terrifying speed.

Sweat broke out beneath her shirt as every fiber of her being concentrated on fleeing danger. All thoughts of a future with CommOptima vanished, all notions of filial duty disappeared. Nothing but sheer survival seemed important now.

Claire and Peanut tore down the trail, rocks flying, foam splattering her knees.

"Jack!" she screamed, so frightened of the beast in the forest that she forgot every harsh thing they'd said to each other. In her terror, Jack's presence defined safety—and she rode like a madwoman in his direction. "Jack!" she screamed again.

Barely keeping in the saddle, Claire hugged Peanut's neck as the little horse took a curve in the trail. They were almost to camp. A few hundred yards, and she was sure she would see the campfire and smell dinner cooking. Once they rounded the outcropping of granite, she was sure they would be safe.

But just as they tore around the wall of rock, a shattering roar split the air above her head. A blur of movement dropped from the outcropping to the path in front of her and a tall figure rose up on its back legs. Claire gaped in horrified amazement, trying to make sense of the vision in front of her, trying to tell herself that she wasn't seeing what she thought she was seeing—a ten-foot-tall lizard, his snout full of teeth, his eyes glowing neon green in the darkness.

While horse and rider flailed to a halt, the creature threw back its head, sucked in a great draught of air, and leaned forward, blasting flames out of his mouth.

Peanut screamed, his shrill voice echoing Claire's as he rose up, terrified of the ball of fire hurling toward him. Claire scrambled for purchase, grabbing Peanut's mane, kicking at the dangling stirrups, clenching her legs in a desperate attempt to keep in the saddle. For a long, horrible moment, Claire felt suspended, as if the world had gone into slow motion. But then in the next sickening second, she realized the floating sensation was the result of her body disengaging from the horse, of being thrown backward through the air, of losing all mastery of her environment.

Claire heard herself screaming as the slow-motion routine ended with an abrupt crash. Her hips and back slammed onto the sandy path, knocking the wind out of her. She felt an awareness of Peanut's struggling mass, as he fought to keep from toppling to the ground. Then Claire heard him grunt, knew he'd recovered his balance, and felt a wrenching pain in her left knee as Peanut lunged to the side, dragging her with him.

Chapter 22

Pulled along the ground, her foot locked in a crazy angle in the stirrup, Claire gaped in fright as the huge lizard swiped at her, barely missing her chest with his small clawed forelegs. She strained toward the stirrup that trapped her, but she couldn't reach her foot. All the while she struggled, she kept an eye on the fantastic creature that lumbered after her, his powerful thighs and cloven hooves unlike anything she had ever seen. But what terrified her most was not the unfamiliarity of the beast or his monstrous proportions, but the gleam of intelligence in his eyes. This was no ordinary reptile, with sluggish thoughts and rudimentary motivations. This was a highly-evolved creature with an uncanny, human-like expression on his leathery countenance.

Rocks dug into Claire's back and hips as Peanut tore into the forest.

"Whoa!" Claire shouted, knowing at the same time that Peanut was running for his life and his fear drowned out her puny human command. "Whoa, Peanut!"

The horse took a sharp curve, and Claire's skull slammed against a fallen tree trunk. She cradled her head with both arms, trying to curl into a ball to minimize the amount of flesh being scraped by the earth as Peanut galloped through the trees. She felt another blast of heat. The lizard was close on their heels.

"Jack!" she screamed over the thunder of hooves and the white-hot pain streaking through her. She clenched her jaw as the world bumped and whirled around her.

What did the lizard want to do? Kill her? Where had it come from? Why had it been following the group? Or was it specifically following her? Did it have something to do with the map? With the tarot cards?

Claire's back flared into an expanse of pain so hot that she closed her eyes, and for a moment thought of giving up, of lying back and letting Peanut drag her to shreds. For a moment she saw herself as a helpless victim, unable to do anything but endure the unmerciful pummeling.

Then she thought of her mother—the quintessential victim, the hard-working, well-meaning martyr who had given up her life to a man who had deserted her, a son whose illness had imprisoned her, an employer who undervalued her, and a country that did not want her. She had taken every blow like a saint and had never fought back.

Suddenly Claire saw herself merging with that vision, of becoming one with her mother, of being anointed into the resigned suffering her mother had worn like a second rosary.

"No!" Claire yelled, curling up a second time, straining to reach for her foot. She would not become her mother—not as long as she had a shred of strength left.

Suddenly a shot rang out, and Claire heard an enraged roar only a few feet behind her. Peanut bugled and galloped into a field of boulders the size of pick-up trucks. Claire fought to keep her skull from smashing upon the granite rocks and hugged both arms around her head.

A second shot rang out. This time the bellow of the lizard was not as loud as the first. Was the creature retreating?

"Jack!" Claire cried as Peanut tore through the maze of rocks. She worried that whoever was shooting the gun might not be able to see her. Her hips crashed into a boulder, gravel scored her back. She choked back a sob, refusing to admit defeat, especially when rescue was so close at hand. But how long could she hold on? She could hear the waver of waning strength in her voice as she called out one more time. "Jack!"

Claire's vision darkened and blurred as tears and dust and pain mingled to blind her. She heard a new sound approaching—the clatter of hooves, the sharp breath of a horse in hot pursuit—but she could no longer see anything but basic shapes. The rider overtook them, passed them like an avenging shadow.

"Whoa, Peanut!" a familiar voice commanded, pulling the stampeding horse to a halt.

Claire's heart leapt at the sound. Jack had heard her. He had heard her and saved her once again. Her terrible ride had come to an end.

"Jack!" Claire gasped, her voice cracking as gentle hands deftly unshackled her foot from the twisted stirrup. Then he knelt beside her, guiding her heel to the ground.

"Oh, Jack!" Claire flung her arms around him, swimming in a flood of shock and relief. His warm, masculine bulk was like a miracle, and she burrowed into him, grabbing fistfuls of his jacket and pressing into the furnace of his wool shirt. She couldn't get close enough to him, couldn't hug him hard enough.

As she trembled and shuddered, his strong arms came around her and held her gently against him, careful not to touch her back. Claire closed her eyes and hugged him fiercely as Jack gave his strength and protection to her, something she'd never known from a man, but something she needed at this moment more than anything.

"What in the hell happened?" he asked.

"A lizard!" Claire tried to marshal her thoughts to explain what had occurred, but her relief at seeing Jack and the punishment her body had just taken momentarily dazed her. Instead of describing the incident from start to finish, all she could blurt out was, "It was a lizard! It tried to get me!"

"Okay, Claire, don't talk." He smoothed her hair. "Try to calm down!"

"It blew fire. It tried to grab me!"

Jack pulled back and framed her shoulders in his hands. "Whatever it was, it's gone."

"Didn't you see it? It was right there!" She pointed behind him to the entrance of the rock maze.

"I thought I saw a bear," he answered. "But I wasn't sure." He tilted his head to study her face more closely. "Are you all right now?"

She met his intense stare and mutely nodded, struck anew

by the realization that she had called out to this man and he had actually come to her. He had saved her life. And he had come to her rescue regardless of the harsh things she'd said to him. She gaped at him in wonder.

He broke off her stare. "I need to check you for broken bones." He urged her to sit still upon the ground. Then he carefully inspected her ankle for signs of damage.

She struggled to get up, but every muscle in her back and abdomen roared with pain. Jack reached out and lightly pressed her shoulder back to encourage her to remain in a sitting position.

"Don't move," he said. "Not until we're sure you haven't broken anything."

Still afraid the lizard might be lurking nearby, Claire glanced around. Darkness was falling quickly, and now even the boulders surrounding them loomed like otherworldly creatures. Visibility was too poor to see much beyond the shadowy shapes. All the while Jack inspected her, she caught herself listening intently for any sound of the lizard.

As she sat there, still in shock, she remembered her phone conversation with Rae Lambers and the woman's tale of releasing the devil from the tarot cards and seeing a man change into a huge lizard. She had claimed the monster was still at large and that Claire was in danger. At the time, Claire had been convinced Rae was a nutcase.

But she'd just seen a huge, very human-like lizard. So what did that make *her*?

Jack felt Claire's left shin, knee, and thigh, his hands steady and business-like. Then he checked out her right leg.

"It was a lizard, Jack!" Claire swallowed, still dazed by fright and pain. "A lizard! A big one! I've never seen anything like it!"

"You must have hit your head," he ventured.

"I did, but—"

"You're delirious. Just take it easy. We'll talk later."

She closed her eyes, perturbed by his explanation, but too banged up to argue with him.

While Jack was still checking her right leg, a second horse galloped into the maze.

"Jack!" a male voice called.

"Here," Jack answered, without looking up from his task.

William Hughes appeared around a boulder, leading his horse.

"Everything okay?" William asked, looking from Claire to Jack.

"Peanut spooked." Jack sat back on his heels. "Claire's scraped up, but that's all."

"Thank goodness."

It was the first nice thing William had ever said to her.

Claire couldn't help but give him a wan, wry smile. "Guess I should have stayed in camp and gathered firewood," she said.

William nodded, uncharacteristically agreeable.

"Think you can ride?" Jack asked, helping her rise to a sitting position.

Claire took a deep breath, but was met with a jagged pain that made the air catch in her chest. Her ribs ached, her knee sang with pain, and her back was on fire. But her only alternative to riding was walking back to camp, and that would be even more grueling. Resolutely, she nodded and accepted Jack's warm hands as he guided her to her feet.

Gently, he boosted her into the saddle, ducked to retrieve the reins, and then placed them in her hands.

"It isn't far," he encouraged.

She nodded again and licked her dry lips, knowing even the shortest ride would be an endurance test.

"Gran's got some whiskey," Jack said. "The sooner we get that into you, the sooner you won't feel so beat up."

"Whiskey?" William exclaimed. "You mean the old woman's been holding out on me?"

Jack swung into his saddle and reached for Peanut's reins. Then he looked at his father. "The whiskey's for times like these," he finally answered. "Not for one of your cocktail hours."

He pulled Peanut to a slow walk, careful not to jostle Claire too much. As they ambled back to camp, Claire was glad for the darkness, grateful that her pain was masked by the gloom. By the time they got back to the row of tents, she was close to tears, and each breath caught in her bruised ribcage like a sob.

JACK WATCHED AS Tobias met them at the edge of the clearing and hurried forward when he spotted Claire.

"Claire!" he shouted, running to her side and placing a solicitous hand upon her thigh.

Jack saw her flinch. Either she was in considerable pain, which no doubt she was, or she didn't want Tobias to touch her. Jack wished for the latter, but suspected her reaction stemmed from a combination of both.

"What happened?" Tobias asked.

"She got thrown." Jack answered for Claire to protect her from having to waste energy on responding to questions. But he also wanted to keep her from blurting out what she thought had happened. If she brought up the lizard sighting, she'd look like a fool, and he wanted to spare her the embarrassment. She'd probably bumped her head harder than she knew and had been delirious when she thought she saw the lizard coming after her. "And dragged," he added.

"Goddamned horses!" Tobias spat. "I told you they were dangerous."

"It wasn't Peanut's fault," Claire put in, reaching forward to pat the horse on the neck.

"Of course it wasn't. It's a lack of training." Tobias directed a burning glare of hatred at Jack. "The horses around here are half wild."

"He spooked," Jack retorted. "It happens."

"Well it better not happen again!" Tobias scowled and then turned back to Claire, his expression softening. "Are you all right, though, Princess?"

She nodded. Jack looked at her, marveling that she could ride so tall in the saddle and hold her chin so high, when she must be in agony. Her hair was littered with twigs, her clothes were covered with dirt, her cheeks were smudged with dust and tears—but her spirit remained fully aflame, bright as ever, in her eyes and in the steel of her spine.

In that moment—which had to have been one of her darkest hours—he thought she was the most alluring creature he had ever seen. Claire wasn't just a princess. She was a queen. And if Tobias Benton didn't see that in her, he was a goddamned idiot.

Before anyone could move, Gran and Susan ran up to the group, and Gran shooed Tobias away from Claire's side.

"Why are you all just standing here jaw jacking?" she barked. "Can't you see the young lady needs medical attention?"

AFTER DINNER, TOBIAS sat by the fire, frowning into his coffee cup, unhappy with the beverage he'd been served, the way he'd been treated by Jack and Claire, and dissatisfied with the entire trip so far. He grumbled goodnight to Susan and William when they left for their tent, and glared at Jack's boots. Then, Grandma Whatsherface walked past holding a plate.

"Where are you going with that?" Jack asked.

"To Claire. She could use some warm food."

Jack rose. "I'll take it. I need to talk to her."

"Suit yourself." Betty handed off the food and turned to go back to her makeshift kitchen.

Jack stepped toward the far tent, carrying the steaming plate, and Tobias jumped to his feet, intending to head him off. If anyone was going to take food to Claire, it was not going to be the cowboy.

But a quick tug at the hem of his jacket made him stop and glance down. Simeon Avare shot him a warning glance and retracted his hand.

"What?" Tobias countered.

Avare bounced his gaze from Jack's retreating back to the log where Tobias had just been sitting.

"What?" Tobias repeated testily, plopping back down to his seat.

"Let him go."

"But—"

"It is for the best, Tobias."

"But—"

"As I said before, you are allowing this woman to cloud your judgment."

"I'm only protecting my interests!"

"Your interests?" Avare raked him with a disdainful look. "You seek to possess her."

"So?"

"There is nothing to be gained in the possession of another being. It will only drag you down."

"I don't see it that way."

"That is because you think you are falling in love." Avare shook his head and poured himself a cup of coffee. He leaned forward, picked up the cup, and then glanced at Tobias. "Have you forgotten everything we have talked about all these years?"

"No." Tobias frowned. He didn't need a lecture. He wasn't a kid. And this guy wasn't his father.

"Tobias, there is no such thing as love. Strike the notion from your thoughts."

"Then what is it we feel? It's so real. So strong."

"It is only a reflection. Like light. People don't really love other people. They love how others make them feel about themselves. Human love is just a reflection. And if you are strong—if you know yourself—you do not require validation from someone else."

Tobias sighed. "I know that."

"You don't need reflection or bondage to another being. They are traps, Tobias, and will keep you bound to the earth. Love is only an illusion wherein you lose parts of yourself."

Tobias nodded. Intellectually, he knew Avare was right. But emotionally and physically, he still wanted Claire to respond to him, and he still had a very real, very burning hunger for her. How could it all be illusion?

"It is because she is so beautiful and so desirable," Avare went on, as if he had read Tobias's mind—which he probably was capable of doing. "That is why you are **ex**periencing such difficulty in seeing through the illusion."

"She is beautiful."

"That is why I thought it best to intervene."

Tobias straightened and glanced at his companion. "What do you mean?"

Avare shrugged and took a sip of coffee. "You needed to be put back along the path, that is all."

"And so you did what?"

"I saw to it that Miss Coulter will no longer perpetuate the illusion that is making you stumble."

"You had something to do with her fall?"

Avare shrugged. "A bruised and broken woman loses all appeal, wouldn't you agree?"

Tobias jumped to his feet. "So you spooked her horse?"

Avare nodded, not at all contrite.

Tobias gaped at him, amazed at his sangfroid.

Avare clucked his tongue. "Come, come. She is not really hurt." Avare looked up at him and smiled. "She will survive. And that's all you need to be concerned about."

Chapter 23

That evening Claire lay in Betty's tent—ostensibly to be near the older woman, the only one in the party with much medical knowledge—but also to remain free of unwanted male attention. Claire was grateful for Betty's intercession, and for the chance to rest far away from prying eyes.

After three shots of whiskey, Claire could breathe easier, and the ache in her battered frame was dulled enough to allow her to lie back and try to sleep. But no amount of whiskey could blot out the image of the lizard she'd seen in the forest. And the more she thought about him, the more sleep eluded her.

She was still going over the attack in her mind when Jack slipped into the tent, carrying a plate.

He knelt down beside her, his wide shoulders and cowboy hat filling the empty space above her. "How are you doing?" he asked, his voice more gentle than she expected from the usually gruff man.

"I'm okay." She managed a tentative smile, never quite sure where they stood with each other, but aware of the ever-present connection between them nevertheless. "The whiskey helped."

"Good." He looked down at the tin plate in his hand. Fragrant steam rose from the food and set her mouth watering. "I thought you might want some pan bread." He leaned closer and offered the plate to her. "Gran just made it."

"Thanks." Claire struggled to roll onto her side and grimaced at the shooting pain that streaked through her. Her ribs couldn't stand the pressure of her weight. Clenching her teeth, she propped herself on her right elbow and then picked up a piece of the golden bread. Her stomach growled as she slowly raised the food to her mouth.

"There's some cheese, too," Jack pointed out, nodding toward the plate as he set it down next to the edge of her sleeping bag.

"Thank you." She shot a quick glance at his face, wondering if he were going to get up and leave, now that he'd completed his errand. Instead, he surprised her by remaining beside her, his left wrist propped on one upraised knee.

Claire chewed hungrily while Jack slowly inspected her. Another man's slow perusal would have made her feel uncomfortable, even violated. But Jack had never assaulted her with his eyes, as so many other men had done. She trusted his gaze enough to keep eating, feeling peculiarly safe with him.

"You're a lucky young woman," he said after a long pause.

She nodded, swallowing a bite of cheese.

"But I think you need at least one day of rest." His dark eyes leveled upon hers. "Maybe more."

Claire stopped chewing and stared at him as his words sank in. "You mean not go on tomorrow?"

"You'll be in no condition to ride."

"You can't be serious!"

"Think you're sore now?" He nodded toward her torso. "Wait 'til tomorrow morning. You'll think a truck ran over you."

"I can take it." Claire struggled to sit up and fought to keep the resulting flash of pain from her expression. "I'll be ready to go, Jack. I will!"

"No, you won't." He sat back with a sigh and swept off his hat, running his right hand through his black hair. Claire kept her stare glued to him, knowing that in her condition she was completely in his power. In turn, Jack sat there studying her so intently he might as well have forced open her jaw and checked her teeth or picked up her foot and inspected her ankle for flaws. In fact, he'd already done that back in the woods, as if she were one of his animals. His control over her, coupled with his impersonal survey of her body and his doubt of her judgment, rankled her.

"I'm not a piece of livestock that has to pass inspection," she countered. "I know my own limits."

"I don't think you do." His reply was more a gentle observation than a challenge, and she looked up at him in surprise. He wasn't going to spar with her this time. His eyes locked with hers, trapping her, as his gentle tone asked for submission and expected her to acquiesce.

She stared at him, realizing how infrequently she had seen his face out from under the shadow of his hat. In the soft light of the lantern, she was suddenly aware of how uncommonly handsome he was with his prominent nose, expressive eyebrows, and sharp bone structure forming his cheek and jaw line. But most startling of all were his unveiled eyes.

His dark brown eyes reminded her of those of his horses: luminous and full of liquid depths, curious but wary, friendly but distant at the same time.

"You're the kind of person who doesn't know when to quit," he continued.

"I'll quit when I'm beat," she answered. "And I'm not beat yet."

"Really?" Jack's gaze remained on her face, his expression easy and kind. "If you don't think you took a beating out there, you must have bumped your head harder than I thought."

"I'm fine." Claire picked up a second piece of pan bread and took a bite. "And I'll be just fine in the morning."

"Let me be the judge of that." His gaze swept into her hair. Then he reached out and picked a small twig from her ragged braid.

"You've got a regular meadow growing in there, you know," he commented, nodding toward her hair.

Trying to show she was still in fighting condition and that she could take care of herself, Claire ran her fingers over the side of her head where his hand had touched her. She brushed off a flurry of little leaves, but the effort made her wince. She looked up to find Jack raising an eyebrow.

"See what I mean?"

Claire sighed. "I know what you're saying, Jack." She pulled the long length of her braid over her shoulder, intending to rid it of leaves as well. "And I would have died out there if you hadn't saved me, but—"

"No buts," he put in, reaching for her wrist. "Claire, listen to me. You can't push yourself so hard."

"I have to!" She tried to pull away from his grasp, but he held her firmly and forced her to look him in the eyes again.

"Because of your brother."

"Yes."

"You're going to be in worse shape than your brother if you insist on this superman shit."

"I have no choice!"

"I'm going to give you a choice then. Force feed it to you if I have to."

"Jack!" She tugged at her wrist and finally broke free. "No!"

"Yes. For your own good." He stood up, his breath coming as quickly as hers.

"Why are you doing this?" she exclaimed, staring up at him.

He studied her for a moment, and then swooped down to retrieve his hat. "Somebody has to care what happens to you. Even if you don't." He plopped his hat over his raven hair. "Turns out that somebody is me."

He stepped toward the entrance of the tent, and Claire stared at his back, speechless, not certain he'd said what she thought she'd just heard. Jack cared about her? Her as a woman? Or her as a client? She watched him stoop to clear the tent opening, and realized she didn't want him to leave.

"Jack?"

He paused, the flap half-lifted in the air, and glanced over his shoulder.

"Stay close tonight?" she asked, her voice smaller than she would have liked. "Near the tent, I mean?"

His gaze poured over her. She could almost feel the warmth of his regard spreading across her skin.

"In case the lizard comes back?" she added.

Jack stood all the way up again and shifted his loosely slung hips. "Is that a demand or a request?"

"A request."

He pushed back his hat. "You're actually asking for my help."

She swallowed the last shreds of her pride. After the run-in with the lizard, she had realized once and for all that she could no longer go it alone. Though she usually considered it a form of weakness to ask for assistance, she knew she needed Jack. She was alone and afraid. And he had proved himself a rock.

Besides, what pride did she have left, anyway? He could probably read the fear in her. He had read everything else about her up to this point, and with maddening accuracy.

"Yes," she said at last. "I'm asking for your help."

"Well, then," he answered. "I'll be right outside."

"Thanks." Their gazes met one last time, and she thought she saw a new light in his eyes, but it could have been the whiskey making her see what she wanted to see. It could have been the golden light of the lantern softening his expression. But in that moment, she thought she discerned a layer of the wall between them melting away.

Jack was the one to break the spell. "Try to get some sleep." He reached for the flap a second time. "Goodnight, Claire." He touched the brim of his hat in a courtly gesture, and then ducked outside.

"Goodnight," she answered, her voice trailing off.

Claire sat there, staring at the void Jack's large frame had left in the confines of the tent, and knew that sleep would be a long time coming.

CLAIRE WOKE MUCH later to a low growling sound coming from the other side of the tent wall, just inches beyond her pillow. At first she thought she was having a nightmare. She blinked, almost too groggy to rouse all the way out of sleep. But when the sound rumbled through the darkness again, she knew she was not dreaming. The creature had found her.

Claire rose up with a start, the hair on the back of her neck and arms prickling with fright, her alarm masking the pain of the sudden movement. Wildly, she glanced around. Jack's grandmother slept peacefully, oblivious to danger, her white hair glowing in the dark. She strained to see the rest of her surrounds, but knew without looking that there were no weapons with which to defend herself.

The creature growled again, and Claire stared over her shoulder at the back of the tent, afraid the beast would slash through the thin fabric. A sheen of sweat broke out beneath her clothes as she reached for her boots.

Without wasting another moment, Claire shoved her feet into her boots and didn't take the time to tie the laces. She had to get out of the tent and draw the beast away from Betty. She was certain the creature wanted her, not the old woman. Claire scrambled to her feet as pain washed over her, so intense her vision blackened for a second and she teetered off balance. But fear propelled her forward, and she stumbled out of the tent, into the blast of cold air that had descended upon the pre-dawn forest.

The chill shocked her to her senses, making her preternaturally awake and aware. Her eyes scanned the clearing and swiftly located Jack, who slept at the base of a tree less than twenty feet away. She could see the glint of a pistol on the blanket near his head. Without looking behind her, Claire lunged toward him, terror choking her. She had to get to Jack. She had to wake him up before the creature killed them all.

Set 9

I am amused sometimes by these humans. They take things so literally! When Horus told his spawn they must be fair and just and all that nonsense, and to keep the bloodline pure to prove they were the sons of the gods so they could enter the realm of heaven, the idiot spawn actually started making king lists and marrying their sisters! I always had to laugh at that. They kept actual lists of who begot whom and whom that person begot, and they spent a lot of time at it, as they chiseled these lists into stone! They didn't bother to write down much history or—God forbid—any philosophy or technical texts explaining their astonishing building achievements, which, by the way, I had taught them over the years. No, they just chipped away at those king lists, misinterpreting everything as usual. All they had to do was provide their DNA when the time came. That was where the idea of mummification came in. Preserving the actual DNA. But they never seemed to get it.

They are all about process, these humans, and never about the big picture.

Set, the Frustrated

Chapter 24

Before Claire had gone more than three steps, she was grabbed from behind. And before she could cry out, a hand clamped over her mouth—a very human hand.

She struggled and twisted, trying to see who held her, and caught a glimpse of a black leather jacket and a whiff of Tobias's ever present cologne. His strong grip alarmed her, and she heard Jack's voice again in her head, telling her she could not control this man, that he was an animal in rut. But was Tobias the creature—the man who could change into a lizard? He couldn't be.

Claire thought back to the breakfast table at the ranch when she had first heard the strange, low vibration. Tobias had been sitting next to her that day and had claimed he couldn't hear a thing. But maybe he'd been lying to her. Maybe he could even project his voice. Or maybe the lizard was a highly-developed robot, like his Mars rover.

Whatever Tobias was, he was dragging her away from Jack. Claire dug her heels into the sandy soil, her thoughts swimming and her alarm rising with every step he took away from camp. But she was no match for Tobias's male strength, just as Jack had predicted. He pulled her through the trees, growing increasingly rougher whenever she thrashed in resistance. The more she writhed in his arms, the more severely he clamped his hand upon her mouth and gripped his arm around her ribcage. Claire thought her chest would collapse from the pressure and pain, and tears squeezed from the corners of her eyes. She felt herself swooning from physical distress.

Tobias apparently took her collapse as a sign of surrender. He released her mouth and let her fall away until he clenched only her upper left arm. Claire opened her mouth to scream for Jack, but the words died on her lips when she spotted Professor Avare stepping around a boulder, leveling a gun on her.

"I wouldn't if I were you," Simeon warned. "One sound and I'll shoot."

"But why? Why are you doing this?" Claire glanced wildly from the professor back to Tobias, and then over her shoulder, half expecting the lizard to appear out of the morning mist.

"It's for your own good, Claire." Tobias finally released her arm, and she stepped backward, rubbing the flesh where he'd bruised her.

"My own good?" she exclaimed, seething.

"Jack told us he planned to remain camped for a few days." Tobias jabbed his thumb in the direction of the tents, which they were far enough away from now to be out of earshot. "I knew you wouldn't want to wait. And frankly, neither do I."

"You think I wouldn't have insisted upon breaking camp in the morning?" She was enraged by his high-handed tactics and smug look.

"Not when you're under that cowboy's spell."

"I'm not under his spell!"

"Bullshit!" Tobias spat. "I saw you kiss him the other night. And don't tell me he forced you into it."

Claire flushed. Tobias had been watching them? She should have known. He had snooped into every aspect of her life before the trip had even begun.

Tobias stepped closer. "Cat got your tongue, Princess?"

She glanced at him, eyes frosty, the steel inside her rising up through her battered body, ready to meet this bastard's challenge. She felt resolve straightening her spine, her shoulders, and the tilt of her head as she returned his angry stare with one of her own. There was no way in hell she was going to apologize for her kiss with Jack.

"Nothing to say, huh?" Tobias continued, aware that his accusation hadn't produced the groveling he desired from her. "And what went on last night in the old granny's tent? He was there long enough."

"Nothing went on," Claire retorted.

"Oh yeah?"

"He's a gentleman," Claire said through clenched teeth. "You wouldn't understand."

"Whatever." Tobias grabbed her arm again. "But he's not calling the shots any more. I am." He turned toward the professor. "Get her horse, Avare."

Simeon ducked behind the boulder and reappeared seconds later leading Peanut, who clip-clopped dutifully behind him.

"Now get up on that horse." Tobias pushed her forward with a shove, made more cruel because her back was scratched and bruised. "And no funny stuff, my love, or the good professor will use his gun."

She gave Simeon a scathing glance. "You wouldn't shoot me! Tobias needs me."

"But he doesn't need all your fingers." He wiggled the gun at her. "Time is of the essence, Miss Coulter." He raised his eyebrows meaningfully.

Trying to mask the agony that echoed her every move, Claire swung into the saddle.

"Put your hands together," Tobias instructed.

"What?"

"I said put your hands together!"

Begrudgingly, Claire obeyed him. Tobias lashed her wrists together with rope from Peanut's saddlebag, and then tied her bound hands to the pommel of the saddle.

"Just in case you try anything stupid," he commented. "To slow us up."

Claire watched him work, his movements tight with anger, and knew it would be useless to protest.

"I assume we're going through Dead Man's Gulch," she said, her voice chilled.

Tobias patted her thigh. "You assume correctly."

"And if you behave, Miss Coulter," Simeon commented, mounting his own horse, "you won't be any worse for the wear."

"But little girls who don't behave suffer the consequences of their actions," Tobias added, smiling up at her. "And I have to admit, this tying-up thing kind of turns me on."

Claire stared straight ahead, refusing to acknowledge the creep or his words.

THEY RODE THROUGH the gray light of dawn and then through the soft light of the spring morning, while dew still glistened in the webs stretched across the trail and dangled from each leaf tip along the path. Without stopping for breakfast, they cantered into Dead Man's Gulch. Within the hour, the path changed from a sparsely forested, sloping valley to a narrow canyon made of sheer granite walls. The floor of the canyon was dotted with boulders, chaparral, and a small zigzagging stream they continuously had to cross. Not one animal appeared, even the usual ground squirrels or noisy jays. Claire swallowed, her throat parched. She had a bad feeling about the place and wondered if Jack had been right about the valley: that it was called Dead Man's Gulch for good reason.

The warm morning sun they'd enjoyed slowly disappeared as the walls grew ever higher on either side of them. Soon they were plunged in shadow. Wind whipped up in the gorge, whistling past them and sucking away their body heat. Claire huddled in the saddle, miserably cold from the sudden drop in temperature. But the ache in her chilled, bound hands was nothing compared to the constant jarring of her injured body. Each step made her head throb, and it took every shred of her fortitude to keep from crying.

As the day dragged on, the sky overhead grew increasingly dark. Though it looked like late afternoon, Claire guessed it couldn't have been much past noon—but try as she might, she couldn't get a good view of her watch without chafing the flesh on her wrists.

She had considered Jack a taskmaster when it came to riding hard, but he was nothing compared to Tobias and the professor. For hours, they kept the horses at a swift pace—until Claire could feel Peanut flagging and heard his ragged breathing as he doggedly matched the pace of the professor's horse ahead of him.

Then, as if she wasn't suffering enough already, Claire heard a roll of thunder in the clouds above them and felt a spattering of rain. She glared over her shoulder at Tobias.

"We've got to get go back!" she yelled. "There's going to be a cloudburst!"

"It's just a light rain."

"Jack said this place can flood easily."

"Mr. Cowboy doesn't know everything." Tobias squinted and wiped the rain off his face in an impatient gesture. "Keep riding."

"What if the storm gets worse?"

"I said, keep riding!" He cantered up to Claire and gave Peanut a sound slap on his left flank.

"THESE PEOPLE ARE more trouble than they're worth," William grumbled, riding up alongside Jack, who knelt on the floor of Dead Man's Gulch and fingered the edge of a hoof print. He recognized the shape and mark of Peanut's horseshoe. Just as he'd expected, Claire, Simeon, and Tobias had ridden this way. Jack stood up. He and his father had ridden after their missing clients while his grandmother and mother had taken the pack animals on the longer route through the mountain pass.

"You were the one who signed them on." Jack stared straight ahead, his mind only partially focused on the conversation, as he wondered how far ahead the others might be and how long it would take to catch up with them. Brutus was fast and had a lot of heart, but a horse could travel only so far at a full gallop.

Sick with worry, Jack mounted up again and urged Brutus to a trot. He didn't know what he would discover up ahead, but by the looks of the darkening sky, he had to find Claire and her cohorts—fast.

An hour later, Jack pulled up, rain funneling off the wide brim of his cowboy hat and coursing down the back of his jacket. The stream swirled around Brutus's fetlocks, rising by the minute. Jack looked up at the sky, where charcoal-colored clouds boiled, heavy with rain. A harsh wind blew, plastering his drenched clothes to his skin.

"I say we go back," William said, sidling next to Jack.

"What if they haven't made it through?"

"Then the hell with them!" William turned his horse around. "It was their damn choice. Let them live with the consequences."

Jack scowled. He couldn't believe Claire had managed to sneak out of the camp in the early morning—that she'd had the strength to do it for one thing, and that he hadn't heard her leave for the other. He'd been so sure of her, that she'd stay in the tent while he stood guard. Last night he had thought he'd seen a change in her, that she'd softened for once. But she'd obviously just been toying with him.

Jack's scowl deepened at the thought of being played for a fool. Still, he couldn't let his clients perish in the wilderness, not even those who had betrayed his trust.

"Come on, Jack!" William shouted over the wind. "Leave it!"

"I can't." Jack nudged his horse to a gallop again, certain he was running into the maw of disaster.

WITHIN A HALF hour, the sprinkles became sheets of rain that blew sideways, stinging Claire's exposed face and hands. Soon rivulets of rain coursed down her hair and over her clothes. Peanut put his head down and slogged forward, through the ever-rising stream swirling at the base of the gorge. No one spoke. No one looked at each other as all three realized the danger they were in. And none of them knew how far they had to ride to get out of the canyon.

The sky turned an ugly purple tinged with yellow, and lightning speared into the valley ahead of them, crackling and echoing off the granite cliffs louder than any sound Claire had ever heard.

"Shouldn't we get our heads down?" she yelled over the wind. "Find shelter?"

"Where?" Tobias shouted back, his hair matted to his round skull. "In the stream?"

"Just keep going!" Simeon barked over his shoulder. "It cannot be far!"

"At least untie me, Tobias!" Claire lifted her bound wrists in his direction.

"No time!" Tobias struggled to maintain control of Bud, who skittered sideways in fear, his ears pitched forward as if he could sense danger approaching.

Claire followed his white-eyed stare. And then she heard a strange rumbling noise. Peanut took a couple of steps backward, his ears flattening against his head.

All the humans paused for a moment as they stared at the winding canyon ahead of them, mesmerized by the unusual sound.

Then Claire saw an unbelievable vision—a wall of churning muddy water at least five feet high, roiling around the bend in the gully, headed straight for them.

"Shit!" Tobias exclaimed. His horse whinnied in terror.

"Tobias!" Claire screamed. "Untie me!"

Chapter 25

Jack heard the wall of water before he saw it through the sheets of rain. Under the rolls of thunder and cracks of lightning, he could hear a constant rumbling, like a freight train coming toward him. His worst fears had been realized: a cloudburst had filled the canyon with water.

Quickly, he glanced around, looking for options, but the walls of the canyon were too steep to scale. Still, his trained eye caught two possible temporary solutions—a ledge on the other side of the canyon where two twisted junipers hung over the precipice, and another ledge jutting out on his side—portions of rock different from the rest, which either chemical makeup or natural placement had caused to erode more slowly than the rest of the surrounding granite.

Jack jumped off Brutus, grabbed his lariat and rifle, and slapped his horse on the flank. The animal needed no encouragement to flee the onslaught of water. He raced off downstream in the direction William had taken, while Jack scrambled up the steep incline to the ledge above his head. Surely the water wouldn't rise to fifteen feet.

He'd only just propped his rifle against the wall of the canyon when he heard the screams of a horse. For a moment Peanut came into view, frantically trying to keep his head above the surface, as ten feet of brown, churning water thundered through the gully. Then Peanut disappeared, his dappled body rolling under the flood.

Jack scanned the torrent for a sign of Claire, his heart sick, his mouth suddenly dry. If a horse couldn't handle the current, there was no way a human would survive it, especially a human in Claire's battered condition.

Then he spotted a dark object bobbing along the opposite wall of the canyon. Jack squinted, every faculty straining to make out the shape in the rain. As the dark object tumbled closer, he could make out Claire's black hair and the soles of her boots as she thrashed in the flood. The water had swelled with phenomenal speed in the last few minutes, from ten feet to twelve. The junipers across the way would be submerged soon if the water level continued to climb.

"Claire!" Jack yelled, his vocal cords straining from the force of his cry. He lunged forward, his first impulse being to jump in after her. But then he checked himself. If he jumped into the roiling water, they would both die. He would never get to her in the flood by swimming.

Sick with dread, Jack gauged her progress and saw that Claire would come very close to the juniper branches hanging over the water.

"Grab the tree!" he shouted, pointing at the other side.

He saw her head move. Thank God she was still coherent. He thought he saw her glance in the direction of the tree, but then she disappeared in a swirl of muddy water.

Jack swore under his breath, the words clogging in his tense throat. He stood poised on the rim of the ledge, ready to plunge in to save her.

Then Claire's head emerged.

"Grab the tree!" Jack screamed.

Water ran off her face and shoulders as she strained to lift her arms and propel herself upward. She grabbed the overhanging limb, struggled to hold on, and nearly lost her grip. Her hands looked bulky, but in the lashing rain, Jack couldn't see them clearly enough to figure out why.

"Hold on!" he yelled, reaching for his lariat. "Claire, hold on!"

She tried to look at him, but the water buffeted her too much to allow any directed movement. Then, to Jack's horror, he noticed the stream had risen even higher. Soon Claire would either have to let go of the juniper limb or be totally submerged.

Reminding himself to keep cool, Jack loosened the loops of the lariat, sliding its familiar curves over the gloved pads of his fingers, just as he'd done hundreds of time before. As he adjusted the rope, he stared at the second juniper across the narrow canyon, letting his mind make the correct calculation for the trajectory from the ledge on which he stood to the one where Claire hung on for dear life.

He swooped the lariat over his head, swung it around a couple of times, and tossed it forward with a grunt. It landed inches from his mark.

"Dammit!" Jack muttered. Swiftly, he reeled in the rope, coiled it in his hands, stared at the juniper, and threw it again.

The rope arced over the flood in a graceful floating motion, unaffected by the wind and rain. For a moment it seemed to hover in midair, and then it landed with a plop over the juniper.

"Bingo," Jack said. Then he carefully pulled up the slack, sliding the noose around an uplifted limb, while sweat and rain trickled down his back and the sides of his face.

He pulled the rope taut and then yanked it hard, testing the strength of the gnarled tree hugging the cliff. It had to be strong enough. He had run out of options, and Claire struggled now to keep her nose and mouth out of the torrent.

"Hold on!" Jack yelled, even though he doubted she could hear him now. He wrapped the thick rope over his gloved right hand and leapt into the water.

He barely felt the cold as the flood dragged him downstream, ripping off his cowboy hat and tearing at his jacket. Jack grimaced and began a grueling hand-over-hand battle with the pummeling current. He ignored how deeply the rope dug into his hands and how his muscles cried out for relief. All he could see was Claire's white face sinking out of view as the waves coursed over her.

Minutes felt like hours as he dragged himself to the twin junipers. As he drew closer, he prayed the small tree would hold his weight and give him enough time to pull himself out of the water. When at last he grabbed the twisted trunk of the old tree, he said another prayer and heaved his sopping bulk out of the stream, scrambling and slipping up the wet rock face to safety.

With rain and fear half blinding him, Jack glanced down at Claire, who was completely submerged now but still miraculously holding on to the tree limb. He could see that her wrists were bound with rope, that the coils had become entangled in a broken limb of the juniper, and that the rope was the only thing keeping her from being swept away. Her crossed hands lay limp and white under the water, her fingers like the splayed wings of a dead bird.

That bastard Benton had bound her wrists for their trip through Dead Man's Gulch. Why? Hadn't Claire wanted to go?

"Claire!" he gasped. He clutched the gray tree trunk for support with one hand and grabbed Claire's arm with the other. Her dead weight, coupled with the raging current, felt like a ton as he strained to lift her upward.

Once he got her torso partially out of the water, he let go of the tree and grabbed her other arm, yanking her free of the limb. He dragged her back to the safety of the ledge behind him.

His heart thudded in his chest as he saw Claire's arms and legs flop lifelessly in front of him. The toes of her boots plopped together like those of a broken toy.

"Oh God!" Jack breathed through clenched teeth. He fell to his knees beside her silent, sodden figure.

He had never given real mouth-to-mouth resuscitation before, but he'd seen it administered plenty of times on television and in movies. He straightened out Claire's body, careful with her head, moving with icy precision even though panic burned through his gut. He'd faced many an emergency at the ranch, but had never felt such an overwhelming need for a positive outcome.

Just like a TV medic, Jack checked Claire's pulse at her neck to make sure she was still alive. Then he quickly inspected her mouth and throat to make sure they were clear, and tipped her head back to afford the best air flow. Next, he gently crossed his left hand over his right and pressed down on her chest. He gave her five chest presses, not sure how many were recommended, and then sat back and inspected her for any sign of life. Nothing.

He rocked forward on his knees, pinched her nose together, and bent toward her slightly parted blue lips. He almost sobbed when he felt her cold, unresponsive mouth meet his. This was not the spirited Claire Coulter he knew, but a wax replica. His heart broke as he blew air and desperation into her lungs.

Again he paused to scan her for the smallest flutter of life, but she lay unmoving, oblivious to the water roaring behind him and the burn in his eyes that demanded she not leave him. Jack set his jaw and placed his hands over her chest again. He wouldn't give up on her. If it took all day, he'd sit here and force life back into this woman.

"Come on, Claire," he urged, staring at her closed eyes, willing her to hear him. "Don't let the bastard beat you like this!"

Jack had no idea how long he knelt at Claire's side, pressing her chest and breathing into her mouth. Like his rope rescue, the process seemed to drag on for hours, and with the sky so dark, he couldn't judge the passage of time by the sun. He only knew that on television and in the movies, he'd never seen resuscitation take this long. But he refused to admit defeat. He refused to accept the possibility that this beautiful woman beneath him, so full of pride, so full of courage, could be so easily snatched out of his life, just when he had realized he loved her.

Yes. He loved her. Jack brushed the stray ebony hair off her pallid forehead and swallowed back a lump of grief. Somehow he'd fallen head over heels in love with this woman in a few short days. But now it was all over. Like the rest of his world, this love had stumbled into the shadow of the Dark Horse Ranch, doomed to fail from the outset.

The kiss they'd shared was the only moment of love he would ever know with her.

CLAIRE AWOKE, BUT not to the storm and the flood she expected to see. Instead, the sky was as blue and flawless as the polished piece of turquoise on Grandma Betty's belt.

The sun shone down, warm and golden, on a vast meadow of yellow salsify and dandelions, and the air sparkled—clear and silvery, a quality of atmosphere she'd seen nowhere else but Tahoe.

When she moved, however, she realized she was still floating. But she couldn't discern the details of her body or what she floated upon—it was like she was in a strange dream. She seemed to be hovering in midair. But how was that possible?

Then she heard the bugle of a horse, and turned toward the sound. A herd of wild horses raced across the meadow toward her. Leading the throng was the massive black stallion she'd seen in her vision when she'd touched Jack.

Unable to move, Claire stared in horror as the horses thundered toward her. She could see the whites of their eyes now. Didn't they see her? Were they going to run right over her? Trample her unresponsive body? A wave of panic washed over her as the horses galloped closer.

Then she saw a familiar shape on the left edge of the herd—a dappled horse with a blond mane and tail, a carefree creature with kind eyes. Peanut! The last she'd seen of him, he'd been swept out from under her by the wall of water.

"Peanut!" she yelled desperately. If only Peanut saw her, he might deflect the onslaught of the approaching herd. But he didn't seem to notice her. Claire strained to rise, to roll out of the way, but she couldn't force her leaden body to comply.

"Peanut!" she screamed.

Chapter 26

Jack's knees throbbed and his back ached, but still he knelt next to Claire. The thought occurred to him that he should give up and accept the reality of Claire's death, but he refused to quit. Again he bent over Claire's chest—and just as he placed his palm on her diaphragm, he felt a spasm beneath his hand and heard Claire cough.

Hope and relief seared through him as he helped her roll to the side, where she sputtered and puked up the water that had nearly drowned her.

"Peanut!" she gasped.

"Hey, it's all right, Claire." Jack gathered her up in his arms and cradled her limp torso in his lap. He stroked the side of her face, so happy she had survived that he could barely keep from whooping with joy. Even so, his hand trembled as he caressed her cheek. Her escape from death had been a narrow one, and the near-miss had shattered him.

"Peanut," Claire mumbled, struggling to free herself.

"He'll be okay," Jack assured her, even though he doubted the small horse could have survived his tumultuous ride through the canyon. He pulled Claire more tightly against his chest and dropped his chin to the top of her wet head.

"Quiet now. Just take a breather."

She hung in his embrace, sopping wet, shivering, and delirious. Jack was sure she was in a state of shock, and knew he had to get her out of her damp clothes and warmed-up as soon as possible. Animals could die of shock and fear. He'd seen it himself. She wasn't out of danger yet.

Carefully, Jack shrugged out of his own jacket. Though it was wet as well, the wool retained warmth more readily than the cotton fleece Claire wore. He draped the coat around her shoulders and then sat with her, his arms and legs wrapped around her, giving her the heat of his body as they waited out the storm. He wished they had decent head covering to keep off the rain, but Claire's ball cap as well as his Stetson had been swept downstream, along with their horses.

HOURS LATER, JACK woke up, startled to discover he had dozed off—not exactly the smartest thing to do when stranded by a storm in the wilderness. His left leg was asleep from the weight of Claire's hip upon his thigh. His arms and back ached with cramps from having cradled her for hours, protecting her from the wind and rain. She sagged against him, her cheek pressed into his flannel shirt, her left hand splayed over one pocket.

After all she'd been through, she needed to sleep—for a few days, not just a few hours—but they had to get up, find shelter for the night, and then catch up with the rest of the group.

Jack glanced around Dead Man's Gulch, surprised to discover the flood had spent itself. All that remained of the storm were scattered snags and piles of limbs and vegetation where the water had come up against the barriers of boulders. The wall of water had dwindled to the small creek once again, although now the stream ran muddy and full of debris.

"Claire," Jack murmured, giving her a gentle squeeze. She didn't respond, and for an instant Jack's heart flopped at the thought that she might have died of shock in his arms. But she'd been breathing, hadn't she? Her body was still warm. God, he had to get a grip!

"Claire, wake up." This time he gave her left shoulder a shake. Groggily she raised her head. Then she slowly looked around until her confused gaze landed on Jack.

"Where am I?" she asked, her lips sticking together. She licked them with a quick flick of her tongue, sending a surge of arousal spiking though Jack, even though he was frozen to the bone. He had to get this woman out of his lap.

"In Dead Man's Gulch," he managed to reply.

"What happened?" she added.

"You almost drowned." He slid his leg out from under her fanny and gently lowered her to the ground. "We've got to get you warm. Build a fire."

He struggled to stand up, his right leg numb from hip to toe.

"How long have I been sleeping?"

"Not sure. A couple hours." Jack glanced down at the floor of the gully, which was a considerable drop. He hoped they wouldn't break a leg getting down. If either of them broke a bone, it would be bad news, as he had no idea how far away his family had ridden. Help could be many hours away, maybe even a day's ride. And they had no horses.

"What about Peanut?" Claire asked, rising to her knees. Immediately after the movement, she caught her head in both hands and swayed back on her haunches.

"Take it easy," Jack warned, wishing he could touch her again, but unwilling to provide her with more puzzling visions now that she was fully conscious. "It's going to be a while before you're one hundred percent."

"Tell me about it." Claire ran a hand across her forehead. "I almost passed out just then."

"Sit there for a minute then, until you gather some strength."

He watched her carefully, trying to gauge how much he could push her. Claire was a fighter, a real trooper, and would probably force herself to keep up with him, no matter the cost to herself. But if she overtaxed herself while in such a fragile state, she might not make it out of Dead Man's Gulch alive.

"I had such strange dreams," she murmured. "All of them about horses. Just like when you and I—"

"You were delirious," he broke in, unwilling to discuss any visions regarding horses.

"Peanut was in one of my dreams. He was running with a wild herd." Claire brushed back a strand of hair which had dried and curled over her forehead. "This huge black stallion came running at me, and then I saw Peanut."

Jack scowled. He didn't want to upset Claire, but he wasn't about to lie to her either.

"That's probably the last you'll see of Peanut," he said gently. "I'm sorry."

She looked up at him, her dark eyes heavy. "What do you mean?"

"I doubt the little guy made it out. He was right in the thick of it."

"No!"

Jack sighed and nodded grimly. "Brutus, too."

"Oh, Jack!"

"All we can do now is try to survive ourselves. We can't let their deaths get us down." He glanced at the gully ahead of them. "We have to go on, Claire. No looking back. It's the only way." Then he looked down at her. "When you think you're ready to climb down from this ledge, let me know."

Without looking at her crestfallen face again, Jack set about preparing for the descent. He checked the lariat tied to the juniper to make sure he could use it for climbing down the rock face. If the juniper had been strong enough to hold his weight and defy the force of the water as well, it would hold him and Claire.

Next, he retrieved the rope that had bound Claire's hands and coiled it into a neat bundle using his shoulder and elbow, all the time picturing Tobias Benton tied with the very same rope and hanging from a tree. The bastard.

"I'm going to get my rifle," Jack announced, slinging the coiled rope over one arm. "It's on a ledge across the way."

"Okay."

He shot a glance at her. The lackluster tone in her voice worried him. Maybe her spirit had been stretched too far this time, and something vital inside her had snapped. He broke off his gaze. He couldn't think about that now.

After pulling on his still-damp gloves, Jack reached for the attached lariat and backed to the rim of the ledge.

"Don't go anywhere," he said, trying to lighten her spirits.

She glanced up at him and then away. "Right."

* * *

HOURS LATER, AFTER darkness had prevented them from walking any farther, Jack told Claire to sit down while he gathered debris for a fire. Though the outer surfaces of the branches were still damp, he knew the wood inside would be dry enough to burn, once he got a blaze going.

While he labored over the stubborn fire, he threw sidelong glances at Claire. She'd collapsed on a large stone and sat slumped on top of it, her arms wrapped around her chest, silent and forlorn, looking lost in the overlarge bulk of his coat. But not once had she uttered a single complaint during their trek. Neither of them had eaten that day or had anything to drink, but she hadn't said a word about it. In fact, she hadn't spoken at all.

After he got the fire going under an overhang in the canyon, he built a framework out of the longest limbs he'd scrounged from a large pile of flood debris. He propped the limbs against the side of the canyon, and kept testing the framework to make sure it was strong enough to withstand wind and weight. When he finished, he ambled over to Claire's huddled form.

"Take off your socks and boots," he said. "And get closer to the fire. See that stretch of sand?"

She nodded, but then glanced over her shoulder, fear hanging in her eyes. "But what if the storm comes back, Jack?"

"It won't."

"But what if it does?"

"Don't worry, Claire." He tried to give her a reassuring smile but felt the sting of his own phoniness. "At the first sign of rain, I'll find us another ledge. It'll be okay."

She studied him for a long moment, branding him with the promise he'd just made, and then reached to untie her boots. Her hands shook, and Jack felt like a cad for not kneeling down to help her. Instead, he reached for his own feet and tugged off his cowboy boots. Then he peeled off his white socks and carried his duds to the fire. Carefully, he draped his socks on the rocks near the fire, and then did the same with Claire's much smaller blue ones. She plopped down on the sand bar and stretched her bare feet toward the crackling fire.

"Oh," she sighed, leaning back on the heels of her hands and closing her eyes. "That feels heavenly."

"Thought it might." He stood for a moment and gazed down at her upraised face. Even with no makeup on a red bruise on her temple, and a line of mosquito bites down her cheek, Claire was strikingly beautiful. A feeling very close to pain wrenched through him. He'd almost lost this woman today, and not until today had he realized how such a loss would devastate him.

Now he knew how difficult it was going to be to return to his solitary life, once this woman's quest came to an end and she bid adieu to the Dark Horse.

Set 10

And another thing the humans misinterpreted, as I see over and over again in the news on television when reporters highlight yet another tomb discovery in Egypt. When Horus told his spawn they would go to heaven in a ship, the humans thought that meant they had to be buried with a ship. How foolish of them! How utterly literal! How much time they wasted, how much human toil was spent for nothing! They were not to go to heaven on a ship of their manufacture. The ship is coming for them. Or at least for me. I count the days.

Set, The Impatient

Chapter 27

Jack cleared his throat, trying to dislodge the lump that choked him. At the sound, Claire's eyelids fluttered open.

He averted his gaze. "There's a candy bar in the right pocket of my coat," he said, nodding at the garment she still wore.

"I could kill for a piece of chocolate," she replied, fishing around for the candy.

"Sorry, but it's a Big Hunk."

"Well," she said inspecting the damp brown wrapper surrounding the taffy, "at least it'll last us a while."

"That it will." Jack smiled in relief. The old Claire was back. There was hope for her yet.

"Before we have the banquet, though," he said while unbuttoning his shirt, "we need to peel off a layer and get them drying."

She nodded and put the candy bar down on a nearby rock. While she took off both of the jackets and her pants, Jack slipped out of his flannel shirt and his jeans. Carefully, he draped the garments over the wooden framework he'd built. This way, the clothing would not only dry faster, it would shield them from the wind by forming a makeshift lean-to.

He noticed Claire scooting closer to the fire and averting her eyes from his nearly naked body. His damp tee shirt and briefs clung to him like a second skin, leaving little to the imagination. In turn, Jack kept his eyes from hungrily devouring the feminine curves of Claire's long, slender legs and the seductive dip where her thigh bone met her hip.

"How about that dinner now?" he said, lowering to the sand beside her. "I'm starved."

She handed him a section of the bar, and he gnawed off a piece of the chewy ivory taffy. "Man, you can cook," he said, chuckling. He glanced down at her and her eyes glinted back at him as she savored her own piece of candy. Jack's heart soared. She was going to be okay.

JACK KEPT THE fire stoked, and Claire let him work without helping. She was just too tired and too stiff to move. After an hour, she actually felt warm. Her hair had dried, as well, once she'd unbraided it and let it hang free.

Jack flipped the outer garments on the wood frame and announced that they were almost dry, which encouraged Claire. She couldn't imagine spending the night in her underwear and thin shirt on the coarse sand of the creek bed. She knew from experience how cold and hard sand could get during the night. Still, she was so weary, she could probably sleep standing up if she had to.

"So what went on?" Jack finally asked, sitting back down beside her.

"You mean this morning?"

"Yeah. Why were you tied up?"

"They thought I'd try something stupid."

"But didn't you want to go through the gulch?"

Claire flushed. "I know I said I did. But I'd changed my mind."

"Why?"

She glanced at the side of his face and then back at the fire. "Because I'd realized it was a better idea to take the long way. Just like you said."

"Oh?" His black eyebrows raised. He looked much younger out from under his cowboy hat and with his hair tousled. "And why is that?"

"Because like you said, Dead Man's Gulch was too risky. And you were right."

He nodded and stared at the fire, surprising her again by his refusal to gloat. He could have taunted her with a well-deserved "I told you so," but he just sat there, silent and contemplative, the firelight dancing across the sharp planes of his face.

"So who tied you up?" he asked at last, his voice gravelly. "Benton?"

"Yes." She remembered the way Tobias had looked at her and told her how it turned him on to bind her wrists, and a cold flush of hatred passed through her.

Jack shook his head and glanced at her. "What is he to you, anyway? How can you even think of marrying a guy like that?"

Claire swallowed. She ached to tell Jack the truth, but she knew she would endanger Emilio if she said anything.

"Because," she replied, her voice glum, "he's going to pay for Emilio's kidney transplant."

"You'd sacrifice yourself to that creep for a medical procedure?" He stared at her, his eyes full of heat and outrage.

"I have no choice, Jack."

"But what about insurance?"

"They won't cover it. Pre-existing condition."

"What about a program to help people like you? I assume your brother's income level is low?"

"Don't you think I've looked?" She glared at the flames, heartsick all over again.

"How can this be? We live in the goddamned United States, the most prosperous country on earth. Surely an American citizen can get help with a life-threatening operation."

"That's just it, Jack. We're not American citizens."

"What?"

Claire sighed and hugged her knees. "We're illegal immigrants. I was born in Mexico and so was my brother. My mother was smuggled across the border with us and never became a citizen."

"Shit!"

"Because of my work, Tobias's company is getting me a green card, but my brother could still be deported. Any day."

"Shit!" Jack swore, still staring at her.

"No one can afford the responsibility of sponsoring my brother, not with his medical problems."

"No one but a man like Tobias."

"That's right."

Jack broke off his stare. "I can see how it will benefit your brother. But, Jesus, what will your life be like?"

Claire sighed again and squeezed her legs tightly. "I can't think about that." She had a terrible premonition that Tobias would figure out how to coerce her into marrying him, and keep her bound to him, fountain or no fountain.

"I bet you can't." Jack put another log on the fire and then sat back. "Shit."

Claire didn't need to look at him to know he wore the same grim expression she did, and that even though he had fallen silent again, he was thinking about her situation as deeply as she was. She only wished she could tell him that everything was going to be all right, as long as she could decipher the code on the door of the fountain and get herself free of Tobias. But she only half believed it herself.

Unlike others who knew of her situation, Jack hadn't looked to blame anyone or to criticize her mother or the immigration laws. He just sat there, sharing her troubles. And if she knew him as she was beginning to think she knew him, he was likely trying to come up with a way to help.

Claire felt a wave of gratitude so strong and sharp that it stuck in her throat and brought tears to her eyes. She blinked back the tears and wedged her chin more deeply between her knees, praying he wouldn't look at her and catch her in one of the rare moments when her feelings were raw and exposed.

Sitting next to Jack in nothing but her underwear had made her vulnerable in more ways than just physical. Sharing her troubles with him had lifted a burden from her shoulders. Some of the darkness had suddenly sloughed off her. His strength, his concern, and his friendship had allowed her to let out the breath she'd been holding for as long as she could remember. She let it sigh out of her, and the pain and loneliness of the past few years spilled from her like the muddy water that had poured out of the canyon.

For the first time in years, Claire felt her heart expanding, as room was made for something other than diligence and despair. For the first time in years, she felt a flicker of hope—and not because Jack would fight her battles for her or solve her problems, but because he had really listened to her and sat next to her as a true friend. She could feel his warmth and concern reaching out to her without even looking at him.

"I'm just wondering where the bastard is," Jack said, breaking the long silence by poking a stick at the fire. Orange sparks spiraled into the air.

"Do you think he's dead?" Claire ventured. "Like Peanut and Brutus?"

Jack shrugged. "If he is, we should have come across the body." He glanced at her. "I saw you and Peanut during the flood, but no sign of Benton or the professor."

Claire nodded. "Everybody spooked. They took off ahead of me. Maybe they found a ledge like you did and waited out the storm."

"Nice of them to come back and check on you."

"They probably assumed I was dead, being tied up like I was."

Jack scowled. "Bastards." He poked the fire again. "Far as I can figure it, they must have gone up the west ravine."

"Where is that?"

"Just beyond the ledge where I found you. They must have taken the west fork, hoping the flood would bypass them—which it would have. The ravine's steep and goes up into the hills. A real nightmare on horseback, too."

"I didn't see that ravine."

"No wonder. You were half-dead when we first started walking."

Claire took another bite of Big Hunk. "What about your family?" she asked. "Are they okay?"

"Yeah. They took the long way. I'm hoping we'll meet up with them sometime tomorrow."

"I hope they have my purse." Claire swallowed the taffy. "It's lucky Tobias didn't think to bring it. I would have lost my wallet, my phone—" She broke off as she thought of the valuable tarot cards nestled in her purse as well. But she'd never tell Jack about them. He'd think she was completely crazy. "Well, everything."

"What about your brother? Will he be worried? You said you call him every night."

Claire nodded. "Yeah. And I didn't call last night, either. He'll be worried sick."

"Shit." Jack threw the stick on the fire and then slowly turned to her. "I've never wanted to be like my parents, slaves to the mighty dollar. You know?"

She raised her chin from her knees and gazed at him, not sure why he'd changed the subject.

"But I wish I'd kept that Wall Street job now. I wish I could sit here and tell you, no problem, I'll help your brother. But I've never made the fortune everyone thought I would."

"It's okay, Jack." She reached out to touch his knee but noticed his wary glance land on her hand, and immediately she retracted the gesture. "I appreciate the sentiment."

"I've never given a second thought to money. Until now."

"It's not your problem, though. It's mine."

"But the idea of you marrying that smug bastard—" Jack jumped to his feet. "It just sticks in my craw."

"I'll find some way to get through it. I always have. I always will."

"And the way he's mistreated my horses—" Jack broke off and threw the stick into the fire. "Hell, I could just imagine—"

"Don't worry." She knew what he was getting at, that a man who could be cruel to an animal could be cruel to a human being as well. "You don't have all the facts. I'll be okay."

Jack stared down at her, his eyes hard. "That's the part that really gets me. Not knowing what's really going on with you."

"Everyone has their secrets." She thought she saw him flush.

"But you don't trust me enough to share."

She glanced up at him. "Jack, I hardly know you."

"Bullshit."

This time she felt herself flushing as he skewered her with

his eyes. He was right. They had recognized something in each other the first moment they had met.

"Look." He broke off the stare and plopped back down. "I want to help you, Claire. But how can I if you're hiding the truth from me?"

"I'm not at liberty to say. I would if I could."

"Because of Tobias?"

"And my job, and my brother."

He sighed. "It's always about your brother, isn't it?"

Claire nodded. "Ever since I can remember."

"And never about you."

"It's my lot in life, I guess." Claire shrugged. "Besides, Emilio is all I have in the world. I would do anything for him."

"But have you ever done anything for yourself?" Jack stared at her, and then ran a hand through his silky black hair. "I mean really for yourself?"

"Like what?"

"Taken a vacation? A break even? Ever fallen in love?"

"I was in love once."

"And?"

"It was a big mistake. It proved how love can blind a person. To everything."

"Really?" His eyebrows shot up. "Sounds intriguing."

"Intriguing?" She could still feel the scalding shame of that memory. "I paid a price for that big mistake. It was a travesty I will never repeat."

"It couldn't have been that bad. We all have affairs that crash and burn."

"Not as bad as this one."

When Jack said nothing, she continued, feeling a sudden urge to tell someone everything—for the first time in her life. "I wasn't good enough for him. That's what it came down to. I was good enough for everything but marriage—that, and meeting his family."

"Doesn't sound like your kind of guy."

"I thought he was." She sighed. "But once he found out I was pregnant, he just disappeared."

Jack's head shot up. "You have a kid?"

"No. I lost the baby." She shrugged and put her chin on her knees again, steeling herself against the memory she had evoked. "I've always wondered, if I had been more happy about the pregnancy, more accepting, maybe I wouldn't have lost her."

"You can't think that way, Claire," he replied kindly. "You can't second-guess Mother Nature."

"But I've always thought it was partly my fault."

After a moment, Jack said, "Well, it explains a lot."

"In what way?"

"About you and Tobias. And why a marriage of convenience doesn't bother you." He shrugged. "It's the easy way out."

"I beg your pardon?"

Chapter 28

It's a way to make sure you'll never risk falling in love again. Never have to lose again."

At his words, Claire fell silent. She'd never thought about the situation in quite that way. Had she dedicated herself to Emilio out of cowardice—instead of self-sacrifice and honor, as she thought she had? Maybe she was just like her mother—playing the martyr to the outside world, but in reality hiding behind Emilio's sickbed so she'd never face humiliation again.

"It explains why you like to keep busy," he continued. "So you don't have time to realize how empty your life is."

"It's not empty," she protested. "I have my work. I love my work!"

"But does it keep you warm at night, Claire?" His voice dropped to the gentle tone he'd used the previous night in the tent. "I know mine doesn't."

Claire glanced at the side of Jack's face, struck again by his ability to read her, to find words that could shoot like a bolt straight into her. She took a ragged breath and stared at the fire, suddenly wondering if the past years of her life had been a senseless waste.

Jack must have thought better of his lapse into self-disclosure, because he rose and busied himself with the clothes he'd placed on the wooden frame. He picked up her jeans.

"Your jeans," he announced. "They're dry."

Claire nodded, not trusting her voice to remain level

should she try to speak. She was on the verge of tears again, and worried that even the tiniest remark could trigger a sobbing episode she knew she'd been repressing for years. She told herself she was tired and hungry, not herself, and that after a decent night's sleep and a hot meal she would snap out of such maudlin thoughts. But cheerleading did nothing to bolster her spirits.

Jack carried her clothes to the side of the fire where she sat and looked down at her. "Why don't you slip out of the stuff you're wearing and put the dry clothes on?" He held out her sweater and jeans. "I promise not to look." He winked at her, but his eyes were full of kindness, not lasciviousness. Again she sensed the depth of his regard for her and his wholesomeness, and it radiated over her like a healing cloud. Her spirits lifted.

"Really?" The sooner she got her mind off the dark side of life, the better. She forced herself to give Jack a breezy smile. "I'm not sure I can return such a promise."

"Why not?" He reached for his own jeans. "I'm just a beat-up cowboy. Hairy and creaky."

"I'll bet," Claire replied wryly, grateful for the change of subject. "You don't look all that creaky to me."

"So you've been checking me out?"

"What else is there to do on a long trail ride?"

"You've been staring at my butt?" He gave her one of his lopsided smiles. "I thought you were engaged."

"A girl can still look." She stood up. "Besides, my relationship with Tobias didn't stop you the other night."

All humor dropped from Jack's expression. "That was a mistake. Forget about it." He turned his back on her and reached for his underwear.

The kiss had been a mistake? What about last night when he'd claimed to care what happened to her? Was that a mistake, too? Did Jack run as hot and cold as she was beginning to suspect he did? Claire immediately turned away from him.

"A kiss like that just happened?" Claire took off her bra, wincing when she pulled it over the bruised flesh of her back. "I've never been kissed like that."

"You were in a state. I had to do something."

"Well, it surprised me, that's for sure." She reached for her stiff sweater and pulled it over her head. Then she struggled into her jeans.

Out of the corner of her eye, she saw him yank his jeans over his small, muscular, and very male butt. "It was meant to surprise you," he said. She heard the rasping sound as he zipped up his pants. "But that doesn't mean we should repeat it."

"Or that you would want to," she challenged, turning to face him.

He shrugged on his flannel shirt. "What is that supposed to mean?"

Claire zipped up her jeans. "Just what it sounds like. The truth."

"The truth? That I wouldn't want to kiss you?"

"Jack, you won't even let me touch you!" She felt a flush creeping back up her cheeks, but pressed on. "Every time I reach out to you, you give me this look."

Jack stopped buttoning his shirt. "What look?" he retorted.

"Like I'm a pariah of some kind." She raised her chin. "Like the look I've received from people since I was five years old—."

Jack stared at her, and she could see her words sinking in, the slow softening of comprehension in his dark eyes.

"Wait a minute," he said. "You've got it all wrong."

"I don't think so."

"It's not what you think. It's not about you."

"It isn't?" She stepped toward him, knowing what he would do, but intent on making him own up to his reactions.

Jack straightened to his full height, throwing his head back as she approached, watching her, his nostrils slightly flared. Most people would have taken one look at his wary expression and stopped in their tracks. But Claire pressed on. Before he could retreat or turn away, she reached up and spread her palms flat upon the thick cotton fabric that covered his wide chest. An image of the huge black horse immediately leapt into her mind, and she sucked in a breath of surprise.

"What is it about you?" she gasped.

Jack clutched her wrists firmly and urged her hands away. "Claire, this is a bad idea."

"Whenever I touch you, I pick up a vision—"

"Not that crap again," he put in.

"—Of a huge black horse. Why is that?" She stared at his face, but he only looked back at her with the same guarded expression. "I never pick up visions from people," she continued, "so why do I get them from you? And always the same horse?"

"How am I supposed to know? You're Dr. Doolittle, not me." Jack released her wrists and stepped back, his gaze locked with hers.

"There you go again," she said, her voice full of frustration, "pushing the world away. Pushing me away."

"Don't," he warned. "Neither of us needs this."

"Why?"

"You're engaged," he retorted, his mouth grim.

"You don't have all the facts about that, Jack."

"Well, until I do, I don't plan to get chummy."

"Why?" She stared at him, knowing how little time they had left and knowing how badly she wanted answers. She raised her chin. "What would it hurt?"

"It would yank my chain."

"Why?"

"Because I don't happen to agree that all is fair in love and war."

"What is that supposed to mean?"

"You have an understanding with a man." He shook his head in disgust. "And I don't butt in on someone else's territory."

"What if the understanding with Tobias isn't what you think?"

"Well, then I'd be confused." He tilted his head and looked deep into her eyes. "And waiting for the smoke to clear."

"What if I wasn't at liberty to talk about it?"

"Then I wouldn't be at liberty to take liberties."

"Jack!" She propped her hands on her hips. "It isn't funny."

"I wasn't trying to be funny."

"God, you're something!"

"Sorry," Jack answered. "But the bastard is still your fiancé."

"Right."

"Until you tell me differently."

As if she could. Frustrated, Claire sighed. "I thought we were becoming friends."

"We are. But that's as far as it's going to go." He looked down and started to button his shirt. Claire plopped down on the sand, chastened, hungry, and dejected.

She had never tried to seduce a man, but she had wanted Jack Hughes to at least respond to her touch, maybe steal a second kiss before pushing her away. But he hadn't taken advantage of her offer. She propped her chin on her knee and stared at the fire, damning Tobias for demanding silence from her and damning herself for agreeing to his scheme. She ached to tell Jack everything, to bare herself to him in all ways.

But maybe Jack was right. Maybe it was stupid to go any farther. He had his life out here in the wilderness, and she had her career at CommOptima. Even if he had responded to her touch, how would she have acted upon the sparks she knew would surely fly between them? Her body was so bruised and her muscles were so sore, she found it painful to even take a deep breath. What kind of lovemaking would she be able to engage in—if it came to that? She would be unimpressive, to say the least. And she wanted more than anything to impress this man.

Depressed and disappointed, Claire closed her eyes. She had so wanted to touch Jack, to feel his arms slip around her, to surrender once again to his kiss and his strong but gentle hands, to enjoy the special connection she'd never known with another human being. But he'd said no. He'd pushed her away. She sat in the cold sand, more dejected than ever—thirsty and hungry, but most of all hurt.

JACK FASTENED THE last button on his shirt and glanced at Claire, wondering what she was thinking. They had been brutally frank with each other and had seemed to reach an uncomfortable agreement. But he could tell by looking at her that she was still upset. Frowning, he pulled on his socks and boots.

Needing to keep busy, Jack ranged close to the fire, gathering more wood for the night and trying to regain control of his good sense. He knew better than to engage in anything with Claire—even as much as a simple kiss—because once that breach was crossed, he would find it nearly impossible to hold back.

He wanted Claire. But he knew the underside of want. He knew how difficult it would be to let her go once he discovered what it was like to truly hold her in his arms. But whatever happened, he knew one thing for sure: he would have to let her go in the end. No woman, especially a woman like Claire, would settle for him if she knew the truth about him. And it would take a very special woman to be able to live in a remote place like the Dark Horse Ranch.

Back at the fire, Jack dropped his load of wood on the ground and ambled to the sand bar. He lowered himself to the ground and nestled his shoulders into the deep, sandy bank, forming a comfortable support for his back. Then he looked over at Claire, who sat silent and unmoving, hugging her knees, her tall slender body tucked in an uncomfortable curl.

Their jackets and underwear still lay drying upon the makeshift rack. All they had to stave off the chill of the mountain night was the fire and each other. It was going to be a long night for both of them. The least he could do was offer her comfort and support after her last two traumatic days.

"Claire." Swallowing his misgivings, Jack held out his right arm. "Come on over here. I'll keep you warm at least."

Surprised, she raised her head and stared at him.

He gestured her closer with a slight wave of his hand. "Come on."

Her gaze swept over his chest and arms and then back to his face, confusion plainly written on her features.

"If you think you can stand the crazy-ass visions you pick up from me," he added.

Claire licked her parched lips, as if buying time to consider the offer.

"You need to sleep," he continued. "Or you won't be any good to me tomorrow."

Finally, she accepted the idea and crawled over to him. Like a child, she clambered into his lap. He settled her sideways against him, her butt between his thighs and her long legs off to the side. She didn't say anything and burrowed into his torso, laying her cheek against his left breast and propping her left hand on his chest.

Carefully, Jack cradled her in his arms, aching with love for her. He wanted to protect her like this forever—not for just one night. He wanted to know what it was like to feel her slender limbs naked against his own, to listen to her talk deep in the night, to feel her heart beating against his own.

At first he wasn't sure where to put his hands, but they soon drifted into position as if they had always known where to land: his left one just under her elbow and his right one on her thigh.

"You're so warm," she murmured.

"That's the idea," he replied, fighting the urge to lean down and kiss her smudged cheek. "Try to get some sleep now."

She nodded her head against his chest. A few moments went by as Jack struggled for control, never having realized the extent of the battle he would face once Claire's willowy body was draped over his.

"You're a good man, Jack Hughes," she murmured again, as she reached up to touch his cheek.

"Claire—," he whispered in warning. Her fingers touched his mouth, sending a spike of arousal down his frame. He turned just enough to brush his lips across her fingertips and closed his eyes as his body cried out for more.

He wasn't a good man. She was wrong about him. He was a freak—a freak on the verge of violating all he knew was right, just so he could slake his overwhelming lust on this woman.

"Don't," he mumbled, as much to himself as to the woman stirring in his arms.

Then her hand slipped up the side of his face and her fingers pushed into his hair as she gently caressed him, just as she had lovingly stroked his horse. How he had wanted to know her touch that night in the barn! And now, here she was, gliding her cool fingertips over his skin with gentle innocence while fireballs roared through his body. Her touch undid him, disarmed him. He closed his eyes again as the most thrilling feeling he'd ever known swept through him, that of this woman turning into him for a kiss.

Then God help him, he kissed her. He kissed her with wolfish hunger, with savage desire held back only by the fact that he could not crush her into him, aware that to enfold her in his embrace would hurt her. Instead, he framed her hips in his hands as she flung her arms around his neck and pressed her breasts into him like weapons of destruction.

She was destroying him, all right. He could feel himself shattering at her touch. He could feel his defenses falling away, the wall he'd built around himself crumbling, and his soul scrambling over the ruins to meet her. He could feel hope and need and joy surging inside him as his self-control cracked and his cock quickened against her belly.

Jack held her hips tightly, gasping with the strain of holding back. He'd never wanted a woman more. Everything throbbed—his temples, his pulse, his cock, even his heart. His ears were buzzing. He thought he would burst into pieces just holding her like this. He was sure that if he looked down, he would see his cock poking out of the top of his jeans, straining for release—that's how thoroughly aroused he'd become.

He was as turned on as a sixteen-year-old virgin with his first lay. And pretty soon he wouldn't be able to refuse this woman anything.

"Claire," he murmured against her cheek. "Wait—"

She straddled him, and he heard her sigh as she slowly sank down upon the part of him that wanted her the most. He arched into her, holding her hips in the vise of his two hands, allowing his mind to go where his body could not.

She dragged over him, her head thrown back, her eyes closed, her lips parted with desire, and her long beautiful throat exposed to the night.

"Jesus!" Jack gasped. Until this moment, he'd never dreamed how thick a barrier two layers of denim could be. He strained against the heat of her, wanting her closer, and it took every shred of his will to keep from unfastening his jeans and freeing himself. All he could think of was tearing away their clothes and thrusting himself into her, feeling her writhing on top of him, capturing her soft curves between the palms of his hands, and tasting the tender flesh at the base of her neck.

A vision loomed in his thoughts, that of the black stallion covering a mare, his great phallus bursting inside the female, his teeth nipping the nape of her neck.

A wave of need washed over Jack, drowning him. He went rigid as he fought back the animal spirit that lived within him. His sight fled, and all he could see was black—the black of the stallion's glossy coat, the black of Claire's raven hair, and the black of his own cursed soul.

"No," he breathed, his heart breaking. "We can't—"

"Jack," she murmured, her lips inches from his. "Please—"

"You're in no condition—"

"I don't care!"

"It's not right."

She pulled back. "You don't want this?"

He blinked as the sight of her face came into focus. Her hair was tousled, her lips looked like crushed, ripe fruit, her smudged cheeks were flushed, and her expressive eyebrows were curved down in confusion. Jack looked deep into her feverish eyes.

"What do you think?" he finally replied, his chest heaving.

"I don't know! You tell me."

"Not until you level with me, Claire."

"God, Jack!" Her hands slid from his chest. "You would pass this up? Because of Tobias?"

"Yes." His stare never wavered.

She swallowed and gazed at him, first in confused frustration and then in disappointed acceptance, and he watched her ruined arousal settling over her like a sudden snowfall, cooling her fire. Then she backed out of his grasp, still staring at him and running the tip of her tongue over her dry lips. He had to look away.

"I don't usually—," she ventured after a moment.

"Neither do I." He glanced back at her, easily reading her expression as she struggled to comprehend their immediate and undeniable attraction for each other and why it could not be acted upon.

"Jack—" Her eyebrows knitted together in consternation. "You must think I'm a—"

"Don't." Jack silenced her words by pressing two fingers against her beautiful, parted lips. "You don't have to explain."

"It's just something about you."

For a long moment she hung before him, gazing at him until he was almost ready to say to hell with previous engagements and honor. Then her eyes changed. He could see the hurt glint harden as her reason returned. She heaved a big sigh, and he knew the battle was over.

"No more of that," he commented.

"Okay."

He reached for her. "Come on. It's late. We need to sleep."

As if her body had suddenly turned to water, Claire flowed back into his arms. She sank her head on his left breast and sighed.

"And no caressing," he said near her ear, half in jest. But even so, he pressed her a little more snugly against his body and closed his eyes as he gently buried his cheek in the tumble of her black hair.

"No caressing," she replied, slowly running her palm across his chest.

Their embraces, which had been hot and searching only moments before, had cooled to safe and tender gestures. But the restrained gentleness of her touch only broke Jack's heart more. This woman was not for him, regardless of whether she was promised to Tobias or not. There was no way Jack's life could merge with hers. This limited fusion—sitting together deep in the night, sharing only the warmth of their bodies—was the only physical joining they could know.

The last thing Jack remembered was Claire's hand coming to rest in the crook of his elbow, like a small bird finding a roost for the night.

The next thing he knew, someone kicked him in the leg.

Chapter 29

"Time to wake up, lover boy," Tobias said, giving Jack another vicious kick.

Jack jerked awake, surprised to discover it was early morning, and even more surprised that he hadn't heard Tobias and the professor approach. Stress must have dulled his usually sharp senses.

Claire stirred awake in his arms and struggled to sit up, squinting in alarm at the men and horses standing above her. Jack released her, his arms and legs still half-asleep from sitting in a single position for the entire night.

"Such a touching sight, the two of you," Tobias drawled, glaring down at them. "And what are these doing off your pretty little body?" He threw Claire's bra and panties at her.

Her panties landed on her left shoulder. She dragged them off as Jack slipped out from under her legs and struggled to his feet.

"Lay off her," Jack growled.

"You just keep quiet, cowboy." Tobias's lip curled into a mocking smile as he raised his hand, displaying a pistol.

Where Tobias had gotten a gun, Jack couldn't have guessed. His blood went cold at the thought of Tobias's mean streak and the man's likely inexperience in handling a firearm—a deadly combination if there ever was one. He stood still, his hands at his sides, unsure what Tobias's next move would be, and not anxious to serve himself up for target practice.

"We are so relieved to find you survived the flood,"

Simeon Avare said, gazing at Claire from his perch atop his horse. He held Jack's rifle propped on his thigh.

"I'll bet," Jack retorted. "And since when did you buddy up to Benton, Avare?"

"I told you to keep quiet!" Tobias waved the gun. He reached for Claire's arm and yanked her to his side.

Pain streaked across her face, but she didn't say anything. She kept her gaze locked on Jack's, her intelligent eyes watching for his instruction, even though he had none to give. He had no gun and no horse—the two prerequisites for rank and power in the backcountry.

"Put on your jacket," Tobias ordered, pushing Claire toward the dead fire where her outer wrap still lay on the makeshift drying rack. She obeyed him, and stuffed her underwear in the pocket of her fleece coat.

"Now get up on Bud."

Claire glanced at Jack, and he nodded at her to obey Benton. Slowly, she mounted the palomino and then glanced over her shoulder at Jack, her back straight and her chin high.

"Take it easy on her, Benton," Jack warned. "She's in no condition to be manhandled."

"Yeah, like you should talk. If you've touched her, cowboy, I swear—"

"Tobias," the professor put in. "Don't waste your energy on this person. He isn't worth your time."

"Right." Tobias swung up behind Claire and wrapped a possessive arm around her waist, pulling her tightly against him. The gesture made Jack's blood turn from ice to fire. He could just imagine the soaring arousal Tobias must be experiencing as Claire's tight ass pressed into him.

"It's been fun, cowboy," Tobias said, yanking Bud's head around with a cruel jerk. The horse danced and arched his neck in protest. "But we no longer need your services."

"You're going to leave me here?"

"You're a cowboy. Deal with it." Tobias smiled. "Make something out of rope and sticks. Be creative."

Then, with a laugh, he, kicked Bud into a trot and left Jack standing in the gully, helpless and angry.

* * *

CLAIRE STRUGGLED TO ignore the pain as they rode hard all morning, stopping only once to relieve themselves and to allow Claire a quick drink and a piece of pan bread they'd filched from Grandma Betty's larder. She gobbled down the food, all the while keeping a watchful eye on her surrounds. Though Jack had no horse, she was sure he would eventually try to rescue her, and she planned to give him as much assistance as she could. She had been a fool not to tell him everything—about the fountain, about Tobias, and her connection to both. She should have put her trust in Jack long ago. And now it was too late.

Every moment along the way, Claire looked for a chance to escape, straining her already overloaded system. Although Claire wanted to find the fountain just as much as Tobias— and apparently now the professor—she intended to explore the place on her own terms, not as Tobias's prisoner. She couldn't believe he'd pulled a gun on her. As Jack had predicted, Tobias had become brazen, and was now handling her with far too much familiarity, oblivious to her revulsion or physical distress. She dreaded the night to come.

By noon, as the sun sailed high in the sky, the trio finally clattered out of the gulch and into a flat, nearly treeless valley. Across the dry stretch loomed a line of low, rocky hills with a notch in the center.

Tobias yanked Bud to a halt. "That's it," he announced. "Medicine Valley."

Simeon lay his left hand over his right on the pommel of his saddle, and eased upward in his stirrups. "So it is."

"Medicine Valley and its Fountain of Youth," Tobias added. "Pretty soon you'll be a new man."

"That I shall."

Surprised by their interchange, Claire glanced at the professor. It was obvious now that Simeon Avare was Tobias's mysterious business associate. She should have guessed. All along she had thought there was something funny about the professor, but his last remark confirmed her suspicions.

"But what about your venom theories?" she chided, put

off by the fact that she'd been lied to by her companions since the day they'd met.

"My theories?" Simeon turned toward her with one of his self-satisfied smirks. His silvery eyes narrowed. "They're untested, my dear Miss Coulter."

"But isn't the fountain untested as well?"

"Historical records support its existence and its efficacy."

"What I've read," Claire said shading her eyes and studying the low range of hills, "is that many men have searched for the Fountain of Youth but no one has ever found it."

"That's because they were uninformed bastards," Tobias retorted. "Idiots lost in the wilderness."

"And they did not think to bring a brilliant cryptographer with them." Simeon lavished her with another smile, but his eyes held no warmth. The expression seemed vaguely familiar to her. She found it chilling.

"I can't make any guarantees," she ventured, suddenly sure she wanted no part of Tobias's scheme, no matter the personal cost. There was something about the professor that she realized had always bothered her—a bad vibe that she picked up from him. She knew she couldn't trust the man.

For the first time on the trip, she felt more than just physical danger. There was a moral evil involved as well. She could feel it on the air, like a dank mist.

"I may not be able to open the door," she added. "There is still much to be learned of the code on the Nimian Stone shard."

"I trust you will do your best," Simeon replied.

"So I take it you are not a professor from the University of Washington?"

"That I am not."

"Who are you then?"

"Me?" He shrugged. "Nothing but an explorer, really." He cut off any further questions with a wave of his hand. "Let us proceed."

* * *

JUST AS THE trio mounted their horses for the last leg of their journey across the wide valley, Claire heard a jingling sound behind her. She turned in the saddle and spotted the Hughes clan coming single file down a rocky path through the trees, with William in the lead. At the sight of the other riders, Claire's heart lurched with hope. She had never been more happy to see Jack's father than at that moment. But when she felt the barrel of Tobias's pistol press into her ribs, she knew she could say or do nothing to alert the others to her predicament.

"Not a word, Princess," Tobias hissed close to her ear.

Grandma Betty trotted up, grinning at the trio. "Well, you're a sight for sore eyes," she exclaimed, assessing the group with a beaming smile. Almost immediately, however, her expression darkened. "But where's Jack?"

"We don't know," Tobias lied. "He must have got swept away in the flood."

"Oh, no!" Susan cried. She reached out to grab her husband's arm for support.

Simeon sidled his horse next to hers. "We spent many hours looking for him, Mrs. Hughes, but to no avail. I'm deeply sorry, madam."

Susan blinked tears back and nodded as she gave the professor a small, shattered smile.

William sat up straight in his saddle, his eyes burning. "I told that boy to high-tail it out of the gulch! The goddamned fool!"

"Jack is no fool!" Claire retorted, amazed that William could criticize Jack even at the news of his possible death.

"He never minded me. Never. Even as a boy. Headstrong idiot!"

"If it weren't for Jack, I'd be dead!"

"I told him not to keep going!" William fumed. "He wouldn't listen. And now look where it's got him."

Claire glared at him. "How can you be so critical?" she exclaimed. "Jack risked his life to save me! He's the finest, bravest man I have ever known!"

"Enough!" William glared at her, his mouth pressed into a hard line. Then his eyes narrowed. "You don't know anything about my family, so keep your goddamned mouth shut."

"I will not!" she flung back. "You're the one that doesn't know your own family! You treat them like idiots! And they're not!"

As if shocked speechless by her tirade, William stared at her. Claire was equally surprised when William made no argument and remained glaring at her, as if he'd never entertained the idea that his son was anything but a failure and a disappointment, and that his wife and mother were anything more than just silly hangers-on.

Grandma Betty took advantage of the lull to reach out and touch Susan's knee. "I'm sure Johnny's survived, Susan. Don't you worry."

"But if he was swept away, he could have hit his head on something—"

"Johnny can take care of himself. If there's a way to get out of Dead Man's Gulch, he'll find it." Grandma Betty turned toward Tobias and Simeon. "What I want to know is why you three went in there in the first place!"

"To save time," Tobias answered.

"And look where it got you!" Grandma Betty rolled her eyes. "You're no better off."

"Yes, well, we spent a considerable amount of time looking for Jack—"

"And Jack could be out there bleeding to death!" Susan cried. She buried her face in her hands.

"Oh, get a grip!" William snapped. He turned to face the other men. "You didn't find his body, I take it?"

"No," Simeon replied. "Not a sign of him."

William looked at Claire, who was dying to let the Hugheses know the truth—that Jack was still alive and had been abandoned by Tobias and Simeon. But she couldn't say a thing, not with a hard circle of steel jabbing her in the ribs, promising retribution.

Simeon crossed his hands over the pommel of his saddle. "May I suggest we split up?"

Claire glanced sharply at the professor. Split up? The last thing she wanted was to lose contact with the others. Without them, she would be at Tobias's mercy.

"I propose that you three wait here for Jack—make sure he is all right," Simeon suggested. "And the three of us will ride on to the fountain."

"You agreed to stop at the edge of your ranch anyway," Tobias put in. "And to let us go on alone."

"Jack would want us to stick together now that he's gone," Claire warned, trying to catch William's eye. But the older man only glanced at her and then looked away, more interested in what her male companions had to say.

"She's right," Susan interjected. "We should keep together."

"And waste time? Jack wouldn't want that." Tobias waved the air with his free hand. "He wouldn't want us to wait for him to show up. It could be days. Do we have provisions for that amount of time?" Tobias looked at the old woman, expecting an answer. "I bet we don't."

"If we don't," she retorted, "we'll make the food last."

Claire arched her back, trying to avoid the pistol and the sickening proximity of Tobias's crotch. "I say we go back and look for Jack."

"I say we go on," Tobias growled, ramming the pistol barrel into her ribcage. "I'm the one paying for this trip. So I'm the one who makes the decisions."

"Here, here!" Simeon echoed.

William scowled at the both of them and then looked over his shoulder at the gulch. After a moment, he turned his attention back to the group. "I don't care who's paying for what, Benton. I'm going back to look for Jack. The women are going with you." He turned his horse's head and the animal quickly rotated toward the entrance of the gully.

THAT LEFT SUSAN and Grandma Betty to ride with the rest of them, although Tobias made it clear that they weren't going near the fountain. Claire slumped down in the saddle again, wishing William had not decided to strike out on his own. Though he had never warmed to-her, she had no doubt that William would defend the women against Tobias and Simeon, if it came to that, and she was beginning to believe it would.

The five riders set out across the wide valley. As with all distances in the backcountry, the trip took longer than expected. The hills flanking Medicine Valley remained maddeningly out of reach as the day dragged on. Only the colors of the range changed, slowly merging from gray into shades of brown and green.

Even in her battered state, Claire picked up on the flagging spirits of the horse she rode, whose good humor dipped as the valley seemed to grow ever wider and his load ever heavier. While the other horses carried only a single human, Bud was saddled with the double burden of Tobias and Claire, as well as the ongoing cruelty of the billionaire's hand. Though Bud valiantly strived to keep up, his steps grew more heavy and his outlook more grim as the afternoon light slowly shifted.

After a few hours, Claire found herself drifting off to sleep out of sheer mental and physical exhaustion as Bud swayed beneath her. But she woke up with a start when she heard Tobias cry out.

"What in the hell is that?"

Set 11

I know in my heart I am a violent soul. I admit it. I'm not afraid to get my hands dirty. I'm not afraid to make tough choices. Sometimes it is the necessary and humane choice to eliminate life. Perhaps that was why I was never considered "evolved enough" to be part of the Golden Ones. I would choose to kill. But I am certainly no slouch, no coward, and definitely no mindless or heartless tyrant. In the end, who will be judged the more evolved being—them or me?

Who has survived? Moi. Little old ruthless me. Perhaps I am the harbinger of a new type of perfection. Hmm. What an interesting thought.

Set, Lord of Avaris

Chapter 30

Claire gaped across the valley to the west horizon where the sun should have been. Instead she saw a wall of darkness against a green-orange sky. At the same time, she became aware of the absence of sound and movement around her. The birds and ground squirrels had fallen eerily quiet, as had the horses, who stood in the valley with their ears flattened against their skulls.

"What is it?" Claire repeated.

"It's a sandstorm," Betty explained. "We get them sometimes around here. Medicine Valley especially. It gets all kinds of storms, matter of fact."

"It looks like it's headed in our direction," Tobias observed.

"In Egypt, such a weather pattern is called a *khamsin*," said Simeon, shading his eyes as he looked at the horizon. "They can be deadly."

"So can our storms," Betty put in, clucking to Ginger, her mount. "We better head for the hills and hope we make it!"

She urged Ginger to a gallop, and Bud immediately followed, straining to keep up with the others. In less than an hour, Claire felt a strange, warm wind rippling through her clothing. Soon the inside of her mouth became coated with a gritty layer of fine sand.

"If you got a scarf," Betty advised, shouting now to be heard over the wind, "put it over your face!"

Claire didn't have a scarf, so she grabbed her underwear in her jacket pocket and pulled them out. Choking on the sandy powder that coated her throat, Claire held the cotton fabric to her nose and mouth while she squinted, trying to gauge the distance to their destination. The sky had darkened considerably in the last half hour, and the sandstorm veiled their world in all directions, including the path they'd ridden from Dead Man's Gulch and the way before them toward Medicine Valley. Soon she could barely see at all as grains of sand stuck to the moisture of her eyes, filling them with gritty, stinging tears.

The horses could no longer see or breathe either. Bud whinnied in fear and came to a prancing halt. Tobias fought him, demanding that the horse keep going, kicking him viciously in the ribs with the heels of his boots.

"Goddammit!" Tobias yelled when the horse refused to continue. "Giddy-up, you worthless piece of shit!"

Screaming in protest, Bud reared up and threw off his riders. Claire hit the earth with a jarring thud that echoed through every bruise and scrape she'd sustained the past few days. New tears welled in her eyes, but she fought them back as she struggled to her feet, disoriented and no longer able to see her companions.

"Betty!" Susan's voice hung disembodied behind Claire. "Where are you?"

"Here!" the old woman replied.

Claire swept the air with one hand, trying to locate the body that belonged to the voice of Jack's grandmother.

Betty's hand grasped Claire's wrist with amazing strength. "Susan?" she asked, coughing.

"It's Claire."

"Betty!" Susan cried again.

Claire could barely keep on her feet as the wind tore at her clothes and blasted her bare skin with stinging particles of sand. In the roar of the storm, she heard the horses bugling and the men shouting, and then nothing but the fury of the wind.

Betty clung tightly to Claire, and then Susan grabbed onto Claire's left arm.

"Can't breathe!" Susan gasped.

Claire reached out, found Susan's midsection, yanked her

shirt out of her jeans, and popped the buttons with a swift
jerk. Then, pulling up one side of the blouse, she held it to
Susan's face until the older woman managed to take hold of
it. For a moment, the two older women huddled around
Claire, buffeted and sandblasted, unsure of how to proceed.

"Angel."

Over the thunder of the storm, Claire heard someone
speak her old nickname, as plain as day. Or was she hearing
the voice in her mind? How else could she hear the word so
plainly?

"Grandmother?" she murmured, only half believing her
ears. How could she hear anything over the torrent of wind?
Her hair whipped across her face.

"Angel."

That was not the voice of her grandmother. It was a male
voice—a strong, rich male voice, but one she did not recognize.

"Reach out," the voice said.

Claire reached out, amazed when her palm met warm
flesh, and by the feel of it—warm horseflesh.

"Hold onto my mane," the voice continued.

Struggling to keep to her feet, Claire grabbed a handful of
the horse's silky mane.

"This way," the voice commanded.

Claire felt a tug on her arm and was forced to take a step.

"Come on!" Claire shouted to the other two woman,
pulling at them. "Grab each others' hands!"

Claire felt Susan trip and almost lost her grip, but she
made sure the three of them were connected before she took
another step.

She had no idea where Tobias and Simeon were. She
could neither see nor hear them. They would have to weather
out the storm as best they could. She, on the other hand, had
decided to put her faith and her life in the hands of her mysterious savior.

They must have walked for at least a half hour, choking
and stumbling through the driving sand, as Claire clung to
the horse's mane. Her hand soon became a chapped claw,

her knuckles eaten raw by the wind and sand, but still she held on, certain the horse was taking them to shelter.

Just when Susan starting sobbing that she couldn't go on, Claire spotted a dark shape looming in front of her, and with a few more steps, all became clear. The horse had guided them to the mouth of a cave with an opening large enough to walk through without stooping over, and extensive enough to provide shelter from the storm. A clear, shallow pool ringed by the rocks gleamed at the center of the cave floor.

Claire unleashed her hold on the mane of the horse and stumbled into the cave, with the other women still holding onto her like a ragged conga line. She marveled at how the whining of the storm dropped to a muted moan as soon as they'd walked a few feet into the gaping cavern.

Susan fell to her hands and knees, sucking in deep draughts of clean air. Grandma Betty pivoted, slowly taking stock of her surrounds, much like Jack would have done. Claire, however, turned back to look at the horse that had guided them through the storm. She wasn't surprised to see the horse had an ebony coat beneath the dust of the storm— just like the coat of the horse in her vision whenever she touched Jack.

No ordinary horse would have appeared from nowhere in the storm. No ordinary horse would have spoken to her or been aware of her childhood nickname.

For a moment she stared into the wild eyes of the stallion, mesmerized by his intelligent gaze. Jack had stared at her in just this way, with the very same intense expression in his dark eyes.

"Claire," Grandma Betty said behind her. "How in blazes did you know this cave was here?"

"I didn't." She turned to look at the old woman.

"Well then, how did you know to come here?"

"I didn't. The horse led us here."

"What horse?" Betty glanced around the cavern as if she couldn't see the large black stallion standing near the entrance.

"The black horse." Claire nodded her head in the direction of the creature at the mouth of the cave. "Behind me."

Both Susan and Betty followed the direction of Claire's gesture, but she could tell by their perplexed looks that they either didn't understand or couldn't discern what she had pointed out.

Claire spun around, only to see the blank opening of the cave and the whirling sandstorm beyond. The horse had vanished as quickly as it had appeared.

"There's no horse," Betty retorted.

"There was!" Claire couldn't believe the animal could disappear so quickly. "I swear!"

"Oh, what are we going to do!" Susan wailed, sitting back on her heels. "We're going to die out here, too. Just like Jack."

"No we're not." Betty shook a finger at her daughter-in-law. "And don't you go thinking like that!"

"Have heart." Claire reached out and gently touched Susan's scrawny shoulder. "Jack isn't dead, Mrs. Hughes. Tobias was just lying to you back there."

"Jack's not dead?"

"No. Tobias and Simeon abandoned him in the gulch, with no horse, no gun, no nothing."

"Those bastards!" Betty sputtered.

AN HOUR LATER, Bud, Ginger, and Susan's horse Lady straggled into the cave, their reins dragging, their coats gray with dust, their nostrils caked with sand and their eyes rimmed in red. The two pack horses wandered in after that, and all the animals ambled to the water to drink. Claire looked for the men, but in the raging storm, she could see no sign of them.

Grandma Betty slipped a canteen off her horse and held it out to Claire. "Here, sweetie. I think you need this more than we do. Seeing things that aren't there—"

"Thanks." More interested in having a drink of water than arguing about the existence of the stallion, Claire took the metal and canvas container in her hands and tipped it up. She gulped down the water until her thirst was slaked, and then handed the container to Susan.

After they'd all had a drink, Betty and Claire set to taking the gear off the exhausted horses. In a surprising turnaround,

Susan rose to her feet to help. She fumbled with every buckle and strap, chiding herself for her own ineptitude, but eventually stripped her horse. She carried the saddle to the side of the cave while Betty and Claire exchanged a glance of amazement.

As Claire worked, she couldn't believe how tired she was. Her arms felt like lead weights, and her feet felt as if she were wearing cement blocks for shoes. Still, she forced herself to keep on task, caring for the horses and then gathering up the dried sticks strewn about the sandy floor for firewood.

After Grandma Betty had finished with her horse, she built a fire and put water on to boil so they could have something hot to drink, and later a meal. Then, she rummaged through her supplies and held out Claire's purse, which she had stowed with the rest of the gear.

"Thought you might want this," Betty remarked.

As soon as Claire saw her leather bag, she was reminded of her brother, of the tarot cards, and of her friend Maria. The weight she'd felt in her limbs now hung in her heart as the shattering events of the last few days came back to her in a dark rush.

"Thanks." Claire took the purse. "I'm going to try calling my brother right now, to let him know we're all right."

She strolled over to the back of the cave, where a smaller tunnel plunged into the depths of the hill behind her. She would have thought the cave would be dank and chilly, but the air wafting around her felt warm and fresh. Facing the darkness, she sat on a rock and opened her purse. A quick check told her the contents were intact, including the heavy deck of cards. Then she slipped out the Lone Ranger phone to call her brother.

Amazingly enough, the phone showed a strong signal, just as Tobias had said it would. Regardless of the creep who had provided her such advanced technology, Claire was grateful for the connection to the outside world. She dialed Emilio's number, but the phone rang and rang and then went to voice mail. Claire left a message and checked her watch. It was four p.m. Maybe Emilio was still at school. She sighed and replaced the phone, worried by the possibility that her brother's silence might mean he was in the hospital again, without her beside him this time.

Claire closed her eyes for a moment, took three deep, steadying breaths, and reminded herself to concentrate on those things she could do something about and not to worry about the things she could not control—the toughest challenge of all for her.

As she sat there with her eyes closed, she thought of Rae Lambers, the woman who had claimed to see the lizard man. Claire fished around in her pocket for the slip of paper where she'd written Rae's number. The paper was tattered and torn—much like herself—and the ink had run slightly, but she still make out the number.

Slowly, she pressed the buttons of the phone. The tones echoed off the surrounding rocks and bounced down the corridor into the blackness.

Rae picked up on the third ring. "Hello?" she said.

"Rae, it's Claire Coulter."

"Claire, how are you?"

Claire could tell by the tone in Rae's voice that she remembered Claire well and was worried about her. Except for Jack, Claire wasn't accustomed to being the object of anyone's concern. The sensation was unfamiliar, but touching as well.

"Trying to survive," Claire replied, keeping her voice down so the others couldn't hear. "It's been crazy around here."

"But you're okay?"

"I'm alive. And lucky to *be* alive."

Claire glanced at the other women to make sure they weren't listening to the conversation. Betty and Susan huddled around the coffee pot, chatting for once. Satisfied their attention was not on her, Claire turned her focus back to the phone call.

"The reason I'm calling," Claire went on, "is because I saw the lizard."

"You did?" Rae's voice cracked. "What did it look like?"

"About ten feet tall, cloven feet, small wings, with a snout like a crocodile. Weird, human-like eyes."

"God, that's him!"

"It attacked me." Claire hugged the phone to her ear, still chilled by the mere memory of the incident. "It spit fireballs at me!"

"But you're okay?"

"Just scraped up."

"Be careful, Claire. Be careful!"

"Don't think I'm not!"

"The lizard can make you see things. It can change form as well. It can even look like a human being if it wants to."

"It seems to be following us." Claire brushed the tangle of her hair away from her forehead. "If it wanted to kill me, it could. I can't understand why it just keeps following us."

"Maybe it wants something of you. My guess is it wants the tarot cards."

"Then why doesn't it just take them?"

"It might not be able to. My experience with the lizard and the man it became was that the creature had some limitations."

"What do you mean?"

"It couldn't see through water, for instance. It hated water, as a matter of fact. Avoided it."

A faint memory pricked at Claire's subconscious, but she didn't have time to explore the mental cue.

Rae continued with her observations. "And when the creature took human form, it was evidently a strenuous process that sapped the being's energy. Sometimes I would see a handsome young man, but other times I would see an ancient being who claimed he had to restore himself."

"You mean renew himself in some way?"

"Yes."

Claire remembered Simeon Avare's last conversation with Tobias, and the hair on her neck rose as a shudder coursed through her. *Business associate, my ass,* she thought to herself.

"Claire?" Rae asked.

Claire swallowed and ran her tongue over her dry lips as facts fell into place—into a very disturbing place. "Rae, the guy you're talking about. This being. Did he have an unusual name?"

"Yes," Rae answered. "He took his name from the ancient city where a temple was dedicated to him in northern Egypt. Avaris."

"Avaris?" Claire breathed the ancient name, balancing it against the modern version Simeon had taken as a surname. "Avare."

"Simeon Avare." Rae finished for her. "So he's there. With you."

"Yes." Claire nodded grimly.

"God, Claire. Get rid of the Forbidden Tarot. Throw it into deep water where no one will find it—ever again."

"But I'm in the middle of a high desert."

"You must find water and submerge the cards. That's all I can tell you."

"But you didn't throw them away."

"No, my sister sold them on eBay to Jonathan Allman." Rae sighed. "And I think Jonathan Allman looked at the cards and drew Set out of my world and into his. Do you want the same thing to happen to someone else?"

"No." Claire glanced around. "There's a pool nearby. Maybe I can find a deeper one where I can hide the cards."

"Do it, Claire," Rae urged. "Save yourself."

Chapter 31

Claire hung up the phone, dropped it in her pocket, and hurried back to the fire. Grandma Betty was frying bacon, and the fragrance made Claire's stomach rumble hungrily, betraying all her deeply held vegetarian beliefs.

At Claire's approach, Betty glanced up from the iron skillet.

"Do you have a flashlight?" Claire asked, dragging her gaze off the sizzling meat.

"Right over there." Betty pointed to the left where she'd placed a canister-type flashlight on a large rock.

"May I use it?"

"Sure. Help yourself."

"What are you going to do?" Susan asked, her voice quavering.

"I just want to explore a little. See what's back there."

"You be careful, young lady," Betty warned. "Lots of critters could be back there, waiting out the storm. Bats, too."

"Oh my!" Susan covered her mouth with one hand while she glanced up at the shadowy ceiling of the cave.

"I'll be careful," Claire replied, reaching for the flashlight. Then she paused and looked at the waning storm swirling beyond the mouth of the cave. There was still no sign of Tobias and Simeon, or William and Jack. Fear and worry clutched at her, as she wondered who would show up first. Logic told her it would be Tobias and Simeon. She turned back to the women.

"Do you have some baggies, Grandma Betty?" Claire asked. "Gallon size?"

"In that blue plastic bin." Betty nodded at a crate near the pile of gear.

Claire located the box of plastic bags, took three out, made sure they sealed well, and slipped them in her pocket. The large plastic bags would hold the tarot deck securely and keep the cards from being ruined by water, as long as the gummy seal was still seated around the lid of the golden box. Though she was wary of the power of the cards, she did not wish to destroy them if it meant trapping the god Set in the modern world. She didn't know enough about the cards to completely destroy them. Deactivate them, yes. Destroy them? Not yet.

"Also, do you have a gun, Grandma Betty?"

Jack's grandmother shot a hard glance at Claire. "Now why do you want to go taking a gun with you? You shoot a bear with a handgun and you're just going to make him mad."

"I don't intend to shoot any animals." Claire adjusted the strap of her purse over her left shoulder. "It's for you. I want you to keep a weapon close at hand."

"Why? No wild animal is going to come close to this fire."

"It's not for a wild animal." Claire glanced at the cave entrance again. "It's for Simeon Avare."

"The professor?" Susan interjected, incredulity hanging in her voice.

"He's not a professor. He's a dangerous imposter."

"What?" Betty stopped fussing with the frying meat.

"He's dangerous. And he's armed. That's all I can tell you. If Simeon shows up before Jack, corner him, tie him up, and don't believe a word he says."

"What in the world are you going on about?" Hot fat dripped from the tines of the fork Betty absently held above the pan.

"And don't trust Tobias either," Claire continued. "He's working with Avare."

"Wait a cotton-picking minute!" Betty dropped the fork in the pan and scrambled to her feet with incredible speed for an old woman. "What are you talking about?"

"I don't have time to explain right now," Claire answered, turning toward the tunnel. "Just trust me, Grandma Betty. I'll be back."

Though Claire was exhausted and starving, she took off at a trot, spurred on by unwavering fear. She had to find a place to dispose of the cards before the men discovered the cave. She hoped and prayed that Rae Lambers's theory was correct—that sinking the cards in water would lift the curse of the Forbidden Tarot and release them from the danger of Simeon Avare. It was their only chance.

Claire snapped on the flashlight and trotted into the strangely warm corridor that snaked into the side of the hill, while her senses snapped on to high alert as well.

AN OMINOUSLY SILENT night had descended after the storm, and a moonless sky pressed down on the now quiet wasteland. Jack half trotted toward Medicine Valley, fear and worry keeping his fatigue at bay. But he came to a stop when he ran across a strange-looking shape lying on the sand. He heard it moan.

"Dad?" he called, dashing to his side.

William lifted his head and then let it plop back down in the sand.

"Jack," he gasped. "Found you."

"Dad, what happened?"

"Horse threw me in the storm. Broke my damn leg."

As his father spoke, Jack's practiced glance swept over the body of the older man. His right leg was bent at a sickeningly impossible angle below the knee.

"We've got to see to that as soon as possible," Jack observed.

"Yeah. Call 911."

Jack was encouraged that his father's sarcasm was still intact, but he was worried that William's leg required medical treatment he couldn't provide. What would be considered a minor injury in town could quickly become life-threatening in the wilderness.

"I got to splint that leg." Jack squinted, searching in the darkness for a branch or shrub sturdy enough to brace his father's leg. He found a suitable stick and hacked it clean with his knife.

"Got a hanky?" he asked, kneeling down at his father's side.

"Shirt pocket." William closed his eyes and clenched his teeth as Jack eased him over onto his back. "Take it easy, kid."

"I'm trying to. Hold on now." As gently as he could, Jack straightened the injured leg and set the branch alongside it, between the knee and ankle. Then he slipped out William's hanky and took his own from his back pocket, and fastened both of them around the branch to form a makeshift splint.

"Now the fun part," Jack said, rising. "We've got to get you up."

He grabbed his father's hands, and at the feel of William's smooth, warm skin, Jack's life swam before his eyes. He couldn't remember the last time he'd touched his father, or the last time the man had held his hand. Had he ever held his boy's hand? Surely Jack would have been able to remember.

"Goddammit!" William cried, as he struggled to his feet. He pulled back his hands.

"Lean on me." Jack slung his left arm under his father's arm and around his back. "Put your weight on your good leg."

He could tell by William's rigid stance that he felt uncomfortable being in such close proximity to his son.

"It's all right, Dad. Just put your arm around my shoulders. I'll carry you."

"You sure? I'm a heavy sonofabitch."

"You ain't heavy," Jack retorted, trying to joke him through his agony. "You're my father."

"I don't know what's worse—that joke or my leg." Grimacing, William reached for Jack and slumped against him.

"We're almost there, Dad," Jack lied, trying to give the old man enough encouragement to continue. "Just let me do most of the work."

JACK FELT THE resonance of the cave before he could actually see it through the swirling sand, and he used the sensation as a homing device. His sixth sense told him to stay away, to not subject himself again to the strange powers of Medicine Valley and specifically to the cave where he'd suffered his shattering mystical experience years ago. But common sense told him to continue to the cave, no matter the cost to his psyche. His father needed medical attention as soon as possible.

Jack shifted William's weight and readjusted his arm around his father's back, using his waning strength to keep the older man's bulk off his broken leg.

"Just a bit more now, Dad," Jack encouraged.

Not once had his father complained during the excruciating walk to the cave. But the longer they struggled toward the hills, the more strenuous the old man's breathing became. He knew his father needed water and rest or he would soon pass out. He would also have to endure the agony of having the bones of his lower leg set—and as soon as possible.

Each step Jack took toward the cavern brought back memories of the night of the lightning storm. He had vowed never to come back here, and to live his life as best he could by ignoring the spirit animal that had merged with him that night. He should have followed his gut instincts and refused to lead the CommOptima group into the valley. It was his own fault he was out in the middle of nowhere, with half his horses gone, his father injured, and the woman he loved in serious danger.

But he hadn't listened to his own good sense. He'd allowed a woman's beauty to cloud his thinking. And since he'd brought them all here, he was also responsible for getting them back to civilization—even if it meant facing the cave again.

CLAIRE CREPT THROUGH the smaller tunnel of the cave, sweeping the beam of light over the walls as she walked, revealing a surprisingly dry and clean granite vault that continued to plunge slightly downward into the earth. She didn't see any bats or bears. In fact, she didn't see a single trace of any wild animal—for which she was grateful. She did, however, discover the imprint of shoes in the sandy path along the cavern floor, and surmised this was the route taken by the first explorers sent out by Simeon Avare—

including the one who had not survived. How had he died, exactly? And where? All she knew was that he had been killed by a booby trap. She only hoped the body had been removed, so she wouldn't come upon it unaware. Surely, someone had taken care of the poor man's remains.

Shuddering nevertheless, Claire continued to walk and forced her thoughts away from the dead by inspecting the geological makeup of the cave. The granite had given way to a dark gray rock she guessed was basalt, and here and there her light caught on the hard edges of metallic crystals. She stepped closer to a cluster and ran a finger over the exposed corner of one of the shining cubes. Pyrite. Fool's gold. A person who came across this section of the cave and didn't know his minerals would have thought he'd stumbled upon a fortune.

Claire kept walking, thankful the cave didn't branch out in all directions, as she had no way to mark her path.

After ten minutes of brisk walking, Claire came to a high blank wall where the path split into a tee. She looked to the right and then to the left, where she saw the deep darkness of a smaller portal. Quickly, Claire swept the left path with the flashlight beam. A large chunk of stone blocked the portal, and the earth all around it was stamped with a jumble of tracks. Was this as far as the first person had come? A shiver coursed through her. She should have been much more careful on her trek through the cavern.

Claire studied the walls above and soon found the shaft where the block had been stored as a booby trap, much like those rigged in the Egyptian pyramids to protect the pharaoh's treasure as well as his expensive sarcophagus and supposedly immortal body.

Frowning, Claire passed the light to the right path, where a separate corridor vanished into blackness. She paused, considering her next move. Since the left path had been rigged with the booby trap, she surmised it was the path that led to the fountain. However, she also knew ancient people were crafty, and never made it easy to find what they intended to keep hidden. There could be any number of false leads and concealed triggers.

Still, she had a feeling the left path was the correct way to go. She squeezed past the block that choked the passageway and slipped into the left corridor, carefully inspecting the ground with every step and checking the walls and ceilings for signs of trip wires, loose stones, or disturbed earth.

Sweat broke out beneath her jacket as she laboriously made her way down the tunnel. Soon she grew so warm that she had to take off her fleece jacket, which she tied around her waist.

Then the tunnel made a second tee. Another tee, another choice. Claire paused, and ran the flashlight beam slowly around the opening of the new corridor, expecting a block to fall any second.

The path to the fountain had failed to remain simple. Claire knew she had to mark her way so she could retrace her steps. She dug into her purse, zipped open her cosmetic bag, and selected the lightest shade of lipstick in the bag. Then she used it like a stick of chalk to draw an arrow on the cave wall. She continued along the dry, winding corridor, her stomach growling and her muscles aching.

Another few minutes and two tees in the trail later, Claire's light glinted off something at the end of the narrow tunnel, and it didn't seem like basalt or fool's gold. A frisson shimmered over her. She stepped closer and soon made out a round metal disk set into a thick wooden door whose unusually wide planks were held together by decorative bronze bands. Symbols ran across the entire face of the metal disk, and Claire strained to make them out from a distance. What she saw made her shudder again. Even from twenty feet away, she could make out the same unusual circle and stick characters she'd studied on the Nimian Stone. This was the door Simeon sought to open, she was sure of it. This was the gate to the legendary Fountain of Youth.

The door was the stuff of fantastic childhood fairy tales, but Claire knew the danger she faced was not part of a child's game, but instead a deadly puzzle of supernatural proportions. She paused and carefully inspected every inch of the walls, ceiling, and floor near the gate, searching for signs of human alteration. Nothing seemed out of place, chipped away, or plastered up. She could find no seams to betray a causeway for a suspended block. Nothing.

She trained the light on the path. Not a single track marked the sand. No living being had come any farther than this since the door had been sealed countless centuries ago.

Chapter 32

Before Claire had made a decision about going forward or going back, she heard a clinking noise in the corridor behind her. She froze, listening intently, and waited for the low ominous tone she associated with the lizard and now also with Simeon. But no such sound materialized.

Wildly, Claire glanced around, knowing that this particular stretch of corridor offered no place to hide. She was totally exposed, like a lone beacon glowing in a narrow alley. Claire snapped off her light and kept her thumb on the switch as the cave plunged into utter darkness. Her heart galloped in her chest as she listened to the muffled footsteps quickly approaching.

Claire flattened her body against the wall and waited, trying to regulate her breathing so no one could detect her presence in the darkness, and prayed that whoever was behind her would take the right turn at the tee instead of the left path she had selected.

She heard the footsteps pause. A ray of light bounced upon the far wall of the tee and ran down to the floor, growing larger and brighter as her pursuer walked closer. Then the light changed as the person turned left at the tee without pausing to make a decision about which direction to take. Her pursuer must have noticed her arrows on the stone.

Claire cursed her own stupidity. She never should have marked the cave wall with her lipstick. At least not in such an obvious way. How could she have been so shortsighted?

Light streamed into her small corridor, catching first on

the toes of her boots. Then the full power of the beam turned upon her, flooding her in a sea of light. Claire flung her right arm up to ward off the blinding glare, but didn't try to run for fear of setting off a booby trap. She'd rather take her chances with Simeon or Tobias.

"Claire!" a familiar voice exclaimed.

Claire almost collapsed with relief. "Jack!" she called out, unable to see anything.

Immediately the light swept down and to the right, and as soon as Claire's eyes adjusted to the change, she made out the tall, lean lines of the man she now counted as her savior and best friend. He carried a flashlight and had a large coil of rope slung over his left shoulder.

"Jack!" she cried again, hurling herself forward and into his arms. "It's you!" she breathed into the base of his throat. "Oh, it's you!"

A soft chuckle rumbled through him. "Of course it's me," he said. "Who else would be crazy enough to run after you?"

Claire smiled and hugged him. "I thought you were Tobias or Simeon."

"They haven't shown up yet." He stroked her tousled hair, and Claire's entire body sang at his touch. With Jack here, everything would be all right.

"Gran was worried." Jack gently ran a hand down her back and then held her slightly apart from him so he could look down at her. "She said you'd been gone for a good hour."

Claire nodded, relief making her giddy. "I've been looking for water."

"Water?" His brows knit together in confusion. "Why? We've got plenty."

"I need to find some deep water."

"Why?"

"It's a long story."

"And about time you told me."

"I will," she promised, switching on her own flashlight. "But first we have to get through a door." She turned and directed her beam of light squarely on the ornate door. "That door."

Jack released her to face the end of the corridor.

"What kind of crazy-ass door is that?" he asked.

"One that I hope will answer most of your questions, once we open it." She stared at the strange symbols and took a deep breath. "If we can open it."

"There's always this." He patted his right shoulder and raised one eyebrow.

"No." Claire touched his arm. "We have to be careful."

She explained how the cave was booby-trapped. Jack listened, and she was surprised that he took in the information without chiding her for believing such nonsense. But she didn't have time for a drawn-out explanation or philosophical discussion. She had to dispose of the cards before Tobias and Simeon found their way to the cave.

"You still haven't told me why you have to find water, though," Jack put in.

"I have to submerge something in it. I'll tell you later what it is and why."

She took a step forward, but Jack grabbed her arm to hold her back.

"Me first," he said.

"But this is my—"

"You're in no condition to take any more chances."

He stared at her, and his hard expression told her not to argue with him, that he'd made up his mind.

Claire sighed and shifted her weight. Jack handed her his flashlight and then slid the lariat off his shoulder and down his arm. Deftly, he formed a small loop in the rope, which he pulled out until it was a yard in diameter. Then he tossed it ahead of them and dragged it back over the sand, checking the path for traps or triggers.

When he walked forward, Claire followed close at his heels. Jack continued throwing the rope, pulling it back, and advancing. In a few minutes, they stood before the door.

Swiftly Jack coiled the lariat and looped it back over his shoulder. Then he reached for his flashlight to study the portal.

"Where's the damn handle?" he asked.

"There isn't one." As she spoke, Claire studied the symbols marching across the metal disk. "There must be a trip mechanism of some kind. A hidden latch."

Jack fell silent and bent down to inspect the wooden barrier while Claire stared at the symbols. The writing was different from that on the Nimian stone in that a delicate, almost-imperceptible horizontal line separated each row of symbols.

"I can't believe it," she murmured.

"What?"

"All this time," she replied, her voice hushed with excitement, "we've had the orientation wrong!"

"Orientation?"

Claire nodded, her gaze running eagerly over the glyphs as clusters of the symbols suddenly made sense. A smile broke out on her face and a strange golden joy diffused through her entire body. She'd never felt anything like it.

"Yes! The orientation of the script." She glanced at Jack who was gazing at her as if she were a complete stranger. "All this time we've been trying to read it vertically, like Chinese characters or Egyptian hieroglyphics. But it runs horizontally! Jack, it runs horizontally! East to west! Horizontally! Listen to this!"

She ran her finger along the line and read the words aloud.

"Here illusion dies. And truth lives. In the—"

She frowned. "I don't know what the next set of symbols mean. 'Prophet arms?' " She stared at the unfamiliar glyphs, struggling to make sense of them.

" 'Singer of songs'?" she scowled and shook her head. "No, that can't be it." She paused, and then suddenly a foreign name popped into her head. Avaris.

Avaris actually rhymed with the second phrase.

Strangely awed, she whispered the entire text on the door.

> *"Here illusion dies.*
> *And truth lives.*
> *In the Oracle*
> *of Avaris."*

She turned to Jack. "That's it!"

"Wait a minute!" Jack clutched her shoulder and turned her

slightly toward him. "You're not just a translator, are you?"

"No. I'm a specialized cryptographer." Claire answered him without looking at him and without violating CommOptima's privacy agreement. "But Tobias made me promise not to tell anyone about my work."

"And you're not really his fiancée either, are you?"

"No."

"Why the lie?"

"So we wouldn't be separated." Claire shrugged. "And because he thought we could have a little fun in the mountains—just him and me—with nobody the wiser."

"Jesus!"

She turned back to the metal disk. "I just can't figure out the last phrase. What is the Oracle of Avasis? I've never heard of it."

"How can you read this stuff?"

She smiled. "I've been working on cracking this code for two years. But the artifacts we've been studying were in bad condition. Nothing like this." She longed to reach out and touch the perfectly preserved symbols, but was afraid to get too close to the door for fear the portal itself was booby-trapped.

"So you're not just a hanger-on vegetarian type?"

Claire shot him a hard glance. "Did you ever think I was?"

"Nope. That's why I could never figure you out."

"Maybe I don't want to be figured out," she retorted, turning back to the door.

"I think you do, Claire. I think you could do with a whole lot of figuring out." His voice came soft and warm behind her, and for a moment Claire looked down as her years of being alone in the world and hiding her secrets came up in a dark rush. She pushed the darkness away. Now was not the time to succumb to any kind of emotional trauma.

"I'll survive," she replied. "I always have."

Before Jack could bring up any more disturbing subjects, she reached out and pointed at the metal disk.

"Wait a minute," she murmured.

"What?" Jack shifted to the side, his shoulder almost touching hers.

"I just noticed something. See that glyph?"

"All I see are circles and lines."

"See the one right there?" She pointed to a circle that looked like all the others but was disconnected from any of the surrounding phrases.

"What about it?"

"It's not part of the text. Maybe it's special. Maybe it's the key to opening the door."

"Now that you mention it," Jack said, leaning closer, "I can see a border around it."

She reached out to press the nickel-sized circle, but Jack grabbed her wrist.

"Claire, wait," he warned.

Claire stopped in midair and looked over her shoulder at Jack. She found his face dark with worry.

"Don't make any sudden moves."

"I don't intend to."

"Don't even touch anything."

"Why?"

"This place isn't just your run-of-the-mill cave."

"I know that." She lowered her hand. "This cave could be the site of the oldest civilization in North America. Maybe even the world."

"I don't know about that." He looked around. "All I know is what the Native Americans thought of the place."

"You don't seem like the type of guy to put much credence in Indian legends."

"I speak from personal experience." His voice dipped to an unusual, hushed tone.

"Oh?" She studied him in the dim light, struck by the sudden huskiness in his voice. "What happened?"

"Like yours, it's a story for later."

"But it has something to do with that black horse, doesn't it?" She reached out for him. "The one I see when I touch you."

He lurched away from her grip.

"What is it, Jack?" she continued. "You can tell me."

"No."

"Why? What are you afraid of?" She took a step closer to

him. "That I'll think you're full of it? That you're crazy?"

"Claire, don't go there. I'm warning you."

"I'm not going where you think I'm going," she retorted. "That horse saved my life. It's the reason I'm standing here, alive. It knew my nickname. How could that be if it isn't part of you in some way?"

When Jack just glowered at her, not answering, she pressed on. "Do you think I'd laugh if you told me you and the horse were somehow connected?"

Jack stared at her, his head thrown back, as regal and wary as the magnificent black stallion that had guided her through the sandstorm.

Determined to break Jack's wall of silence, she added, "Do you think I would think you were nuts?"

"Maybe."

"Jack, it's me. Claire." She thumped her chest with her fist. "The person who picks up images from animals. The person who thinks Egyptians came to America. Of all the people in the world you could tell something like this to— it's me!"

Set 12

I found my first lesion today, on my inner thigh. My theory is correct: human females carry a deadly virus. And now I am infected, as my brothers and sisters were infected before me. But I remind myself to look at the bright side. In a few years I will be free of this place and will be healed of all blights the moment I translate my being into the blessed kingdom to which I have longed to return for all these millennia. Ah, how sweet it will be to finally be home again—and even more sweet will be my personal triumph!

Set, Lord of the Red Earth

Chapter 33

Jack took a deep breath, studied her face, and let the air out in a long, thoughtful sigh. Still, he said nothing.

"Maybe your former girlfriend laughed at you and dumped you," Claire continued, bracing a hand on her hip. "But from what I've been told, she wasn't worth your time or your trouble."

He nodded, looked down at the floor of the cave, and then back at Claire.

"And I'm nothing like her. Nothing. So tell me!"

"Yeah. Okay." He cleared his throat. "I had an experience here. Here in this cave. When I was thirteen."

Claire turned away from the door to fully face him. "What happened?"

"I ran into the cave during a storm. It was an electrical storm, the worst I'd ever seen." He paused, obviously visualizing that day, and Claire waited for him to continue. He pushed up a strand of rope that had slipped down to his elbow.

"I was standing in the entrance of the cave, worried about trespassing in a sacred place, but worried about getting struck by lightning, too. And then, in a flash of lightning, I saw a herd of horses coming toward me—the big black stallion in the lead. I had nowhere to go. I didn't know if they were real or imaginary. Hell, I was only thirteen—and hadn't eaten anything for three days."

"Why? Were you lost?"

"I was on a spirit quest. Know what that is?"

Claire shook her head, confused.

"It's something the Native Americans did. Maybe still do. A kind of coming-of-age journey. You would usually get a new name at that time. You'd fast and wander off into the back country. And if you were lucky, you'd be visited by a spirit that would impart a valuable piece of wisdom to you. That spirit animal would become your totem for the rest of your life."

"So you do believe in Native-American lore."

Jack shrugged. "I did when I was thirteen. I wanted to believe in something. And I sure as hell didn't believe in what my parents stood for."

"So you rode out to Medicine Valley."

"Not directly. But that's where I ended up."

"And you were caught in a storm, much like we were today."

Jack nodded, brushing his fingertips over his upper lip as if to wipe away beads of sweat. "And standing there in the entrance of the cave, I was struck by lightning."

"Were you hurt?"

"Amazingly, no. But I lost consciousness. The next thing I knew I was back at the ranch with Gran leaning over me, shouting my name. I was buck naked. And I had managed to get back to the ranch in a phenomenally short amount of time for a kid on foot." He ran a hand over his dark hair. "Ever since that incident, I sometimes black out—especially when confined in a small space or if I'm in a large crowd. I believe when I black out, I release the spirit of that black stallion."

Claire stared at him. She didn't know what to say in response to his far-fetched story. But the last thing she wanted to do was show evidence of doubt. She didn't move. Not a single eyebrow.

"My totem became part of me, Claire," Jack continued. "That's the only explanation I can come up with. During that burst of electricity in the storm, the black stallion's spirit somehow got tangled up with mine."

Claire shook her head in wonder. "Coming from anyone else but you, I'd say your story was unbelievable. Or that you'd had one too many peyote buttons."

"Anyone but me?"

"Jack." She reached for his arm again. This time, he didn't flinch or pull away. "You are the salt of the earth. The rock of Gibraltar. If you say a horse spirit lives inside of you, then it must be true."

Claire saw his eyes change. The wariness softened for a fraction of a second.

"Do you mean that?" he asked, his voice almost a whisper.

"Yes." She looked up at him, her gaze never wavering. "I've never met anyone like you. Never."

Then, in the next instant, his eyes changed back to their usual hardness and the warmth vanished. "You don't know what you're saying, Claire."

"Oh, yes I do."

"You don't know me. And it's best if you just keep your distance." He shrugged off her hand, but she refused to let him back away again. She grabbed his sleeve one more time.

"Why?" she challenged, hurt by his continual rejection of her. "Is it because of my background? Are you afraid of what your parents think of me? What they might say?"

"Hell no!"

"Then what?"

"There are things about me. I can be dangerous."

"What do you mean, dangerous?"

"The horse spirit makes me want to do things. Things I wouldn't ordinarily do."

"Like what?" Her words caught in her throat as she suddenly picked up a vision: the stallion pawing the earth and staring at her, his breath coming hard and fast, his chest muscles flicking, his coat glistening with sweat.

"Dominating people. My father, for instance."

"Is that why you always walk away when he treats you like shit?"

"Yeah."

"I thought you were just avoiding confrontation."

"I know you thought that." Jack clenched his teeth. "But I know what the stallion wants. He'd trample my father to shreds if I let him."

"Then the horse spirit is evil?" Claire asked. "I just can't see that. Animals aren't inherently evil."

"Not evil. Just acting as nature intended. There's only one stallion in a herd, you know. All the others are either run off or killed."

Claire slowly nodded, struggling to digest this new and startling information.

"The stallion wanted me to kill Tobias the other night," Jack added grimly. "And then there's you." His voice dipped lower.

"What about me?"

"The stallion wants to dominate you as well."

Claire's heart skipped a beat, and she looked up at Jack's face, surprised and shocked by the fire she saw burning in his dark brown eyes.

"I can't let him do that to you." Jack backed against the wall. "I can't just let him take you—"

"How do you know it's the stallion?"

"Because it's an overwhelming feeling. I can barely hold it back. And I've always been able to hold back."

Braver now, Claire stepped closer to him, determined to demolish the wall that had risen between them and to show Jack that he was human after all. "So it's the stallion's fault then—this attraction you feel?"

"I don't know." Jack licked his lips as if his mouth had suddenly gone dry. "That's what I live with constantly, not knowing what kind of feelings I'm experiencing—human being or wild animal."

"Jack!" She touched his face, realizing at last the fear and confusion he must have endured since he'd been a teenager. "It's okay."

"No." Jack grabbed her wrist to keep her from touching him. "No it isn't, Claire! It's not okay!" His eyes glinted with heat and need. "You don't know how close I am to breaking."

"Maybe you should break. Maybe what you're feeling is human for once, Jack. Maybe it's real this time."

"How in the hell am I supposed to tell?"

"Because I feel it, too."

Knowing Jack would never make the first move for fear of violating her, Claire set her flashlight on the ground and stepped closer to his tall frame, which was still pressed against the wall. He went still, every muscle frozen, as she slid her hands up the front of his flannel shirt and then up the sides of his throat. His body seemed forged from the earth around him—rough granite, towering pine, and warm, smooth flint. She cradled his head in her hands, urging him to stand before her and look at her.

"Claire—" he croaked, his voice gravelly and full of anguish.

"Jack. You're feeling this. *You* are. The man. It's healthy. It's right!" She rose up on tiptoe while she brought his head down, aching for his mouth to meet hers.

"How do you know?" he asked, his breath puffing across her lips.

"Because I'm in love with you."

She closed her eyes as their lips touched. She reveled in the warmth of his skin and the strength of his neck and shoulders, and waited for him to return her heartfelt kiss.

At first he resisted, but then she heard him groan and heard his flashlight thud to the sand. His arms came around her. She sighed as his mouth dragged from her lips to her neck, where he pressed fervent, starving kisses along her jaw and all the way up to her ear, as if he were feeding on her acceptance of him. Starbursts of pleasure shimmered through her, lighting her up inside. She flung back her head, and he kissed her neck and caressed her, pulling her hard against him, where she could feel the physical evidence of how much he had lost his grip on his formidable self-control.

"Claire," he gasped, his breath coming as hard and fast as the stallion's in her vision. "Are you sure?"

"Yes, Jack. Yes!"

She embraced him as he rolled away from the wall, taking her with him, seeming to consume her body with his, infusing her with the driving need of the stallion. She'd never felt anything like it—the blazing insistence that erupted between them in their searching hands, hungry mouths, and burning skin, both of their bodies crying out to be touched.

Claire's only lover had never inflamed her this way. He'd been a man of rituals, of dinner and candlelight, of hot tubs and careful protection—a predictable and mechanical lover who had never made her feel the way Jack was now: breathless, eager, and half-mad with desire.

The next thing she knew, Jack had pulled her legs up and pinned her to the wall, grinding into her and growling in the small of her neck. His hands clutched her bottom as he took possession of her in every way but one. She thrilled to the thought of the power she'd unleashed in him, and by the fact that she had no idea where they were going with each other—only that this time, she intended to take it all the way.

Then he kissed her as she had never been kissed. He ravished her with his mouth, pinning her with his hips and with one hand while his other hand slid up her rib cage, over the fullness of her breast, up her neck, and into her hair. He clutched her skull, trapping her with his big, male hand.

Yet she had no desire to escape this man. He was everything to her—friend, confidant, and protector—and she wouldn't let him go until he became part of her and she of him.

In the back of her mind, she knew they should be disposing of the tarot cards and searching for the fountain, but suddenly nothing mattered more than making love with Jack, of showing him that his desire for her was part of the human world. And her hunger for this good man—this upstanding and brave man—was a thirst that suddenly demanded to be slaked.

Claire pulled his shirt out of his jeans and slipped her palms under his warm tee shirt. His abdomen was smooth and hard and muscled, like a span of rock rippled by water. His chest was a furnace, his nipples hard as pebbles. While she caressed his bare skin for the first time, amazed at how her own body wanted to merge with his, she felt his hands at her belt buckle.

She began to throb for him, to ache with a sweet yearning she'd never felt before, and gasped as his fingers slipped into the front of her jeans. She moved against his fingertips, wanting more, wanting everything.

She knew they couldn't afford the time to make love, and ever since her disastrous affair long ago, she had vowed never to have sex without ensuring she was safe from conceiving. But here with Jack, all precautions faded into the background as blinding desire roared up, pawing the air as she swept her hands across his glorious fiery skin.

"Jesus!" he whispered, gathering her into his arms again and staggering backward, kissing her all the while.

Claire couldn't get enough of him—the taste of him, the feel of his silken hair and skin, and the way his hands could change from a vise-like grip to a tender stroke that spread wildfire wherever he touched her.

Then in one fluid movement, he sank to his knees with her, pulling down her jeans as they dropped to the floor. He let out a sigh as his hands swept down her bare thighs and away.

"Jack!" Claire cried, thinking he was going to break it off as he'd always done.

He glanced at her, his eyes feverish with desire, and then unfastened his gun belt and his big silver buckle. Deftly, he released himself. He wasn't backing off this time. There was no turning back for either of them now.

Claire gasped at the sight of him, at the sheer magnificence of him. But she had only a second to gape at him before he grabbed her hips and turned her around, as if he didn't want her staring at his unusual length. Before Claire could protest, he slung one arm under her and gave a quick upward hoist, tipping her bottom in the air. She struggled to brace herself on her palms as he pulled her against him.

He was on fire, so aroused that he moved against her backside in blind desperate strokes, lost to the primal dance he had finally succumbed to. She felt his manhood sweeping between her buttocks and then stabbing between her legs, missing the mark, but making her want him all the more. He was huge, and so distended that she could feel the tip of him brush her belly.

"God," he whispered. "Claire, I'm too—"

"Jack, just do it—"

She broke off as he clutched her hips in his big hands and suddenly pushed into her. Claire gasped at the sensation, at the incredible size of him. He groaned and took hold of himself, working to push into her more deeply, but careful not to hurt her. He strained to hold back. She could hear him swearing under his breath and panting. Little by little, with every stroke, he pushed deeper and deeper into her until she'd taken all she could of him. Then, with a long moan, he held her in his hands and found his rhythm.

Claire closed her eyes, almost weeping with need. She was transported by the vision of what he was doing with her, merged with a vision of the stallion throwing his forelegs onto the back of a white mare, thrusting into her again and again, until his haunches shuddered.

Just as the stallion climaxed in the vision, Jack bent over Claire, clasping her breasts in his hands, bucking against her, his body curled around her, his shaft curved into her, their bodies singing and straining, until he stopped with a cry, crushing her into him as he came in a shattering, surging stream.

Chapter 34

For a long moment Claire and Jack hung together, fused and gasping for breath. Then Jack slowly pulled away, taking his blazing heat with him. But just as Claire made a move to shift her legs, she felt him kiss the small of her back. The glow he had fired in her flared anew as he leaned down and embraced her with infinite tenderness.

Again she was struck by the hardness and softness contained in this man, amazed that such driving passion and gentle tenderness could live inside a single human being.

"You don't know what that meant to me," he said, his soft voice next to her ear. Then he kissed the back of her neck. Tingles sparkled through every cell of her body.

"And the next time we'll do it right," he added.

Claire turned in his arms, ignoring the pain of her bruises and scrapes.

"Jack, that *was* right."

"You know what I mean. For you."

He kissed her, closing his eyes, and Claire kissed him back, her heart pouring out to him.

Had he heard her when she said she loved him, or had he been too upset to notice? She longed to know if he loved her as much as she was coming to love him. But now was not the time for such questions.

She stroked his cheek, rough with two days' growth of his heavy beard. "We should get back on track," she said, her voice still breathy from lovemaking.

He nodded and got to his feet, and reached down to help

Claire get up. Then they both straightened their clothes and brushed back their hair.

"I'm kind of a mess," Claire admitted, the smell of her sweat mingling with his seed. "I could use a shower."

"We'll find some water soon." Jack snatched up his flashlight and trained it upon the door. "Now which circle was the special one?"

"The one in the center, and just to the left."

Before she could say anything more, Jack pressed the circle with the tip of a forefinger. They heard a deep, metallic click, and Claire looked wildly around, sure a trap had just been activated. But nothing happened. They exchanged a puzzled glance. Then Jack reached out and shoved the door with his hand. With a loud creak, the portal swung open.

Claire rushed forward, but Jack stopped her with a hand to her chest. "Age before beauty," he said. He slipped a revolver out of his holster and held it in front of them as they slowly passed through the door. Claire felt the hair on the backs of her arms and scalp rise. She kept one hand on Jack's arm as they walked through the doorway and into another narrow corridor. Both of them paused on the other side to take the time to run their lights over the surfaces of the new territory.

Two doors faced them a hundred feet away, and two more corridors intersected the main one about halfway up the path.

"I thought we'd find the fountain here," Claire remarked, unable to hide her disappointment.

"Looks like it isn't going to be as easy as you thought." He put the gun back in the holster.

"No, it doesn't." Claire frowned. "Are you going to do your rope trick again?"

"Yep." He handed the flashlight to her and slid the lariat off his shoulder.

Like before, Jack threw the big loop of rope, dragged it back to the toes of his boots, and then moved forward with Claire. On the third throw, Claire heard a ping and grabbed Jack's arm, pulling him backward as a huge blade swung out of a crevice in the rock, cut through his lariat, and barely missed slicing off his toes.

"Jesus!" Jack exclaimed, struggling to maintain his balance and Claire's.

Fear as hot as their lovemaking seared through her, leaving her legs trembling. A few wrong steps and that blade would have cut right through one of them, or possibly both of them, as the metal disk had been carefully angled to swing through the greatest arc of space.

"What next?" Jack looked up at the ceiling. "Poisoned arrows?"

"I wouldn't joke about it," Claire warned.

He looked down at her. "I wasn't."

With a hard tug, he retrieved his rope and fashioned a new knot and loop. Claire noticed his hands were as deft and as steady as ever, while hers were cold and shaking.

"Ready?" he asked, giving her a quick but warm backward glance.

"Yes."

Jack threw and withdrew his lariat without incident until they made it to the second set of doors. Claire stepped to Jack's side and trained her light on the writing carved into the plaques that were fastened to each door, just like the first one they'd encountered.

"I'll look for the magic button," Jack said, stepping closer. "While you crack the code."

"Okay."

Claire gave him back his flashlight while she tried to focus her attention on the door. But her mind was sluggish—too filled with thoughts of Jack making love to her and the blade that could have ended their lives. She felt numb, as if she were slipping into a state of shock.

"You all right?" Jack asked, once again picking up on her emotions.

"Just a little shell-shocked." She glanced up at him. "Sorry."

"You're allowed." His gaze swept over her face, pouring his special brand of warmth over her. She could feel his strength and kindness renewing her, as if she'd stepped into a soothing, fragrant bath.

He clutched her elbow and leaned down to kiss her, just as

a metallic click behind them shattered the moment. Claire jerked around, and much to her surprise and dismay, spotted Simeon and Tobias standing in the passageway at the intersection. They held flaming torches of pitchy pine boughs in their hands.

Simeon raised a gun. "That's what I like to see," he purred. "Real teamwork."

"Hands off her, cowboy!" Tobias ordered, lunging forward.

Jack straightened, his right hand slowly moving downward toward his pistol.

"And throw your weapon down," Simeon added, walking toward them, his steps unhurried. "Now!"

Jack sighed and pulled the revolver out of its holster. Tobias held out his hand for the gun, smirking, while his gaze darted over Claire as if inspecting her for signs of violation. Claire held her chin high beneath the scrutiny, daring him to challenge her about where she'd been and what she'd been doing. She'd had enough of Tobias Benton and CommOptima. She couldn't work another day for such a bastard, not even if it meant giving up the Nimian Project, not even if it—

Claire swallowed, staring at Tobias, unable to complete the thought: that she would give up on her brother. Giving up on Emilio was something she could never do, no matter the price. Even if that price was her.

Seemingly, Tobias read her mind, for he gave her a knowing smirk and pulled her away from the door.

"How'd you get here?" Jack asked the other two men.

"We found a back door," Tobias replied. "After getting detoured in that storm."

"A great turn of luck," Simeon put in. "And I am relieved at seeing you have survived, Miss Coulter."

Claire didn't respond. All she could think about when she looked at Simeon was that underneath his charm and style was a lizard that had tried to kill her, or at least scare her out of her wits.

"I'll take that flashlight." Simeon threw down his torch and held out his hand. Claire had no recourse but to relinquish her light. Tobias grinned his gummy smile and took Jack's flashlight as well, which he gave to Simeon. Claire stood in the corridor, feeling oddly naked, knowing that should they be separated from the other two men, she and Jack would never find their way through the dense blackness of the cave.

Simeon beamed his flashlight backward, in the direction Claire and Jack had just traveled. He trained his light on the ornate door they had left open. "Ah," he exclaimed. "I see that you have come through the door. You broke the code!"

"No, she didn't," Jack retorted. "I just used this." He patted his right shoulder.

"You're lying!" Tobias spat.

"Want to see me do it again?" Jack countered, turning for the first door. Claire said nothing, realizing Jack was doing anything he could to gain the upper hand, or at least get out of range of the guns.

Simeon leveled his glinting eyes on Jack and studied him for a moment. "No need for useless repetition," he finally remarked. "Two doors remain for you to brutalize, Mr. Hughes."

"But which of these leads to the fountain?" Tobias stepped closer to the doors, all the while making sure his weapon was directed at Jack. He quickly scanned the carved figures that marched across the portal.

"We shall let Miss Coulter decide," Simeon said.

Claire clenched her jaw. If it wasn't for the adrenaline rush of danger, she knew she would be on the verge of collapse. She couldn't remember the last decent meal she'd had or the last time she'd got an adequate amount of sleep. Only fear of Simeon and worry for her companions kept her from crumbling out of sheer exhaustion.

"We don't have all the time in the world." Tobias shoved the flashlight in her face. "So have at it."

"It might take a while," she warned, trying to buy time. She had no wish to assist Simeon in finding his fountain of youth.

"I shall give you five minutes." Simeon turned his wrist and glanced at his watch. "After five minutes, I will shoot one of Mr. Hughes's feet. And so on."

Claire glared at him. "You wouldn't!"

"I would." He waved the gun barrel at the left door. "Now proceed. The clock is ticking."

Claire hurried to the first door and inspected the rows of circles and lines that represented the language of a people long since dead. The characters swam before her eyes. She was so worried and exhausted that she couldn't hold the combinations in her head long enough to decode the message.

"Two minutes, Miss Coulter," Simeon put in.

Her hand trembled as she brushed back her dusty hair and put her nose closer to the writing, looking for the telltale release button, the circle that didn't fit in with the surrounding characters. There it was, in the center of the text, a little to the left.

"One minute," Simeon said.

Claire steeled herself and blotted out everything around her, using her power of concentration to focus on the code, just as she had used her focus to blot out the rest of the world when life and her brother's illness had been too much to bear. Sweat dripped down her temples.

"Ten seconds, Miss Coulter."

Suddenly the code crystallized, as if her brain had compensated for her physical distress.

"Truth," she blurted, racing ahead in the text to double-check her translation. "Truth is—" She paused.

"Truth is what?" Tobias demanded, sweeping the light of the flashlight across the text.

"Everything." Claire looked over her shoulder at Simeon. "Truth is everything."

"That's it?" Tobias exclaimed, obviously not impressed.

"It appears the door is part of a puzzle." Simeon waved his gun at the right portal. "Now, the other door, Miss Coulter. And perhaps the choice will be made more evident."

"What did the door back there say?" Tobias asked, blocking her path with his forearm, as he nodded toward the portal she and Jack had opened.

"No bastards allowed," Jack replied.

Tobias turned in Jack's direction and smashed the blunt end of the flashlight into his cheek. Jack reeled back in agony, both hands to his face.

"I didn't ask you, cowboy!" Tobias yelled, hatred mingling with the white froth of anger at the corners of his mouth.

"Shall I shoot him?" Simeon raised his eyebrows as he raised his gun higher.

"No!" Claire cried. She couldn't take the chance of calling Simeon's bluff, well aware that Jack was expendable. "It said something about illusions dying. I couldn't get it all."

Simeon frowned, obviously considering her translation, and then indicated that she go on to the second door.

Claire trudged to the wood and bronze portal and focused on the script before her.

"Five minutes, Miss Coulter."

"Shut the hell up!" Jack shouted. "Just let her work, dammit!"

"You shut up." Tobias rammed Jack in the chest with the barrel of the flashlight, knocking the wind out of him.

Claire exchanged a worried glance with Jack. There was no reason for him to needlessly endanger his life. Tobias was waiting for a reason to kill him, or at least hurt him. She tried to tell that to him with her eyes, but Jack only looked away, his expression hard, his body stiff and poised for action.

"Four minutes, Miss Coulter."

She swallowed and set to work on the code, running her gaze over the characters until they raced through her mind in a jumbled frenzy. This message was shorter, which made it more difficult to decipher.

"Two minutes."

"Everything," Claire ventured, certain the translation was correct from her work with the left door. She stared at the remaining symbols until they seemed to melt together. Something inside her head buzzed, interfering with her thought processes.

"Thirty seconds."

Claire crossed her arms. Why couldn't she figure out what the last cluster represented? It seemed as if the two doors said the same thing: Truth is Everything. Everything is Truth. Why would the carved figures say the same thing only in reverse?

Then she realized the release button was not in the middle of the text, but at the end.

"Time's up!" Simeon crowed.

"Everything is true," Claire exclaimed, sure now that she was correct.

"Wait a minute." Tobias glanced at the first door and back again. "They say essentially the same thing. Is that what you're telling us?"

Claire nodded, frowning. It certainly wasn't clear which door was the right door to open.

"Truth is everything," Simeon murmured. "Everything is true. Hmm." His eyebrows drew together above the ridge of his fine nose. "One door might lead to the fountain, the other to a trap or death."

"So which one do we open?" Tobias asked.

Chapter 35

Hungry, tired and out of sorts, Tobias glared at the two doors. Nothing on this trip had gone as he had planned. Nothing. He'd been shown up at every turn by the cowboy, and he'd never really got close to Claire, not in the way he wanted. Frustration burned in him, an echo of his physical hunger. Not even seeing the Nimian Stone script on the doors had excited him. All he could think about was the way he had lost the woman of his dreams to a rube from the back country. It just didn't seem possible.

He glanced at her again while bitterness washed over him. Women were all alike when it came to certain common denominators, like falling for the wrong guy, making impractical relationship decisions, and pledging their loyalties to causes they knew would fail—losers like Jack Hughes.

He had thought Claire was different—special—but she had proved herself to be like all the others: a stupid, illogical female. She didn't deserve him.

He watched her exchange a quick but intimate glance with the cowboy, and his dark mood blackened. Claire had made her choice. It was obvious. Well, now she'd have to live with that choice. He would show no mercy to someone who displayed such a blatant lack of intelligence, and to someone who had disappointed him so thoroughly. A sharp feeling twisted inside him, like a knife in his gut.

Tobias took a step back from the doors and leveled his

burning glower on Claire. "You decide," he barked, finding it difficult to speak through the venom clogging his throat. "You decide what door to open."

"Me?"

"You're the so-called expert of these Nimian people. Which door?"

She shot him a wild, questioning stare. "I don't know!"

"Then start knowing," Tobias growled. "Or I'll shoot Cowboy Jack, and not just one of his toes!"

Claire paled and turned back to the doors. Tobias felt a slight amount of satisfaction from watching the color drain from her pretty face and seeing the deadly earnest expression flare in her eyes. Finally, she was realizing he was serious and to be feared—something she had failed to recognize ever since the start of the trip.

He moved up to stand directly behind her, so she could feel his breath on the back of her neck. He could smell something different about her, a musky male scent mingling with her own light, womanly fragrance. Had she and Jack had sex? Here in the cave? Under his nose?

Enraged, he glanced down the back of her trim figure, wondering what she'd done with Jack, and his body produced a throbbing—almost excruciating—erection in answer, an erection made more intense by his years of sexual frustration.

Tobias took a deep breath as he felt his vision going red. All he could think about was the woman standing in front of him, inches away—and the fact that he wanted her so acutely he felt as if he were going to burst into flames. He could hear his own breathing intensifying, could feel his blood pounding in his temples and his crotch.

"Which will it be, Miss Coulter?" Simeon asked, breaking the silence as if he were aware of Tobias's inner turmoil. "The right door or the left?"

"How am I supposed to know?" she snapped. Then she held out her hand. "I need better light."

Simeon relinquished his flashlight, and Claire took it, stepping back for a better view of both doors and almost colliding with Tobias.

He jerked to the side. Had she so much as brushed the front of him, he would have lost control and ravished her on the spot, no matter the consequences, no matter that two other men were present. He staggered back, struggling to regain control of himself.

CLAIRE SWEPT THE beam of light over the doors, looking for something—anything—to give her a clue regarding the correct path.

As she searched the doors, her sight was overtaken by swirling recollections of the last few days, snatches of visuals overlaid with bits of conversation. She saw the stallion, felt the roaring of Tobias's Porsche, watched poor Peanut rolling in the flood, heard Jack asking if she meant what she said, saw the lizard shooting fire at her, and heard Rae Lambers telling her to get rid of the tarot cards. Was she about to die? Was this her life passing before her eyes?

Suddenly something caught her attention, snagging on her subconscious sense which constantly worked in the background collecting, analyzing, and synthesizing data, no matter how tired or disconsolate she was. There was something in the rock above one of the doors, something different from the rest of the surrounding stone. Years of searching for nuances and patterns, and making sense of jumbled concepts and symbols, made her sweep the light across the rock for a second time.

The soft light bounced off the edges of two subtle markings in the rock, easily missed because they'd been carved so high above the door. The symbols seemed vaguely familiar, and Claire struggled to recall where she had seen them before. Then she suddenly remembered—in the corners of the tarot card she'd looked at! One was the astrological glyph for Scorpio, the other was the glyph for the Sun. Had the tarot card ordained all of this?

A chill spiked through her exhausted frame.

"So, what's the verdict?" Tobias inquired, moving closer to her. She eased the light down, hoping no one else had noticed the glyphs.

Claire now had to make a decision. If the Sun and Scorpio glyphs marked the correct path, which she assumed they did, should she direct Simeon and Tobias to the wrong door, and hope their greed would prove their undoing? It might be her and Jack's only hope of escape.

"Well?" Simeon added, his voice laced with impatience.

"That one," Claire announced, pointing to the left door.

"Why that one?" Simeon narrowed his glittering eyes.

"Because—" Claire searched her sluggish mind for a reasonable explanation for choosing the left door. "Truth is everything," she said, and then glanced to the side. "The other door states a falsehood. Everything is not necessarily true."

"It could be true somewhere," Tobias countered. "In a universe with different physical laws, for instance. Or seen from a different perspective."

Simeon frowned, studying both doors and then studying Claire. His regard made her skin crawl.

"The left door," he stated. "You believe it to be the correct choice."

She nodded.

"Very well then." Simeon turned to Jack. "Mr. Hughes shall lead the way and apply his brawn to the door."

Jack trudged forward.

"Wait!" Claire cried. She hadn't predicted this. She had thought Tobias would have rushed forward with Simeon at his heels, anxious to be the first to see the fountain.

"There's no need for brute force," Claire put in, struggling to hide her panic. "There's a hidden release."

Simeon slid her an evaluating glance that turned to ice and promised death if she thought to trick him.

Her heart surged into her throat, choking her. She knew with nauseating certainty that she wasn't dealing with a human being. How could she think she could outwit a creature who had been alive since the dawn of Egypt? She was a mere mortal, a babe in comparison.

She knew from Simeon's dark look that she was doomed.

"Show the release to Mr. Hughes," Simeon hissed. "And quit wasting my time!" His eyes glinted at her, cruel pieces of ice set in a deceptively charming face. Why hadn't she noticed his real personality in time? She'd picked up so many odd vibrations from the man. And yet, what could she have done differently? Taken a gun and shot him in cold blood? That wasn't her style.

Tobias shoved Jack toward the door.

"No! Wait!" Claire flung herself between Jack and the door on the left. "It's the right door!"

"I thought as much," Simeon purred, his eyes narrowing to slits. "You thought to trick me, Miss Coulter, didn't you?"

"Stupid bitch!" Tobias gave a sharp laugh as Simeon advanced toward her. "You don't know who you're dealing with!"

"You have the nerve to think you can trick me." Simeon walked up to her and slapped her on the face so harshly that she spun sideways and tumbled to the ground, landing painfully on one hip. "Fool!"

"Bastard!" Jack lunged for Simeon, but Tobias quickly stepped in his path and raised his gun.

"Keep coming, cowboy," he taunted, his mouth pulled into an unfriendly smile. "Give me a reason to shoot you."

Jack stopped in mid-stride, seething, the whites of his eyes glowing against his tan, his shadowy beard and tousled black hair making him look every inch a wild animal trapped in human form.

Claire gazed at him, knowing they might not survive the next few minutes and knowing that every look that passed between them might be their last. Her gaze feasted on him as she scrambled to her feet. Jack might think his animal nature was a curse, but she thought it made him what he was—undeniably beautiful, proud, and dangerously unpredictable. She also knew Jack and the wild stallion inside him would sacrifice their lives to protect her.

She had never loved him more than at that moment.

"We do not need such interference." Simeon pointed to Jack's lariat lying on the sand. "Tie him up, Tobias."

Claire could see the wildness flare in Jack's eyes as Tobias bound his hands behind his back, his every movement
rough and designed to cause pain. She remembered Jack's
confession, that the horse spirit regaled against being
forced into confined spaces or surrounded by crowds.
Would Jack be able to endure being tied up, without losing
his mind?

She could see beads of sweat glistening on his forehead,
but he refused to look her way, as if being tied up had
stripped him of his manhood. Then Tobias kicked him in the
back of his knees. Jack fell heavily onto the sand, unable to
cushion his fall with his hands, and rolled to the side,
coughing.

"Now show me how you really passed through the first
door," Simeon said, motioning Claire forward.

"What about Jack?" she asked.

"What about him?"

"We can't just leave him," she protested. "Not alone, not
in the dark."

"He is no longer useful, Miss Coulter."

"But what if something happens to him?"

Simeon shrugged. "His fate is not our concern." His voice
was cold. "He chose to come to Medicine Valley. He must
find his own way now."

"But—"

"No buts," Tobias put in. "If you don't do what Simeon
wants, I'll shoot Jack. I mean it, Claire."

Claire slanted Tobias a sharp glare of hatred. She had no
choice but to turn her back on Jack and obey Simeon's request to open the door.

Claire walked to the door, her spirits plummeting. She
feared for Jack's life. She feared for her own. Raising a
trembling hand, she pressed the release button and heard the
now-familiar metallic clink.

"Well?" Tobias craned his neck to see if the door had
moved.

"You have to push it open," Claire commented.

Tobias shoved the door open with his foot, disregarding

the age and worth of the portal. As the door creaked open, Claire expected to see another corridor and another set of doors. What she glimpsed before her eclipsed any fantasy she could have imagined.

Set 13

I throw myself toward this supposed fountain of youth as a last resort, desperate as I am to find a magical place in this singularly un-magical world. Perhaps the spring will return my youth to me. Perhaps it will heal my lesions. I must find and possess the fountain. I will do anything to slough off this decaying form—even if I have to kill for it.

Set, of Aging *Khat* but Ever Vigorous *Akh*

Chapter 36

"I'll be damned!" Tobias swore, stumbling through the portal, his gaze riveted on the awesome vision before him. The door had opened a wonderland of quartz crystals, a sparkling fairyland set upon layers and layers of agate.

The vault they entered was huge, and lit by a strange lilac glow that emanated from deep in the heart of the crystals hanging from the ceiling, pushing up through the translucent agate floor, and encrusting the vaulted walls. Tobias estimated that some of the crystals were at least ten feet long, each formed in a rainbow of colors from smoky silver to lilac, to a deep purple.

"My God!" Claire gasped, slowly twirling around, her head tipped to the ceiling, her lips parted in wonder. "What is this place?"

"It's like a giant thunder egg blasted out of a volcano," Tobias answered. "A *mother* of a volcano."

"And look!" Simeon exclaimed, pointing to an alcove on the far wall. "The fountain!"

Tobias turned to follow the direction of Simeon's finger and spotted what he first thought was a giant sculpture of three horses. But then he saw the sprays of celadon-colored water bursting from around the hooves of each beast and falling into a pool—the color of which he'd never seen before. The water was an intense turquoise color glowing neon green around the edges, and it was strangely opaque, as if the pool were bottomless. Everything glowed, as if lighted from within—even the pool.

He stepped closer, barely noticing where he put his feet, his every sense mesmerized by the fountain. The horse sculpture had been cut from what appeared to be an immense, amethyst-colored crystal, expertly hewn in the shape of three gigantic steeds. The center horse was shown rearing and the two on either side were pawing the ground, their manes flying and their necks arched as if in deference to the huge stallion—an amazing accomplishment considering the material used for the sculpture. All around the animals sprayed turquoise streams, glinting seafoam and indigo in the changing light, and refracting off the crystal into thousands of rainbows. This crystal miracle made the Trevil Fountain in Rome look like a crude and colorless attempt at a backyard water feature.

For a moment Tobias couldn't move, he was so awestruck by the work of art before him.

"This makes my temple seem like a stable in comparison," Simeon commented, his eyes alight. "Truly, this is a marvel! A wonder of the world!"

"What type of civilization could make such a thing?" Claire murmured, her voice hushed with reverence. "The horses look so real!"

"A clever, clever people," Simeon replied. "I am not usually surprised these days. How refreshing to feel such awe!"

Tobias ventured closer to the turquoise water. He held out his palm to touch one of the feathery cascades.

"Careful," Simeon warned. "Like everything, it could be booby-trapped."

Tobias quickly retracted his hand.

Simeon looked down. "Ah, yes. There is a plaque. And two goblets. How interesting." He turned and glanced at Claire. "Miss Coulter?"

Claire didn't respond, seemingly absorbed with her magical surroundings. Her gaze hung on the pool, as if it were hypnotizing her.

"Claire!" Tobias grabbed her elbow, using any excuse to manhandle her, to punish her for her stupidity.

"What?" Her voice sounded vague, as if her mind had drifted somewhere else. Tobias could just imagine where.

He could smell the male musk on her again, and he squeezed her arm harder than necessary. He felt her flinch and try to pull out of his grip.

"Pay attention. The professor needs you to read something."

"He's no professor," she retorted. "He's evil, Tobias. Why do you do whatever he says?" She stared fearfully at Simeon as he slowly turned in her direction. "He isn't even human!"

"So?" Tobias sneered. "What's so good about being human? I haven't met a sorrier lot than the human race."

"You're human, Tobias." Claire jerked out of his grip and fell back a step. "Why are you playing traitor to your own race?"

"Why not? There's something better out there," he retorted, waving his arm in a large arc. "A new world. And I intend to be part of it."

"What are you talking about?"

"A new future, Claire. One with no physical boundaries as we know them."

She gaped at him, as if he were insane.

Tobias smirked. Let her think what she wanted. She wasn't capable of seeing a larger world view—she'd shown her limits well enough on this trip. He should count himself fortunate he hadn't linked his life to hers as Simeon had advised him against. Until now he hadn't realized just how conventional and small-minded Claire was.

God, he'd nearly been duped by a pretty face. Just how evolved could he be? He felt a flush of self-loathing but immediately reminded himself that he had triumphed in the end, after all. He hadn't succumbed to her. Not completely.

"We are wasting time, children," Simeon interjected tersely. "Read the plaque, Miss Coulter."

Claire's tired face turned even more grim as she gazed at Simeon standing near the plaque, imperiously pointing down at the metal square. The cool blue light of the crystals accentuated the lines of exhaustion in her face, the bruises on her skin, the mosquito bites on her cheek, and the circles under her eyes. How could he have ever thought she was beautiful?

And yet, one look at her soft lips, her delicate profile, and the vulnerable slenderness of her neck, and he felt himself growing hard all over again.

"May I remind you," Simeon said, breaking into Tobias's fantasy. "That I don't have—as they say—all day."

CLAIRE WALKED TOWARD the pool, her heart thudding in her chest as she stealthily reached for the strap of her purse. The pool looked fathomlessly deep, the perfect place to submerge the Forbidden Tarot. She had to get as close as possible and fling her purse as accurately as she could—far enough so neither man could retrieve it before it sank, and close enough to land in the water and not on the crystal statues.

She would have only one chance, one throw. She prayed Rae Lambers was right—that in submerging the tarot deck, she would free herself from the curse of the cards. Claire's pulse thundered in her temples. She had one chance to save Jack and the rest of the world from the damage Simeon Avare could inflict, and she couldn't blow it.

Simeon stepped aside as she approached the edge of the pool, where an agate wall a foot high ringed the water, looking like a long piece of ribbon candy.

This was her moment, her chance to throw the purse. She wouldn't get any closer to the water than she was now. In one quick motion, Claire whipped her purse strap down her arm and flung the bag outward, just as Tobias caught her elbow. His interference caused the bag to veer to the left, and Claire watched in horror as the purse sailed too high and curved off the mark, its strap snagging on the outstretched foreleg of the giant stallion. She couldn't have managed such a feat if she had tried a hundred times.

Dread and terror flooded over her as she watched her purse swing in the air and come to rest, dangling five feet above the water.

"Claire!" Tobias shouted. "Why'd you do that?"

"Because she's an idiot!" Simeon roared. He grabbed her neck from behind and threw her forward. Her knees slammed into the solid rock of the cavern, and she only kept herself from falling into the water by bracing her hands on the rim of the agate wall.

"Read the plaque!" he commanded, his fingers clamping down on her neck until she thought he would sever her head from her shoulders. He pressed her down until her nose smashed into the metal plaque. "Now!"

She didn't make a sound, even though spikes of agony shot through her knees and neck. He was going to kill her. After she read the plaque, he was going to kill her.

"Read it!" Simeon thundered.

"I can't," she said, her voice muffled by her flattened nose and lips. She knew she was a dead woman. All she could do was play for time, hoping a miracle would occur to save her. There was nothing left for her to do. But with the hopelessness of her plight searing through her came a reckless kind of courage. She had nothing to lose. No matter what she did, she knew Simeon was going to kill her. She would be damned before she made it easy for him. She pushed against his hand.

"Let me up," she demanded.

He allowed her to rise a few inches, but his hand was still a vise around her spine.

"Make haste!" Simeon spat.

"It takes time," she retorted. "Do you want me to make a mistake?"

"Of course not. But no more of your games!"

"I thought you liked surprises," she countered.

"I warn you, Miss Coulter—" His fingers squeezed harder. She refused to cry out.

"Hey," Tobias leaned closer. "You're going to break her neck."

"She's trying my patience!" Simeon hissed.

"Let her go, Simeon. We need her to crack the code."

With a hard shove, Simeon released her. Claire caught her balance and rotated her head, trying to ease the pain in her neck and shoulders.

"She's stalling," Simeon growled.

"Then I'll go shoot Cowboy Jack," Tobias suggested. "And see if that hurries her up."

"No!" Claire cried.

"Listen to you." Tobias's lip curled as he gazed down at her. "Simeon warned me about human affection. How it can cripple a person. How stupid it is. Look at you, Claire. You're caving for a cowboy." He shook his head, but she only glared at him, refusing to allow his comments to affect her.

"Do you think for one minute that Cowboy Jack would give up his life for you? For you, Mexicali Rose?"

Claire raised her chin at the insult. "I know he would."

"You're pitiful," Tobias replied. "A fool for love." His smile turned into a disgusted sneer. "Now get to work."

He'd pulled a trump card in threatening Jack. Claire would do anything to save Jack, and he knew it. Claire heaved a sigh and stared down at the Nimian script before her.

Odd, how the specter of death crystallized her thought processes and made her mind soar. Or was it the strange power of this cavern that lent wings to her thoughts? She decoded the entire text on the second pass.

"Life begets life," she stated, her voice a monotone.

"What in the hell?" Tobias blurted.

"Blood begets life."

"I see," murmured Simeon.

"Life unlocks the fountain."

"Ah, yes," purred Simeon.

Claire looked up at the man, unsure what the words on the plaque meant, and worried that Simeon seemed to know.

"What?" Tobias demanded. "What does it mean?"

"Life is just a bunch of riddles, isn't it?" Simeon smiled, his eyes glittering. "But there's nothing much new in the world when it comes right down to it." He reached down and grabbed Claire's right wrist, pulling her to her feet and keeping his hand locked securely around her arm. "It's all about death and resurrection in one form or another."

Tobias swept the air impatiently. "What are you talking about?"

"I'm talking about immortality, Tobias. About recharging

batteries." Simeon smiled at Tobias, his anger gone, his face calm and charming once more. "About winter and spring. Cycles."

"Cycles?" Tobias scowled. "I'm not following you."

"It always comes down to sacrifice, Tobias. Just like the plaque said. A life for a life. That's the way of the world. Timeless. Perfect. Poetic, really."

Claire stared at him, not sure what he was talking about, but certain it didn't bode well for her. She stood still in his grip, refusing to tremble, refusing to show an ounce of cowardice when it came her time to die.

"The fountain wants blood, Tobias. Do you not understand?"

Tobias glanced at the glowing water, then at Simeon, and finally at Claire. She saw his lips open with incredulity as the realization hit him.

"Yes. She must die," Simeon said, his voice as matter-of-fact as if he were reciting the current temperature. "Shoot her, Tobias."

"You can't be serious."

"Oh, I am." Simeon replied. "How do you say it? I'm deadly serious." Then he chuckled at his own pun. "Shoot her in a couple of places. There must be plenty of blood."

Tobias stepped backward, holding his gun away from his body. "Wait a sec, Simeon! You can't expect me to just—"

"Do it, Tobias!" He dragged Claire closer. "Remember, she's nothing to you! She's meaningless! Her body is meaningless. Her death will be but a blip in time, like millions of deaths before her's. Nothing more! Shoot!"

Tobias raised his pistol. Claire could see his arm shaking and his mouth trembling. She stood trapped by Simeon's hand, knowing she had nowhere to run and was staring death in the face.

In the end, at the very last moment of her life, she closed her eyes and turned to her mother's God, the one she had ceased believing in long ago. She prayed for someone to watch over Emilio, for Jack to survive the cave, and for the world to find a way to stop Simeon.

Then, when her fervent prayer was done, she opened her eyes, saw Tobias's expression harden and his fingers tighten around the gun. A second later, her world burst into a million painful pieces of light.

Chapter 37

"No!" Jack bellowed, his neck bulging, every muscle in his body straining against the ropes that bound him. They'd shot Claire. Three times. He had been forced to stand helplessly by, listening to Simeon's twisted philosophies and then to the gun being fired.

They had killed her. Jack dropped to his knees in the sand, and then let his forehead sink to the earth as his anger was overcome by grief. Claire hadn't made a sound. She hadn't begged for mercy. And now she was dead, her life cut short to benefit that madman, Simeon Avare.

Her brave silence had shown once again what she was made of: pure steel. Through this whole ordeal, she had been nothing short of admirable. He'd never met a woman like her and knew he never would again. But he had lost her. She had died without knowing how he felt about her. And he should have told her. He should have protected her better. Tears stung his eyes.

"No!" he cried again, his tears mingling with rage, ripping him apart. He couldn't bear the thought that Claire's life spark had gone out, that he would never talk to her, look into her luminous eyes, or feel her gentle touch again.

How could she have died so easily? How could he have been caught by surprise two separate times, and been left powerless to help her?

"No!" he roared, raising his head from the sand, his tears evaporating in the heat of his rage. "No!"

He threw back his head, and for the first time in his life, he called upon his spirit guide to take him, to possess him, to avenge the woman he had loved.

"HOLD HER UP!" Simeon commanded. "We must take her blood while her heart is still beating."

The scenario had turned a bit gruesome for Tobias's taste. He had a sudden and queer revulsion when it came to touching a person he had just shot. He had ached to embrace Claire, to hold her in his arms like this, but not when her body was smeared in crimson and hung limp. This was no longer Claire. Something crucial and specifically Claire had vacated the premises. He could only guess it was her soul.

"Hold her head down, Tobias!" Simeon barked, pressing one of the goblets to the ragged hole in her neck.

Tobias grimaced. Even though the woman was close to death and unaware of what was happening to her, he still considered it degrading to hold her nearly upside down.

"Hurry up," he muttered, wanting to get this distasteful deed over with, and wanting even more to leave the cave behind, and all that he had done here. The atmosphere had suddenly changed—the air had gone deadly quiet. Simeon didn't seem to notice, but then again he was preoccupied in capturing Claire's blood in the golden goblet. The hair on Tobias's forearms rose, and he glanced around, wondering what he was sensing.

"That should be enough," Simeon crowed, rising to his full height. His eyes glowed with anticipation, and with a hunger that alarmed Tobias. If the guy could live in the ether without physical boundaries as he claimed he could, why did he seem to want a younger body so much?

Slowly, Tobias lowered Claire's lifeless form to the ground. He straightened her legs and then settled her lids over her staring eyes, feeling the same stab of horror he'd experienced when he'd pulled the trigger—and she had opened her eyes to look at him. He'd almost faltered when she'd stared back at him.

But he'd managed to get through the killing, and as Simeon had said, once he'd got over the initial shock of taking a life, it hadn't been that big of a deal. Claire had surrendered her life with remarkable ease and bravery. He had to wonder if he'd die as well as she had, when it came his time. He didn't intend to face death for many years, though—or at all, if this fountain was everything it was cracked up to be.

"Goodbye, Princess," he murmured.

Her blood-spattered left arm sprawled on the agate floor, fingers pointing to the gun he had used and left upon the ground, her gesture like a deathbed accusation.

Another wave of shame and horror at what he had done washed over him. He swallowed and stared at the weapon for a moment, doubting he would ever be able to touch it again without vomiting.

"Welcome to the world of carnivores." Simeon congratulated him with a pat on the back. "The real world. You've just killed something with eyes."

"Yeah." Tobias fought back a surge of nausea as he rose to his feet.

"And now I'm going to consume what you killed." Simeon stepped back. "The moral of the story, Tobias?"

"I'm dying to hear it," he drawled, only half listening.

"It doesn't pay to be vegetarian."

Tobias shot him a dark smile, struggling to emulate Simeon's admirable sangfroid, but falling far short of the mark. He watched his companion turn and dip the second goblet into the turquoise water of the pool.

"This is it, my friend," Simeon murmured, holding the goblets in his hands. "The moment we've worked so hard for."

"It better do the trick," Tobias retorted. "I had to kill one of my best employees for you."

"And you have done a fine job, Tobias." Simeon smiled at him. "More than that, you remained strong, unaffected by the woman."

Tobias nodded, knowing in his heart that he wouldn't have been strong if Claire hadn't been so adamant about pushing him away and if Jack hadn't protected her so fiercely. Where was the strength in that?

"Now for the test." Simeon raised the goblet of blood. "The real test!"

Slowly he poured water into the goblet that held Claire's still-warm essence. "First, I will add water to her blood."

Tobias heard a hiss and a gurgling noise and watched as a pink mist rose up from the goblet. Effervescence ran up and over the sides of the cup and down Simeon's hand, like pastel-colored dry ice.

"It seems to be working," Simeon announced, his eyes gleaming.

"Bottoms up," Tobias remarked, wondering if he would have the stomach to drink human blood.

"To my health!" Simeon replied, his expression hopeful, almost joyous. He tipped the cup to his mouth and drank greedily, his Adam's apple climbing up his throat, sinking, and climbing up again as he drained the contents of the goblet.

Tobias stared, every muscle taut, not knowing what to expect, and expecting anything.

As Tobias stared at Simeon, watching his companion for signs that the potion was working, he heard a startling sound—that of a horse whinnying. How had a horse got in the cave?

He jerked around, astonished to see a huge black stallion galloping toward him, hooves clattering on the agate floor, his wild eyes burning like fireballs.

"What in the heck?" Tobias's voice trailed off as he half turned toward the animal. The horse appeared as if it were going to run right into him, and by the look in the creature's eyes, it was going to try to hurt him.

Tobias forgot all about the transformation of his associate. Frantic, he glanced around for an escape route. He could either jump into the fountain—which might not be the smartest thing to do since he didn't know yet what physical effect the water would have on a human body—or he could run to the left where Claire's body lay on the ground. Even better, his gun lay beyond Claire, and the gun was the only defense he had against the rampaging stallion.

He took only a fraction of a second to decide, and then scrambled sideways, barely avoiding the hooves of the enraged horse as it struck out at him. He dived over Claire's body and slid across the agate floor to the pistol he'd abandoned and had thought he would never use again. With shaking hands, he snatched up the weapon, barely able to keep a grip on it, and then swung around to face the horse. He had three bullets left and knew he had to make each of them count.

Then Tobias saw something so astonishing, he wondered if fear had made him delirious. As he turned with the gun, he saw a huge, olive green dragon where Simeon had been standing only moments before.

The creature was at least ten feet tall, sitting on its haunches, and it had monstrous black wings that looked like bat wings, which it flapped suddenly to unfold and stretch to their full span.

The movement distracted the horse. Bugling, the stallion rose up on his hind legs and lunged for the dragon. For a moment Tobias gaped at the two animals as they sparred near the water's edge, but then realized he was wasting valuable time. He and Simeon needed to leave before the dragon attacked *them*. But where in the hell was Simeon? Desperate, Tobias looked around for his mentor, but Simeon was nowhere to be seen.

He could only conclude that while his back was turned, he had missed seeing the dragon appear. It must have frightened Simeon off, or maybe even eaten him.

"Oh, God!" Tobias gasped, his stomach roiling at the thought that he might be the only one left. Nausea and a feeling of doom welled up inside him. Where had the dragon come from? An adjoining chamber? The fountain? Was it a guardian of some sort like the ones in his video games?

Tobias knew he couldn't spare the time to analyze the situation. He had to get out—and get out quick—before the horse or dragon noticed his absence. He plunged toward the door of the corridor where they'd left Cowboy Jack. Though Tobias hated the man, he hoped and prayed Jack was still alive. The cowboy would help. Jack would never let him die. He only hoped he could untie him in time.

As Tobias dashed for the door, he heard the ear-shattering roar of the dragon behind him.

Tobias froze. He'd never been as scared and unsure of himself as he was at that instant. It felt like a dream. Then again, it was more like a video game. A very real, very frightening video game, and one he wanted to quit playing—immediately. But in this particular scenario, he had no idea where the "end" button was.

Shaking and sobbing with fear, Tobias turned at the door, so terrified that his thought processes froze. All he could do now was react. Grimacing, he raised his quaking hand. He could see the gun wobbling far out there, at the end of his arm. But he had to take a shot. He had to try at least wounding the dragon, or it would come after him as soon as it finished with the horse.

Tobias tried to marshal his strength, to quit shaking, to keep from slobbering with fear, but he no longer had control of his physical self. As he stood there, holding the wavering pistol, he felt his bladder release and a shaming stream run down his left leg.

In answer to his own pitiful weakness, he squeezed the trigger. The shot went wide, totally missing the dragon. Tobias almost sank to his knees in despair. He fired again, missing once more, but the bullet made a funny pinging sound, and he soon realized it had ricocheted off the wall. He followed the second ping and guessed the bullet must have hit the horse sculpture, for all of a sudden a bunch of fractures shot through the crystal, making strange cracking noises. Tobias gaped at the three horses as lines raced through them with amazing speed. In a few seconds, it looked as if millions of spiders had spun webs inside the crystal.

Tobias heard a light ringing sound, as if someone had struck a water glass with a spoon to call for attention at a banquet. He paused, the gun dropping in his hand, as the three magnificent horses cracked into tiny pieces and cascaded into the fountain like a thousand diamond dominoes. Then, as if in slow motion, Claire's purse dropped to the water.

The moment the purse hit the pool, the dragon roared, his enraged rumble echoing through the cave around them. Tobias stumbled to the side in fright as the creature turned his way, his small eyes bright with intelligence, his forelegs clenched in anger. Then he dropped to all fours, swept the stallion aside with his massive tail, and lowered his head. Fireballs hurled through the air, rolling toward Tobias.

Tobias staggered backward, and like a fool fired his gun, wasting his last shot in a useless defense against the creature. He knew as soon as he squeezed the trigger that a mere bullet would never pierce the thick scales of the beast. He swore at his own stupidity.

The third bullet ricocheted just like the last one, and Tobias froze in place as the lizard seemed to dissolve into space right before his eyes. Then Tobias heard an odd crack above him. He tore his stare off the fading image of the dragon long enough to glance upward, long enough to see a three-foot quartz crystal break from the ceiling high above.

He had no time to react. No time to roll out of the crystal's path. It hit him in the skull like a torpedo.

Chapter 38

Jack was still screaming inside as he came-to on the floor of the cave, naked and bruised. Even though he had blacked out, he had dreamed about Claire, seeing her shot again and again while he stood bound and helpless beside her.

Grief hung in his throat—a weird metallic taste—as he struggled to his feet. He had awakened in a fantastic cavern full of crystals, which ordinarily he would have thoroughly explored. But right now he had other things on his mind: Claire.

Rope burns stung his wrists and something had happened to the stallion that had left a gash in his right thigh. He hobbled across the floor of the cavern toward Claire's lifeless body, but paused when a movement caught his eye. There in the doorway of the cave stood Peanut, his saddle hanging to one side, his reins dangling, but looking very much alive.

Jack was so dumbfounded and shell-shocked from the past half hour that he didn't say a word. How the animal had found its way to Medicine Valley and then to the fountain was nothing short of a miracle. But he wasn't going to look a gift horse in the mouth. Jack smiled grimly to himself. Claire would have chided him for making jokes about something so serious.

Claire.

He took stock of the situation. Claire lay dead. Tobias's boots were still twitching, but he would never survive such a massive head injury. And Simeon was nowhere to be seen—

the bastard. Jack looked around, sniffing the air, listening, coming fully aware of the place.

He felt an eerie calm. The thundercloud of danger had passed overhead and had gone on. He was left now in a fabulously beautiful place with death all around him, and only a small horse as a companion.

Jack limped over the agate floor and heard the quiet clip-clop of Peanut's hooves as he followed his master.

"Claire." Jack murmured her name out loud, and the word stuck in his throat as he gazed down at her blood-spattered body. "Ah, Claire—"

He sank to his knees beside her, surveying the devastation of the beautiful woman before him. She was like a patch of rare ladyslippers he'd once found carelessly trampled by hikers, never to bloom again.

As a last hope, he placed two fingers on her pale, white throat, searching for a pulse but finding none. He hadn't expected to. He sat back on his heels, gazing at her, struggling to hold back tears. She had been much too young to die, too vibrant, and she had had too much to live for—her brother, her life's work, which had only just begun, and him.

Peanut clip-clopped closer, knocking aside one of the goblets. It rolled in an arc to Jack's left knee and came to rest beside his leg. Jack looked down, and the thought occurred to him that Claire's life might not be over just yet. Not if the fountain was all Simeon had claimed it to be.

Jack grabbed the goblet and leapt to his feet, ignoring the pain in his leg. If anyone deserved a second chance at life, it was Claire Coulter. If anyone deserved the gift of the fountain, it was she. And if anyone deserved to give up their lifeblood for another, it was Tobias Benton.

Quickly, Jack retrieved the second cup and hurried over to the billionaire who lay amidst a field of broken lavender crystal. Jack lowered to one knee, his kneecap crunching into the pulverized stone, and held the cup to Tobias's temple where a stream of blood still trickled.

Jack waited, his heart pounding, his gaze avoiding Tobias's crushed skull. When he'd managed to get a few tablespoons of blood in the goblet, he pulled away the cup, anxious to get away from the man.

"Thanks," he said to the insensate billionaire. "You've finally done something decent."

Then, following the instructions he'd heard Simeon convey to Tobias, Jack limped to the fountain and dipped the empty second goblet in the water. He was so tense, so worried, that sweat dripped down his naked back. The fountain was Claire's only chance. He prayed he had the proportions correct and that he was performing the procedure correctly, for there would be no more blood from Tobias, unless he scraped the guy's blood off the agate floor. He glanced back at the billionaire, who lay in a grisly mosaic of crystal and congealed blood, and then limped quickly back to Claire.

"This is it, Angel," he murmured. He poured part of the water into the first cup and watched as a pink fizz rose up and over the rim. Jack grimaced, not wanting Tobias's blood to touch his flesh.

"Sorry, it's Benton's blood," Jack commented, slowly lowering to one knee and talking to Claire even though he was certain she couldn't hear him. "But he owes you."

Carefully, Jack set aside the goblets and reached for Claire's head to cradle her in his lap so he could guide the precious fluid into her mouth. When he lifted her torso, despair stabbed him as he felt her leaden weight and cold unresponsiveness. He held her, careful to protect her head from falling back too far on her fragile neck.

"Oh, God, Claire!" For a moment, he was overcome by grief. He hugged her close to his chest, tattooing his naked skin with the crimson brand of her violent death. Then he gently placed her head and shoulders in his lap, opened her jaw, and tipped the fizzing goblet to her lips.

"Please," Jack prayed, staring down at the pink froth slowly easing into her mouth. "Please let her live again. She has so much to give still. And I love her so much. Please don't let her die like this!"

Peanut leaned down, softly nickering as he passed a whiskery investigation over Claire's forehead and hair, his ears flicking back and forth at the smell of life and death combining, going against every law of nature they both knew and lived by.

Some of the concoction trailed down Claire's chin, but most of it stayed in her mouth and gradually slipped down her esophagus. Jack held her, intently searching for signs of recovery. But after a few minutes, nothing had changed. She was still cold. She was still deadly pale.

He sighed. "It must not really work. It must be a hoax after all, Peanut."

The little horse shook his head, rattling his bridle. He sniffed Claire's face again, and pushed gently at the side of her head with his muzzle. Jack watched, his heart breaking all over again, as the horse valiantly tried to rouse his mistress. She had loved Peanut, and apparently he had loved her just as much.

"Maybe it wasn't enough potion," Jack said, more to himself than to the horse. "Maybe I should try again. Give her more."

Carefully, he set Claire's body back down on the floor. Then he grabbed the goblet, which was still dripping with pink froth, and hobbled over to Tobias.

The billionaire's blood had almost stopped flowing as his heart slowly pumped in weaker and weaker pulses. But Jack managed to get a few more spoonfuls in the cup, careful not to waste a single drop.

Peanut raised his head as Jack walked back to the fountain and set the goblet on the agate wall near the plaque.

"Peanut," Jack said, reaching for the saddle. "I need your blanket, boy." Deftly he unfastened the girth and hoisted the heavy saddle to the ground. Then he dragged off the still-warm blanket striped in blue and white, and slung it over one shoulder. He knew from years of dealing with emergencies in the backcountry that if he did manage to revive Claire, she'd need something warm to prevent her from slipping back into deadly shock.

Dutifully, Peanut trailed Jack back to Claire's side. Jack looked down at her ashen face, at her mouth smeared with pink, at her clothes stained with her own blood. He knew in his heart that Claire was dead and was going to stay dead. There was nothing he could do.

For the first time in his life, Jack felt truly helpless. He couldn't saddle break death. He couldn't ride it down. And he sure as hell couldn't shoot it. Those were his skills. That's what he could bring to the table. And in Claire's case, it just wasn't enough.

Tears rolled unbridled down his face as he held the useless goblets in his hands. Unable to take another step, he stared at the far wall, his spirit struck dumb by unutterable sorrow.

CLAIRE OPENED HER eyes and was startled to see Jack standing over her, naked except for a striped horse blanket draped over his shoulder. He held two golden goblets in his hands, and was looking toward the wall, his expression unspeakably sad. She could see tears glistening in his eyes.

For a moment, she stared at him, surmising that she hadn't really awakened and must be dreaming. Like a strange tableau, the tarot card she'd chosen—Temperance—had come alive before her. Everything she'd seen on the card was displayed before her eyes, even the starburst behind Jack's head, formed by light reflecting off the crystals behind him.

But Claire knew in her heart she wasn't in a dream. She had fallen victim to the Forbidden Tarot, and now here she was, seeing the image of her card one final time as a reminder of her transgression before she passed out of the mortal world. Peanut was even there to assist her in her spiritual journey.

She gazed at the happy-go-lucky creature. He stood so close to her that she could feel his breath on her face. A wave of love for him washed over her.

"Hello, my friend," she said, shocked to hear the words rasp out of her throat in a whispery croak.

"Claire?" Jack jerked around to peer down at her.

She raised her glance to meet his, wondering if he'd been able to hear her, and wondering how she appeared to him—

if in reality she lay in a pool of blood, her body a tattered mass of wounds. She didn't feel transformed—but she felt no pain whatsoever, so she was pretty sure she was floating on a different physical plane than Jack. She was probably experiencing one of those out-of-body incidents that people claimed to have had when they had nearly died.

Still, even in her altered state, she was able to think and feel exactly the way she did when she'd been alive. And the sound of heartbreak and hope in Jack's voice made her ache to connect with him, even though she knew she was on the way out.

"Jack?" she whispered, hoping the effort to communicate with him wouldn't fail.

Peanut nickered and sniffed her nose and eyelids as Jack fell to his knees.

"My God!" he exclaimed. "Claire?"

He dropped the goblets with a clang, and she saw his big left hand come toward her to brush away the hair from her face. She could feel the warmth emanating from his skin.

"I can feel that!" she gasped. "I can feel your hand!"

"I can't believe it!"

"Jack, whatever happens—" She stared up at him, not knowing how much time she had, but determined to make the best use of it this go-around. "I want you to know I—"

"Don't talk." He cut her off. Had he guessed what she was going to say? That she loved him? That she never wanted to spend another day without him?

As if he meant to divert her from another intimate confession, he gathered her in his arms and held her to his fiery-hot chest. "Save your strength, Claire."

She could feel his warmth and vitality streaming into her, radiating over her like a cloud. How could this be? How could she feel anything of the mortal world? Out-of-body experiences weren't supposed to be like this. She was supposed to be floating near the ceiling, watching but unable to connect with those below.

Then the last thing she expected to happen occurred—a roar of desire for Jack swept through her. She couldn't believe it. She was dead. Or almost dead. How was it physically possible for her to feel desire? It didn't make sense.

Too confused and shocked to try to explain what was happening to her, Claire flung her arms around Jack's neck and held him tight. This would be their last embrace, their final farewell, and she intended to take full advantage of it. She could feel her heart thudding against his, and she sank her nose into the small of his neck. She kissed him and drank in a great draught of his male scent—the outdoorsy fragrance laced with pine, musk and horseflesh—a smell that, to her, defined the essence of belonging. For her, Jack's arms were home. And she wanted to breathe her last breath while she was tucked securely against him.

As she held him, she felt Jack's body start to quake, and she realized he was sobbing. His embrace tightened, as if he thought he could keep her in the mortal world by applying brute strength.

She had thought she could endure anything, but the sound of this big, tough cowboy crying tore her heart in two.

Chapter 39

Claire lifted her head and ran her hands up the sides of Jack's face. His cheeks were wet with tears, and his eyes were red and bleary.

"Jack," she said. "It's okay. It's not so bad—physically I mean."

He stared at her, obviously not understanding.

"I don't feel any pain." She caressed his face as he stared down at her. "Really."

He swallowed and blinked, and she saw one eyebrow drop in confusion. "What are you talking about?"

"Dying. It's not so bad."

"Dying? Who's dying?" He blinked again and seemed to snap out of his emotional daze. "Wait a second. You need to get bundled up." He snatched the horse blanket from his left shoulder.

Claire smiled as he settled her gently on the agate floor, touched by his desperate moves to keep her in his world when she knew that she was bound for another. Carefully, he tucked the blanket around her.

"Better?" he asked.

She nodded. She could actually feel the insulating effect of the thick wool. Odd. She would have thought her body impervious to such an earthly sensation. Reacting to Jack was one thing, because she loved him so much and had always sensed the deep bond that connected them. But she couldn't explain being able to feel the blanket.

Jack sat back on his heels and studied her, just as he had

many times before, his face lined with concern, his brown eyes opaque with worry.

"God, I thought you were gone," he said, wiping the last of his tears away with the back of his hand. "You were a mess."

She nodded in agreement, not wishing to contradict him and further upset him.

"Benton shot you. Three times."

She glanced around. "Where is he, by the way?"

"Dead." Jack nodded in the direction of her boss. "From what I can tell, a bullet must have gone astray and cracked a crystal, and it fell on him."

"Oh—" Claire broke off, horrified at the thought.

"He deserved it, Claire. It was karma in action."

"And Simeon Avare?" she asked, after a moment of silence.

Jack shrugged. "I don't know what happened to him."

"You didn't see him?"

Jack shook his head. "I know he drank the potion. But that's all. I, uh—" He ran a hand through his hair. "I kind of blacked out."

"Because of the stallion?"

"Yeah." He paused and looked across the cavern before he leveled his gaze on her again. "I asked the spirit to come into me."

It was her turn to be surprised. Claire stared at him, knowing how Jack feared and resented the horse spirit that was linked to him. "You did?"

"I knew it was a long shot, but I thought he might be able to save you. I was too late, though."

Lovingly, Claire touched his cheek. "At least we got this chance to talk before I go."

"What do you mean—go?"

"How long do you think I have in this state?"

"I don't know." Jack covered the hand that cupped his face. He squeezed her fingers gently. "A day. A year—"

"Surely I won't last that long."

"How do you know?" He pulled her hand away from his

face. "Do you know what the fountain's true powers are—something you didn't tell Avare?"

It was her turn to be confused. "What?"

"The potion—does it have a side-effect you didn't tell Benton and Avare about?"

"Wait a minute!" She scrambled up on both elbows. "What are you talking about, Jack?"

"The potion. How long does it last?"

"You gave me the potion?"

Jack nodded, his expression dark and serious.

"You gave me someone's blood?"

"I had to!"

"You made me drink blood after I had died?" The horror and the marvel of it took her breath away.

"Maybe you weren't dead, Claire." Jack edged closer as if he had a sense she was going to bolt away. "Maybe there was a spark inside you that was still alive. You never did know when to quit."

Claire swallowed, her mouth suddenly dry. She knew Jack wouldn't lie to her, but she had to see proof for herself. With a trembling hand she felt the left side of her skull where the first bullet had grazed her. She could find no mark, no tender flesh, no caked blood. Then she slid her hand over her neck where the second bullet had plunged through her flesh. She suspected Tobias had been aiming for her head again but had missed. She dragged the pads of her fingers over her throat but felt only skin and tendons. Just to be absolutely certain, she checked the other side of her neck. Nothing.

Her heart thudded even more loudly as time seemed to stand still and no one made a sound. Quickly, half hopeful and half dreading what she might discover, she raised her shirt and looked down at her torso where the third bullet had torn through her internal organs and out the other side. Not a sign of any gunshot wound marred her flesh. In fact, she couldn't see a single bruise or scrape from being dragged by Peanut or being half-drowned in the cloudburst. Her clothes showed no evidence of bullet holes or blood. It was as if she had never been shot.

"What in the world?" she gasped, shooting a confounded glance at Jack.

"It healed you," Jack replied. "Your goddamned fountain brought you back to life!"

BY THE NEXT day, when the CommOptima chopper had touched down to pick up the survivors, Jack had come to his senses. He'd spent the night looking after his father and taking care of the horses, keeping himself occupied so he wouldn't torture himself with thoughts of Claire. All he wanted to do was slip away and spend the night making love to her. But it wasn't the time for self-indulgence, and didn't he know it.

He watched Claire greet the CommOptima pilot, Benton's doctor, and the county sheriff. Her shoulders were straight and her chin was held high in that proud, alert stance the fountain had returned to her. She walked with her fellow employee toward the cave, and Jack could tell by her hand gestures that she was explaining what had happened to her boss.

All four of them walked up to Jack, who straightened from his task of saddling Bud for the long ride home. He brushed his hands on his dusty jeans.

"Hey Jack," the sheriff greeted, holding out his hand. "Sounds like you've been having some excitement up here."

"Yeah." Jack shook his hand and then glanced at the doctor.

"This Dr. McAndrew," Claire put in, motioning toward the small balding man with glasses standing by the pilot.

"Claire tells me your dad fractured his leg?"

"Yeah." Jack shot a grateful look at Claire, and she gave him a calm smile.

"Well, let's have a look at him first. From what Miss Coulter says, it's too late to help Mr. Benton."

"Thanks." Jack led the physician to the fire, where his father lay covered with two horse blankets and with a bundle of duds cradling his head.

While the doctor bent to check William out, the sheriff pushed back his cowboy hat.

"So how about a quick run-down on what happened?" he asked, looking over at Jack.

"Like Miss Coulter probably told you, I was tied up and left in another part of the cave." Jack held out both wrists to display the angry red rope burns on his arms. "I didn't break free until the very end. After it was all over."

"But you think Mr. Benton was trying to kill Miss Coulter when the rock fell on him?"

"It was a crystal," Jack corrected. "And yeah, I believe he was going to kill her."

The pilot's eyebrows raised toward the fringe of his crew cut. "That doesn't sound like Benton."

"Places like this bring out a person's true nature," Jack replied.

"You bet," said the sheriff, nodding. "And it's best to just stay away."

Jack glanced at Claire, who stood at a proper distance from him and displayed no familiarity toward him. The space between them seemed colder than the rest of the surrounding air, and he was suddenly reminded of how great a gap existed between them in their normal lives.

She was a high-tech scientist living in Silicon Valley. He was a simple horseman trying to save a ranch. How more disparate could two people get? In the light of day he could see how hopeless a romance would be between them. And how either one of them would suffer if they were stuck in the other's world.

They'd been thrown together by danger and adventure and the strange spell of the cave, but now in broad daylight with outsiders encroaching, Jack could feel the magic falling away and doubt creeping in. He knew it was only a matter of time before Claire would begin to see him in a different light as well.

She'd made him feel like a warrior, a hero—the first time in his adult life he'd felt as if he'd come into his own at last. It was the reason he had finally made peace with the spirit inside him. Yet tomorrow or the next day when she stepped back into civilization, into her familiar routine, she would look at him and see him for what he really was—a freak of nature. And she'd thank her lucky stars she'd got out in time.

"So Jack?"

The sheriff's voice broke into Jack's dark thoughts, startling him back to reality.

"Yeah?"

"I said, would you mind showing us the body and describing what happened? What you saw, anyway?"

"Sure."

"You too, Miss Coulter, if you don't mind."

Jack turned to lead the men through the labyrinth to the crystal cave. He didn't look back at Claire. He didn't need to. Her pale face and serious countenance were branded into his memory forever.

THE INVESTIGATION DID not wrap up until close to noon. Jack was grateful for the fantastic surrounds of the cavern and its lavender glow, which had been helpful in detracting the men from CommOptima. They didn't notice the patch of agate that had been washed clean of Claire's blood or the two goblets that had been carefully rinsed and set aside in an alcove. He and Claire had looked everywhere for her purse, but they hadn't found it. They surmised that it had dropped into the pool along with most of the ruined horse fountain.

Not that he and Claire wished to lie to the sheriff or the doctor. Claire just didn't want them to know the truth about the cave. She had insisted upon covering up all traces of her miraculous revival and blood drinking, which any outsider would view as suspicious, to say the least. She had been adamant that once the secret got out about the cave, it would be overrun by strangers who would destroy the place. It had been damaged enough by Benton's stray bullets.

The sheriff found one of the slugs embedded in the agate, enough to provide proof for a ballistics lab that Benton had fired the pistol still locked in his hand.

"What I can't figure out," the sheriff drawled, rising up from his knee, "is why Mr. Benton wanted to kill you, young lady."

"It was plain and simple, really," Claire answered. "And will probably surprise a lot of people."

"Go on," he urged, taking notes.

"Tobias brought me out here to help him find this place. But also to seduce me."

The sheriff flashed a sharp glance at her.

"He harassed me sexually the entire time," Claire continued, her brisk tone never wavering. "He told everyone we were engaged."

"And you didn't raise a fuss?"

"He threatened me. He told me if I said anything, I would lose my job."

The sheriff raised his eyebrows and scribbled something on his tablet.

The doctor stared down at his deceased patient.

"He thought I had developed feelings for Mr. Hughes," Claire explained. "He became insanely jealous."

"Actually," the doctor said looking up, "I could believe that, knowing Mr. Benton's medical history."

"And what would that be?" the sheriff asked.

"The information is confidential. But if the court asks for his records, I've got information to support Miss Coulter's statement."

"I assure you," Claire put in, firm as ever, "I'm not making any of this up. If Jack hadn't stepped in, Mr. Benton would have forced himself upon me on two separate occasions. He just snapped here in this cave." She shrugged her shoulders and gazed down at the unrecognizable figure of her former employer. "He just snapped."

The sheriff nodded. "Well, we'll finish up here and get Mr. Benton home. You folks can wait for us with the others."

Claire nodded and then glanced at Jack. He slowly walked toward her but didn't touch her. He longed to take her hand or put his arm around her shoulders, but he didn't want to risk showing the depth of the relationship that had developed between them. Even more, he knew it was best to pull away and stay away. Better for them both.

Silently they walked with each other to the main cave and joined his family. An hour later, the doctor, pilot and sheriff carried out Benton's bagged body on a stretcher and loaded him into the helicopter. Jack's dad was carefully transported to the chopper on a second stretcher. The rest of his family clambered in behind him.

The rotor blades sliced through the brisk spring air, throwing up dust and sand and making it nearly impossible to talk. Jack was thankful for the quick goodbye, as his throat was clenched with a desperate need to tell Claire that he loved her. Had he been able to say anything, he would have begged her not to leave him, not to climb in with the others and leave him alone again.

But he knew Claire had to go. She had her brother's health problems to attend to and a job to return to. And he had to guide the stock back to the Dark Horse Ranch.

Claire was the last passenger to approach the helicopter. At the last minute she turned to Jack, who was standing at the periphery of the blades, his hair swirling around his head.

"Bye, Jack," she said, holding out her hand, her lips moving as the words whipped away in the wind.

Her eyes were full of the things she wanted to say but could not. All Jack could think was that she was leaving him. It was as if she were dying all over again.

Jack could barely look at her, too afraid he would break apart in despair. He thought he saw her mouth the words, "I'll call you," but he couldn't be certain. Maybe he was only thinking he saw what he wanted her to say.

"See you, Angel," he replied, knowing she couldn't hear the endearment. He gave her delicate hand a quick shake. Then he turned on his heel and trotted away so the chopper could lift off, and he could dash back to the suffocating safety of his solitude.

Set 14

Ah. The fountain did its work, at least partially. The lesions are gone and I feel invigorated. But I still posses the *khat* of an old man. Alas, the fountain could not take me back in time and restore me to my youth. It apparently could only restore good health to whatever shell I arrived in

I am not daunted, however. It is only a matter of time—a small drop of water in the sea of forever, which I have certainly sailed all these centuries. This aging shell will last until I make the transfer into my soon-to-be born son.

Set, of Aging *Khat* but Ever Vigorous *Akh*

Chapter 40

That afternoon, as Claire walked to Tobias's car back at the ranch, she nearly broke down. Everything she saw reminded her of Jack and the stabbing desperation she'd sensed in him when they'd parted in Medicine Valley. Though no one could have detected his emotional state from the hard look in his eyes, she had picked up a staggering vision from him the moment he'd clasped her palm in their goodbye handshake.

In that moment, she'd glimpsed the black stallion again, standing alone on a high outcropping of rock, his coat glinting in the sun, his right hoof pawing the ground, his proud emblazoned head shaking back and forth, tossing his silken mane as if refusing to let her go. But she'd been forced to leave him. There had simply been no way to remain.

And they had left so much unsaid.

The image of the wild horse still tore at her heart as she unlocked Tobias's Porsche. She was going to take Tobias's belongings back to Silicon Valley, including the Porsche, and then drive Emilio to the doctor as soon as she got home. Somehow, she would find a way to tell her brother that the offer for his operation had been rescinded due to Tobias's untimely death. There would be no kidney. No green cards. They were back to their old lives and their old fears.

But not everything would be the same. Part of her would

always be here at the Dark Horse Ranch. Part of her would not rest easy until Jack got safely back to the ranch and they decided what it was they meant to each other.

"Here, dear." Grandma Betty's voice startled Claire. "I made you a sandwich for the road."

Claire turned around, surprised to see Jack's grandmother holding out a brown paper bag. "Thank you," she said. She accepted the bag and pulled open the car door.

"When Jack gets back," she added, "would you have him call me?"

"Sure, dear."

Claire set the lunch bag on the passenger seat and searched through Tobias's wallet for a business card. She gave one to the white-haired woman. "He can call the main number there and leave a voice mail for me at my voice mail box."

"I'll do that."

"Just so I know he's safe?"

Grandma Betty nodded but her eyes twinkled knowingly.

Claire dragged her gaze off the smug expression of Jack's grandmother and pulled out the wad of bills she'd seen in Tobias's wallet. "And here, take this and get a dog for Jack's horse."

"Mr. B?"

"Yes. It's very important. Do it as soon as you can. Before Jack gets back, even."

"Why?"

"It's for Mr. B's mental health. You'll see." She watched Grandma Betty stuff the money in the pocket of her jeans.

"If it isn't enough, call me."

"Not enough for a mutt?" Grandma Betty waved her off. "Don't you worry about a thing now," she said. "You just see to that brother of yours." She pulled the car door wide and waited for Claire to slip into the sports car. "And try to get some rest yourself. This last week hasn't exactly been a picnic for you, young lady."

Claire nodded, anxious to see her brother but reluctant to leave the Dark Horse Ranch.

"Thanks for everything, Grandma Betty." She held out her hand and shook the strong hand of the old horsewoman.

"You take of yourself now."

"I will." Claire pulled the door closed as Betty gave it a push for good measure and then stepped away from the car. Claire turned the key and the engine rumbled into action, as powerful and as eager as the black stallion who was never far from her thoughts.

Then in the streaming sun of late afternoon, she pulled out of the parking space and sailed down the gravel driveway, gaily tooting the car horn to cover up her tears.

THAT NIGHT, CLAIRE called Rae Lambers to let her know what had happened at the cave.

"Rae, it's Claire."

"Hi, Claire."

Even hundreds of miles away on the phone, Claire could hear the despair in Rae Lambers's voice.

"Rae, what's wrong?"

"It's my sister." Rae broke off, and Claire felt a hot wave of dread wash over her.

"What about her?"

"She's dead. Angie's dead."

"What? Oh, Rae!" Claire hugged the phone to her ear as she sank down to her couch. "How? What happened?"

"The baby came early. Angie had a rough time of it. The pregnancy had taken a lot out of her, you know."

Claire nodded, thinking of the lizard fathering a child with a mortal woman, and she shivered in disgust. "So what happened?"

"She didn't have the strength to hang on. She died during delivery."

"Oh, God!" Claire clasped a hand over her mouth. "Couldn't they have done a C-section?"

"They tried. They were in the process. I guess it was too much for Angie. Just too much."

"Rae, I'm so, so sorry."

For a moment neither of them spoke. Claire heard Rae sniff.

"What about the baby?"

"It's okay. It seems . . . human."

"Are you going to be all right?" Claire asked. "Do you have someone there with you?"

"Michael's here." Rae's voice was thick with tears. "And a friend of mine, Maren Lake."

"Good. I was hoping you weren't alone."

"But I'm worried, Claire, about Simeon Avare."

"The creep." Claire sighed, frustrated by the lack of closure with the man. If karma had truly been in action, it should have ordained that Simeon perish with Tobias in the cavern.

"Where is he?" Rae asked.

"I don't know. He just disappeared."

"Did you throw the tarot cards in water?"

"Yes. I think it's over, Rae."

"I'm not so sure," Rae said. "I've got to protect Angie's son from Simeon. I feel strongly that I must hide him away."

"Where?"

"I'm not sure yet." Rae sighed. "But it's got to be really remote—the last place he'd ever look."

"Somewhere totally unconnected to your present life," Claire added.

"And the cards." Rae sniffed. "Plus we don't have much time. Less than twelve short years to get ready."

"Ready for what?"

"I'll tell you when I see you. I am going to see you soon, aren't I?"

"Yes. When I can leave Emilio."

"Good." Rae seemed to have mustered her usual strong spirit. "We'll talk more when I see you."

"I'm so sorry about Angie, Rae."

"Thanks. I've got to go now." She hung up the phone, leaving Claire in a stunned daze.

Another person had fallen victim to the Forbidden Tarot. Another mystery had roared up to worry her. What had Rae meant—they didn't have much time? What loomed on the horizon?

* * *

A MONTH LATER, Claire's doorbell rang. She brushed back a strand of stray hair and stared down the hall to the front door. The last time she'd had a visitor was the last time she'd seen Maria. Who could be ringing her bell? No one visited them. Not many people even knew where Claire lived.

Was it Simeon Avare? The chimes rang again. Claire bit her lip, her heart pounding in her chest, unwilling to risk opening her world again to the curse of the tarot cards and the threat of Simeon Avare. But surely, he thought she was dead.

When the doorbell rang a third time, Claire realized the visitor wasn't going away, and that the chimes might wake up Emilio, who had suffered all night with excruciating cramps in his feet and had just now fallen asleep.

Frowning, Claire tiptoed to the door, peeped through the fish-eye lens, and was surprised to see the Hughes family standing in the corridor outside her apartment. Everyone but Jack.

Claire pulled open the door.

"Surprise!" Susan Hughes exclaimed, throwing something into the air as she rushed into the living room. Pieces of paper floated all around Claire and fell to the floor of her tiny foyer. It took a few seconds for her to realize the papers were fifty-dollar bills.

"What in the—," Claire gasped as Grandma Betty pushed forward, a huge smile on her face. William brought up the rear, swinging along on crutches and sporting an uncharacteristic grin.

"What's this all about?" Claire asked, shock and surprise mingling in equal parts.

"Sit yourself down, young lady," Betty ordered, pointing at the couch.

"Got anything for a toast?" William asked, glancing toward her small kitchen.

"A toast?" Claire stood in the center of her living room, stunned by the Hughes visit, their altered family dynamics, and the strange way they were acting. It was as if they thought it was somebody's birthday and she should be all excited. But the only member of the Hughes clan she really wanted to see was Jack. And he hadn't joined the party.

"A toast!" William repeated. But instead of berating her for being deaf or not paying attention, he waved the air and smiled good-naturedly. "You know, bubbly. Champagne."

"The only bubbly thing I have is Diet Pepsi."

"That'll do," William replied.

"I'll get it." Susan hurried into the kitchen and came back with four cans.

Claire accepted her Pepsi can and held it without flipping it open. "Is somebody going to tell me what this is all about?"

"In good time," William replied, opening his can with a sharp whoosh. Everyone followed his lead. He held his soda aloft.

"First off. I'm getting my cast off today and we're finally going home to New York."

"Here, here!" Susan exclaimed.

"And secondly, and more important—" He held his can in front of Claire. "I'd like to thank you, Claire, for that lecture."

She gaped at him, aware that her mouth had dropped open at the unusual goodwill she read in his expression. "What lecture?"

"The one where you told me I was treating my family like shit. You were right. I was."

Grandma Betty nodded in agreement.

"I always thought I was surrounded by incompetents," he continued. "Always one step away from disaster. It drove me nuts." He glanced down at the cast on his leg. "It wasn't until I really met disaster in Medicine Valley that I found out how wrong I was." He looked back up. "Jack saved my life. Susan has been the best nurse a person could ask for, and Mother has held it all together back at the ranch. Without me."

"He's like a changed man." Susan beamed. "Our life together has never been better."

"I'm glad," Claire replied.

"Should have broken his leg a long time ago!" Betty winked, and everyone chuckled.

"So here's to you, Claire," William announced, holding his soda can aloft. Then they all drank to her while she blushed, still confused about the reason for their visit and the money on the floor, and still disappointed that Jack was not with them.

Grandma Betty lowered her drink and looked over at Claire. "You did a good thing for Johnny, too," she said. "Telling me to get him a dog for that horse of his. It was like a miracle."

"You should have seen it." William adjusted the crutch under his arm. "That horse turned into a puppy himself— overnight."

"They're inseparable," Susan put in. "It's so cute."

"But more important for Johnny," Grandma Betty went on, "is that Mr. B started to run again. Did you catch the Kentucky Derby?"

"I'm afraid I didn't." Claire glanced down, the money swimming in a blur at her feet as the memory of the last few weeks blurred in her thoughts. Emilio's condition had deteriorated so much she'd had to miss a lot of work. Progress on the Nimian Project had also stalled now that Tobias was dead. Even the exciting discovery of the cave in Medicine Valley had had to be suppressed, as she wasn't sure whom to trust at CommOptima, or if she should tell anyone at all in the company. In every part of her life, it seemed she'd come up against barriers.

"It was quite a race." William edged closer, bringing her attention back to her guests. "Neck and neck almost all the way."

"Are you saying that Jack ran Mr. B in the Derby?"

William nodded. "It took every waking moment to get Mr. B up to speed for it, but he didn't disappoint."

"He placed, then?" Claire swept the air to indicate the money on the floor.

"Placed?" Grandma Betty snorted. "Lord! He won!"

The news dumbfounded Claire. She turned and gaped at

Jack's grandmother, at the fifty-dollar bills on the floor, and then back at William, wondering if she'd heard correctly.

"He won?" she gasped.

"Thanks to you and that dog. We even took the mutt to the track."

"That's wonderful!" It was Claire's turn to grin. She felt the expression tugging unused muscles in her face, and realized she hadn't smiled for weeks.

"Not only that," Grandma Betty touched her elbow. "Remember that wad of money you gave me?"

"For the dog?"

"Do you know how much you gave me?"

"Not really." Claire shrugged. "It was whatever Tobias had in his wallet."

"Well, it was a sight more than I needed for a dog. So I bet that cash on a dark horse so to speak." She squeezed Claire's arm gently. "I knew you would have backed Johnny, so I put the whole wad down on Mr. B."

A chill coursed down Claire's spine. Grandma Betty had placed a bet on Jack—on Mr. B—both dark horses in their own right. She would have done the same, just as Grandma Betty had said.

"The odds were fantastic," William put in. "Everyone thought Mr. B was a has-been. A one-trick pony. And until the last seconds of the race, so did I."

"But Mr. B gave it all he had, right at the last," Susan chimed in, grinning. "Like a new engine had kicked in, and he won by a length."

"That's just wonderful!" Claire gulped her soda, happy that Jack's fortunes had turned. He deserved it. "Maybe now you'll have enough to fix up the ranch."

"But this isn't for the ranch," Grandma Betty countered. "This is yours. Part of it, anyway."

"Mine?"

Betty nodded. "The way I see it, that Benton character owed you."

Grandma Betty didn't know the half of it—that Tobias

had killed her, and only Jack's quick thinking and the magic of the fountain had brought her back to life.

"Now you can get that brother of yours his operation," Susan added, delight glistening in her eyes.

"Thanks," Claire replied, glancing at the smattering of fifties on the wood floor. "But a kidney transplant will take a bit more than this."

"Oh, there's plenty more," Grandma Betty replied, her eyes sparkling. "Enough to get your brother a new kidney, and enough to fund a little time off for you."

"You know, a sabbatical." William put in. So you can study that stuff in the cave. Jack said it was quite the place. For someone like you, that is."

Someone like her? Claire shot him a hard glance, wondering if he were taking a jab at her again.

"You know—," he added hastily. "A scientist."

Claire stared at them all in turn, struggling to take in all that she had just heard.

"You and your brother could come and live at the ranch while he recovers." Grandma Betty raised both her white eyebrows, waiting for Claire's reaction. "If you want to. We'd love to have you."

"Mr. B won that much money?" Claire murmured, still in shock.

"You bet."

"And he's going to win more." William grinned, his eyes crinkling to slits. "You can just see it in him."

Grandma Betty rolled her eyes. "He had it in him all along, Bill. But only Johnny could see it."

"Jack *and* Claire," Susan added, smiling gently at her.

Claire sank to the couch, too shocked to remain on her feet. She could afford the operation? She could afford to take time off? Such a turn of fortune was so outrageous, she couldn't believe it. Not entirely.

"So how about it?" Grandma Betty asked.

Claire glanced up at her. "It's a generous offer. But what about Jack?"

"What about him?"

"What does he have to say about all this?"

"Jack's going to be so busy this season." William drained his soda. "He won't know what hit him."

"Still, I wouldn't dream of showing up at the Dark Horse without Jack's blessing."

"You don't think you have it?" Grandma Betty asked.

Claire shook her head. "He's not here, is he?"

As if William had sensed the dismay she struggled to conceal, he said, "Blessing or no blessing, the man will hardly be around until fall, what with the traveling he'll be doing. Why would he mind if you and your brother were at the ranch?"

Still, Claire felt a lump hardening in her throat. Jack's silence these last few weeks had been a harsh surprise for her. She had thought the two of them had forged a very special connection—one that she had longed to explore. But apparently she'd been only a diversion on the trail for Jack.

It was nice of his family to show up and offer her shelter and support—sweet, even—but she could never accept their generosity, knowing Jack was in the background, dark and silent and aloof for reasons she would probably never understand.

Claire felt Grandma Betty's gaze on her and finally looked up at the old woman, who reached into her jacket pocket.

"Well, whatever you decide to do, Claire, I'm going to write you a check. And if you change your mind, you come on up to the Dark Horse. The door'll always be open."

THREE WEEKS LATER, Claire sat in her brother's hospital room, waiting for him to return from a last round of tests so they could finally leave the hospital. As she sat in the room with his suitcase packed and ready to go near her chair, she felt a wave of total desolation sweep over her.

What kind of life would she return to? Everything she had known had collapsed. Though Emilio's life had just begun, she couldn't help but worry that hers had ended, that she would have to start over, and painfully scratch her way to the top again. The dark hand of the Forbidden Tarot had shattered her world more than she ever would have dreamed.

She had lost her best friend, Maria. Her boss at CommOptima had told her that she'd better look for a new position, now that the Nimian Project was on hold. She'd fallen in love with a strangely-gifted cowboy who had apparently decided he could not return her affection. But even more shattering was the information she'd been recently given.

Before Emilio's operation, his doctors had informed her that she could not donate one of her kidneys to her brother, as they had always planned. Antigen tests done to ensure a good organ match had shown a startling lack of similarity in their DNA. She and Emilio could in no way be related. In fact, the doctors had also informed her that an unusual marker had shown up on her results, and they wanted to do more tests on her to make sure they hadn't made a mistake.

Claire sighed as she thought of the brisk, technology-dependent doctors, the stifling hospital, and the tubes, pills, and injections that had been forced upon her brother after he'd received his new kidney. She'd had quite enough of the medical industry over the years and more than enough new and disturbing information. The doctors and their tests could wait for another day.

Emilio was free of tubes now. Free of dialysis and pain. The winnings from Mr. B had set him free of his disease, and given him a second chance at a normal life. She should be ecstatic. But always, behind her happiness for her brother, loomed the disappointment of Jack's silence and the way they had parted without really saying goodbye.

As she sat there, she felt a faint prickling sensation pass down her spine, as a strange and sudden awareness set her on alert. She raised her head as she slowly rose to her feet, still expecting Simeon Avare to track her down and kill her.

The awareness bloomed into ever-increasing prickles. Someone rapped softly on the door. Claire straightened, glancing around for a way to escape, but knowing there was nowhere to run.

The door opened slowly, and Claire froze, watching it swing wide.

Chapter 41

Jack Hughes came into view. He was dressed in a tan suede jacket, jeans, and boots, with his Stetson hanging near his left knee. She'd forgotten how tall he was, how imposing his horseman's figure was. He nearly filled the doorway.

He stood on the threshold, his right hand on the latch of the door, his dark eyes fastened on her, his mouth a grim line, his expression unreadable.

Jack was the last person she had expected to show up at Emilio's hospital room.

Then he shot a quick glance at the empty bed and back at her, the obvious question hanging in his eyes.

"Emilio's fine." She had to pause and clear her throat. Seeing Jack had nearly taken her breath away. "He's, uh, having some final tests done." She indicated the rest of the hospital behind the wall of cowboy in front of her. "Giving that last drop of blood." She licked her lips, which had suddenly gone dry. And numb. "Before he's discharged." She broke off, hearing her stilted phrases echoing as she fought through a roiling mass of conflicting emotions. She wanted to run into Jack's arms. She wanted to kiss him. Hold him. And then again, she wanted to slap him for the way he had broken her heart.

Jack nodded. He fingered the rim of his hat, the only sign of nervousness he betrayed.

"I brought the truck," he stated.

"Truck?"

"Gran said you would need it."

Claire frowned and crossed her arms. "And why would I need your truck?"

"For moving out to the ranch."

"What?" Claire stared at him, amazed that he could show up like this, never saying a word about their fizzled relationship, and stand there expecting her to pack her things and go with him—just like that. "I never told her I was coming."

"She thinks you are." His jaw flinched as he clenched his teeth. "And she's gone to a lot of trouble for you."

"Like what?"

"Doing up the bunkhouse, for one. It's become a real showplace. State-of-the-art everything."

"But I told her I wasn't moving out there. That I couldn't."

"Because of me."

She raised her glare and met his gaze. Her eyes felt hot, and she knew she was close to tears. The last thing she wanted to do was break down in front of Jack and allow him to see how much she had suffered since they'd parted near the helicopter.

"Because of me," he repeated. "Right, Claire?"

"Yes, dammit!" She turned her back on him and squeezed her eyelids shut, forcing back the threatening tears. How could he stand there like that—the heartless bastard—and act so innocent when he damn well knew his presence would upset her.

She heard him heave a sigh and take a step toward her. But he didn't say a word. She could feel his stare on her back, could tell that he was studying her, and the sensation was as strong as if he had reached out and touched her.

"You never even called me, Jack," she said, her lips sticky with emotion.

"I couldn't," he replied, his voice as deep and as gravelly as she remembered.

"Why? Lose my number?" Bitterness and sarcasm dragged through her words.

"It wouldn't have been a good idea."

She pivoted to face him, unable to take any more of his frustrating self-control. "Says who?" she demanded.

He just gazed at her. She'd forgotten how he could rile her with his solid unwavering gaze.

"Why is it always up to you?" she exclaimed, stepping backward, out of the power of his eyes. "Why couldn't I have any say in the matter?"

"Because I knew it could only go one place, Claire."

"And where is that?"

"Nowhere."

"Why?" Her voice came out in a strangled whine, and the sound made her feel like a child. Still, she had to press onward, to make him say the hurtful truth he'd obviously planned to keep from her. She had to hear it out loud, see him say it, before she'd believe that he didn't love her. "Why nowhere?"

"Because." He tossed his hat on the nearby chair, and it landed with a muffled plop. "You're a highly educated scientist. And I'm a simple horseman—in every sense of the word."

"Opposites attract." She hugged her arms more tightly around her ribcage as the thought of the tarot card flitted through her mind.

"Maybe. But it wouldn't last."

"That's your opinion, Jack. Not mine."

He set his jaw again and stared at her.

"I thought we had something, you and me," she continued, raking him with her burning glare. "Something special."

He paced across the floor toward the window as if trying to escape her claim. She watched him, waiting for him to agree with her or tell her she was full-of-it. Jack braced his hands on his hips and stared out at the parking lot below him.

"What was I supposed to do, Claire?" he finally replied. "Call you up? Have you drive four hours and meet me for a picnic? Show you my latest shoeing job?" He snorted. "Sounds like a real fun date to me."

"I would have been happy just to hear your voice on the phone."

He fell silent. Didn't move.

"To hear that you'd made it out of the valley in one piece," she went on. "To hear if Brutus ever made it back to the ranch. To find out what's blooming on the high meadow by the Two Sisters, hear if the American River is warm enough for swimming yet." She paused and studied his broad back and the stubborn set of his wide shoulders. "You know—the big things. The little things. And all the stuff in between."

Jack looked up at a spot between the wall and the ceiling. She couldn't tell if he was interested in what she had to say or just waiting for her to finish. She stepped closer, frustrated by his silence. She hadn't forgotten his penchant for silence.

"Do you think that just because I'm educated, I can't appreciate anything but the high-tech world? Do you think I'm that one-dimensional?"

"I never said you were one-dimensional."

"Well, that's what it sounds like to me!" She was so close to him now that she could see the collar of his jacket lift up and brush the ends of his black hair as he breathed. "Do you know what Josef Mendel's daily routine was?"

"Pollinating peas?"

"No. Documenting the weather. The Father of Genetics spent his time recording the temperature every day. That was his job. And he lived in a monastery. Talk about remote."

"Eventually you'd get bored."

"How do you know?" She grabbed his arm. "Are you a fortune-teller as well as a shape-shifter?"

"Don't go there." He glared down at her and tried to withdraw his arm, but she held fast. "I mean it, Claire."

"Where do you get off making my decisions for me, telling me what I'll like and won't like?"

"I just know females."

"Bull!" She flung herself away from his arm, desperate to make him understand how she felt. "I'm not your typical female anyway. And you know it!"

"That's right. And I'm not your typical male. So let's just leave it at that."

She shot him a sideways glare. "You'd be satisfied with that? After what we felt for each other in the cave, on the trail?"

"I never said I was satisfied."

"Then you admit you want more?"

He turned to face her, and she could see the familiar blaze

in his eyes. "Hell, yes, I want more. But not at the price I'd have to pay for it."

"What price?"

He stared at her and then looked away again, unable or unwilling to answer her.

"What price, Jack?" she asked, softening her tone as she saw his shoulders wilt, albeit almost imperceptibly.

He faced the window. For a moment the air stretched between them, silent but thick with their unresolved business. "The price of watching you go again."

Claire gaped at his back, stunned by the rawness in his voice, the strangled emotion in his words. She wanted to run to him, fling her arms around him and kiss away the devastation that hung in the air between them. But his back was like a wall between them.

Until he reached out for her, she wasn't going to violate the defenses he'd build to protect his all-too-vulnerable heart. One wrong move and she knew she would lose him forever.

"It's not something I aim to go through again," he added.

Claire swallowed and stepped closer to him. "So because of the unknown—the future—you'll deny yourself the present."

"It's better that way. No big surprises. No one gets hurt."

"Says who?"

He glanced briefly to the side at her, as if confused by her words.

"I'm hurting right now," Claire explained, holding back from touching him. "And I've been hurting since I realized you weren't going to return my call, that you weren't even going to say goodbye."

He sighed and looked down at the tips of his boots.

"No one can predict the future, Jack. Even the people we think are perfectly suited to each other often slip up. It's a crapshoot. Life and love is a crapshoot."

"I know that," he growled. He shifted his weight to his left leg.

"So what if I have an unusual occupation and an advanced degree." She stepped closer again, encouraged by the slight change in his body language. "So what if you have an unusual alter ego and live out in the sticks. So what?"

"There's an inherently high failure rate in that combination."

"You'd let statistics decide for you? Not your heart?"

"I'd be a fool not to."

Claire gazed at him, not knowing how else she could convince him that she could be perfectly happy living at the Dark Horse Ranch, studying the mysterious cave and getting to know Jack better. But the odds were that she'd never get her heart's desire. Once Jack made up his mind, he was the most immovable object she'd ever encountered.

Exasperated, she sighed. "Then I guess the tarot card was wrong after all."

"What tarot card?" He pivoted slightly on his heel to look at her.

"The one that I looked at a while ago. The one that started this whole thing."

She told him about the card, about her friend Maria, and how they'd both looked at the card with the two goblets. Temperance. Maria had predicted that opposites would attract, that two disparate forces would combine to produce a far better whole.

"For a little while, I thought the card referred to Tobias. But now I know it was a reflection of you and me."

"You would base your future on a tarot card?"

"Not just any tarot card, Jack."

The hard light in his eyes tempered to a softer, more accessible glint. "Right."

"Besides, I'm not basing the future on a tarot card. I'm basing it on what I know of you as a man. What I've seen. How you've acted. And how I feel about you."

"Claire, we spent less than a week together."

"That week was full of more living than most people experience in an entire lifetime. You even said yourself once that we knew each other—from the very first moment."

He fell silent again and found something to study on the opposite wall.

Claire stared at him, searching for a way to get through his thick hide.

"Yes. We're opposites," she continued. "But I believe we bring out the best in each other. I feel as if I can trust you, confide in you, and that you will never turn anything back on me. I've told you things I've never told another human being."

"People often let down their guards to comrades in arms. You're no different."

"I disagree. I told you those things because I trust you, Jack. I trust your intelligence, your judgment, and your sense of honor. You'll possess those qualities come rain or shine."

She saw the steel in his back ease. "And you trust me, Jack. I know you do. You trusted me enough to tell me about your special gift."

He shrugged. "You're the only person who would see it as a gift."

"It is!" She clenched her jaw, trying to restrain herself. But she was unable to hold back any longer. In a quick movement, she rushed to him and flung her arms around him, pressing her cheek above the wings of his shoulder blades.

"Jack, I love you! I don't care where you live or what you do. I love you! I love the man in you. And I love the spirit of the horse in you. Both of you."

"Claire, it just can't—," he breathed, his voice thick with emotion.

"Look what we've done for each other and *with* each other. My brother is on the road to recovery. So is the ranch. We could accomplish a lot together, you and me. I just know it!"

He sighed. He looked up at the ceiling, breathing heavily, his shoulders rising and falling as he struggled with his self-control.

"Please, Jack. Don't deny the way we feel about each other. Don't be afraid of me. I will never hurt you. Not intentionally. I love you. And I know you love me!"

She squeezed him with gentle strength, infusing him with the soaring love she felt for him, a love that bubbled up and flowed out of her like the fountain they had searched for together. As she embraced him, she could see the stallion in the distance, standing on an outcropping of rock, his head held at such an angle that she knew he was listening.

Jack the man might never drop his defenses and admit how he felt. But the stallion would forever stay true to his nature. And the stallion knew exactly what he wanted.

Come to me. Claire prayed to the horse in an unspoken language she knew he could understand. She closed her eyes and visualized the shining black horse. *Come to me,* she called. *Take me to the mountains where I belong.*

The horse turned his head while the wind played in his mane. He looked right at her as if he could see across the vast miles between them.

Take me with you, she continued, speaking to the wild part she knew lived within Jack, the part that placed no human limitations on heart or spirit. *Take me home.*

The horse reared up, and then with a smart kick, launched himself forward, galloping full-out toward her, never once taking his intense gaze off her.

At that moment, Jack's self-control cracked, and the steel in his spine melted. "Ah, God," he murmured.

"Jack!" She hugged him even tighter, until he turned in her embrace and caught her up in his arms.

"I do love you, Claire," he confessed, crushing her against him and pressing his cheek against hers. "Since the first moment I saw you."

She closed her eyes as his hands swept over her back.

"I thought I could live without you. But it's just not—"
He broke off.

"It's just not what, Jack?"

"It's just not right without you." He pulled her tighter. "I've just been going through the motions of living. It's not the same without you."

Her heart burst with joy as he embraced her and kissed her, filling himself up with the love she poured out to him. After a long, breathless kiss, he pulled away, just enough to hug her against his large frame again.

"I love you so much, Claire!"

"Then you'll give it a try?" She pulled back slightly and

looked into his dark brown eyes, which were melting now with love for her, full of luminous depth. "You'll give us a try?"

"Not just a try, Angel," he answered, leaning down for another kiss. "I'm going to give it everything I've got." He smoothed her bottom lip with the pad of his thumb. "I've been in a living hell these past weeks, missing you so much. I love you, Claire. More than you'll ever know."

"Oh, Jack!"

"And you're right. It scares the shit out of me."

Set 15

And what of the Golden Ones' DNA, you might ask? Once Those Who Live Forever come back to swoop up their own, using DNA profiling, will they find the remains of the Golden Ones? Will they use that DNA to recreate their precious comrades—their best and brightest—who did not survive their stay on Earth? In a word—no! Archeologists have recently discovered that the tombs of the founding dynasty of Egypt were burned.

Of course they were. It was an act of pure genius, actually. When the Golden Ones were interred and forgotten after a few centuries, I simply burnt their bodies. No DNA? No trip to the heavens—for my brothers and sisters as well as all their earthly spawn. And all those king lists laboriously chipped into stone? Useless. Sorry, Golden Ones. Sorry spawn. If you had been more charitable toward me, things might have been different. But your own glory blinded you, and you foolishly misjudged me. You thought I was a mere servant. A chauffeur. A driver. Well, my dears, the joke is on you.

Set (Set 'er Down), Captain of Starship Celestia V

Turn the page for a preview of

THE
MIDNIGHT
WORK

BY KASSANDRA SIMS

Coming from Tor Romance
in December 2005

Sophie knew city life was such that strange strangers and odd behavior tended to be below noticing, or simply gaped at and forgotten again instantaneously. Yet, she was still surprised at how totally oblivious people could be to a beautiful man standing on a street corner, turning in a Widdershins circle, reciting Shakespeare in pig-Latin, while his female companion wiped blood from her neck with handy wipes at exactly midnight.

Perhaps, she reflected, it was remarkable while being witnessed, but not nearly the weirdest occurrence in the day of a city-dweller. Not when, upon second glance, they were gone anyway.

Sophie wasn't sure how she'd react herself to witnessing such a thing; last week maybe she'd have been a little freaked out for a minute, and then walked on. Now she was the female companion, actually *doing* the weird things.

"Who would have known you were fluent in pig-Latin?" Sophie gazed around what appeared to be an art gallery connected through vaulted arches into other galleries on either end.

"It took me forever to memorize that password. I think I got an extra hard one since I pissed the guardian off once." He ran a hand through his hair and approached one of the doorways, touching a mark etched in the wood.

Sophie gazed at the nearest painting hanging on the beige wall directly in her line of site—a village at night, thatched houses set close together with candles burning in each window, when she squinted she could make out three figures hanging in the grey sky, astride brooms—when the painting faded and recongealed into a macabre scene of a woman in habit with her neck set at a strange angle, blood pooling between her legs. The picture next to it was a child's scrawl of a Dracula character, complete with blood dripping from its fangs onto the ground.

"What is this place?" She turned to Olivier, who was already watching her ogle the artwork. The art here was almost as scary as Norah hungry. Next to the kid's sketch was a parade of men and women, most with one or both of their eyes gouged out, hobbled at hand and foot, being led by men on horseback dressed in knightly regalia, Templar crosses emblazoned on pennants and surplices.

"All of the art in the world." His face gave away nothing. "We're somewhere I haven't been before." His voice sounded off slightly, the pitch wrong, neither his crushed velvet whisper nor his sexy-stranger timbre.

Sophie considered that for a second. Why not? Who knew what the guy thought, really? "How does that work? Seems like a lot of art has been made in all of time." The answer was, naturally, magic, but she was curious how he would explain it.

"Some things are so beyond comprehension pondering them leaves you with more questions than you began with." Waving his hand for her to follow, he exited the gallery and strode through the next. Sophie spotted a child's drawing of what appeared to be a pear tree with an ax embedded in the trunk, a half-recognized tableau of fruit, pomegranates and apples, in a bowl with a hovering fruit fly, and a brace of dead rabbits next to a couple of leeks before they emerged into a completely different sort of gallery.

Fire blazed from the confines of every frame in the room. One depicted a ship alight in the midst of a night battle. Various public buildings and palaces burned in every state of immolation from recently alight to near collapse. Directly to her right was a twenty-foot tall tableau of a witch burning, the victim's mouth open and swallowing flame. Sophie watched Olivier purposefully stand with his back to that work. In the center of the room a real fire burned low in an open ring of stones containing several bricks of coal.

Olivier approached the stones and coals and fire. Sophie followed him and watched as he dropped a wondrously detailed sketch of someone's ear into the coals. She blinked rapidly as a tiny figure coalesced amid the shifting flame. Its torso burned a white so bright she had to avert her eyes to its extremities where the flickering limbs waved first blue then yellowish orange at the tips. The creature leapt from a coal directly onto the paper Olivier had dropped with what seemed to be considerable glee. In a flash the drawing was nothing but ash as the tiny, flaming feet rushing over it, stomping out a fiery jig.

"You bring me the best gifts." A voice like snapping wood rustled out of the creature. He turned a mainly indistinct face to Sophie. "Oh, *her*! Let me burn her again!" He stamped around his coal floor in a circle waving his arms above his head.

Olivier's expression turned blank, hard, unreadable. "Your jokes don't amuse me. Words like those will cause me to leave you without my gifts forever."

"Poor blood-drinker, lost them all to the flames." The coal the imp stood upon glowed orange where his feet made continuous contact. Sophie couldn't tell if he was mocking or commiserating with Olivier. "I will always have you here with me."

There was so much going on Sophie didn't understand here. Her mind tripped over her thoughts trying to order the questions she had. Burning her again? *Again?* Olivier lost everyone to fire? Who was everyone?

In the painting on her left, a picture of a dancing bear kicking a gypsy into a bonfire melted into a portrait of a very angry-looking Luc done in superb Italianate style. She focused, came up with a coherent question—Olivier could paint like that?—then decided she was better off not thinking about any of this.

"*Those* you can't consume with your vicious dancing." Olivier's voice was colored by a mocking thread, a tone she had never heard him use. This was not the same man who was patient and curious, but always kind. Except for that whole turning her into a vampire and stalking her part. Which could be his version of patience.

Tiring of crouching over, Sophie dropped to her knees next to Olivier.

"True, true. Did you come to tell me a story?" Hopping from coal to coal, the imp stoked up the fire enough to make Sophie uncomfortable. "Give me more to consume, more, more, and I will answer a question!"

Olivier grinned and pulled out two more drawings. These were far more detailed and perfectly rendered than the ear. The one in his left hand was of Sophie sleeping in a chair, her head back exposing her neck, her hands oddly clasped together politely. The one in his right hand was of Norah laughing uproariously at something, Luc's hand on Norah's shoulder, her posture bent in mirth.

The imp jumped in place. "Yes, yessssss. Those. Give them to me!"

"One question for each picture. One for me, one for her." He waved the papers in the air.

"Yes, two questions! I agree." Almost the entirety of his miniscule body glowed white and blue at the prospect of the sketches.

Olivier dropped them both in at the same time, and the imp whipped around in circles, cackling, his feet beating out a rhythm only he comprehended.

"He enjoys destroying beautiful things." Olivier's murmur zinged her straight in the belly. Sophie watched the paper curling into ash from the center out, each little footprint smoking as the fiery creature raced along.

"Not destroying—consuming." She could see that, he fed on the sketches like they fed on blood. Needfully, heedlessly. "Why is he here with all the art in the world? That seems pretty stupid." She turned her eyes back to the painting of Luc dressed in a black velvet smock shot through with silver thread and beaded around the neck in pearls. His anger flared in oil and egg tempura, in perfect shading and light on dark contrast. He was a masterpiece.

"This is his jail. He's serving a sentence for one of the

great medieval fires. I don't know which." Olivier drew a breath, and the imp shrieked.

"*Rome! Rome! Rome!*" the crackling voice remonstrated. Sophie tore her eyes away from the fearsome Luc, the after image of the imp's figure still flashing in front of her retinas, and gazed on the figure sort of sideways.

"I give her my question. She has them both." Olivier whispered in a low, gravelly tone.

"YES!" The imp hopped up and down.

"Ask him a question." Olivier nudged Sophie.

"Like what?" What did one ask a fiery critter that appeared to have limitless knowledge?

"Anything you want."

"Have I lived another life? Is this the first time I was born?" The dreams, she'd always had the dreams, since she could first remember she'd wondered if they were more than that.

Olivier looked extremely peeved.

"*Auto-de-fe!*" The imp did a somersault over that thrill. "You have lived before, blood-sucker, as have all of your kind. Over and over and over!"

"Ask him something else," Olivier grated out. The anger throbbed off him, she could taste it bitter like lemon peel.

"Are my friends okay?"

The flames stilled somewhat, the flickering slower. He leapt in place instead of running in circles. "Ask something more specific."

And that wasn't reassuring. More specific how? Was it the work "okay"?

"Are they in danger?" She couldn't bring herself to ask if Suki was alive; she knew Norah wasn't. She'd killed Norah herself—although that had turned out pretty all right, as far as Sophie was concerned, what with the vampirism and all.

The feet began to move again, round and round, the flames that simulated hair flickering orange. "Danger!! No one you know is not in danger! He will come! Oh, yes, he will come! She can't save you. *No!*"

Sophie's skin turned to gooseflesh even as she sat inches away from glowing coals a living fire. He? Everyone was in danger?

COMING FROM TOR BOOKS IN JANUARY 2006 . . .

"With the sleekness of a supernatural *Alias*, Cunningham's novel is a fast, fun read with a likable, hip heroine."

—*Booklist*

"In the first of the Changeling trilogy, Cunningham delivers urban fantasy with a straight face (*C.S.I.* via Tolkien), employing the quicksilver pacing typical of such suspense authors as Vachs, Gardner and Koontz . . . This is an auspicious debut for a cool crime-solver who could teach Anita a thing or two."

—*Publishers Weekly*